THE Physician's Tale

THE Physician's Tale

ANN BENSON

Delacorte Press

THE PHYSICIAN'S TALE
A Delacorte Press Book / December 2006

Published by Bantam Dell
A Division of Random House, Inc.
New York, New York

Book design by Ellen Cipriano

Delacorte Press is a registered trademark of Random House, Inc.,
and the colophon is a trademark of Random House, Inc.

Library of Congress Cataloging-in-Publication Data
Benson, Ann.
The physician's tale / Ann Benson.
p.   cm.
ISBN-13: 978-0-385-33505-8
ISBN-10: 0-385-33505-9
1. Physicians—Fiction. 2. Healers—Fiction. 3. Great Britain—History—
14th century—Fiction. 4. Plague—Fiction. 5. Survival—Fiction. I. Title.

PS3552.E547659P48 2006
813'.54—dc22   2006046260

Printed in the United States of America
Published simultaneously in Canada

www.bantamdell.com

BVG   10   9   8   7   6   5   4   3   2   1

For Jennifer Robinson and Jackie Cantor
Pros in prose

The author wishes to express her extreme and
eternal gratitude to editor Anne Groell for her
insightful help in bringing this book to fruition.

THE Physician's Tale

Prologue

It was the first spring after the long, hard winter that marked the second coming of the plague called DR SAM. The sun was April bright, but the wind seemed stuck in March; it roared down the mountainside with the ferocity of a lion, blowing ripples on the surface of the river's fast-moving waters. Slender shoots of green struggled upward through the tenacious bits of ice that were stuck along the riverbank. The water was nearly opaque with the silt and debris that nature washed downstream, as she did every year. By June her tirade would be over and it would be clear as glass, all the way to the bottom.

Janie Crowe and Tom Macalester—husband and wife—sat astride their horses and stared at the bridge, beneath which were the Encampments.

"I don't know," Tom said. "I don't like the looks of what's down there."

"I don't either," Janie said.

Trolls were supposed to rule the land underside the bridges of the world. But beneath the bridge that connected Northampton to Hadley, there were colonies of ne'er-do-wells, escapees of DR SAM who could not—or would not—fit into any of the survivor groups that had formed in the valley. They were the rogues, the bad seed that no one wanted. They had banded together into a frightening and unpredictable enclave of maladroits who extracted anything they could from those who needed to pass over the bridge.

Tom looked up and down the river. "God, you'd think by now someone would have started a ferry service...."

"Maybe someone tried," Janie said. "Maybe they were chased off."

"I don't see any other way to get across." He pointed upriver. "In August we could probably wade to the other side. There used to be a ford about a hundred yards up. But now..."

The water was simply too fast-moving, however strong the horses might be.

"I guess we cross on the bridge, then."

"Yeah, I guess we do."

For a moment, Janie looked south along the riverbank. In the time before, it had been a playground, a wonderful community resource open to anyone who could get there. The banks of the shallow river extended well outward, so children could play waist-deep in water as far out as fifty feet; it was only in the very center of the flow that larger boats could navigate. And so it had become a gathering place for smaller pleasure craft of all kinds: motorboats, canoes, kayaks, Jet Skis, pontoons. In the heat of August, it was the best way possible to spend a day in Massachusetts.

Now it was an obstacle, a cold and forbidding challenge. To get to their destination, Tom and Janie would have to cross.

"We go now or we turn back," Tom said. "We have to time this to make the best use of the daylight."

Ten seconds passed. "Go now," Janie said.

"Okay," Tom said. "We ride fast, and we don't stop. You understand?"

His wife nodded solemnly.

"All right. Ready?"

"Ready."

He whipped his horse with a leather crop, and the gelding took off

like a champion. Janie heeled her own mare, who cast off the docile nature her rider had come to love and took on the persona of Seabiscuit.

The horses' hooves pounded thunderously over the bridge, down
below, renegades came awake and bolted to awareness. As Janie and
Tom neared the downslope of the bridge, where it met the road on the
other side, the trolls who lived under the steel and concrete poured out
onto what was left of the pavement. They streamed toward the center
of the road, where the horses ran; with grabbing hands they tugged at
the frightened animals, looking for any kind of handhold that might
dislodge the rider and thus expose the horse to their claim.

Janie felt hands upon her thigh and slapped them away with her
crop. Then she saw a filthy ragged man reach up and take hold of the
bit in her horse's mouth. She pulled one foot out of the stirrup and
kicked at him with all her might. He fell back, clutching his jaw.

Up ahead, she saw Tom, who had fought off his own ravagers and
now waited at the edge of the road for her to catch up.

"Come on," he yelled. "You're almost here...."

Janie could not look. She closed her eyes and trusted the horse.
There was nothing else that could be done.

Somehow, they found themselves safe and dry on the other side,
the trolls vanquished—for now.

"You're a warrior," Tom said to her.

"No," she said. Her entire body was shaking. "I'm not."

"Hey. We made it. We're over the bridge. The rest of the trip will
be easy."

Janie thought it was a good thing that the remainder of the trip to
the book depository would take an hour; she would need that much
time to regain her composure so Myra Ross wouldn't see her in such a
state of upset. But her anxiety abated as they neared their destination.

And it returned when they arrived, for the place looked deserted.

Janie Crowe hugged her coat around herself as she stepped carefully through the pile of sticks and leaves in the recessed entry of the
book depository. She shaded her eyes with one hand and peered
through the streaked glass into the vestibule, hoping for signs of life.
Seeing no one, she tried the door.

"Locked," she said to her husband. She pounded, hoping someone would come. No one did. She pounded again, harder, using the side of her mittened fist. The glass vibrated under her attack. "No one," she said.

Tom climbed down off his horse. "Is there a back entrance?"

"Yeah, but it's a fire exit—no outside handle."

"Okay, let me try," Tom said. He pulled on the handle with all his might, but it wouldn't give.

He looked at his wife, his expression forlorn. "You really want to go in?"

"We've come all this way."

"I can break the glass, but if I do that, the place won't be secure anymore."

Janie stared at the door for a few moments, thinking of the treasures that lay within. To the average pilferer, the books and manuscripts would have little value. No one but a curator of antiquities was likely to steal them.

"If she's in there," Janie said, "we'll be taking her back with us, so we don't have to worry about her. If she's not...I don't know. The things she's collected can't be replaced."

"Neither can she," Tom said.

Janie pressed her nose against the glass and peered in one more time.

A small figure shuffled through the shadows.

"I see someone!" She knocked furiously, but the figure did not reappear.

She turned back to her husband. "We have to go in."

"Okay," Tom said. He pulled out his handgun. "Stand back."

He shot the glass of the door near the handle.

The glass cracked but did not shatter.

"Damn," he said. "She wasn't kidding when she said this place was armored. You're *absolutely certain* you want to do this?"

"*Yes,*" she said.

"Okay," he said. "I just want to be sure before we use up bullets we can't replace."

He shot the handle once more. The echo of the report rang in their ears and a new series of cracks appeared, but there was no further breach. Muttering to himself, Tom grabbed the rope that was draped over his saddle horn. He doubled the rope, slipped it through the door handles, and tied it around the saddle horn securely. Then he got back on the horse and spurred it forward. The animal lurched ahead, snorting in protest. After he managed a few struggling steps, the doors pulled open, glass tumbling like geometric ice onto the concrete landing.

Janie stepped over the shards and tried the inner doors, which opened easily. Tom tied up the horses, then he and Janie stepped inside, finding themselves in the familiar hallway.

"Hello?" Janie called. Her voice echoed off walls that were bare of the exhibits she remembered from the last time she'd been there—in the time before.

They walked a few yards down the main hallway. Suddenly Tom grabbed Janie's arm to stop her and pointed to his left.

Janie looked where he'd pointed. In the dim light, it was hard to make out even the most basic architectural features, but she noticed a movement as well. A head popped out of a doorway, then just as quickly went back in.

"You stay here," Tom said quietly.

Janie clutched his arm and whispered, "Whither thou goest, remember?"

He knew better than to protest. They stepped quietly down the hallway, hugging the wall until they were just outside the door.

With his gun raised and ready, Tom peeked just far enough around the door frame to see a thin, smallish figure.

"Hello?"

A raspy but defiant voice answered, "Stay away. I've got a gun. There's nothing in here but old books, so go away."

Still, there was no mistaking the accent. "Oh, my God, Myra, it's me, Janie, and Tom...."

A long moan of disbelief followed. Janie got one step into the room before her friend from the time before spoke again.

"Stop! Please! Don't come any closer."

"But why—"

"I'm sick."

Janie came to an instant stop, as did Tom. In unison, they pulled up the breathing masks that hung around their necks.

A match flared; Myra Ross lit a candle. She raised the light until it revealed her face.

Janie could not suppress a gasp of shock. She took one step forward. "Maybe I can help you...."

Myra managed a bitter laugh. "So, my 'daughter' the doctor, have you been able to help anyone else with this problem?"

Janie didn't have to answer. "How long have you been sick?" she asked in a quiet voice.

"Since last night."

Only hours, and already she was this bad; she wouldn't be one of those people who lasted several days. She'd go quickly.

Janie knew it was a mercy.

"Myra, I...I'm so sorry."

"Yeah. Me too. All I've lived through, and this gets me. Go figure."

"Maybe it *won't* get you," Janie said, voicing a hope she did not truly feel. "Some people do get better."

"Not old ladies," she said. "No, *Maidie*, this is my time." She coughed into her hand and wiped the resulting phlegm onto her pants leg. "My mother, rest in peace, would *platz* to see me do that. But I'm all out of hankies. So, is this a social call, or do you have some other business?"

Janie and Tom looked at each other. A silent understanding passed between them that their plan to bring Myra back to their compound was moot. Finally, Tom said, "We came to get the book, if you'll be willing to part with it. You know we'll take good care of it."

"Willing?" She made a small effort at laughing; it came out dark and bitter. "I'd be on my knees thanking God right now, if I thought I could get up again. Please, take it. I'll die happier knowing it's in good hands." She coughed more deeply than she had just a few minutes before, the sound wet and rattling.

Myra put one hand on her chest. "It's—filling up—my lungs," she said. Between words, she gasped for air. "I can—really feel it—now."

As Janie's heart sank, she cursed herself that they hadn't come sooner. Mentally, she replayed the conversation between herself and Tom, several months back, shortly after their wedding.

She could come to live with us on the mountain.

She'll never leave her books, you know that.

Please, Tom, I won't be able to sleep at night—she's been like a mother to me.

You don't know what we'll run into . . . not everyone is dead out there.

His wariness had been wise; their encounter with the people living in encampments under the bridge had proved that. Nevertheless, the difficult discussion still rang in Janie's ears.

Myra's been isolated, so she might still be okay, but she'll be alone and scared and—

We're easy prey. And besides, with your situation now, we need to be careful.

I'll be all right, Tom.

"It'll be all right, Myra," she said aloud.

"How will it be all right?"

There was a heavy silence until Tom said, "Where is it?"

A cough rumbled up from deep within Myra's chest. "In—the safe." She made a motion with her hand, as if to indicate that they should follow her. "Stay—back."

"Tell us where it is, we'll find it."

The frail woman managed one long slow breath without coughing. It seemed to restore her. "Please," she said, measuring each word. "It's a blessing to know I'll go out on a *mitzvah.*"

She made another gesture, bidding Tom and Janie to part, and when they moved aside, she walked between them in small, pained steps. As she passed through, Janie saw with horror the gravity of Myra's illness. She had always been svelte, but now she was emaciated. What skin remained on her bones was dark and wrinkled.

She led them farther down the main hallway and into a suite of offices that were now devoid of the furniture and equipment they'd

once held. Children had once crowded these halls, full of their enthusiastic chatter, always happy to be away from the prison of school for any
reason at all. Now, lacking the laughter, vitality, and much of its former collection, the Hebrew Book Depository seemed a hollow, empty
place.

Myra struggled forward; purpose seemed to give some strength to
her steps, and for a moment Janie detected in her voice a small remnant
of the woman's legendary pluck. "I held them off for a long time, you
know," she said as she shuffled along. "Just me. Just like when I was a
young woman, in Israel." But then she stopped walking and shrank
again into the sick old woman she'd become. "But they got in eventually. Four men. Boys, really. I was outside for a few minutes. I was so
sick of myself I just needed to hear some birds and wind. I got lazy—
one time—and left the door unlocked. They must have been watching.
Blew right in and helped themselves."

She stopped walking and pressed her hand against the wall for balance. As she rested, she said, "One of them was coughing. The little
bastard."

After a few raspy breaths, she pointed. "Inside that door. Go in
there, and I'll call out the combination. It looks like a water cooler."

Tom looked at Janie and said, "Go ahead. I'll stay here."

She nodded. A few steps later she was kneeling in front of the safe-
in-cooler's-clothing.

"Ready."

Janie turned the knob after each number, squinting to see the dial
in the thin light. After the last turn, she heard the sweet click of the
tumblers falling out of their pinholes.

It took all of her strength to work the handle, which had stiffened
with neglect. Inside, she found a pile of books and manuscripts. She
took the lot out of the compartment and placed them on the floor in
front of her. Halfway down, by its familiar feel, she found the journal.
She closed her eyes and clutched it to her heart for a few moments. And
despite the urgency of their mission, she allowed herself one moment
to feel its wonderful heft in her hands.

She came out of the safe room with the volume gripped tightly in her arms.

Wax dripped onto Myra's hand as she held the candle high, but she didn't seem to notice. "Okay," she said, "you've got it; that's good." She coughed hard, her abdomen bending with each spasm.

She looked up and made a little shrug of acceptance, and Janie saw on her face an understanding of what was to come.

"Back to my blankets now, I think."

Myra turned slowly, candle in hand, and shuffled back the way she'd come. Janie and Tom watched in aching frustration as she lowered herself onto the pile of blankets that would be her deathbed. It took a painfully long time for her to arrange herself, but finally she lay still.

"Go," she said. "Get out of here."

"We'll stay with you until . . . you know. . . ."

"No you won't. Leave me in peace. I don't want anyone to see this."

Janie moved into Myra's line of sight. "We'll bury you when . . . it's over."

"No you won't. Don't you dare touch me. . . . I won't have God asking me when I get to heaven why I let you get sick too."

Janie said nothing for a moment, then, in a small voice, "Are you scared?"

She took a very long breath and spoke slowly, pausing for smaller breaths after every few words. "No, *Maidie*, not now. Old women are supposed to die. I'd like a little more time, but in a better world than this one. . . . I was scared in Auschwitz when I was a little girl." She nodded at the book that Janie held in her arms. "My work is done."

After a few seconds, Janie said, "The hair and the skin flakes you gave me from the other manuscript—they worked."

Myra raised her head up slightly.

"Worked—for what? To help those little boys?"

"Yes, for that, but there's more." Janie could not help but smile. "I'm pregnant."

Myra let her head fall back onto the blankets. Janie could hear the whispered prayer but did not understand the language. "God in heaven—is it true?"

Janie nodded.

"Now I can die happy."

She closed her eyes. Janie and Tom stayed and watched over her from a distance. Her coughing became more frequent for a while, then began to diminish. In less than an hour, it ceased entirely. She drew in one long wheezy breath, then let it out, her last movement in this world.

One

In the time of *pestis secunda*, Alejandro Canches knew too well the dread that came with a sharp knock, so he tapped gently on the door of William and Emily Cooper. Emily opened it, her eyes red and wet.

She nodded gravely and tucked a stray strand of hair into her white cap. "I have sat with him all night," she said when she saw the physician on her doorstep. "He struggles, but he holds on. Come in, see for yourself."

"His resistance is remarkable," Alejandro said as he entered. William Cooper had long since traversed the threshold over which one passes to reach the death stage of plague, but he was clinging ferociously to the last few bits of his life.

The woman led him by candlelight to the bedside. The cooper's face was all Alejandro could see; everything else was covered. The sweat that his wife had so dutifully wiped away during the night had accumulated anew in her brief absence, and in the candlelight, the sheen of fever was visible on Cooper's forehead. The man's eyes were closed and did not open, even on hearing a voice.

Alejandro covered his nose against the putrid plague smell and put his head to the man's chest. The heartbeat, though faint, was still surprisingly steady. He palpated the swellings in the man's neck and armpits with his fingers. Though he was gentle, Cooper moaned in pain.

"Sorry," Alejandro whispered. "I did not mean to cause you pain."

First do no harm, he reminded himself. The swellings were firm, but no more so than they had been upon his last examination two days prior. The dark blue coloration seemed virtually the same.

"A fortnight," the physician said to Emily as he stepped back. "It is beyond my ken. You have done a fine job in caring for him."

"It cannot be the result of my efforts," she said. "I do nothing more than wipe the sweat from his brow."

Alejandro dipped his hands in the bowl of water that Emily had brought and dried them on the towel that hung over her forearm. It had become a practiced ritual between them over the course of William's illness, only this time she refrained from commenting on his obsession with hand-washing.

"And there is nothing more that *can* be done. It is in God's realm now." He did not add what seemed obvious to him—that Cooper's fate had belonged to God for some time. "That he has lived so long in this suspended state seems almost an aberration of nature."

But years of rendering medicine had shown him many such oddities, and he had come—over time—to the conclusion that such aberrations might often be part of the divine scheme. He wondered what Guy de Chauliac might say to that notion and wished, for the thousandth time, for an opportunity to discuss it with his friend and mentor.

As he went to leave, the woman took him by the arm and said, "My husband has said we ought to pay you."

He had never asked her for money; he knew they had barely enough to get by. "No," he said, "I will not accept payment. I lack for nothing. But please—tell me one thing. In all the time I have known you both, we have never spoken of why it is that your husband chose to bring you here to live among the Jews, when as Christians, all the rest of Avignon is available to you. I would know the reason."

She hesitated briefly, as if judging his trustworthiness. Finally she said, "We had to leave our village, a place called Eyam, at the foot of the Peaks. It bordered on one of the king's favorite hunting reserves." She wiped her eyes with the back of one hand. "It was a very hard winter; we were cold and hungry."

Alejandro saw de Chauliac at his door in the desperate winter of 1357 and shuddered without realizing it as the memory of the biting cold and their desperate hunger overtook him. He recalled in his mind the bitter words he had said to the Frenchman that day:

You are not wanted here.

No, de Chauliac had replied, *but I am needed.* The food he brought from Paris saved their lives.

"The gamekeepers caught my husband hunting," he now heard Emily Cooper say. "They said he was within the boundaries of the reserve, but he was outside, he swears it! It didn't matter; the king would have ordered him hanged anyway."

Alejandro eyed her curiously. "But—he did not."

"No. He was robbed of the opportunity. Our son went to rescue Will; they had only put my husband in a pen, not within the irons. One of the guards was drunk, so the boy managed to free him."

"A brave and worthy son," he said.

"Aye," the woman said sadly. "A lost son." She pulled up the corner of her apron and wiped her eyes again, one after the other, then looked at the physician. "The warder awakened and put an arrow in him as he climbed over the wall behind his father."

He lowered his gaze respectfully. "I am truly sorry."

Emily nodded her acknowledgment of his sympathy and returned to her husband's side. She wiped his brow with the wet corner of her apron, then sat down on a chair at the bedside. A hard and distant look came over her—an expression Alejandro had never seen her wear before. She cast one last look in his direction, and the physician felt an unspoken accusation.

For a few moments, he considered giving the cooper's wife some of his own gold, but he did not wish to embarrass her. It was best simply to depart.

·   ·   ·

"My lord," the page said, bowing deeply to the king.

"Ah, Chaucer. Always so prompt. I trust your lord Lionel can spare you for a moment."

As if there could be any question of it. "Yes, sire. He and Lady Elizabeth are taking some air."

"Good. 'Tis a fine day for air. My own scribe is occupied at the moment with other matters, and I have need of some transcription."

Meaning, Chaucer knew, that the scribe had taken a bit too much of the drink again and could not be trusted for accuracy. He had corrected many of the man's mistakes of late; most might have been considered amusing had they not involved affairs of state.

"Of course, sire," the young man answered. "I shall be honored."

King Edward III gestured toward a corner of the chamber. "You will find what you need there, in the secretary."

As Geoffrey Chaucer gathered pen and parchment from the marble-topped desk, the king added, "I trust that you will keep this correspondence in strictest confidence. My son speaks very highly of your discretion. Now, please—these are letters critical to our welfare—record my words precisely."

He cleared his throat and began to speak. "Your Holiness," he began. A long and flowery greeting followed; Chaucer silently mouthed it in unison with the king, for he had written it many times.

And then the king got to the heart of the matter:

We are pleased to announce that our beloved daughter Isabella has agreed—of course, pending your approval—to accept a proposal of marriage from the Baron Enguerrand de Coucy. We ask your permission to call the banns for their nuptials at the earliest possible date.

Chaucer nearly dropped the pen. He fumbled to regain it and had to examine the page to see if there were any accidental markings. He saw none, so he scribbled furiously to catch up.

At the same time, I wish to ask a great personal favor of you. I have a child, a daughter, born of a woman who once served my cherished queen. I wish to acknowledge her as my own progeny and to accept her into my household as a princess of England. I confess my sins and humbly ask your intercession with God in heaven that I may be forgiven, not only for my depraved act of adultery but as well for my failure to embrace this daughter properly before now. Surely this is a sin as grievous as that which resulted in her conception.

The king paused, as if he were considering what to say next. He looked at the young page and said, "What say you, Chaucer—you are clever with words. Do I convey a proper sentiment, not too bold, but not too humble?"

Chaucer could barely speak. "Regarding the princess Isabella and the Baron de Coucy...you speak your intent plainly, yet you allow the pontiff room to make you sweat a bit. Very wise."

The monarch smiled. "I thought so myself."

"But may I be so brazen as to ask, sire, is the child you refer to the lady Kate?"

The king eyed him with some suspicion. "You may, and my answer is yes."

"Oh, then, undoubtedly, sire, your sentiments are proper. Heart-felt, but yet not too honeyed. You make your request respectfully, but you do not grovel before the pope, which in view of your personal majesty would of course be inna—"

"Thank you, Chaucer." The king cleared his throat and continued.

I wish for this daughter to be wed also. She is once married but is now a widow, so we need not burden you with concerns over an annulment. Her fecundity has already been demonstrated. In view of this and other valuable qualities she possesses, we are currently discussing a suitable arrangement with a prominent French family allied to de Coucy. As always, we remember that such arrangements are made pending your approval and blessing. My queen, despite her knowledge of my sin, has graciously agreed that this is the proper course.

There was more; Chaucer scribbled, trying hard not to let the shock of the news distract him. It was only with the greatest of effort that he contained himself. At last, the disquiet was unmasked! For weeks the atmosphere at Windsor Castle had been strained and stiff, and Chaucer had begun to wonder if a life of service to the royals was a wise choice. On occasion, the king and queen, normally an affectionate pair, had even been seen behaving in a most belligerent manner toward each other. There was much speculation among the servants and attendants that the queen had discovered the liaison between the king and his most recent mistress, her lady Alice, and was wreaking her havoc on both, just as she had brought misery to the lady who had been Kate's mother. But everyone thought surely she must know already—the king had made no great effort to conceal his admiration for the younger woman. All were agreed—it must be something more.

A great deal more, now that it was revealed! Chaucer recorded the other small matters that the king presented to the pope, though he could barely pay attention. When he was done, he handed the scroll to King Edward, who quickly read it through, then scribbled his signature.

The monarch held open his palm. "Wax," he said.

The young man hurried to the secretary, fumbled around until he found the wax, and came back. The king folded the parchment in thirds and used a candle to melt the red wax onto it, then affixed his seal. He allowed a moment for cooling, then picked up the message and gave it an exaggerated kiss.

"For luck!" he said. "Let's hope for the best this time, eh, Master Chaucer?"

"Indeed, sire. One always does." He bowed his way out of the room, then ran off.

The young woman who was the subject of the king's request had nearly heaved out her innards on the channel crossing when the soldiers of the king brought her from France, seven years before. Chaucer, himself also only seventeen at the time and newly ransomed from the French, had watched her with pity as the boat tossed in the waves of the cold sea. She wore chains of a common criminal on her legs, and it pained him to see the blood that dripped down her ankles and over her shoes. No one had offered her any sort of comfort, though she was mightily in need of it. He would have gone to her himself, had he not understood that this journey was part of her punishment.

Punishment for what, he had wondered at the time; she was brave and intelligent, a great beauty, and she had lived her life with far more grace than seemed possible under the circumstances. At seventeen, Katherine Karle was already a widow, and barely healed from the strain of a difficult birth—could the gods be more heartless?

Indeed they can, he thought. She had not seen her son since the day he was born. Moreover, he considered the words he had just written on behalf of the king.

Specifically, the Baron de Coucy has asked that the alliance between our families be cemented further by a union between his cousin the Baron de Benoit and an "Englishwoman of prominence," by which I take to mean a member of our near family. What nearer kin than my own child? You know, Holiness, of the difficulties we have had in arranging a truly suitable marriage for our spirited Isabella; I will spare you a recounting of her delicacies herein, as I am sure they have reached your ears on other lips. I am loath to allow the match between Isabella and de Coucy to be damaged by a failure regarding his cousin, for whom he seems to hold an uncannily deep affection.

De Coucy's cousin Benoit was a sniveling, hairy coward who overcame his many shortcomings with beastly rages when things did not go his way. That the king should settle the wondrous Kate upon him seemed an entirely unholy thing. *But he has run short of grown daughters,* Chaucer realized. *He has to conjure up another one somehow, to seal the arrangement for Isabella.* The queen was all dried up; Alice Perrer's children by the king were mere babies. Joanna was long dead, carried off in the first visitation of plague, in the year of 1348, after the Battle of Crécy.

Hope for the best, indeed! The spoiled and insolent Isabella was thirty and three, a princess, and yet after five attempts at a match, she remained a spinster; it was unnatural.

But not nearly as unnatural, Chaucer thought, as the events that were about to befall her half sister.

Emily Cooper pulled the linens off the straw on her husband's pallet and bundled them into a ball, then threw them into the hearth as the physician had instructed her to do. One blanket she kept; she would need it for herself. They'd come for the cooper's corpse not an hour before, in their hawkish beaks and dark hoods.

"Don't be thinking those things will protect you," she told the men as they carted her dead husband out the door. She followed them out to the street, the better to continue her warnings. "I've seen many a muler go down to the pest, and they fairly wrapped themselves in shrouds to keep it at bay!"

The hooded drovers did not respond, for neither understood English. Finally, when the cart was once again covered with the cloth that shielded the dead from the horrified eyes of the living, one of them shuffled back to her and said, in the detested French she barely understood, "*C'est votre mari qui est morte, non?*"

"Eh?" she said, wishing he would speak to her in English.

"Widow," the man said, having found one word.

"Yes." She nodded.

"*Allez à la palace toute de suite,*" he said. "*Il sera un pension pour vous.*"

He inclined his head slightly, then turned and mounted the driver's seat.

Pension, she understood. And *palace.*

The widow wasted no time in doing as he advised, for when she counted the coins remaining in her husband's purse, she found it was a dismayingly small number. She wrapped a shawl around her shoulders and headed out of the *ghetto* toward the pope's majestic abode, in search of mercy.

Avignon's narrow streets put her to mind of London; she'd been there once with her husband to visit his sister, who'd married a manservant to one of the king's distant cousins and now cooked in a fine house. The recollection brought a stab of jealousy, for the sister lived her life on stone floors, not the hard-packed dirt of Eyam. Still, Eyam was home, and she missed it keenly.

"*Pension,*" she said to the guard who stood at the gate of the papal palace. The tall white towers of the ornate castle loomed up behind the guard, making him look terribly small in his red mantle. The man grunted and pointed her to the right. She pulled her shawl tighter and began to walk around the palace perimeter. White gravel crunched under her steps; the sound distracted her, until it was overshadowed by the clop-clop of hooves on cobblestones. She looked up to see a party of couriers riding into the palace courtyard, under the banner of King Edward.

She tucked herself into a shadow and watched for a few moments, then realized the silliness of it and stepped back into the warmth of the sun. As if after all these years they should waste their time looking for her! They were a comely group, all decked out in their armor on fine strong horses, and she began to think with longing of England, of the familiarity of the people and the ease with which she could understand them.

No one there would know her as the wife of a poacher—she would be just another invisible old woman in need of alms, completely unworthy of notice. Her heart began to ache with homesickness. The passage across *la Manche* was dear and dangerous, but there was nothing for her in Avignon, or in all of France, for that matter. She had no relatives, and her only possible ally was the Jew physician, himself also a fugitive from English justice—

A terrible thought entered her mind as the English party paraded past in all their splendor: How much might they pay for a few choice words about him?

Certainly it would be enough for passage and a new start.

No, she chided herself, *it would be an unholy betrayal of a good man.*

But was he, after all, good? Her husband had died, despite the physician's attentions. He was hiding a child, a little boy with blond hair and blue eyes, whose mother was some sort of English noblewoman, even perhaps royal. It was her duty, she decided, to report him. She was still an Englishwoman. And her survival was at stake. She picked up the pace of her steps and followed the traveling party. Just before she reached them, she crossed herself and whispered a prayer for forgiveness.

·   ·   ·

Alejandro heard the midnight knock through a dream; he was crashing through dark woods with vague ogres in pursuit—an all-too-common occurrence—when the banging brought him abruptly to his mind's surface. He opened his eyes but saw nothing through the darkness.

He had heard nothing from the cooper's wife in several days and wondered immediately if the man's time had finally come. He rose from the narrow bed and wiped his hand over his beard. He tucked his long dark hair behind his ears and set his feet on the hard-packed floor of the room he shared with the boy Guillaume, who in the innocence of childhood had slept soundly through the knock. His knees ached, if only for the briefest time—a harbinger, he feared, of what was to come as he aged.

But he would accept it all with gratitude and offered up a quick prayer that he would live long enough to experience every misery that age could inflict, if only he could see once again the girl he called daughter. Girl indeed! By now she was a young woman. He allowed himself a few seconds of missing this young woman who had, in the agony of bereavement, given life to this child seven years before. She was as precious to him as any daughter who might have sprung from his own loins—of which there were, sadly, none.

The deep ache in his heart made that ache which he felt in his knees seem trivial. He chided himself, for if missing a person could evoke proximity, the young woman would now be in his household where she truly belonged, not among those whose blood she happened to share, through some monumental error on the part of God.

Forgive me, he prayed. *I mean no disrespect in pointing out Your over-sights.* "But why is it," he said in his quietest voice, "that such knocks as these come only in the unholiest of hours, when one cannot help but imagine some foul demon on the other side of the planks?"

The ill-defined dread he felt was all imagination; beyond the door would be a small, tired Englishwoman. He ducked through a low passage-way, and before he could stand fully, the knock came again.

He stood slowly and stared at the door. The firm pounding he heard could not have been made by the frail fist of a sorrowful old woman but by someone with much more strength of hand. And, judging by the rapidity and force, a good deal more urgency.

He tiptoed the rest of the way to the door and positioned himself to one side. "Never stand directly in the center of a door," Eduardo Hernandez had once told him. "A decent sword well thrust can come right through the boards. Imagine," the old soldier warned, "what a *fine* sword in the hands of a master might do to your gut. Even you with all your skills will be helpless."

But who else would come with dawn still hours hence? Strangers rarely traveled through this quarter of the city during daylight, let alone at night. He peered with one squinted eye through a crack along the edge of the door, hoping for a glimpse of the caller, but it was impossible to see anything in the darkness.

"Who knocks?" he said finally.

"I seek the physician Canches" came the reply.

Had they found him? His heart threatened to thump out of his chest. "One moment," he said. The words came out far more timidly than he would have liked. He cleared his throat, then added, "I'll see if he can be awakened."

He barely heard the grunted response on the other side of the door; he rushed into the bedroom and shook the boy urgently.

"Guillaume," he whispered. "Guillaume! You must wake up!"

The boy rubbed his eyes as he came awake. "But why, *Grand-père*—"

"Ask no questions now." His own voice sounded sharp, even to himself, and he tried to soften it. "Just make ready as I have showed you before—we may need to leave quickly."

As if he had not understood, the boy said, "But, *Grand-père*, where are we—"

"Shhh! Now hurry."

"Yes, *Grand-père*." He threw off his coverlet and stood up, wavering sleepily as he rose.

Alejandro steadied him. "Good boy," he said. "Now listen carefully. Watch from right here." He pointed to a spot just inside the room. "If I make the signal we have practiced, you must run out the back door and go to Rachel's house. She will take care of you until I can come to get you."

On one of the many occasions when they had practiced for this dreaded event, Guillaume had tearfully asked, "What if you do not come to get me?" Alejandro had not answered. He had never considered the possibility that he might not be able to do so.

The boy nodded solemnly. Alejandro gave him a reassuring touch on the cheek and slunk back to the door. He took in a long breath before turning the wood latch.

The door was not shoved inward on the turning of the latch, which would certainly have been the case if King Edward's men were on the other side. When the creak of the hinges stopped, the physician saw a youngish man with a familiar crest emblazoned on the front of his red mantle. He slowly let out the breath he had been holding.

"You are de Chauliac's man."

He received a nod in return.

"I am Canches."

The soldier looked relieved to hear that. "My master says you must come to the palace." He held out a sealed scroll. "I am not to return without you."

On taking the scroll from the soldier's hand, Alejandro said, "He might have requested my presence at a more reasonable hour."

As the physician read what was written, the soldier said, "You are to come immediately. My master says you are to bring the boy with you."

Alejandro stepped back as he considered the contents of the message. He and de Chauliac had discussed and planned for an urgent situation through secret letters over the years, but now that a crisis seemed to be upon him, he felt ill-prepared. "How much time is there?" he asked quietly.

"He only said immediately."

After a few seconds' pause, Alejandro took the man by the arm and drew him inside. "I must see to two matters before we leave," he said.

"But already I have horses waiting at the end of the street," the soldier protested.

"Bring them here and through the house," the physician whispered. "There is a narrow alley behind us where no one will see."

The soldier looked surprised but dutifully turned and went back down the dark street. Alejandro left the door slightly ajar for his return. Then he went to the hearth and put the scroll into the embers. He fanned it with his hand for a few seconds until the parchment caught fire. He watched the wax seal melt as the flames consumed the message, written in de Chauliac's own hand. He said to the small pile of ash, "Thank you, my dear, dear friend."

"Father, wake up. We must leave immediately."

On the best of days, Avram Canches took a very long time to awaken fully. On this night there would be no such luxury.

"Wake up!" Alejandro said as he shook him.

"What..." the old man said.

Alejandro helped his father to a sitting position. "I must take you to Rachel."

On hearing this, the father's face filled with fear. "Truly?" he said.

"Yes, truly. And immediately."

In his confused state, Avram Canches said, "Have you killed someone again, boy?"

"No," Alejandro said gently. "Not of late." He turned away and called for Guillaume. The child appeared in the room within seconds. He was fully dressed and carried a small satchel in his hand.

Alejandro would have smiled, had there been time for such a show of pride. But instead he simply nodded his approval and said, "*arrière-grand-père's* things..." He pointed to a leather case in one corner of the room.

The boy hastened to gather up the old man's belongings. The case was heavy and the child had to struggle, but he did what was required. Alejandro took hold of his father, nearly carrying him. Within seconds, the three were heading out a rear door, into the darkness of the small street that led to Rachel's home just a few doors away. Behind them, the physician heard the sound of hooves stepping into the house and the protesting snorts of the confused horses.

Alejandro did not bother to knock on Rachel's door; such formalities were not necessary with the widow who had been more of a mother to Guillaume than the physician had any right to expect. The boy ran in and out of her house at will, as if it were his own home. On the night of their arrival in Avignon seven years earlier, she had taken Guillaume out of Alejandro's arms and, without so much as one question, put the fair-haired baby to her breast. The milk that would have gone to her own darker child still flowed; she had lost both that child and her husband to plague only days before. Since then, Alejandro's generosity had kept food on her table, but Guillaume's need for her had been far more nourishing.

As she came into the kitchen she wrapped her shawl around her shoulders. Her feet were bare below the white nightdress, and her long dark hair hung loose around her shoulders. For a few precious seconds, he stared at her.

His father was right. She was a beautiful woman.

But urgency reclaimed his attention. "We must go," he said to her.

Rachel nodded sadly; she needed no additional explanation. With a look of terrible unhappiness, she reached out to Alejandro's father. "Come, Avram," she said softly. "I will take you to the bed."

She supported Alejandro's ancient father with great tenderness as he walked unsteadily beside her. Guillaume followed with the bag of possessions. It took a moment for her to settle Avram comfortably into her own bed. Alejandro heard her reassure the old man that she would arrange for his own familiar bed to be brought over on the morrow and that she would sleep by the hearth tonight. He heard the soft rustling as she arranged the covers over Avram. Alejandro looked into the room and saw the heartbreaking confusion on his father's face.

Rachel came out of the room. Alejandro took her by the arm and pulled her aside.

For a few moments their eyes were locked together; neither one said a word. They had been thrown together by fate and had passed more than seven years in a strange sort of intimacy, as comfortable as that which passed between many husbands and wives, perhaps more so. Yet Alejandro had not allowed himself to slip too close to her, for fear that he might one day be forced to leave.

Now that day had come.

"I—I cannot thank you properly. You have been like a daughter to my father."

He saw the sad accusation on her face. *But not a daughter-in-law.*

"I will return as soon as I can." He took hold of her hand and pressed a bag of coins into it. "As long as my father lives, you shall never want, if it is within my power to see you comfortable."

She looked away; he knew her heart was breaking.

"Please," she whispered, "can we not go with you?"

A moment passed; she added, "For your father's sake."

"No," Alejandro said gently.

Her expression turned bitter. "You had best say your good-byes to him, then. God may take him at any moment."

Alejandro said nothing. He left her and went to his father again. He sat down on the straw and tucked the blanket up around the old man's neck.

"I will return as soon as I can, Father."

The response was barely audible. "God willing."

"Yes. Rachel will care for you while we are gone."

Avram looked into his son's eyes. He managed the faintest smile. "She is a good woman. She would make a good wife. You should think about this before it is too late. By the time you come back, you may be so old that she will no longer want you."

The gentle humor of his father's chiding was bittersweet; both of them knew that his return was far from assured.

Alejandro patted his father's hand and said, "You have always given me good advice."

"You have never taken it."

It was true; he had studied medicine against his parents' wishes, far away from their native Spain, and—to his father's complete horror— had never married.

"Well, there is time yet," he said with a smile.

"God willing."

Alejandro leaned over and placed a kiss on his father's forehead. As he rose up to leave, the old man turned away.

Two

Goats were gold—mostly for their milk, since only a few of the cows had survived. Everyone dreamed shamelessly of cheeseburgers—which, unlike all the other assorted creatures they ate, did not taste like chicken. Even chickens didn't taste like chicken in the new world. There were no more plump, seasoned Perdues, just skinny, tough fighters you had to chase around the yard to kill.

"Wiry," Tom would say. Janie Crowe stared down at a textbook example of that wiriness, which lay on a platter in front of her. It was a good-size bird and would feed them all, but it would be nothing but bones by the time dinner was through. She snipped the feet off the already headless bird with a large pair of shears and tossed the clawed appendages into the compost pot, grimacing as she considered that in China someone knew how to make them palatable—assuming anyone was left there, that is.

But of course someone was left there. It was unthinkable that everyone had perished, though no traveling minstrels had come up the mountain with news of that empire. When the minstrels were still coming, there had been reports of Europe and South America, both struggling mightily like North America. If the world ever resumed its connections, everyone surmised that China would roar like a lion to the head of the pride, because when you start with too many people, the elimination of more than eighty percent of them wouldn't be a crippling blow.

Janie glanced out the kitchen window and saw the green tips on the forsythia bush near the compound's main gate. Her heart warmed at the sign of spring. New Englanders were known for their toughness, but even the most hardy souls were felled when DR SAM made its second pass through the world. And among those who'd survived, the unprepared didn't make it through that first bitter winter without power or food, or protection from the bands of marauders who scavenged their way through every Middlesex village and town.

God bless Tom, she thought. It was due to her husband's uncannily thorough planning that they were staying afloat in their mountain compound. Their minimalist life was often rich and rewarding in ways that surprised them. But there were still moments—far too many of them—when Janie's finger itched for a clicker. She was not alone in that longing. "Remote denial syndrome" became—until it ceased to seem funny—the standard laugh-off to the daily chores of survival. Janie missed the comforts of her Before Plague home, as well as her wonderful vehicle, phones, stereos, constant refrigeration, air-conditioning, insect repellent, heat that didn't require stoking, and, and, and . . .

Out of the corner of her eye she saw a blur of motion through the steamy glass, so she wiped away the moisture with the cuff of her sweater. Through the wet streaks that remained, she caught a glimpse of her son, Alex, running in the snow. Sarah would not be far behind. A smile rose, unbidden, onto her face, and all those luxurious comforts she pined for seemed suddenly unimportant.

At seven, Alex was lithe and sure-footed, though he had his share of little-boy moments and, to his physician–mother's dismay, the usual allotment of bumps, bruises, and scrapes. From the moment of his birth, he had been a thing of beauty, a source of joy when there was no other place to find it. In the dark days of winter, he could always be counted on for a laugh and a smile. He seemed to know through some instinctual wisdom when Janie or Tom was distressed and, with one toothy grin, could restore them.

His existence was the result of two combined forces: strong will and miraculous science. When they closed the doors to the outside world and hunkered down for the storm of DR SAM eight years before, Janie had been well past the natural years of unassisted conception, nearing fifty—and she had had a tubal ligation. There were many days when she wondered what she could have been thinking when she begged to have this being implanted in her womb. Child-rearing in a world without machines, she had come to discover, was the work of young women.

He is so beautiful, she thought as she watched him at play. She tapped on the windowpane and her son looked toward her. The sweetest smile came onto his face. As he waved, the snowball he'd been forming fell out of his hands. He tried to catch it but only succeeded in crushing it. Janie saw but could not hear his laughter.

He bounded through the snow toward the back door. In a moment Janie heard the creak of the hinges and the lovely sound of children laughing.

"Wipe your feet!" she called out, "and wash your hands!" Once upon a time, when her daughter Betsy—

rest in peace

—was a child, she would have overlooked the mess on the floor, because a few moments with the central vac would magically make the dirt disappear. Now Janie and Sarah's mother, Caroline, swept with straw brooms they made themselves and beat the rugs with switches, like prairie housewives; it was the only way to vanquish the dirt.

Laundry might as well be pounded on the rocks for all the effort it took without bleach and detergent, though they did have a solar dryer—the long rope clothesline that ran between two thick tree trunks in the courtyard. Tom and Caroline's husband, Michael, would come in with the other men from their chores when the light faded; they took off their sweaty socks, put on their sheepskin slippers, and settled themselves at the table. Dinner would appear, prepared by their wives. After dinner, the men would sit with the children and check their schoolwork while the women cleaned up.

Just like the good old days.

Janie transferred the headless, footless carcass of the chicken to a roasting pan. Turnips and carrots would accompany the sorry thing, but not much else; they were rationing the potatoes so they'd last through spring. Already they'd set a few potato eyes in liquid nutrients to sprout, so the plants would be ready when the soil softened.

She glanced out the window again at the hated snow and thought, *If it ever does.*

Alex came roaring into the kitchen and gave her a big hug. His brown eyes darted around the room, touching on each flat surface in a search for available food. "What's for supper?" he said.

"*That,*" she said, pointing at the chicken. "It'll be another hour and a half before it's ready, though. Just enough time for you to finish that math you started yesterday. But you look like you want something to eat." She turned and picked up a plate of sliced apples on the counter behind her and offered it to him and Sarah.

He beamed as he grabbed a few slices. "Thanks, Mom!" He turned to his playmate. "Come on, Sarah, *math*!"

Sarah squealed in delight and ran after him. Some things about this new world, Janie mused, were all right.

When they were gone, Janie did what she could with the bird—a descendant of the scrawny bloodline that had proved resistant to avian flu. A few crumbled twigs of dried oregano would improve the flavor, if not the texture. No one would care that it was chewy. It was good food, and they were lucky to have it.

Janie washed and dried her hands, then headed toward the lab Tom had set up before they closed the outer gate on what was left of the world. It was small and crowded with equipment, most of which had been state-of-the-art when they first came eight years before. For all they knew in their isolation, it was still just as up-to-date; the world probably hadn't seen much science in the time since DR SAM's most recent iteration. In one corner, there were three climate-controlled cases—more like terrariums—in which dwelled, respectively, a coffee tree, a lemon tree, and a cacao tree. All were healthy and apparently thriving in their perfect little atmospheres, created by small but precious bits of electricity. The northern sun was simply not strong enough at this time of year to warm the air inside the cases.

"Bloom, dammit," she said under her breath as she inspected the trees from beyond the glass. "You have everything you need; now do your thing."

She thought about her last lemon, acquired the day before they came here. She'd scored the skin with her own teeth and rubbed the fruit on her face and hands so she could remember the smell. A memory of another lemon, one she'd been given in London, snuck in; she shoved it away.

The last time they'd ventured outside the confines of their compound, Tom and Michael—the compound's two official explorers—had returned with a dozen or so of what they called, with dark affection, SAM-pulls, which were simply cotton swabs that had been swiped over, dipped into, or smeared with something that might yield a trace of drug-resistant *Staphylococcus aureus mexicalis*. In the beginning, nearly everything they brought back was contaminated in some measure with the voracious bacterium that had crashed the world. As time passed, the percentage of contamination had decreased; the last batch before this one was twenty-four percent.

She had to stop and think about when that last batch was taken. Time ran differently after the plague; they kept a calendar, but no one paid much attention to it except for holidays, which they tried to observe so the habit would be intact if normalcy ever returned. Within each day, the hours moved according to how much daylight was left. The dark was no longer casually illuminated, so daylight was precious. The vernal equinox was just around the corner, and everyone in the compound seemed to be relaxing a bit as more light time became available each day.

Janie leafed backward through the stained and ragged pages of her notebook—her own equivalent of Alejandro's journal. Following his medieval example, she'd kept it faithfully all these eight years. She ran her finger down a page from the previous year. April 24 was the date of the last group—almost a year—and she sighed with dismay on seeing that there had been an eleven-month gap in their journeys outside.

Their life was, sadly, like a medieval siege. They were the hunkered-down keepers of the castle with foes camped openly at the base of the wall, waiting for some indication of weakness or vulnerability, knowing that eventually the food and water would run out. Their foes were not soldiers but something much smaller and far more deadly—vicious, fast-growing bacteria that had proved resistant to every pot of boiling oil they'd thrown over the wall. She thought about Alejandro's journal and what he'd written of his time in Windsor, how he had recorded his observations of his confined world when there was little else to do. Only once during that time—at least that he'd written about—had he left the safe haven of Windsor Castle, in a desperate mission of mercy to soothe the tortured conscience of the king who'd commanded it. The journey had not turned out well, as such journeys had a habit of doing.

She put on a mask and pulled on a pair of vinyl gloves, hoping that the last use had not been the straw that broke the camel's back. There was no telling how many more uses she would get out of them. When they were gone, there was little she would be able to do to protect herself beyond washing her hands when the work was done. Tom had supplied the lab well; there had been dozens of boxes of gloves when they first came there. But who knew their hibernation would last eight years, with no end in sight?

She pulled the sixteen samples out of their toothbrush cases one at a time and poked the stick end of each swab into a lump of modeling clay so the cotton tips couldn't touch each other or anything else. As she did this, she wrote in her notebook the location where each sample had been found, which Tom and Michael had recorded as they gathered them from what remained of the surrounding towns. The numbered toothbrush cases would be sterilized in boiling water before they were used again, and the swabs themselves burned to powdery ash— two time-tested methods of bacterial eradication, just as cheap and effective as in Alejandro's time, though few beyond himself and de

Chauliac seemed to practice those methods, according to the notations in the journal. If her expectations were correct, three or fewer would show signs of infestation, and what bacteria presented itself would likely—though not certainly—be weak and shriveled. One by one, she streaked the cotton surfaces on glass slides, each of which would go under the microscope in turn.

A sense of anticipation came to her as she did this task that she loved so much; it reminded her of the work of her previous life. Not that she didn't get plenty of work in their compound; she'd done several surgeries, including one emergency hysterectomy—a bloody mess that pushed the limits of her tools and equipment. More than once during the procedure, Caroline had had to hold their copy of *Gray's Anatomy* open in front of Janie's eyes so she could look at some detail of a woman's internal parts. It was some help, but not much, because when she opened Lorraine's abdomen, she found a heartbreaking crop of tumors. There were blood smears on the pages now, a reminder, each time she looked in the book, of the draining day that had tested her skills so dramatically. She thanked God that day that she'd had the foresight to bring in enough anesthesia to last.

"Rest in peace," she said quietly. She missed her departed friend.

The focus on the microscope was manual—automation took too much electricity—so she turned the ridged dial slowly until the slide came into focus. She peered into the eyepiece, expecting to see the business-as-usual assortment of odd dead cells, until something moved in one corner of her view.

Her first thought was that she'd seen one of her own eye floaters; they'd been more frequent of late, which was a minor cause of concern. She moved the view on the slide until what had been in the corner was centered. "Okay," she said under her mask, "let's see you do that again."

It obliged with a heave of its sides.

She increased the magnification.

"All right, I guess you're alive, so let's see who you are." A guilty sense of excitement slipped into her psyche; she was a scientist, and it was her nature to dig into things of interest, regardless of how vile and deadly they might be.

In focus on the slide in front of her was a living bacterium, one that looked familiar.

"But you're not DR SAM," she whispered. She watched with fascination as it went through the stages of mitosis and emerged as two separate beings.

It was something new. *And on the very first slide*, she thought with surprise as she pulled it out of the clip and set it aside. *What are the odds of that?* She wrote a small history of that slide in her notebook before putting the next one in place. The next two slides proved predictably boring and unremarkable.

But the three after that were all contaminated with the same microbe.

With a heightened sense of urgency, she worked through the remaining samples. And when she was finally finished, she went through the entire process again, just to be certain that her findings of a contamination rate of nearly seventy percent were correct.

She covered the sample tray with a glass bell and removed her protective gear. She scrubbed her hands at the lab sink until they were red and shook them dry. Before returning to the kitchen, she looked in on Alex and Sarah just long enough to realize, for the thousandth time, how the sight of them could make her ache with love. They were working innocently on slates, talking quietly to each other, and never saw her.

She took a quick peek at the chicken, which was just beginning to brown in the woodstove and filling the lodge with a wonderful aroma. At the back door she put on her boots, then headed out, buttoning her coat on the fly. As she trotted through the courtyard, she passed Terry, who was stacking wood, laying it carefully in neat rows so the logs would dry. She waved; he waved back.

"Where's Elaine?" Janie said.

"Grinding flour."

A Stanford Ph.D. in economics was grinding flour. *Go figure*, Janie thought, finding the irony sublime, because no one understood the value of her own physical labor better than Elaine.

"Tell her dinner will be in about an hour, if you see her."

"Will do."

Tom would be at the power plant, checking to see that everything was all right; it was his daily routine to tuck the camp safely into darkness. As she crunched down the path through the snow, Janie saw the beginnings of a sunset through the mist of her own breath. It was pink and dreamy, almost apocalyptic in its stark loveliness.

On any other day, Janie would have stopped at the vista point for a moment to take it in. She had come, after the plague, to understand the sweetness of each moment of unexpected beauty—for they were outnumbered by moments of hardship and cruelty in this new world. But today she kept moving, because the information she had to deliver seemed urgent.

The door to the power plant was ajar; she looked inside, but Tom was not there. There were fresh footprints in the snow outside the building; she followed them and found her husband removing snow from one of the connections that led to the windmill. He was hatless, despite the cold—a condition not ameliorated by his thinning hair. He'd grown leaner and stronger over time, from the physical requirements of survival. He often quipped that law school hadn't prepared him for this phase of his life, but he was unfailingly good-natured about their circumstances.

His smile was as youthful as ever. As he crunched through the snow, he said, "My beautiful wife. How nice."

Janie did not melt into his embrace as she usually did. She hugged him quickly, then let go. Tom pulled back when he felt the tension in her body.

"What is it?" he said. "Is someone sick?"

"No," she answered with a quick shake of her head. She shivered as a chill went through her, and he pulled her closer.

"No," she repeated. Her voice was little more than a whisper. "At least not yet."

Three

The papal palace looked much the same as it had the last time Alejandro had seen it, some seven years earlier. At that time, the infant Guillaume had been strapped to his chest, rather than sharing the saddle. Their traveling companion on that flight from Paris was a small white goat, who had obliged them with a steady supply of milk. The physician had been dirty and ragged from his journey, and, dressed as he was in common clothing, he was hardly worth notice.

He had stopped in this very square to ask a question of a passerby. *Where do the Jews live?*

Rue des Juifs, naturellement, was the stranger's reply. There, he was reunited with his aged father, and for seven years had lived with him and Guillaume in the *ghetto*, never once venturing outside the borders—which, though invisible, were as distinct as those of any fortress.

Perhaps de Chauliac was wise to send his messenger in the dark hours, he thought.

I will open the door for you, the young soldier had said. He'd given Alejandro detailed directions on where to wait, in a secluded spot at the rear of the palace—a wood door to the right of the stables, with a red pull for the bell. They waited there now, still astride the horse. Guillaume's small arms were around Alejandro's waist, just as his mother's arms had been when they first came out of England, before she grew into a fine young woman.

In the bitter plague winter after her husband's death, when there was little to keep them sane but the telling of tales, Kate had told him of the remark the young page Chaucer had made when he first saw her in Paris.

Why, you might be a twin to my lord Lionel.

"*Grand-père,*" the boy whispered.

Alejandro snapped back to the present. "Yes, Guillaume?"

"Are we where we are going?"

Where *were* they going? He could not yet say.

"For the moment."

"Then why are we still upon the horse?"

Alejandro pondered the appropriate reply. He did not wish to frighten the boy; neither did he wish to dismiss the danger of their situation. Finally he settled on a response. "We may need to continue on," he said. "We will know shortly."

"Ah," the boy said. He seemed satisfied with the answer and rested his head against Alejandro's back. "I am very tired, *Grand-père*. When can we sleep?"

"As soon as it is advisable. Very soon, I hope."

Guillaume leaned against Alejandro's back. Alejandro felt the boy's grip relax as he drifted into a semisleep. He kept very still as they waited in the dark, silent shadow of the palace. After a short while, he heard noise on the other side of the door, and within a few moments the door opened with a long, slow creak of the iron hinges. Alejandro could not see the face of the opener in the dim predawn light, so he put his hand on his dagger and stayed very still until, with great relief, he ascertained by the voice that it was the same young man who had escorted them from *Rue des Juifs*.

He nudged the sleepy boy awake and handed him down to the soldier, who placed the boy on the ground with more tenderness than expected. He wondered if de Chauliac had told the soldier about the boy's true identity, and thought not; such knowledge would only be imparted when there was a need to know, especially by one as cautious as de Chauliac.

After Alejandro dismounted, the soldier took the reins of their horse. He gestured in the direction of the open door, saying, "*Monsieur* will come shortly. Wait inside, but do not wander from the door."

The physician hesitated, but the soldier gestured again for them to enter, as if to indicate that it would be safe. They stepped inside; as the door closed they heard the sound of the horse's hooves on the paving stones as the animal was led away. The soft darkness enveloped them, and Alejandro could hear the beating of his own heart in counterpoint to the *drip drip* of water in the deep passageway. Guillaume clung in silence to the physician's leg. Alejandro could feel the boy's trembling and hugged him tight to his side. Seconds felt like hours with the senses so deprived, but finally they heard the faint sound of footsteps. A dim light came into view in the passageway; its approach kept pace with the footsteps. Soon the figure was close enough to see, but the light of the torch obscured the bearer's features.

What if the approaching figure was not de Chauliac? He pulled Guillaume even closer to him and gripped the handle of his dagger again.

The figure stopped a few steps in front of them. He held the torch high, forcing Alejandro to shield his eyes with a raised hand. When whoever was there said nothing immediately, Alejandro pulled the dagger from its sheath. The sound of the blade scraping along the leather might have been thunder in the stillness that surrounded them.

There was a soft laugh—one that Alejandro recognized instantly.

"You will have no need of that weapon, colleague."

Alejandro could not see de Chauliac's smile, but he sensed it just the same.

"Still always ready for a confrontation," the Frenchman said. "God bless your constancy. You might consider that you are not as young as you once were. But I must say, you are looking rather well for a man of your advanced age."

As his tension drained out of him, Alejandro said, "I would say the same to you, if only I could see your face. And might I remind you, esteemed colleague, your own age is quite a bit more advanced than my own. One wonders if you hide behind that torch for a reason."

When the flame was lowered, the light shone upon the same commanding figure he had last seen in Paris on the night of Guillaume's birth. De Chauliac's chiseled-looking face was more lined and his hair nearly all white now, but the sharp intelligence in his blue eyes had not lessened a bit.

De Chauliac stepped forward and put a welcoming hand on Alejandro's shoulder. "It is good to see you, Physician," he said with unmistakable sincerity. "I have yearned so many times for your company when there were thoughts to be shared." He reached down and touched the top of the boy's head. "And you, young Master Guillaume, have become quite a fair boy."

The boy looked up at Alejandro as if to ask, *Who is this man, who I do not know, who somehow knows me?* Alejandro leaned down and said, "Monsieur de Chauliac has been a loyal friend to us and has helped me personally many times."

"I was present on the day of your birth," the Frenchman said to the boy.

Guillaume looked first at Alejandro in surprise, then at de Chauliac. "You know my mother?" he said eagerly.

De Chauliac cast a quick glance at Alejandro. On his nod of approval, the Frenchman said, "I do, indeed. She is a good woman and her heart would burst with pride if she could see her fine son. But we will speak more of her later; now we must hasten to my quarters."

Alejandro was surprised. "Is it wise? I mean, will you—"

"Have no fear, colleague. I have taken the necessary precautions."

They hurried through the basement corridor by the light of de Chauliac's torch, slipping through the shadows past the kitchen, where—even at that ungodly hour the work of preparing the day's food was well under way. Alejandro kept hold of Guillaume's hand as they made their way up a narrow, winding staircase. More than once the child nearly lost his footing on the damp stone steps. Finally, they emerged, several stories up, a few paces away from de Chauliac's private quarters.

The rooms in which his colleague lived and worked in the papal palace were every bit as much of a sanctuary to their occupant as when Alejandro was first brought there, a frightened young Jew on the run from his crime of passion. He was alone then—a fugitive with no country, no home, no family. He had the sense again that he entered a private lair of a man who, were he less fastidious in his demeanor, might have marked it off as a buck does his piece of the forest. The appointments were a reflection of the Frenchman, who left an indelible mark on nearly everything he touched. The same exquisite tapestries graced the walls; the sumptuous carpets hushed every step, and the furniture gleamed in the torchlight like the still surface of a pond. Guillaume was as awestruck as his grandfather had been on his first occasion there as his eyes traveled slowly over the marvels, drinking in their exotic beauty.

While the boy was absorbed in inspecting his surroundings, Alejandro led de Chauliac far enough away so the child would not hear.

"Speak, my friend, and tell me why we were called here so urgently."

De Chauliac looked in the boy's direction. "Will he sleep?"

"As soon as he calms. He has never seen such things as these before."

"We will speak when he is abed. You must stay the day here, in any case. It is not safe to leave just yet."

"Leave?" he said. He disliked the word before it left his mouth. "Where are we going?"

"To Paris, where you will be safe."

It was the last destination he would have considered. "To Paris? *Safe?* From what?"

"From those who would hurt you, and the boy."

"They have discovered us, then."

De Chauliac said nothing but glanced toward the boy.

"Ah, yes," Alejandro said, acknowledging the need for discretion. "When he sleeps." He leaned closer. "I have been away from the larger world for so long that I am no decent judge of it. Even so, Paris would not be my chosen haven."

"I understand your sentiment," de Chauliac said, "but you must trust me now. You are safe for the moment, and you will be safe there."

Their eyes locked. Once before he had trusted de Chauliac with his life and more.

And I am still alive, he thought. *So is Kate, and so is Guillaume.*

"Please. Forgive my impatience."

De Chauliac nodded. "It is your nature, after all." His eyes settled again on Guillaume. "The boy seems to have found something of interest."

They moved across the large salon and stood on either side of Guillaume, who ran his hand back and forth on the polished surface of a table with quiet awe. He looked up at Alejandro and said, "*Grand-père*, the wood is so smooth—I can see my face!"

He moved his small fingers over the carved edges of the table, examining their shape and texture with a light and reverent touch.

De Chauliac leaned over—with some difficulty, for he was extremely tall—and said, "I will have a special treat for you later, but first you must take some rest. Young boys need sleep, for it is in repose that you grow."

The child looked up at him, and then at his grandfather. "Really?" he said.

"Really. Now," he said, extending his hand, "if you will but follow me, young man, we shall find you a soft place...."

The boy allowed himself to be led into the separate bedchamber. Alejandro watched through the door as de Chauliac settled Guillaume onto a *chaise longue*.

"He seems to trust you," Alejandro said when de Chauliac returned.

"The boy follows your lead—in all things, one imagines." He pointed to the same shiny table that Guillaume had admired. "You have been known to admire a thing of beauty. Now, sit, colleague. There is much to discuss."

Alejandro did as bidden; de Chauliac went to the very same table and picked up a sheaf of parchments, first carefully removing the stone weights he had placed on both ends against the inevitable curl brought on by Avignon's often damp weather. He carried the lot to where Alejandro sat and offered it to him.

Wearing a look of confusion, Alejandro took the offered pages and placed them on his lap. He read the opening lines on the first page:

> In God's name, here beginneth the inventory or gathering together of medicine in the part of surgery, compiled and fulfilled in the year of our Lord 1363 by Guy de Chauliac, Surgeon and Doctor of Physik in the full clear study of Montpellier. . . .

He looked up in astonishment. "Colleague . . . what treasure is this?"

"A manual of surgery," he said with quiet pride. "I have begun one, at long last."

Alejandro began to turn the pages, now wearing a look of joy and wonder, but de Chauliac placed his hand on the stack of sheaves.

"This is the reason I have given to his Holiness to explain my sudden need to travel to Paris. We will speak more of this work in time. But right now we have more immediate matters to discuss."

Kate aligned the ivory combs on the dresser in the specific order preferred by her sister Isabella. She stared at the arrangement, which rested precisely on a brocaded silk scarf, and wondered if Isabella had ever actually touched any of the combs herself; her hair was always dressed by one of the many ladies who clucked incessantly around the royal apartment, meeting the princess's every need with stunning immediacy. *Her world consists of lotions and silks and lace*, Kate thought. *She knows nothing of her people, who live beyond these walls.*

She used the tip of her finger to move one of the combs ever so slightly, until it was just visibly out of line with its companions. It was a peevish gesture but one that would send her older half sister into a wild rant. She regretted that she would not hear it; by then, the soldiers would have come to take her away again. Poor Nurse—dear, venerable, faithful Nurse—would have to listen to the diatribe that followed, despite the queen's mandate to Isabella that she treat the old servant more tenderly. It was an instruction that the Plantagenet princess—the only marriageable daughter of King Edward and his lawful queen—chose to ignore. Despite Nurse's best efforts, Isabella had grown into her father's daughter more than her mother's; she was a demanding, self-absorbed, and petulant woman, shrewdly devoted to the pursuit of all that she desired. She wore arrogance as visibly as a harlot wore rouge and kohl, without even the slightest attempt at subtlety.

But for all her similarities of temperament, Isabella bore only a passing physical resemblance to her father, King Edward. Not so with Kate, who had, since her abduction from Paris by her half brother's retainers, made no secret of her hatred for Edward—or for Isabella.

She knew the king's knock when it sounded and wondered why he bothered, for he never waited to hear *Entrez*. He would simply enter, without a decent interval, for his daily attempt at reconciliation, though she could not for the life of her understand why he wished to reclaim their kinship after so many years of denial.

"You need not bother to knock next time," she said defiantly. "Save your knuckles."

He walked across the room with long strides. "Such anger, such contempt," he said. "It is not fitting for a princess." He made a point of emphasizing the last word. As he glanced around the salon, his eyes came to rest on a pile of rumpled garments in one corner. He walked over to it and picked up the ivory velvet mantle that lay on top. "Nor is this mess. Why are my gifts in a heap on the floor?"

"Because the window is barred, and I could not throw them into the courtyard."

The king's voice darkened. "Do these riches not please you, daughter?"

Her reply was spoken without hesitation. "You are no father to me."

She saw the anger flare in his eyes and shrank back, but he lurched forward suddenly and took her by the arm. The Plantagenet king yanked the defiant young woman he had sired to the looking glass and held her still in front of it. She closed her eyes against the pain of his grip, but he squeezed her arms until she cried out.

"Open your eyes and look into the glass, or I shall squeeze harder. Better yet," he added, "I will summon one of those burly Celts who escort you to and fro. Perhaps they can convince you to take a look. Or maybe," he said, "I will send them out to collect your son." After a pause for effect, he said, "The boy is well within my grasp."

She opened her eyes and stared straight ahead but would not meet her father's stare.

"That's right," the king said as he tightened his grip on her flesh. "Even you cannot fail to see the resemblance between us." He let go of her arm and shoved her away.

She rubbed her arm and fought back the tears, lest he see her weakness. "Indeed," she said, "you have left more than a passing mark on me."

The king grabbed hold of her hair and pulled her close. She squeezed her eyes tightly shut.

"I gave you life," he hissed into her ear. "You would be wise to thank me for that gift."

"You may reclaim that life," she whispered back, "when you find it convenient. You will hear no complaint from me. That would be the most desirous gift you can give me."

He pushed her away again, almost violently, and she fell to the floor. "You forget to whom you speak!"

She pushed herself up and looked directly into his eyes. "I speak to the man who denied me as an innocent child, and now, after years of abandonment, would claim me as his own. Well, you shall not have me. My father will come for me. You might prepare yourself."

The king laughed aloud. "Your father?" he sneered. "A stinking Jew, a coward who has not shown himself in seven years! He stole your son—my grandson—and yet still you speak of him as if he were the Savior himself! You dwell in delusion, daughter. He will not come. And if he should foolishly attempt it, we will take him prisoner."

Kate's voice trembled; she could not hide it from the king. "He will come."

"You sound as though you must convince yourself."

Barely above a whisper, she said again, "He will come."

The king stomped off but turned back at the door. "He had better hurry, then." He strode out, slamming the heavy door behind him.

De Chauliac and his protégé were finally alone.

"I sent for you because there is news on two fronts. First, the king has written to the pope requesting the approval of a match for Isabella."

For a moment, Alejandro said nothing. "I shall say a prayer for her bridegroom," he finally offered, his voice bitter. "The man will soon find himself in need of grace."

"Indeed," de Chauliac said. "But it may be Isabella who will need your prayers."

"I shall not pray to any god for her happiness."

"She is to marry de Coucy."

Alejandro nearly leaped to his feet. "Dare you say!" The long rows of desperately wounded soldiers of the ill-fated *Jacquerie* came into his mind's eye, and he revisited for a brief moment the atrocities that de Coucy—under the command of the Count of Navarre—had carried out in quashing their rebellion. Though de Coucy was but a young baron of eighteen at the time, he had displayed a ruthlessness more fitting for an older, embittered warrior. By the time sun set on that terrible battle, Alejandro and Kate were drenched in the blood of the fallen comrades of her husband, Guillaume Karle, whose own head had perhaps been taken by de Coucy himself. The only reason that Kate herself was still alive after de Coucy and Navarre descended upon them was her swift and sure placement of a knife at de Coucy's crotch when he grabbed her from behind.

He saw now the image of this monster at the side of the wretched and scheming Isabella. What a fitting couple they made—two demons of the dark.

May they dance at their wedding in shoes of hot iron and make their marriage bed on hot coals.

"Surely God cannot allow such a horror as this to take place!" he seethed.

De Chauliac put a hand on Alejandro's shoulder and gently pushed him back to sitting. "Please, colleague, you will take a shock with your outbursts, and I have need of you yet. Sit, and calm yourself. There is much more to tell."

The tall Frenchman poured himself a glass of brandy. "Will you have one, for your constitution?" He did not wait for the reply but poured anyway. "His Holiness will naturally approve the match, since *la famille* de Coucy have always supported him. This is an excellent match for them. Quite excellent. Of course, they would expect nobility in their son's bride, but royalty should have been beyond them—the daughter of a king, the king of England, is too much to be hoped for. But as we all well know, she is an evil shrew, worthy only to be Satan's bride, and he is a hostage in Edward's court, against a ransom. Edward will do everything in his power to see that it takes place." He paused before saying, "Word has it, incredibly, that they are very much in love, despite the difference in their ages."

Alejandro sat back in his chair and imagined Isabella as she might now be—a woman of thirty-three or perhaps thirty-four years, whose sharp beauty would certainly have begun to harden. With four failed matches behind her, she would be on the verge of desperation. De Coucy at twenty-six would be in the fullness of his manhood, swarthy and dark, a steely and well-muscled warrior.

"Love, between such a pair? Indecent. And love is of no import in such arrangements, or so you have stated before. Therefore, you must tell me, de Chauliac, what importance this has to bring me out of the *ghetto* with the boy. Let Isabella and her beastly bridegroom spend their honeymoon in hell. My only concern is my daughter."

De Chauliac wanted to remind his comrade that Kate was not truly his daughter, but this hardly seemed the time. "Therein lies the main reason for my summons," he said gently. "It seems that the king is seeking to legitimize her, so she can be wed as well. He has written to the pope with that request."

Alejandro gripped the arms of the chair and leaned forward. "This cannot be true," he said.

"I have seen the letter myself, Canches, and I know it is true."

"But who . . ."

"De Coucy has asked that she be given to one of his retainers, a distant cousin, a count whose name is Benoit. There is little known about him other than that he is a fellow of some means and property, most of it in Bretagne, where Edward has little influence. And so by giving her to him he accomplishes two goals: He cements his bargain with de Coucy and puts his fingers on Bretagne."

"I will rip him from neck to navel if ever I see him again!"

"Whom shall you rip—de Coucy or the king?"

"Both," he snarled, "given the opportunity."

"You must learn to curb your temper, my friend. Your impetuous acts have cost you dearly in the past. This excess of emotion is unhealthy and will be your undoing."

Alejandro ignored his friend's warning and pushed himself out of the chair. He paced back and forth on the thick oriental carpet in de Chauliac's salon, muttering to himself. Then he turned to de Chauliac and said, "I must depart immediately. I will take her out of the castle and bring her back here. She will be safe in Avignon, among the Jews. . . ."

De Chauliac saw his friend's distress and agitation. "Calm yourself, colleague; now is the time for temperance, not tempestuousness. I brought you here as soon as the news arrived, so there is time yet to formulate a plan and then to act. The pope has not yet given his approval for the match, though I am sure he will agree. The message has only just arrived. There is much to be gained in delaying his response. The king will become nervous and perhaps conciliatory on other matters. This is a game they play with each other."

"I cannot delay. I must go now, to afford myself every advantage." The anger in his voice changed to regret. "I should have gone for her before."

"You would have failed. The time was not right. There was too much strife in the land, and there is plenty still! Soldiers are all about, and though they are fewer in number than before, they are no doubt still seeking you, with no war to distract them."

Alejandro slumped back into the chair again. There was defeat in his voice. "So," he said, "how shall I proceed, then?"

"Go first to Paris with me. Bring the boy. You will be safe there, I assure you. When we arrive, I will put some of my retainers to the task of gathering further intelligence on these events. Then we will take measure of what you ought to do next. There will be many travelers heading for England as soon as the betrothal is announced. You might be able to lose yourself among them."

"Or be recognized."

"There is, of course, that risk."

"And what shall I do, with a small child in tow?"

"If we deem it advisable, he can remain in Paris, in my home, and we will house him among the servants." De Chauliac paused, to let Alejandro consider the things he had said. "His Holiness is in good health for the moment, and he is not as demanding a patient as his predecessors, so I will ask for permission to travel to Paris to work on my Cyrurgia. I have no doubt that he will oblige me. You can travel as an assistant to me; no one will be the wiser."

He did not say, as he might have, that a certain intelligence had already come his way that the king's soldiers had been told to double their efforts to find the Jew physician and bring him to England. There would be time for that bitter news later, when they were safely in Paris.

The Frenchman shuddered, then coughed. Alejandro's eyes were upon him in an instant.

"You are pale, colleague." He came forward and placed a hand on de Chauliac's forehead. "And you are feverish."

De Chauliac pulled Alejandro's hand away. "Excessive emotion," he said. "See how it affects one; you must take my advice and proceed in a calm and cautious manner, or it will take its toll on you as well."

Alejandro said nothing to this dismissal; it was de Chauliac's nature to command him, and he would not allow himself to take offense, as he might have done long ago. He returned to his chair and lay back in the chair with eyes closed. The gravity of his situation descended upon him in a terrifying darkness. *Once again,* he thought miserably, *I am torn from safety. Once again, I must flee.*

*f*our

"Could it be just an anomaly?" Tom asked. "A statistical blip?"

Janie hesitated for a moment before answering. When she did, her tone was equivocal. "Of course. There could be any number of explanations. Clusters of an unfamiliar bacteria don't necessarily mean there's a problem."

"We'll talk to Kristina. Right after dinner."

A silence fell, the sort that settles over two people when each is engaged in private worry over the same matter. Each one would fret along a separate route to arrive at the same disturbing place, namely: *How do we survive?*

Husband and wife walked hand in hand along the path that led to the lodge. They reached the same vista point where the sunset had beckoned to Janie; down in the valley through the still-bare trees, the last of the day's light danced in orange and gold steps on the calm water. Tom tugged on Janie's hand, holding her in place.

"We need to get back," she said.

"Wait. Just enjoy this with me."

He pulled her closer; she leaned against him. A flood of warmth and safety rushed through her, dispelling her worry for one brief moment.

"I wonder if the sunsets will be this beautiful when all the pollution filters out of the atmosphere," Tom said.

"What makes you think it will?"

He gave her a surprised look. "No buses, no cars, no coal-fueled power plants."

"They might be out there somewhere."

"You're a dreamer, my love. It's all gone."

"We don't know that."

Tom gave her hand a squeeze and said, "Well, I hope you're right and that whoever is still out there is friendly."

They soaked up the glowing peace for a few moments. Janie said, very quietly, "I feel so small when I look out from here. I mean, I feel small in general these days, but this is a better kind of small."

"Yeah," Tom said. He slipped his arm around her waist. "Part-of-the-larger-universe small, not part-of-the-food-chain small."

That brought a smile to her face. "Speaking of food, there's a chicken roasting, such as it is."

They left the sunset to its own demise and set out at a brisk walk.

They were barely inside the door when Alex came running around the corner and leaped into his father's arms, completely disregarding Tom's one-boot-on, one-boot-off condition. Tom caught him up in a hug.

Sarah wasn't far behind; Janie put an arm around the girl's slender shoulders. She looked down on the amazing red hair, the sea of freckles, and the gap-toothed smile.

"Show me those dimples," she commanded. Sarah complied by squeezing her eyes shut and grinning widely. Two distinct indentations, one on each cheek, were proof that she was Caroline Rosow's daughter.

"Wanna see me roll my tongue?" the little girl asked excitedly.

"Show-off!" Alex said.

"You can't!" Sarah teased.

"So what?"

"That's enough," Caroline said as she came around the corner. "It's not a talent, Sarah, it's a genetic trait, and a pretty useless one at that. Get over it. Now go wash your hands. Dinner's ready."

Alex stuck out his nonrolling tongue; Sarah wrinkled her nose up at him. Then she turned to her mother and said, "But we already washed our hands when we came in."

"Wash them again," Caroline repeated, "or you can go sit in your dark bedroom while everyone else eats dinner."

Alex looked up at his mother.

"You too," Janie said.

They ran off, grumbling. Janie smiled and said, "That was pretty medieval."

"Hey, they knew how to raise kids back then." She turned to Tom. "How's Jellybean doing?"

"The hoof still seems to be a little tender, but I saw Ed walking her this afternoon and she looked like she was doing well. The crisis seems to have passed, thanks to your TLC."

"That's a relief. Well, we should probably eat."

They all went off in different directions momentarily, but within a few minutes the occupants of the compound began to drift to the long table, drawn in by the sounds and smells of supper. Flour-dusted Elaine and wood-scented Terry worked at settling his Alzheimer's-afflicted mother into a chair at one end of the table. She would not lift her leg over the bench, even though she could, so the same chair was always reserved for her. Elaine and Terry's daughter, Patricia, sat to the old woman's right. She tucked a napkin into her grandmother's collar and patted her fondly on the shoulder. Ed Golochuk, a former FedEx driver who'd always been a bit of a loner, squeezed in next to her and gave her a little smile. Food was passed politely from person to person; conversations began about the day's activities.

Positively Waltonesque, Janie thought as she regarded the scene from the kitchen door. The news she had to deliver after dinner would alter that precious and ethereal dynamic, so hard-won among a "family" as large as theirs. She grabbed the last of the platters, this one loaded with mashed turnips, and slipped into the space that Tom and Alex had left between them just for her.

Janie could see the relief on Caroline's face as Tom elaborated on his report about the mare, which was bolstered by Ed's agreement. The task of treating the ailments of the horses might more naturally have fallen to herself as a physician, but they'd learned in short order after arriving at the lodge that chores were often better doled out by passion than time before vocation. Caroline, a research biologist, didn't want to be in the lab, but she'd happily taken on the job of caring for the occupants of the barn and the stables. She milked the goats, sheared the sheep, and hovered maternally over the last two cows of the twelve they'd originally had. In time they determined that a mutation of the DR SAM bacterium had felled them, starting as an infection in the udder of one animal. The disease had spread from one stall to the next, showing symptoms that mimicked the human version of DR SAM. When there were seven left, they isolated them all, in the hope of staving off the spread. Five more died anyway.

Janie watched and listened as her husband spoke about the horse's foot. This kind and generous man had once been on the short list for a vacant seat on the federal bench; in the time after, he had become the clan's tinkerer. Tom fixed and fashioned with limitless energy, showing patience that amazed everyone as he worked and reworked and then re-reworked his creations until each device was as sublimely functional as it could be. He'd put together carts with removable wheels to move the dead cows; the wood slabs on which they were transported would have to be burned along with the carcasses. They had a whole forest full of wood, but only a few wheels.

Janie heard deep laughter from the other side of the table as Michael Rosow responded to his daughter's rolled tongue. On a sharp glance from Caroline, he winked at Sarah and said, in his thick English accent, "Put that thing away, will you, love, and eat your turnips?" He gestured with his continentally held fork toward the steaming golden pile on her plate. "Ed and I went to a lot of trouble to grow them nice and tasty just for you, so be a good girl now and eat up."

Michael was one of their two farmers—a far cry from the cop he'd once been, but he would often say, with his patented flirtatious wink, "Once a copper, always a copper."

But Janie would forever and always think of him in a more defined way, as a biocop.

The green suit he wore in the time before was packed carefully away in protective plastic bags, each little part thoroughly scrubbed. Some of the parts to that amazing suit—the ones that could withstand the heat—were steamed before storage. He'd had it on only a few times since they'd come into the compound; one of those times was the day they dragged the cows out for immolation. Janie knew that it could not have been fun to do that heavy work inside a sealed suit on a hot day, but there was only one suit, and he was the only one who knew how to use it. The others—especially the men—watched guiltily, as he labored for the benefit of the entire group.

Across the Atlantic he'd come, tracking her and Caroline from London to the Berkshires. His superiors hadn't wanted him to follow the lead in the mysterious plague incident to America; there was too much red tape involved in traveling from one country to another in the era of DR SAM, even when it was official business. But she and Caroline had information on the death of an old man in London, so the British biocops let Michael go, and he'd found Janie and Caroline rather handily with a few clicks on the keyboard in a state-police barracks. He showed up on Janie's doorstep one afternoon and, after a polite and proper introduction, explained that he was in need of additional information on the demise of one Robert Sarin.

We questioned your friend Dr. Ransom on the matter already—picked him up at Heathrow when he was bounced back by your Customs—but he wasn't able to tell us much.

Though she didn't fully understand why she was inclined to trust him, Janie let Michael Rosow in and promptly called Caroline. Many times since then, Tom had chided her. *You should have called your lawyer—that would be me—first.*

"But it turned out okay," she'd replied in her own defense. "Well, in fact."

Luckily.

Janie recognized the attraction between Michael and Caroline instantly, though it took the pair themselves a bit longer. It was Tom who arranged the necessary visas, allowing Michael to stay in the United States. He went back to the familiar green suit, but this time in a strange new land.

But he was still a British biocop when he first questioned them. "You dug the sample out of the ground near Sarin's house, and then you sent it to the lab to be tested. For plague, you say?"

"Yes."

In retrospect, their explanation seemed absurd. She could hear herself still, cringing as she recounted the events, pleading to be believed.

I was working on a paper, and I needed to determine if the Great Fire of 1666 had a purifying effect on the soil. I needed samples from a grid of locations throughout London. One of them landed there, in that park near where he lived.

And it got loose from the lab at the institute?

Unfortunately.

Was Dr. Ransom involved in that incident?

No! It was his boss who caused the accident. Bruce was really just trying to contain it.

He finally came to believe her after she showed him Alejandro's journal, before she brought it to Myra for safekeeping in the Hebrew Book Depository. But every now and then, Michael would still ask questions. Across the table, he and Sarah were trading funny faces. Farther down at one end, Tom's daughter, Kristina, smiled and laughed to watch them.

It was Kristina who had deciphered the puzzle of the mutation that got the cows—she with her incredible brilliance, who could recite the periodic table of the elements and write out the genetic-code sequence of DR SAM from memory—the same young woman who had to write down her own birthday because the neural path that once led directly to that memory was no longer in existence. And despite the odd, sometimes debilitating flaws in her memory, it was she to whom they would present the problem of the bacterial cluster. As soon as they all got through washing and drying the dishes.

. . .

There was never any food left after a meal, so the cleanup was quick. No one was fat; body energy was more easily acquired and spent than electricity, though their generator and windmill produced just enough of that for the essentials.

And my fruit trees, Janie thought as she turned on the fluorescent bulb in the small table lamp that would illuminate their discussion. The light of the fire would not be enough tonight. The adults—Kristina was twenty-five, depending on how you counted—gathered around the table with a slab of white enameled metal, a drop leaf from a table someone had brought along. They discovered, quite by accident, that pencil markings could be washed away, leaving the surface white and writable. Alex had initially been scolded for the act that led to this discovery, but he'd been thanked many times since. Paper was no longer an option.

Janie began by explaining what she'd found and why it seemed remarkable to her. "The numbers were going down consistently, and all of a sudden there's this new thing. It looks a lot like the bacteria that causes plague, but it can't be, not at this time of year. I don't know if it's a mutation of DR SAM or what. It just seems unlikely that it would be a natural anomaly."

"But it could be, right?" Tom looked back and forth between Janie and Kristina.

The two women glanced at each other for a brief moment, then looked around at the hopeful faces of their clanmates.

"I'm not sure," Janie said. "I didn't take enough statistics in school to answer that question."

"Could be," Kristina said after a moment.

A small sigh went through all the others.

"But I'm guessing it's not."

In the silence that followed, she gave an explanation, accompanied by a John Maddenesque map on the enamel, with circles and arrows and paths of progress. She pointed out the locations of previous sampling points, then scribbled a tight circle to indicate the location of the one Janie had examined. It was well inside the rough ring of previous samples.

"These are all DR SAM spots," she said. "They're close to the places where we found this new one. Maybe this is a mutation, but I don't know...."

Michael was the first one to lean back out of the light so he could process his thoughts; the others all followed shortly. After a few moments, Kristina spoke again. "I think we need to go to these two spots and take additional samples." She pointed to two locations on the map. "Something's coming back, or starting up, whatever this is. We need to verify it."

"But how?" Terry said. "And why now, after all these years?"

"One problem at a time," Patricia said. "Let's concentrate on *if* before we give any energy to how and why."

There was silence in the entire group for a short while. Finally, Michael rose up. "Well," he said, "guess what day tomorrow is?"

People glanced back and forth at each other in mild confusion, wondering why such a question would be asked at this moment. Finally Caroline said, "Someone's birthday?"

He gave her a smile that seemed almost sad. "No, love. It's March seventeenth. Saint Patrick's. A good day for the wearing of the green."

ƒive

The high-stepping horses ridden by the papal guards wore the same red regalia, matching the mantles of their riders, as Alejandro recalled from fifteen years back. But before they'd gone ten leagues, the fretted borders with gold fleurs-de-lis were caked and brown by the splatter that rose up from their hooves. Then, as now, he rode in the company of the pope's soldiers, but this time—unlike before—he was dressed in the simple traveling garb of a common man, not the embroidered mantle and breeches he had worn as the pope's emissary to the English court. And on this journey, de Chauliac himself was among the travelers. As befitted his station, the Frenchman wore the flowing burgundy-colored robes and squared hat of a master physician. His white hair stuck out in stark contrast. He would attract all the notice as they passed through town after town; no one would pay any attention to the quiet dark-haired man at the rear of the procession, who carried a small child on the horse with him.

Guillaume was quite subdued and grew more contained as the distance grew between him and the only home he'd known. His customary exuberance was replaced by a staid and somber demeanor. For miles at a time, he said nothing, and though his grandfather was relieved—*we must not do anything to attract attention to ourselves*—he was also concerned and a bit saddened to see the change. He was pained as well that though he and de Chauliac were at long last reunited, they could not speak of their shared passions during their travel. He longed for an opportunity to discuss the things they had each learned, separate from the other. Their secret correspondences had been precious, detailed, and satisfying, but they were limited to parchment, without the spontaneous give-and-take that had marked their discussions. To have the friend there in person—to provoke, respond, and challenge—would have been glorious. As the familiar road unfurled before them, Alejandro considered that when he first rode this way, de Chauliac had been the master, and himself the pupil. He had been in awe of the depth and breadth of his mentor's knowledge. Yet, it was Alejandro Canches who stunned Guy de Chauliac with the insight that would prompt their most compelling discourse.

Rats.

What do you mean, rats?

It is rats that cause plague.

Nonsense!

Think of it, de Chauliac. Where there are rats, there is plague.

De Chauliac promptly pronounced the assertion an insanity:

There are rats everywhere.

"Precisely," Alejandro said aloud.

Guillaume turned his head and made a curious face, as if to ask, *What did you say?*

"Nothing," Alejandro said, knowing the boy's question without hearing it. "Nothing of any import."

Not far north of Avignon, they were put upon a barge and poled up the Rhône until the cascade of spring flow from *le Massif Central* made the current too much to battle; they put back ashore again and continued their journey on horseback until they came to the village of Valence, still on the river. Therein lay the monastery where they would pass the first night of their travel. De Chauliac was bowed into the courtyard by several footmen and a dozen or so brown-clad monks and then promptly disappeared through the door in the company of a prelate in a red robe and a mitered cap. His fellow travelers—Alejandro and Guillaume among them—were left in the care of a groom, who showed them to the stables where they would bed in straw among the horses.

The town itself was only a short distance from the monastery. Guillaume could not keep his eyes off the lights spilling out of the tavern's windows, and when Alejandro tried to guide him inside the stable, the child resisted.

"We must stay hidden," he said to the boy.

"But, *Grand-père*, there is music—can we listen, please?"

"No, Guillaume, we must make sure that no one sees us."

"But just for a while; no one will know us there."

He was right, of course; there was little real risk in going to the tavern. It might, in truth, be more noteworthy if they did *not* go there. The only soldiers about were those in their own party. Half remained *en garde* in full regalia; the other half, save one, went to the tavern as soon as they were at liberty. The slight-looking soldier who stayed behind seemed ill at ease among the others and slipped quietly into the stables as the rest departed. Alejandro thought to invite the fellow to come along but decided, based on the soldier's purposeful retreat, against doing so.

But if this was a papal guard among comrades, why was he staying back when there might be jollity ahead?

This moment of suspicion slipped away when he saw the look of curiosity on Guillaume's face. He was not surprised to see the excitement; the long ride from Avignon to Paris in 1348 had been a huge part of his own education in the ways of the world, and he would never forget one bit of it—even those horrors that were better forgotten. The little boy in his care had never been outside the Avignon *ghetto*, except for his birth and the hard journey Alejandro had made from Paris to Avignon with the infant strapped to his chest. What sort of education was that for the grandchild of the king of England?

"All right," he said to Guillaume. "We shall have some music, but you must promise to be careful not to speak to strangers."

He held Guillaume behind him at the tavern door until he could look around; seeing nothing remarkable, he let the boy come forward. Guillaume's eyes, wide as saucers, darted hungrily from one fascination to the next, taking it all in. The women in the tavern wore clothing that would have been considered shameful among the Jewesses of the *ghetto* for its scantiness and bright color. They sported laces and jewels, outrageous hats, and pointed shoes.

"Why do the women all have such tall foreheads?" Guillaume asked.

"They pluck back their hair because the high forehead is considered a sign of elegance."

Guillaume shrugged. "I don't see why," he said. "They look odd to me."

"Myself as well," his grandfather admitted.

The jocund behavior of the French bourgeoisie—singing, dancing, brawling, the enthusiastic *causerie*—all held the child rapt.

"Are you hungry?" Alejandro asked him.

"Oh, yes!"

"Then let us sup." He motioned to the landlord with one hand. When the man came, he asked for bread and cheese and, for himself, a draught of ale.

"You shall have your first taste of ale tonight, Guillaume."

Guillaume took the flask eagerly but made a face when the bitter liquid touched his tongue.

"The boy is right sensible in his taste."

Alejandro turned toward the voice and saw an elderly man with white hair and gray whiskers. When the old gent grinned, his face crinkled with a thousand lines, but his eyes were clear and blue and full of vitality.

"Don't like the ale in this place much myself," he said. "But drink it I do, for the water is not to be drunk, not for love nor money."

Alejandro's interest was instantly piqued. "And why is that, good sir?"

The man looked around, as if he might be overheard. "Well," he said when he was satisfied that no one was within distance, "it makes a man sick to drink it. But the landlord won't admit that his well is bad."

The physician moved closer, ignoring the elderly man's rancid breath. "What signs of sickness does one have after drinking this water?"

The man peered into his eyes and said, "You have the sound of a Spaniard."

After all his years in exile, he'd thought all traces of his origin had been erased. But this man had deciphered him, after just a few sentences.

"I have lived in many places," he said cautiously, "among them Spain. I suppose my tongue took a liking to the sound of the language. But pray, continue—sick, how?"

"Those who drink from it all develop *la grippe*," the old man said. "They cannot contain themselves, one end or the other, if you understand my meaning." His eyes fairly twinkled with the unsavory revelation.

"I do, indeed," the physician said. "But surely such a malady cannot be entirely attributed to the water?"

"And why not? Strangers who come to town even for a visit of short duration leave clutching their sides. They rush off into the woods to relieve themselves, and we never see them again."

"But what of those who dwell here? Surely they are not continuously afflicted."

"Ah! Untouched," the old man said. " 'Tis curious, indeed."

"Yourself?"

"Untouched." He grinned mischievously. "But then, I do not drink the water, as I told you. Only the ale." He lifted his flagon in salute and then drank it down in one long pull. He set the flagon down and wiped the froth from his mouth with one sleeve. "And where might ye be coming from?"

"Montpellier," Alejandro answered.

"Grand—"

The physician shushed the boy with one stern look.

"And your destination?"

"Strasbourg," he answered.

This time Guillaume said nothing about the lie Alejandro told.

"A long journey," the old man said.

"Indeed. And a strenuous one."

"Well, I bid you Godspeed," the old man said. He started to rise but gave one last tipsy caution. "Remember, do not drink from the well." He leaned closer. "The Jews have poisoned it, they say."

And with that he departed, leaving Alejandro speechless and angry.

They ate their bread and cheese quickly and returned to the stables. The small soldier who had stayed behind was the only one there, already abed, with only his hooded head visible above the blanket that he'd pulled tightly around him. Alejandro glanced briefly at the boots standing straight upright between the soldier's pallet and the next, toes and heels aligned, curiously neat.

Entirely too neat—it was as if this soldier had created a little wall between himself and the comrade who would lay beside him.

And why had this soldier not spoken? The man seemed to shrink back when words were exchanged among his fellows.

He settled the boy in the straw, but Guillaume was fidgety; he tossed and turned in a way that would never have happened in his own bed in Avignon. Finally, Alejandro spoke to him.

"What is the cause of your agitation, Guillaume?"

The boy sat up on one elbow. "Are we really going to that other place you said?"

Instantly, Alejandro put a finger to his pursed lips. "Shhh," he said in a whisper. He glanced over his shoulder at the small soldier, who seemed already to be asleep. Nevertheless, he lowered his voice so no one else could hear.

"No, child, we are going to Paris."

The boy took his grandfather's signal and whispered as well.

"Then why did you tell that man something else?"

"Because we must be very careful not to be discovered."

"But why?"

The physician did not answer immediately. "In time, you shall know why," he said. "But for now you must be satisfied to wonder. It is a hard task for a boy, I know. Will you try?"

"Yes, *Grand-père*," came the reply, but there was disappointment in the boy's voice.

"Patience, Guillaume, all will be well."

He wished he could believe that himself.

The door to the ladies' quarters was opened by Isabella's ancient nurse. Her face, framed as it was by the stiff white headpiece, was a map of wrinkles.

"What do you want, boy?"

"Ah, good Nurse, I beg you to reconsider your wordage. *Lad* is so much preferable to *boy*. It hints of impending manhood. Grant me at least that."

She looked him up and down with great misgivings. "As you wish, then. What do you want, *lad*?"

"I would speak with the lady Kate, if that is permissible."

"At the moment, it is not. She is currently attending to the princess," the nurse said.

There was a tone of bitterness in her voice that was not lost on Geoffrey Chaucer. He had, in fact, expected to find her thus engaged. "And when do you think she might be done with said engrossing activity, if I may be so bold to ask?"

"You may, but I cannot give you a direct answer. She will be done, I fear, when it pleases the princess for her to be done."

"Then might I leave a note for her?"

Nurse held out her hand. He handed her the paper he had written in anticipation of this outcome.

"I will await her reply, when it is convenient, with much eagerness."

Nurse tucked the paper into one of her billowing sleeves, wishing to God that she had the audacity to read it.

.   .   .

Kate stood and watched with several other ladies of her sister's house-hold as the princess paraded out an army of dresses for comment. Her disgust swelled to near bursting as opinion after opinion was issued by Isabella's attendants, but only after Isabella's own thoughts on the gar-ment were safely revealed by her enthusiasm or lack thereof. To a one, the ladies parroted back what Isabella herself seemed to think.

One was too garish, another too bright, still another too subdued—not one among the dozens of dresses seemed to satisfy her. She pulled the last dress out of the chest brought by one of her tailors and held it up for everyone to see. It was long and simple, made of pale silk in the color of a rose that had been pressed between the pages of a book and allowed to dry, a soft and creamy shade of pink. There were ornate em-broideries in the same color all around the hem and cuffs. Kate's eyes were drawn to the beautiful handwork; she admired the skill it took to create such a treasure. Isabella took note of her interest, and, when she rejected the dress for herself, she tossed it to Kate.

"Perhaps this will be your nuptial dress, since you seem to admire it so much."

Kate picked up the dress and folded it over one arm, smoothing the silk as she did so. "I have no plan to marry," she said quietly.

"Perhaps not," Isabella said. "Our father will make those plans for you."

"With the same luck he's had in making such arrangements for you, one hopes."

Twenty dainty hands rose up to ladies' lips in perfect unison, but they failed to dim the faint chorus of snickers that followed Kate's stinging remark. Isabella's brow wrinkled, showing her age, as her anger grew.

"I shall be sure to tell our father how you admire his diplomatic skills."

"He is no father of mine, but please, do tell the man! I cannot wait to hear his comment."

"His comment shall be made with a switch on your behind, were it up to me!" Isabella snarled. "Now, be a good little girl and try the dress. Let us all see if it suits you or not."

Kate stood still, with the dress draped over one arm.

"Go on, *sister*. I command it."

She had refused to obey Isabella's commands when she was first brought back to Windsor. Her stubbornness lasted only until her guards demonstrated its consequences. She was unable to use her left hand for nearly a month after they were through with her. And every time she exhibited more than passing resistance to the indignities they put her through, she was reminded of the vulnerability of her son. She dragged the dress along the floor as she went behind the curtain, causing a twitter among the other ladies. But when she emerged a few moments later to show the dress, a stunned hush came from the observers.

"Well," Isabella said finally, "it seems to suit you far better than it does myself." She stood up and walked closer to Kate. "I am feeling exceedingly generous today. You shall have it for your wedding."

"I say again, *sister*," Kate said, "I have no plans to marry."

"We shall see," Isabella said. "Now, all of these carryings-on have made me late for an appointment with my jeweler. The poor man will be in a faint by now." She picked up her skirts and walked briskly away, followed in step by a trail of young women, none of whom would look Kate in the eye as they passed.

As soon as they were gone, Nurse came forward. She looked around the corner to see that the ladies were all out of hearing, then whispered to Kate, "There is a message for you, from the lad Chaucer." She pulled it out of her sleeve and handed it over.

Kate grabbed the paper and nearly tore it open.

Fairest Lady Kate, may I call upon you in your quarters this evening? I wish to discuss those histories in which you had an interest. If it is agreeable, please send word to me through your nurse.

What histories? The young man adored an intrigue, sometimes to a fault. She recalled the first words he had ever spoken to her, in Paris, in his hostage days.

You might be a twin to my lord Lionel. He made this comment to her just before she and Guillaume Karle, at the time not yet her husband, tricked him into participating in Alejandro's escape from de Chauliac, before their alliance had solidified. Remarkably, Chaucer did not seem to hold the deception against her. He had spoken to her many times since her arrival in Windsor, and though she often saw the young man staring at her, she wondered at those times if there was something more he wished to say.

"Nurse, of what age is Master Chaucer?"

"Of an age with yourself, I think, child," Nurse said.

She would always be a child in the old woman's eyes. "And what of his family?"

"Wine traders, I believe, from London."

"He is an interesting young man."

"Indeed, right brilliant, by the sound of his speech. He'll go far in this world on that alone, mark my words."

"I believe you are right in that assessment, good Nurse. Please send word to Master Chaucer that I will gladly meet with him. He may come to my quarters, and we will speak on the balcony overlooking the chapel. My keepers will be able to see me, but our words will be private."

The traveling party stayed well back of the circle of stones and watched from the safety of the forest as a crowd of flagellants dressed only in loincloths whipped themselves and one another with willow switches. They danced in frenzied fashion around three stakes, each one set in the middle of a pile of twigs and branches. Strapped to each stake was one man; on each man's jacket was the bright yellow circle that screamed JEW to any and all who saw it. The moaning of the captives was horrifying; Alejandro watched in shock as one of the flagellants came forward with a torch and lit all three pyres. Smoke came first, then flames, and before long the tongues of fire were licking at the legs of the captive Jews.

We must stop them!

But the captain of the escort would not interfere. *I am duty-bound to see your safety* was all he would say.

Alejandro pulled an arrow out of his own quiver and nocked it into the bowstring. He aimed carefully, as Hernandez had taught him to do, and let the arrow fly. It struck one of the captives square in the chest. The man shuddered for an instant, then his head drooped down.

The flagellants turned as one in the direction from which the arrow had come. Seeing the party in the forest, they raised their fists in anger and began running toward the travelers. Alejandro turned his horse and heeled him in the sides, but the animal's hooves seemed mired in quicksand, and he could not run, and soon the flagellants were upon him, and—

"*Grand-père!* What is wrong?"

Alejandro sat up straight in the straw, his heart thumping wildly in his chest.

"*Grand-père*, were you dreaming?"

He rubbed his hand over his face to be sure that he was indeed awake. "I was, child, I was."

"What did you dream? You were sorely disturbed!"

"I cannot recall just now," he lied. There was no reason to frighten the boy; the journey would find ways to do that without his help. "Perhaps I will remember later. It cannot have been a pleasant dream, so maybe God will be good enough to let me forget it." He looked to one of the windows and saw the light streaming in. "It's morning, anyway. We should be rising soon. No doubt Monsieur de Chauliac will want to depart as soon as possible."

He turned his head and saw the small, quiet soldier staring at him, but he looked away before Alejandro could decipher the expression.

They washed in a cold-water basin brought by one of the grooms. The man had a sack of apples for the horses but shared them with Alejandro and the boy, who used them to break their fast. When de Chauliac emerged from the abbey, refreshed by his soft bed and resplendent in red, the entire party was waiting for him.

The Frenchman cast a quick glance in Alejandro's direction. When their eyes met, he gave his colleague a brief nod of recognition, which Alejandro returned discreetly. Then, to Alejandro's surprise, the Frenchman cast a glance in the direction of the soldiers, focusing for a moment on the very same one who had stayed behind the night before.

He suspects him as well!

The banner rose under a dark and threatening sky, and the party assembled in proper order beneath it. The protection of God and the pope went before them. Alejandro could only hope it would be enough.

Kate stood on the balcony outside the ladies' quarters at Windsor. Below her was the chapel, its tiled roof not twenty feet down.

A long drop, but not impossible with a tether of some sort . . .

And then where would you go?

Her position at the balcony wall afforded her a fine view of the countryside. Small plumes of smoke dotted the landscape; beneath each one would be a hearth. An apple tree stood at the crest of a hill; many years before, when they had looked out over the same vista together, Alejandro had promised to make her a rope swing from one of its stout branches. She thought about the country folk who inhabited the cottages in the near surrounds; most of them were tenants to Windsor itself. They would not be unlike the folk she had come to know north of Paris while she and Alejandro hid in that region. There would be pots hanging in the hearths, boiling turnips, perhaps a pheasant or a goose strung from the rafters to ripen for a special repast. In all of these cottages, the housewife would possess a rough broom—probably fashioned by herself—which she would wield with great endeavor to chase out the mice and rats, or to beat the rug, if she was fortunate enough to have one. The straw of their bedding would be bug-infested in summer, dank in winter, and when it was finally discarded for new, the cows would eat it, lest it go to waste. It was a mean and frugal life at best, fraught with uncertainty.

And now I sleep on silk, I never touch a broom, and I dine on the finest delicacies. But, oh, the freedom . . .

The view was lovely and captivating, especially as the sun set. She let her eyes wander over it and found a small measure of peace. She hoped the effects of the moment would linger in her soul.

"Good evening, my lady Kate."

She turned and saw Geoffrey Chaucer standing a few feet away from her. He was a pleasant-looking lad with an open expression; light-brown curly hair framed his youthful face. He wore a blue mantle with wide sleeves that draped to a point behind his wrist. In his hands he held a small clutch of flowers. He bowed deeply, then approached with a smile.

"Good evening to you, Master Chaucer." She took the offered flowers. "Such a beautiful bouquet—how kind of you!"

"Beauty to beauty," he said. "It is only fitting that you should be the recipient."

Kate made a show of enjoying the fragrance. "I was pleased to receive your request for this *rendez-vous*." She moved a step closer and lowered her voice. "As you perhaps know, I am a keen student of history, as it must be repeated if it is not learned. Or so says my *père*, who is a wise man indeed."

Chaucer stepped closer and took hold of her hand. He pulled it to his face and kissed it dramatically. "By which do you mean your father, King Edward?"

She smiled bitterly as she withdrew her hand from his. "I think you know that I do not." She pointed to a stone bench near the balcony wall, well away from the door, on the other side of which were her detested guards, whose attention through the glass never wavered.

They sat down together. "Well," Kate said, "let us not waste time. You must illuminate me on the nature of this—history."

"I hardly know where to begin, lady," he said. He leaned closer to her, as if in confidence. "As you most likely know, I serve the king and queen on occasions when their own servants may be unavailable. This puts me in a position of—trust, I suppose. I am often privy to things that a man of my lowly station might not otherwise hear. I was recently called upon to write a message for your—for the king. Naturally, I am sworn to secrecy regarding all of the royal correspondence." He sighed deeply and stared at his hands for a few moments. When he looked up again, he continued. "I am loath to betray the trust of my patron, but I cannot hold my tongue at present. The consequences of doing so may be . . . dire, if I might use that word. The message was written to His

Holiness himself, so I am doubly pained, as I am a good Christian, and I do not in any way wish to jeopardize the sanctity of my immortal—"

"I understand," she said impatiently. "You have expressed your dilemma with admirable detail." She smiled politely, adding, "I see that you are still fond of words."

Chaucer reddened. "Indeed, lady, my apologies, but I feel that I must lay the proper foundation on which to excuse my own sin."

Kate laughed softly; she found Chaucer wonderfully entertaining. "How very wise."

"I aspire to wisdom. Perhaps someday I will actually acquire some, through the grace of God and no effort of my own. In any case, the message the king dictated concerned your sister, as well as yourself. The king seeks the pope's permission to formalize an engagement between the Princess Royal and the Baron de Coucy, of which you are already aware, but there was another request also—I do not know how to say this properly, but you are, apparently, to be 'legitimized,' for the purpose of—"

Chaucer stopped speaking when he saw the look of shock on Kate's face.

"My lady, are you ill? Is the night air too much for you? If so, we can go inside—"

She vetoed this suggestion with a wave of her hand and rose up quickly from the bench. "He would not dare!"

Chaucer rose as well and looked directly into her eyes. His tone of voice was more urgent now. "He does indeed dare. The letter was sent nearly a fortnight ago. I have agonized since its sending on whether I ought to speak to you or not. I expect it has already reached Avignon and that the matter is under consideration."

"But why would he...I mean, of what use could it be to make me his daughter after all these years?"

Chaucer's voice softened. He revealed less than the entire truth. "A daughter is a tool of diplomacy to a man who wishes to solidify his kingdom. De Coucy has vast lands in France, as you well know, and the same is true of his kin—in particular, one cousin, a certain Count

Benoit. He is here, among the celebrants. Our king still presses his claim to the French throne, and should he desire to press it more vigorously, he will need the support of the French nobility. What better way than to curry favor with the overlord of a territory as vast as that of de Coucy?"

He glanced at the guards again. They seemed completely disinterested in the intimate conversation taking place before them. "Benoit is a weasel.... Why one would claim such a kinship is beyond my ken. But he seems to love the man well, for whatever reason. Benoit's family lands are in Bretagne, though surely not as vast as those held by *la famille de Rais* in that region. The king would cause a stir there if he could, for instability among the local lords would help him in his quest for the throne of France. As I was saying, I suspect—if you will forgive me—that the king would incite all this with another marriage. For that he needs another daughter."

She made no comment on the notion of another marriage, but her voice was dark when she said, "It might well have been de Coucy himself who put the sword to my husband's neck."

"I know that, lady, and it pains me to speak of him in your presence."

Kate was quiet for a moment. "The king has already spent one daughter on diplomacy," she said. "I was just a small child, but I remember still how they wailed and cried in this household when Joanna fell to plague on her bridal journey! When the news of the tragedy came, Nurse could not be consoled for what seemed an eternity; she was my only joy in Windsor, and I was frightened by her great sorrow."

She paused and looked out at the sky. "I have since learned even more fully what it means to be in the depths of sorrow."

Chaucer reached out, with some hesitation, and took hold of her hand. She did not pull it away. "They say your husband was a brave man."

She met his eyes again and saw sympathy and kindness. "More than most will ever know. But history will speak only of de Coucy and how he preserved the monarchy in that battle. They will not remember how my husband gave his life to throw off the chains of servitude that held his countrymen. His legacy is forfeit."

"Except through his son."

"His son," she whispered bitterly. "I have not seen his child, *my* son, since the day he was born."

"Such sadness cannot be imagined by anyone who has not experienced it."

"That wisdom to which you aspire seems to have found you, Master Chaucer." She looked down at the chapel roof again. "You've come forward as a friend in my time of need." Then she turned and stared at him. "I would know what compels you to do such a dangerous and forbidden thing."

Chaucer paused. "I will tell you the truth—though you may find it odd. I developed an admiration for your *père* while he was in Paris. There is something pure about him, something almost noble. He is an intriguing fellow, and I liked him immensely. He treated me well—far better than Prince Lionel and Lady Elizabeth."

"Were you punished for what happened?"

"No. Lady Elizabeth was angry, but she was equally embarrassed by the events of that afternoon. Of course it was her own fault—she flirted with your *père* shamelessly, and had she an ounce of sense, she would have recognized him for the man of high morals that he is. She would have known that he would not enter into an actual assignation with a married woman, only a charade." He hesitated briefly, then asked, "May I speak frankly, lady?"

His candor made her relax a bit. "A true friend always does, Chaucer. Speak your peace, I beg of you."

"She was horrified to learn that she had been touched by a Jew, though she did not know him to be a Jew at the time. He looks so—"

"Ordinary?" Kate said.

"Indeed. So normal. So unlike a Jew. Why, he is handsome and well appointed, a man much taller than other Jews I have seen. And elegant in his demeanor, fastidious to a fault . . ."

"Well, he is human, after all. Jews are not animals, I assure you. He is the most fastidiously clean man I have ever known. They ridicule me here for my habit of bathing, which I acquired from him. And he is fearless! A most exceptional example of masculinity and fatherhood, though he owed me nothing when he took me out of here, nothing at all. I only hope that my son is still with him, so he might be properly fathered himself."

"By your description, one would take him for an adventurer rather than for a physician."

"A true assessment."

"What a tale his exploits would make!" Chaucer sighed, then continued. "In any event, I was not punished. My position within the household is secure." He leaned closer. "Unless, of course, my revelations to you are themselves revealed."

"Never," she whispered. She let her glance stray briefly to her guards. They were watching the interchange intently.

"You must kiss me," she said.

Chaucer pulled back momentarily and looked into her eyes, as if to ascertain her sincerity. "Lady, I hardly know what—"

"Just lean forward and kiss me, tenderly."

He raised his eyebrows in surprise, then shrugged and did as she asked. She grabbed hold of his mantle and pulled him close, and then held him in the kiss for a long moment. Chaucer gave himself willingly to the intimacy; he put his arms around her waist and drew her closer.

He opened one eye just a slit and looked in the direction of the guards, who watched with great interest.

Finally, after their dramatic moment, she let go of his mantle, and he of her waist, and they parted. For a long moment, Chaucer stared into her eyes. "Your kiss is as sweet as the dew on the honeysuckle. I am blessed to have tasted it. I will admit to you, lady, that I am also compelled to come to your aid simply because—well, I *admire* you."

She blushed slightly. "You have my admiration as well. But please do not think me brazen in kissing you—I am in dire need of your help, and I beg you to continue to come to me as you have today, so that I may have your aid in plotting my escape."

"But you cannot escape from here; it's impossible!"

"Would you have said that it was impossible for *Père* to escape de Chauliac's men in Paris?"

"Well, yes, but—"

"And was the plotting of it not exquisite?"

"I must avow, it was a masterpiece of theater."

"Then take this challenge, and plot with me now. You have a sublime intelligence, and you can help me!"

He stepped back from her for a moment but could not take his eyes from her.

"All right," he said quietly, "I will help you. God save me, but I cannot resist the intrigue."

She embraced him again, this time without pretense. And once more, she kissed him on the lips.

"I will owe you a debt of such enormity that it will never be repaid."

"We shall see if that is true. Repayment often comes in surprising ways."

"Thank you, from the bottom of my heart. Now you must depart, for propriety's sake. Come to me tomorrow. It will give me some time to think of how we might accomplish our intent."

He bowed slightly and began to turn. She caught his hand and placed it lightly on her chest.

"Your heart—it beats wildly," he said with genuine surprise.

"Your kiss did this to me," she told him. "There was no theater in it."

Six

Caroline had squelched Tom's suggestion that the suit be saved for a rainier day by pointing her finger in his face and suggesting that he himself go into a known hot zone without it. This was, in her opinion, a monsoon.

Now one rigid black boot sat on the table; plastic crinkled as Janie unwrapped the other. She put it down next to its mate, then carefully folded the bag and set it aside. She grabbed the boots by the tops with one hand and placed them on the floor. "I forgot how heavy these things are," she said.

"Very," Caroline said. "I can't even imagine wearing them." She turned and took another plastic bag from a hang-hook on the wall behind her, then reverently laid it out on the table surface. Janie went to one side of the table, Caroline to the other, and together they unzipped the bag from opposite sides. Caroline pulled back the front flap and stared at the green suit.

She looked at Janie and said, "I remember my mother doing this with her wedding gown."

"Mine too," Janie said with a dreamy fondness in her voice. "What was that blue paper supposed to do, anyway?"

"I don't know. Keep it white, I guess. Didn't they add something blue to the white laundry? Maybe it was the same kind of thing."

"It was probably just another wives' tale." A little laugh slipped in. "God alone knows what will turn out to be our wives' tales a hundred years from now."

The rest of that sentiment remained unvoiced in Janie's head: *May it please the Force that there will still be wives' tales a hundred years from now.*

"They're bound to be doozies," Caroline said. She sighed heavily. "Well, here we are, just like samurai women, preparing the armor for our warrior."

That sobering simile put an end to the girl talk. Janie skirted the edge of the table with quick, small steps and put her arms around Caroline. She felt her friend's shoulders trembling. "It'll be all right," she whispered with the hug. "He'll be okay."

Caroline wiped tears away and said, "He has to be. I can't even think about what it would be like without him."

Janie tightened her hug but did not speak. The idea of their little tribe losing one of its adult males was not something she wanted to consider either.

The map covered the central and western part of Massachusetts in fairly good detail. It was secured to a long wall on one side of the large meeting room, a space that had once hosted the board of overseers for Worcester Technical Institute. Above the map was a hand-lettered sign:

THINK GLOBAL ACT LOCAL

"Glob*ally*, local*ly*," the scar-faced man said to himself. He'd often wanted to correct it, but the sign had been there long before he arrived and it had seniority. He turned his attention back to the map.

If I just stare at it long enough, let my vision just go where it will, mused the man, *if I let that rapid eye movement thing take over, then some kind of pattern will appear, something to explain what's happening.*

Dozens of yellow-tipped pushpins lived on this map, each one inserted at a point where the probes had detected a positive result. The dates of discovery were printed neatly in small block letters beneath each pin.

His eyes were tired. He wiped his hand downward over his face to revive himself and felt the hard tissue that had replaced his once-smooth skin.

He pushed himself up from his chair and went to the bathroom, where he splashed water on his face and dried it with a towel, taking care not to rub too hard—cracks were a constant problem in his leathery skin. He caught a glimpse of himself in the mirror and looked away quickly. He considered it a good thing that he didn't come into contact with too many children, because he would surely frighten them. He frightened himself.

My kingdom, such as it is, for a surgeon.

His self-pity was interrupted by the sound of his assistant calling him.

"Hey, boss, you all right?"

"Fine," he answered into the mirror. The word echoed back at him accusingly. *A fine liar.*

"Just checking. We need you, don't forget that. You're the heart of this organization."

At their first encounter, Bruce would not have taken him for a geek; Fredo looked more like a biker bodyguard than a braniac. He was large and long-haired with a full mustache, and he had colorful tattoos running from his wrists to his elbows. His huge hands appeared to be a better match for a football than a trackball. When he walked into the ICU of the abandoned Boston hospital looking for spare computer parts, Fredo was wearing a leather vest festooned with all manner of studs and unidentified metal things. His voice was deep and scary.

"Anyone home?"

Bruce had remained hidden in his supply closet and watched as Fredo sat down at the nurse's station and started opening drawers.

After a time he'd stopped searching and, having found nothing of value, moved on to his next task, lunch. He pulled a hunk of bread from one pocket and tore off a piece of it with his teeth. He chewed with what appeared to Bruce to be annoyance.

"I hate this eating-alone crap."

Again, Bruce had watched through the door slit as Fredo engaged in a fascinating conversation with the computer that sat under the counter at the nurse's station.

"So how come you don't have a USB port I can take? I come all this way, and you don't have a decent port? Jee-zus. What's this world coming to?"

As Fredo ate his lunch, Bruce decided that he was not the only human being who craved conversation. He couldn't recall, precisely, how long it had been since he'd engaged in repartee with another human being. He'd kept a calendar for a while but had given it up after several months, in part because he didn't trust the accuracy of what he'd recorded; as his burns healed, he'd dosed himself pretty heavily with painkillers, and there had to have been days that he'd missed in his belladonic haze. But there was another reason why he'd stopped keeping track of the days: They were all the same, silent and solitary.

He'd opened the closet door and presented himself. The first thing he'd thought to ask of the enormous stranger was "What are you doing here?"

Fredo had started to get to his feet but, on seeing Bruce's face, had sat back down again with a stricken look. "Trying to find some computer parts." Then, after a pause, "I guess I don't have to ask what *you're* doing here. What the hell *happened* to you, anyway?"

"Plane crash."

Fredo had been mortified. "Aw, man, I'm sorry, that was so rude. God, I'm glad my mother didn't hear me say that. Jeez, that's awful. Were you on one of the planes that crashed at Logan?"

Bruce explained how they'd already crossed into U.S. airspace when the controllers deserted the tower at Logan Airport. The pilot had managed to lift the aircraft just enough to avoid hitting the small plane that taxied unannounced into their landing runway—just after the point of no return—but there wasn't enough runway left after that for the plane to come to a stop. The craft had crashed through a concrete barrier and skidded into Boston Harbor, killing the cockpit crew and many of the passengers who'd been seated near the front.

"I got three kids down the slide, and I was going back for the mother when the plane exploded."

"But you got the kids out?"

"They went into the water, but it was pretty shallow there. I don't know if they made it. I hope so. I'd hate to think I got this face for nothing."

"How'd you end up here?"

"Someone brought me here, I don't know who. They brought me inside the ER door and then left."

"All alone?"

"They probably didn't realize there was no one here. And I'm guessing they thought I was going to die anyway. In any case, I'm grateful to whoever it was, because here I am."

Fredo had brushed away a tear at the end of the story. When he found out what Bruce did for a living in the time before, he insisted that he come along.

We have a group starting up. In Worcester, at Tech. We're pretty disorganized, but things are beginning to come together. . . .

When Bruce got there, he realized just how right Fredo had been about disorganization. No one objected when he took on a leadership role. It brought him back to life; he was no longer depressed by his condition, because he had something to occupy his mind—a purpose, a goal, not just the pain of each day.

"Three new locations this week," he said as he emerged from the bathroom.

"I saw," Fredo said. "Pretty far west."

"Certainly farther than we've seen before. What do you make of it?"

"I don't know. It could just be spreading naturally."

"Come on, Fredo, you don't really believe that, do you?"

"I guess not."

"Good. I would lose faith in you if you did. No, someone's got to be sending it out to those locations."

"But why? What's the point in taking out all the rest of us?"

"We're infidels, remember? This is the new jihad. The second coming of the Final Solution."

"It still doesn't make sense to me. They're putting this new thing out there, but it could come back on them, just like DR SAM did. I can't believe they'd let it go without having some means of protecting their own people."

"They might just lay low and let it do its thing. They already isolate themselves, just like the Taliban did in Afghanistan, just like Al Qaeda—so they wait and let it run its course until there's no natural reservoir left."

Tests he'd done on certain birds had showed that they could carry the disease but did not succumb to it. But there were many things that birds would succumb to, when the need to eliminate the reservoir they provided arrived.

He thought of the avian flu and shuddered.

"We have to warn the deltas," Fredo said. "If they're putting together another round of meetings, we need to know if they're going to do another one here."

Yes, we do, Bruce thought as he looked up at the map again, *so we can act locally. Because that's all any of us can do.*

Janie was alone in the main room of the lodge, fussing over the minutiae of the suit, when Michael came in. "Top of the marnin' to ya," he said with a big smile. He further thickened his fake brogue and added, "I'll be lookin' forward to some corned beef and cabbage when I get back."

"Pork and turnip," Janie corrected him.

"Well, I'll just imagine it's a boiled dinner, then." He regarded the waiting suit for a moment. "Looks downright inspectable. You ladies did a nice job with it." He glanced around. "Boots?"

Janie said, "Your wife has them."

Just then, Caroline came in with the boots, which gleamed as if they'd been spit-shined. She set them down and planted a light kiss on his cheek, but her face was worried. She rubbed his arm lightly. "Want some breakfast before you go? Eggs, maybe?"

Michael gave his wife a one-arm hug. "No, thanks, love. I'll eat when I get back."

"But you'll need some fuel."

"Yeah, but it gets hot inside that thing. You don't want to be cleaning eggs off the inside of the helmet."

After about ten minutes of zipping, snapping, and hooking, he was properly enclosed. Everything but the helmet was in place.

He stood, like an astronaut, with the helmet cradled in one arm and the gloves in one hand. "Well, how do I look?"

Caroline managed a smile. "Like a hero."

Janie took that as her cue to disappear. "I'll go get the kids," she said, and left Caroline and Michael to their good-byes.

They were still asleep when she went into their room. The room that Alex and Sarah now shared with hand-hewn bunk beds had started out as a nursery. Two years prior, they'd tried to put them in separate rooms, thinking it was the proper thing to do. After a series of nights dominated by crying, requests for a drink, and bad dreams, Janie pointed out that the original Alejandro—according to his journal—had slept in the same room with his sister, had dressed in front of her, and he'd turned out all right, hadn't he? The children were, after all, more like sister and brother than friends.

"Rise and shine," she said. She pulled back the curtains and let in the light.

Sarah, always the first, came up on her elbow almost immediately. Alex required the customary gentle shaking. "Come on, sleepyhead," Janie said to her son. "The day's a-wasting."

She loved this part of the morning, because as soon as Alex emerged from the fog of sleep, he would smile and reach out his arms for a hug, and the warmth of his small body would just flood through her. It was always with reluctance that she let him go.

"Come on out," she said.

They both scrambled out of the covers in their pajamas. Sarah climbed down the ladder but jumped past the last two rungs. She landed on the floor with a thud and a grin, the perfect little gymnast who'd just nailed her landing in front of the cheering crowd. Janie winced without comment; as they ran out the door, she quickly straightened the covers on both beds. Mothers worried, mothers cleaned; some things never changed.

When she came into the main room, she saw Sarah hugging Caroline's leg, another thing that did not change. The look on the little girl's face was a combination of both awe and fear. Janie realized that Sarah had never seen her father in that suit before, at least not as a verbal being. The child's previous encounter with the suit would have taken place in a time when she had not yet developed an understanding of what was scary and what was not. Now, even though her exposure to the outside world had been limited, she would realize without much explanation that there were implications to the armor her father wore.

Alex, however, was right next to Michael, touching, prodding—always fearless, Janie thought. Just like his—

His what? In the years since her son had reentered the world, she still hadn't come up with a satisfactory term to describe his relationship to Alejandro. *Father* wasn't right; Tom was his father. *Original* fell short. *Twin* was the best she could come up with, but for some reason she couldn't pinpoint, it didn't satisfy her.

Not important, she reminded herself. What was important was that he was healthy, reasonably happy, and completely himself, despite his origin.

The little boy didn't turn when his mother cleared her throat, but maintained his focus on Michael's exciting attire. He ran the tip of his finger slowly down one of the suit's reinforced seams, feeling each stitch. Janie imagined a rush of adrenaline into his brain and tried, vicariously, to feel the same excitement. But her own experienced brain understood too much to let the marvel break through. She was excited for her son, nevertheless.

He turned and looked at her, his eyes wide with wonder. "Mom, this is so *cool*!"

Where, she wondered, had he come up with that expression?

"Does Dad know about this?"

They all laughed; it was a welcome—if brief—respite from dread. Tom came into their midst from the next room, laughing himself. "Yes, I know about it. Pretty amazing, huh?"

In his hands he carried something wrapped in a dark cloth. He laid it on the table and said to Michael, "Clean as a whistle, all ready to go."

Janie and Caroline both knew what was wrapped in the cloth. It was a handgun, not the same one Janie had with her on the last ride to the compound, so many years before, but another of the same model.

"Six," Tom said quietly.

Michael nodded his approval. "Just in case." All eyes were on him now; even Alex had stepped back. He met the gaze of each one in turn, then said, "Well, I guess that's it, then. I'll just be off to the parade."

The women and children stood in pairs on either side of the gate. Tom would go with Michael as far as the top of the mountain. What was left of the road up to the peak—now just a series of frost heaves and pavement chunks—would still be icy. Spring came late to the mountaintop, though the winter had been somewhat mild. They would all be relieved to know that Michael had made it safely to that point.

They watched in silence as Tom helped Michael onto his horse—the stallion they called Galen, after the ancient Greek physician and healer whose theories and practices still ruled medicine well into Alejandro's time. They had taken the name from a page in Alejandro's journal. Tom himself would ride Jellybean, named for the treat Janie used to train her when they first came to the mountainside. The moniker stuck when the treat ran out. They tested her again by riding around the compound courtyard; her limp magically disappeared with someone on her back, a condition she seemed to love.

As she watched the men approach, Janie whispered to Caroline, "How did pioneer women do this?"

Caroline shook her head slowly. "I don't know."

Snakebite. Bears. Footfalls—there was so much to fear. In the time before, air bags, cops, and supermarkets numbed the edge of wariness that all humans carried in their primal selves. They all understood those dangers now, as they worked their way back to the surface.

Suddenly, Alex said, "Wait! We need swords!"

"What?" his mother said.

"To make a tunnel!"

To Janie's quizzical look, he said, "You know, like they did when knights left their castles!"

Of course. An arch! She jumped out of formation and put up a hand to halt Michael and Tom.

"What's going on?" Tom said.

"Wait just a minute!"

She ran across the courtyard and into the house and returned with an armful of mops and brooms. She handed them around quickly and got back into her place. A few moments later, Tom and Michael passed under the dust and the drips and out into the larger world, with their hopeful but worried clan cheering them on.

What was left of the road curved frequently to accommodate the mountainside. It was more of a foothill, in comparison to the real mountains of Utah and Colorado, but it did have its own brand of challenges, one of which presented itself about halfway up. A large boulder had tumbled from above and now sat in the middle of the road, surrounded by its own miniature mountain of debris.

"Not too long ago," Tom said when they came upon it. "The mud all around it is pretty fresh." He pointed toward the area just above the mess. "I think up will be easier than down," he said.

Michael urged Galen to a better vantage point and looked down at the slope below the road. "I think you're right." He kneed the horse lightly in the sides. The animal climbed around the rock, tentatively at first, and then with more assurance. The ground underneath was wet and unstable, but the horse seemed to understand what was necessary and persevered, despite the fact that he was sinking into the mud up to his ankles.

Jellybean had a harder time of it. After a few unsuccessful tries, Tom called out to Michael, "I don't think she should go any farther. I'll tie her up here and go with you on foot."

"No you won't," Michael said. "Go back. I'll go on alone."

Tom would not agree at first but eventually capitulated.

"I'll be back before sunset," Michael said.

"Put the visor down," Tom replied. "And be careful out there among them English."

Michael laughed and pulled down the plexishield on the helmet. He gave Tom the thumbs-up and got Galen moving again.

The horse worked his way cautiously around the pile of rocks. Step by steady step, he played the mule, astonishing Michael with his uncanny balance. They made it past the obstruction and followed a natural break in the brush, but there was no easy way to return to the road; the woods, though bare of leaves, were thick and scrubby, not something he wanted to press through in a rippable garment. He patted the horse on the flank reassuringly and said, in a voice muffled by the helmet, "Just have to wait for the next deer run, won't we?"

They paralleled the road for another short distance. Ahead on the left Michael saw what appeared to be an opening in the brush. He felt a surge of hope that he would soon be back on easier ground. He urged the horse onward again, and they were almost out of the rough section when the outcropping of rocks and dirt on which they were riding gave way. Michael held on tightly as he leaned in the opposite direction, battling against gravity to maintain his balance as the horse slid downward.

But gravity won, and Michael tumbled off as the horse went down on his side. He landed with a thud on his back; the wind rushed out of him. He lay there just long enough to realize that Galen's legs were thrashing wildly in an attempt to right himself. He sat up and slid back out of range just in time. After a few moments of wild struggle, the horse rose up, snorting and stomping in the ignominy of having fallen.

Michael groaned, testing each limb as he slowly rose to his feet; nothing seemed to be broken. He began to brush the debris away. The gloves made it difficult to do a proper job of it, and he was tempted to pull them off, but he decided against it and persevered.

His thumb caught on something. He twisted as much as he could and looked down at his thigh.

"Bloody hell." There was a tear about three inches long in the plasticized fabric of the suit.

"Bloody, bloody hell," he said louder. He pushed up the visor and yanked off his gloves, which he threw to the ground in a fit of anger. Sounds flooded his previously sheltered ears; he heard birds singing and a distant wind rushing down the other side of the peak. And then he heard something he would never have expected.

"Don't move."

He spun around in a crinkle of plastic and was greeted by a shotgun barrel, aimed directly at him by a smallish woman in a sheepskin jacket. His right hand went naturally to his hip, where his weapon would have been had he not been wearing the suit. He'd stowed the handgun in a strap at the front of the saddle; his eyes went quickly to Galen, but from the horse's position he couldn't see if it was still there.

"It's on the ground," the woman said. "I'll get it in a moment." She sat with visible assurance on the back of a dappled gray horse. The limp bodies of two or three foxes—he couldn't see clearly enough for an accurate count—were draped over the back of the horse. Wisps of her long, light-colored hair swirled around her head in the spring wind. Her eyes, in line with the barrel of the gun, were trained steadily on him. She seemed to know what she was doing.

Slowly, he raised his hands; it seemed the only thing to do in that moment, and he understood, for perhaps the first time, what it felt like to be under the control of someone with a weapon. He'd trained his own chemical rifle on one bad guy or another hundreds of times. Right now he needed to convince his captor that he was one of the good guys.

"I...I..." he stammered, until finally the words spilled out: "I'm a cop."

The woman surprised him by laughing. Still, her gaze never wavered. "I can see that," she said. Her grip on the shotgun relaxed and she lowered it slightly. Michael saw her face; she was pretty, if a bit weathered.

"And by the way," she said, pointing to his garb, "nice suit."

Seven

A serving girl tugged at the sleeve of Kate's nightdress.

"Wake up, m'lady," she said urgently. "The princess has commanded your presence."

Kate opened one eye and looked into the young girl's face suspiciously. "For what reason?"

"I only know that she commands you to dress for a day's riding."

She sat up in her bed; though she rankled at the command, a surge of excitement welled up in her. Riding—another opportunity might present itself!

"Where are we to ride?"

The flustered girl could not answer. She seemed embarrassed to be making the demand on such short notice. "Begging your pardon, m'lady," the girl said, her tone quite apologetic, "I don't know. If you please, *hurry*, for your sister awaits you."

"Where are my guards?"

"Outside the door, as always," the girl said.

Kate went to the bed stand, where a fresh pitcher of water awaited her. The girl stood by and offered a cloth as Kate splashed the sleep out of her eyes. She dried her face, then went to the window and looked out.

Below, through the early-morning mist, she saw the assembly of grooms with horses prancing in anticipation of the ride. A number of guards were already in place, with horns tucked under their arms and hounds straining on their leashes. A tall standard bearing the crest of the Black Prince was held high by the lead rider. A shiver, beyond her control, coursed through her bones.

Her heart sank on seeing the guards. There would be no possibility of escape; there were just too many of them. With a sigh of resignation, she pulled a simple gown from the chest, one with a wide skirt, though she preferred breeches for riding—she had grown accustomed to them in her travels with Alejandro. She recalled Isabella's angry words when she had first requested a pair:

We shall not abide a woman in breeches in our presence.

The serving girl helped her with the buttons and ties and then handed Kate a brush. She ran it through her hair—something her pampered sister seemed incapable of doing for herself—and tied it back into a tail with a cord of black leather, all without ever once gazing into the glass.

"You'll be needing this, m'lady," the girl said as Kate passed by her. "There's an unaccountable chill."

Kate noticed the girl's sympathetic expression; she saw it often on the faces of all those who served her. She took the offered cloak and thanked the girl. In the ladies' salon, a party of chattering women were already gathered. At their center—predictably surrounded by her clucking admirers—stood Isabella, beautifully attired in a handsome embroidered riding cape, which served as the subject of the effusive commentary.

"Ah," Isabella said. She looked her younger sister up and down. "My beloved sister. We see that you have given the customary twinkle of attention to your appearance."

Kate responded with an icy stare.

Isabella made a small, grunting laugh, full of disdain. "Well, let us join the others," she said. "You know how gentlemen hate to be kept waiting."

If what Chaucer had told her was true, then de Coucy might well be among them. Her guards followed her as she descended the stairs into the courtyard. She commanded all of her emotions to bury themselves deep within her psyche, for on this day she would be subjected to an encounter with the man who had most likely put Guillaume Karle to death. It would be the first time they had come face-to-face since the fateful day, nearly eight years before, when he had sent her headless husband back to her.

Hatred—for both of them—filled her as she watched de Coucy kiss her sister on the hand.

She turned away from the sight, thinking, *They are a match made in hell.* She positioned herself so she would not have to come into contact with de Coucy. She would rip the skin off his face, and then her son would be motherless, indeed.

Her eyes settled on a short, stocky man on horseback who had placed himself well within the main party but did not seem to be involved in the repartee. Instead, he stared at her in a most unnerving manner. Whenever Kate glanced in his direction, the man's eyes seemed to be upon her. Once he even smiled, revealing a mouthful of blackened teeth.

When the man nodded and blew her a kiss, Kate came to a horrifying realization—this man might well be Benoit, her "intended."

She turned her head to the side and spat, quite deliberately, making as much noise as she could. When she glanced back at the monstrous little man who'd been eying her, he was whispering to de Coucy, with an expression that indicated a complaint.

The Black Prince himself was among the group, accompanied as usual by Sir John Chandos. The stalwart warrior, who had always been kind to her—even in this captivity—rode up to her and greeted her with a polite nod.

"My lady," he said. He smiled at her rough clothing. "I can see that you are outfitted for a hunt."

"And why not, good sir? If one is to hunt, one must be properly prepared."

It was all so very silly; she would not be allowed any sort of weapon. Anything she managed to catch on this expedition would have to be taken with her bare hands. Chandos knew that in her years with Alejandro, she would have learned to use a sling and stone, to throw a knife, to wield a club, to peel the skin off her prey before the creature's last heartbeat. Once, in an afternoon of sport, he had watched her place arrow after arrow in the center of the target, to the astonishment of her guards.

Chandos held her glance for a moment more, and then said, "I wish you a most pleasant hunt." He glanced in the direction of de Coucy and the dark little ape at his flank. "Our company seems a bit rough today. Rest assured that I shall personally watch over you, so you may be returned safely to the castle."

With a smile—Kate wondered if it was sympathy or amusement that she saw in it—Chandos turned his horse and rode back to the group of men. Kate watched him with the bitter understanding that while he would certainly oversee her safety, it was her return to captivity in Windsor that would be foremost in his mind.

On the surface, it was an altogether splendid group that departed the castle heading north that morning to enjoy a day of hunting and birding. The ladies, for the most part, were there merely to watch as the men wielded their strong bows and well-balanced slings against the animals in the king's reserve. Kate envied those men their weapons. Memories of hunting with Alejandro—not for sport, but sustenance— drifted through her mind. She had brought in many a meal during their years in France, that dangerous and unforgiving time, when food and shelter were never certain and every rider they passed was a potential enemy.

Compared to this captivity, those times seemed heavenly.

She pulled her cloak around herself and blessed the serving girl who had suggested that she take it. They rode north, stopping now and then to allow the gentlemen to take small game from the brush, whetting their appetites for the larger game that awaited on the reserves. As the sun rose higher in the sky, the day warmed, and soon the party stopped again, but this time with the purpose of shedding their over-garments—not an easy task for a lady on horseback. In her simpler garb, Kate was able to remove her own cloak without help from anyone else, and indeed without much effort on her own part. She draped the wool cloak over the back of her horse and sat there impatiently while servants and valets fussed around their masters and mistresses, all so the great ones would not have to be bothered to raise up their arms.

She found herself, for a precious instant, unguarded, her keepers had been enlisted to help the other lords and ladies. A quick glance off to the west revealed a dense stand of trees. She peered at the thick green brush of springtime and realized that it would make excellent cover. Without any sharp movements, Kate nudged her horse to change its direction so they faced more toward the stand of brush. She kept an eye on the traveling party, looking for one precious opportunity to slip into the woods unnoticed.

With each breath, she inched closer to making her move. She tapped the horse very lightly in the side with her heels. The animal re-sponded by moving a pace westward. After a moment's wait to see if anyone had noticed, she decided that no one had, so she nudged him again and gained a few more inches. Twice more she did the same; the trees were tantalizingly close. She was perhaps only one more step from bolting to freedom when she glanced back and saw Sir John look-ing in her direction.

She froze as still as a statue. Her heart sank, and with it, her hopes.

The good knight broke away from the group and moved toward her quite casually, his eyes never leaving hers. When he was close enough that his words would not be heard by anyone but Kate, he said, with a slight smile, "Take care of the woods, m'lady. There are dangers within."

Smiling in return, Kate said, "I know this only too well, dear knight."

"From your travels, no doubt. Well, take heed, then," he said. "I should hate to have to answer to the king if anything untoward were to happen to you."

She noted with silent gratitude that he had not said "your father." *He understands*, she thought. *He knows how I hate the man. And why.*

"No such unhappy event shall come to pass," she assured him. With a few gentle heels, she directed the horse away from the trees and back toward the group.

On the third day of their journey, de Chauliac's party came to the town of Cluny, in the low mountains that lay to the northeast of *le Massif Central*. The monastery they found there was lovely in its idyllic setting, with the gardens just beginning to show small and welcome bits of color. As the sun left the sky, they rode into the courtyard, dusty and tired from the grueling passage over the hills.

De Chauliac disappeared as he had on each of the nights before into the comfortable custody of whatever cleric was there to greet him. But this time the rest of the party was invited inside to dine with the nuns and brothers who made their home within the monastery walls, while de Chauliac and his host bishop dined privately. They were led through the abbey to the rooms that lay behind and ultimately to a small but comfortable dining hall. Down the center of the table there lay a scarf of the most exquisite lace, running its entire length. A candelabra shed a warm light on the food the nuns brought in a seemingly endless stream of steaming platters.

As the party arranged themselves around the table, Alejandro saw, out of the corner of his eye, that the elusive small soldier was speaking quietly with one of the nuns as she set her plate down. The nun nodded slightly, and Alejandro surmised that the soldier was, for some unknowable reason, begging to be excused.

Lest your English accent give you away, spy, he thought bitterly. *So be it*, he thought as he watched the discourse. *I will avail myself of your secrets some other time.* Before the soldier departed, he reached out and fingered the beautiful lace of the tablecloth and, for the briefest moment, studied its details.

·   ·   ·

By mid-afternoon of the hunt, the flanks of the horses were draped with the carcasses of birds and small animals, and even one deer, and the air was thick with the coppery smell of spilled blood. The hunting grounds kept by the king were always well stocked, and rarely did one of his guests return without evidence of hunting prowess, whether merited or not.

As the group was making ready for the return to Windsor, a ragged-looking man astride a mule appeared out of the woods. The guards were upon him in an instant. Sir John rode forward and greeted the man, perhaps a bit more rudely than he might have were he not watched by so many critical eyes.

"Halt, fellow," he said. "You pass through the king's reserves."

The man had a terrified look on his face but did not stop. He heeled the mule and tried quite foolishly to ride directly through the party. He was a foul-looking man and he stank of manure, even from a distance. The ladies covered their noses and mouths with gloved hands and turned their faces away as he attempted to press through their midst.

"I say, halt," Sir John repeated. He raised his hand in a signal that produced an instant response from the archers. In the blink of an eye, the poor traveler found himself at the point of a dozen arrows, with no choice but to stop.

"Please, sir," he said, fairly blubbering, "I mean no disrespect, and I'll not be poaching any game from His Majesty. I only mean to travel through."

"It is well-known in these parts that His Majesty prefers travelers to take a route *around* his lands, not through them."

"Indeed, sir, I know this, though I am not directly from these parts. And I beg your lordship's forgiveness, but—"

"Forgiveness is not mine to give. These are the king's lands, and I am but his humble servant. Now be off with you, before you suffer the consequences. Surely I do not need to remind you that the king's justice is swift and harsh."

The man looked behind himself, then turned back to Chandos with a terribly distressed look on his face. "I cannot go back, sir."

"Indeed," Chandos said, "and why not?"

"I am afeared of plague!" he blurted. "They say it has come once again to the Peaks!"

"We have heard nothing of plague's return thereabouts, though we know it is in Europa," Chandos said in a scornful voice. "We are not aware that it has crossed *la Manche* as of yet. And in any case, if it has, we are too far north to be concerned." He leaned over his saddle pomme and eyed the man closely. "Unless, of course, you yourself are afflicted."

Kate nudged her horse closer so she could fully hear the man's words.

"I am not, I swear it, but I dared not remain there!"

"You would leave your home and ride so far south for this reason?"

"I have no home, sir. I am a beggar." He opened his arms to show his ragged clothing.

Chandos eyed the mule skeptically. "Beggars do not ride," he said.

"This animal belonged to my best fellow. When he died I put him in the ground and took the mule's care upon myself. I've given him a good home, just as a Christian man ought. Seemed only right. He would have willed the beast to me anyways."

"Very generous of you," the bemused knight said. "And of him as well. But perhaps you now carry his disease with you, since you ride his animal."

"Oh, no, sir, not I...I am unafflicted." He pulled down his cowl, revealing horribly wrinkled flesh, but no buboes. "My friend spent his last days in the care of the brothers of Christ—he was taken in to pass his last hours in comfort."

"But—if he carries plague, then all the brothers shall die if they are in close quarters to him!"

All eyes turned to Kate, who had voiced this concern in one untethered blurt.

The man looked directly at her and said, "Begging your pardon, m'lady, but if it's God's will, there's naught anyone can do about it."

All were momentarily silent; everyone had heard stories of monasteries wherein the monks had locked themselves, thinking to keep plague out, but instead had enclosed themselves in its grasp.

"This is a fool's tale!" Chandos finally said. "Why should I believe you?"

The man crossed himself and raised up his hand. "I give you my oath, sir, the word of a Christian believer."

Upon hearing this declaration, Chandos laughed. But his smile faded quickly. "Then against my better judgment, you may pass. In honor of our princess's nuptials." He glanced in Isabella's direction and made a small nod of respect. Isabella sat taller astride her horse as the eyes of her party fell upon her. The beggar, following Chandos's lead, bent deeply at the waist and muttered vague congratulations that no one else could hear or understand.

Chandos then said to the man, "But before you may depart, come forward."

With visible reluctance, the man heeled the mule until he came alongside Chandos. Before anyone could even gasp, Chandos had his knife out and had cut two neat slashes in the man's cheek, in the shape of an arrowhead. Blood oozed out of the cuts; the stricken man pressed on his cheek to stanch the flow. He pulled his hand away and looked at it in horror, then looked back at Chandos again.

"Those marks are the means by which I shall know you if I ever see you on His Majesty's lands again," Chandos said. "Now get out of here, before my resolve to do away with you returns."

The traveler kicked the mule viciously in the sides. The animal brayed and took off, this time in a westerly direction. He disappeared into the thick woods, as Kate had wanted to do earlier in the foray. She followed him with her eyes, while her heart was filled with envy. When he finally disappeared from view, she turned her eyes back to Chandos. The knight sat still on his horse with a cold expression on his face.

My only ally, save Chaucer, she thought as she watched him turn his horse around.

When the meal was through, the nuns removed themselves from the table before their guests and began to take the empty plates away.

"Well, Guillaume, that was quite a fare, was it not?"

"Yes, *Grand-père.*" The little boy rubbed his eyes.

"You are very weary, I suspect. This was a long day of travel."

Again, he said, "Yes, *Grand-père.*"

"And you are quite agreeable."

"Yes—" The boy stopped, and smiled at his own repetition.

"Let us find you a place to lay your head." They rose up from their bench and followed others from their party, who seemed to have acquired some sense of where they ought to go by following one of the monks. As they wove through the dark, narrow halls of the abbey by the light of a torch held high by the first monk in the procession, Alejandro saw one of the nuns approach. The woman walked slowly, balancing a pan of steaming water in her hands. Under one arm was folded a white cloth of some sort, perhaps a towel, with a small bit of lace peeking out.

She padded quietly past them, keeping her eyes discreetly low, though Alejandro tried to catch her notice. She stopped finally and tapped on a door. Alejandro heard a muffled reply. The nun balanced the pan against her hip, then opened the door with one hand. He turned in time to see her slip into a brightly lit room, and heard her say, *"Voici l'eau chaude, Mademoiselle."*

Alejandro stopped short; they were at the very rear of the entourage, so no one stumbled into him. Guillaume stopped as well, but Alejandro patted him on the shoulder and said, "Go ahead, child, I will catch up shortly."

The boy did as he was told, though he glanced back reluctantly as he left his grandfather. Alejandro remained where he was, listening at the door to the quiet conversation within. Two women—one the nun he had seen entering, and another, unknown, with a clear, sweet voice—spoke of womanly matters. He wondered if the younger-sounding voice belonged to an initiate, and if she was being prepared for entry into the order. How strange, he thought, that they would give up their young women to a life of servitude, when there were children to be made and cared for!

He heard the quiet dripping of water and assumed that the younger woman, whom the older nun seemed to be attending, was bathing herself. This thought pleased him, and he smiled, though there was no one to appreciate it.

He listened for a few moments more, but it was fruitless, for he learned nothing of note. When the dripping came to a sudden end, he thought it best to leave, for the nun might have finished her duties to the woman and could come through the door at any time to catch him in his pointless espionage.

But the sound of their voices was strangely soothing. *A few more words*, he told himself. *And if she comes to the door, I will pretend that I am merely walking by.*

"Here is your towel, *Mademoiselle*," he heard the nun say.

"Thank you." There was a brief moment of quiet—perhaps as she dried herself—before he heard the younger woman say, "The lace is so beautiful. Just like the tablecloth."

As he tiptoed quickly away, Alejandro knew he would be waiting at the door, well before the sun rose, to see just who it was that came out.

The child was still abed when Alejandro slipped out of the straw in the morning. He found his clothing in the darkness and dressed quietly, then tiptoed away without waking anyone. Whoever was in that room, he reasoned, would rise early as well, if there was something to hide. He whispered a prayer that no one else would be about at that ungodly hour and stepped very quietly through the halls and passageways to the room where he'd listened the night before.

A pang of discomfort arose in him as he recalled his short stint with his ear to the planks. After all, what business was it of his if a lady enjoyed bathing? Such healthy behavior was to be encouraged, especially among the stinking French. He assuaged his own guilt by telling himself that there might be some perilous plot afoot, some kind of duplicity taking place among the guards, and that de Chauliac ought to be made aware of it for his own safety and the success of their journey. If

Alejandro discovered something untoward, he would find a way before they set out again to take his mentor aside and deliver the intelligence he had acquired, however shamefully.

He heard stirrings within; they grew louder with each passing minute. Nevertheless, it seemed a lifetime to the physician until the door began to open. He stepped back a few paces and watched, with his back against the cold stone wall, as the room's occupant emerged.

"Dearest God," he said aloud to the small soldier. "You are—a woman!"

She took him by the arm with surprising force and pulled him into the room with her. When they were both completely inside, she shut the door, then whirled around to face him.

In flawless French, she said, "And you, sir, are a Jew."

For a moment, he was speechless.

"How do you know this?" he said.

"How did you discover my sex?" she demanded.

"I—I spied upon you last night, by putting my ear to the door as you were having your bath. I overheard your conversations with the nun."

"But I do not understand—what prompted you to do this?"

"I thought you were—" He could not bring himself to say *an English spy*, so great was his relief to discover—if her speech was any indication—that such was probably not the case. "The tablecloth," he said. "You aroused my suspicion with your admiration for the lace. I thought perhaps you might just be a man with a liking for niceties— there are many such men, I know—but I could not convince myself that you were one of them."

"You are very clever," she said. "I shall have to exercise more care in my admirations."

"As for explanations," he said, stepping closer, "what you have said of me just now demands one."

"Father Guy told me."

He searched her eyes for some clue about who the person she had named might be. A deep concern entered his heart; was there one among the guards who knew who he was, and had that guard revealed it to one of the brothers? Of course, there would be a handsome reward from the English king for such information.

"I must assume you refer to one of the brothers here," he said. "But how could—"

"No," she said. "Father Guy. Your teacher."

"*Father* Guy?" For a moment he was stymied. Then he said, "You cannot mean Guy de Chauliac?"

"I can, and I do."

"But he is not a priest. I know this with certainty."

"No, not now, but he was once. How else do you think he could enjoy such proximity to the Holy Father?"

Alejandro said nothing for a moment as he digested the astonishing information he'd just received. "One assumes it is because he is the best physician in Europa."

Now the woman laughed lightly; the sound of it was sweet and lyrical. "He would say, I think, that you yourself occupy that exalted position."

A surge of pride went through Alejandro to hear those words said, but this was not a time to let such utterances swell his head. "He would be wrong," he said, "and there are too many other things to consider at the moment to let such flattery fog my thinking. On my mother's soul, I would never have suspected this. He said nothing to me in all the time I have known him of having taken holy orders."

He stepped closer to her again. "Nor did he say anything of a woman on this ride. Some say it is bad luck. Therefore, if I am to be cursed on yet another journey, let me at least have full sight of the source of the trouble to come." He reached forward and pulled on the bowstring that held her tight cap in place. She made no move to stop him. The cap came off, and her hair fell free; she shook it loose and brushed it back behind her shoulders with an annoyed look on her face.

"It took me a great deal of time to put all this hair into that cap. Now I shall have to do it all over again."

"Why bother?" he said. "You are discovered. Appear as the beautiful woman you are."

She seemed to shrink a bit when she heard that. In a less defiant voice, she said, "I am discovered by you, but my fellow soldiers are still blind—I think and hope—to my true nature. I have many good reasons for continuing my charade, and for the safety of all of us, it must remain that way."

Alejandro stepped back and crossed his arms over his chest. With a very slight smile on his face, he watched as the woman went through the laborious process of replacing the cap on her head and tucking the stray locks into place.

"I shall not reveal you," he said as she completed the task. "My name, though you perhaps already know it, is Alejandro Canches." He bowed slightly. "I am pleased to meet you, though I suspect that the time for formal introductions is past."

"Philomène de Felice," she said. "You have my deep gratitude for your discretion." Then she became the soldier again. "On this journey, I am called Philippe. I will be most grateful, as will Father Guy, if you would call me by that name, should the need arise." She replaced the helmet over her cap.

"As you wish," he said.

But it would not be easy, having seen Philomène.

He managed to corner Guy de Chauliac for a few brief moments before they all departed.

Standing just far enough away from his mentor so they did not appear to be in conversation, Alejandro said, "I have met Philippe."

De Chauliac's head turned quickly in his direction.

"Most interesting," Alejandro said. "A soldier of many talents. Indeed, many faces, one might more accurately say."

"Indeed," de Chauliac said quietly. "We will speak more of this when we are in Paris." Then his tone became more urgent. "Say nothing to anyone of this. You do not understand the importance, nor will you, until more is revealed. For now you must trust me."

"You have said this before," Alejandro told him.

"To your great benefit. Never forget that."

"I shall not, Father Guy."

De Chauliac gave him a perturbed stare, then turned his horse and found his forward position in the party. Alejandro got onto his own horse, then took Guillaume by the hand and pulled him up. The soldiers of the pope rode by them, one by one.

"*Bonjour*, Philippe," he said quietly as she passed him.

"*À vous-même*, Alejandro" came the reply.

They stopped on the riverbank to water their horses before noon. Alejandro set Guillaume down on the ground to run and stretch his legs, then brought his mount alongside Philomène's. He stood next to her at the water's edge with no one else near. "If circumstances permit," he said quietly, "may I call upon you this evening?" He qualified his intent by adding, "For conversation, of course. Depending on the nature of our lodging, if it happens to be advantageous."

Their reflections rippled as the horses drank. Philomène did not respond, but he did not see a discouraging look upon her face.

"If you do not think it ill-advised, that is."

After a time, she said, "I would be amenable to some conversation. Of course, there are realms that I will prefer not to discuss, but one does long for good company on occasion." They stood quietly together, watching the little waves in the pond, until the horses seemed satisfied. "You should know before you come to me," she said, "that the other soldiers will talk if we are seen together. So you must be especially discreet. They think me odd and will think the same of you by association."

He almost laughed. "One can only imagine what they would think if they truly knew."

Her reply was blunt and humorless. "They would think me fair game for their appetites."

"Well," Alejandro said, a bit flustered by her frank response, "I have no doubt they would think me fair game for their hatred, were they to know about me what you already do. I shall be especially careful, for both of our sakes."

The rest of the party began to remount. The physician called to

Guillaume, then took up his horse's reins. As he left Philomène's side, he looked back and said, "Until this evening, then."

The captain of the English guard pressed a purse of coins into the palm of the cooper's widow. She made no pretense of gratitude, but hefted and squeezed the linen sack to judge the value of the sum it held. It was well more than the thirty coins of silver that signified another betrayal. Her passage and resettlement into England were assured, and she would know comfort there.

He has left Avignon in haste and has taken the boy with him. Yes, the boy has golden hair and eyes of blue. I know not where, but they left several days ago, on horseback.

She stuffed the purse into the pocket of her apron and headed immediately for the public stables. *The next party that goes to Calais*, she told the stableman, *I would go with them.* She pressed one of her coins into his hand and told him where he might find her when the time came.

The better part of that afternoon was passed in completing the arduous descent from Cluny to the edge of the plain. Digoin lay to the west, which town—with some luck—they would reach before the sun fell. As the terrain leveled, the party came closer together again, for it was no longer necessary to ride in single file as they had been forced to do on the rocky hills, where the roads were little more than paths. Words could once again be exchanged between riders without shouting. The day was fine, with full sun and a sweet breeze that carried the scent of meadow flowers to their noses.

Alejandro felt his tension ease at last, for it was no longer necessary to look down with each step his mount made. The weight of his journey's purpose never left his heart, but in this moment it seemed less of a burden than at other times. Guillaume began to nap against his back as the horse's motion smoothed. The boy's arms were warm and welcome, much the same as Kate's small arms had felt when she was of the age her son was now. Up ahead, Alejandro saw Philomène among her fellows; she kept with them, though she did not seem to interact beyond riding in tandem.

He allowed himself to think about her, to let this new intrigue have its due. Thoughts of the evening's rendezvous were a pleasant diversion to the monotony of the ride. Would she wear a woman's clothing when he came to call upon her? He doubted it. Should she be required as a soldier to react to some kind of emergency, she would be revealed, for the skirts of a woman were cumbersome and often difficult to remove. He tried to remember how old Kate had been when she began to complain of the complexity that folds of fabric created in riding a horse. At some point she had fashioned herself two pairs of breeches from one skirt and had worn them unabashedly in their travels.

The ease with which Philomène wore her soldier's mantle and breeches seemed more reasonable as these thoughts came back to him. The short sword at her belt, the arrows in her quiver—he had seen his own daughter wear them with something akin to enthusiasm. She often hunted their meat in the deep woods around the little cottage they'd shared, before Guillaume Karle stumbled upon them, dragging his wounded comrade. As Alejandro stood well back, ready to strike a blow if needed, the sixteen-year-old Kate had opened the door. Guillaume Karle seemed a giant as he strode in, carrying his comrade, whose wounded arm had to be removed to preserve his life. It had been a futile attempt. The forces with whom de Coucy rode had found them and had slain the wounded man, who had to be left behind as his would-be saviors fled.

All because they desired their own little pieces of French soil! With such vast holdings as were theirs, how could Navarre and de Coucy reasonably deny them? In the end, it was a simple matter: With the English breathing down the neck of the French king, Charles of Navarre had tried to press his advantage and steal the throne for himself, and he needed all of his lands to bolster his strength. His efforts—despite bloody enthusiasm and a victory over the *Jacquerie*—had eventually been for naught.

Alejandro patted Guillaume's hand lightly as he remembered the day when their entire world was turned, in an instant, upside down. The boy did not stir but rested quietly, his breathing regular and deep as he slept. Alejandro's vision settled on a dragonfly not an arm's length from his face. The wings fluttered as the beautiful creature rose up and down, side to side, jerking in every direction—

—until the whoosh of an arrow blew it away.

The missile found its mark in the neck of one of the soldiers, who had been riding a few paces forward and to his left. Alejandro turned toward what he thought would be the arrow's source, only to see another whiz past. He shouted a loud warning; Guillaume came awake instantly and clutched at his back. Up ahead he saw an outcropping of large rocks on the side of a rise.

"Hold me tightly," he said to the boy, who responded by clutching at his grandfather's waist with all his strength.

The rest of the party was already on its way to the rocks. Alejandro spurred the horse hard and brought it alongside the horse on which the wounded soldier now slumped. He grabbed the reins of the man's frantic horse and pulled it along as he rode, with Guillaume clinging perilously, toward the haven of the rocks.

An arrow flew behind them but caught the wounded man's horse in the flank. The animal rose up on its hind legs; Alejandro's horse did the same. He fought for control and felt Guillaume begin to slip. He grabbed the boy's arm and threw himself against the horse's neck. His weight brought the animal back down just in time to keep himself and Guillaume from being thrown. They reached the rocks a few seconds later; hands came up from all sides to help the boy and the wounded man down to the ground.

Alejandro dismounted quickly, and for a few moments, he leaned over with his hands clutched around his belly, panting hard to catch his breath. As he did this, Guillaume slipped between him and the side of the rock, where he cowered with his hands covering his face.

"Free companies," he heard someone say. Alejandro's heart sank. He had hoped their reign of terror had passed by now, but such was apparently not the case; in his sheltered *ghetto* life, word of the bands of rogue knights who roamed the roads in search of easy victims had not reached him. With so many of France's overlords taken at Poitiers and the skirmishes that had come after, hundreds of knights were left without a means of obtaining the plunder by which they made their livings. And so they had banded together—in companies free of allegiance. They made themselves the scourge of all honest travelers; this group was so desperate that they had chosen to fall upon a group traveling under the protection of the pope.

As four of the guards sent their own arrows in the direction of the marauders, two more stood directly in front of de Chauliac. Another pair were on the ground, attending to their wounded comrade. One of those was Philomène.

All of these observations swirled through Alejandro's brain in an instant. He turned and took Guillaume by the shoulders. "Are you hurt?"

There was stark fear in the child's voice. "No, *Grand-père*...."

"Then stay close to this rock while I see to the man on the ground. Do not run from here, or you will have no protection. Do you understand?"

On the boy's frightened nod, Alejandro hugged him for a very brief moment of reassurance. Then he bent down close to the fallen soldier, who lay on his back with his arms and legs twitching. He pushed himself between Philomène and her stricken comrade. The shaft of an arrow protruded from the side of the man's neck; the point did not protrude from the other side.

"It is well embedded; I have seen such a wound before," he said, hoping to explain away what he was about to do. "We must pull the arrow out slowly and keep a cloth against his neck, to stanch the blood."

"No," he heard someone beside him say. To his great surprise, it was Philomène. She deliberately lowered her voice when she said, "First we must shift it, so his shuddering will stop. If we do not, then the cord that binds the rest of his body to his neck might be severed. We must be careful to do him no harm in trying to help him."

First do no harm. These words were part of the oath he had taken upon finishing his studies at Montpellier.

He moved aside and let Philomène do her work. He glanced back at de Chauliac, who watched the soldier in disguise intently over the shoulder of his guard. The look on the Frenchman's face was one Alejandro had seen many times himself: critical, appraising, pedantic, and, at the same time, proud. Alejandro knew then that he was not the only student in the party.

Eight

"What do you have on underneath that suit?" the woman asked Michael.

"Underwear," he said.

"Then I guess you'll have to leave it on." She moved toward the horse; Galen did not protest as she poked at the saddle and rummaged in the saddlebags. She dwelled momentarily on the toothbrush containers with their cotton swabs but put them back in the bag. The extra clip of bullets went into one of her pockets. When she had apparently satisfied herself that there were no other weapons, she bent over, her eyes still trained on Michael, and picked up the gun that had fallen free. She examined it in the blink of an eye and tucked it into the other pocket.

In response to his visible dismay, she said, "Don't worry, it's going to a good home."

"I feel ever so much better now," Michael said bitterly.

"You're a Brit," she said.

"How kind of you to notice. You're a Yank."

"And proud of it," she said. "You can get back on the horse."

Michael did as he was told, though it was a mighty struggle in the bulky suit. She made no offer to help but motioned toward the peak with her hand. "That way."

"Where are you taking me?" Michael asked.

She didn't answer his question, saying only, "Stay on this path—it's pretty clear all the way to the top; better than the road. I'll be right behind you. Since you're a cop, I'll assume I don't have to explain what will happen to you if you try anything stupid."

"No," he muttered. "You don't."

"Be careful," she warned him. "The footing can be bad."

"I wish you'd been around to tell me that before," he said angrily.

"I was," she said.

He looked at her in surprise.

"You just didn't know I was there."

The remark seemed an insult, delivered as it was with a little grin. "When we get where we're going," he said, "perhaps you'll oblige me with some lessons."

They progressed slowly up the slope. It was rough going, and several times Galen didn't seem to want to move forward. Michael tried to reassure him with pats on the flank, but the horse seemed also to feel what his rider was experiencing—the raw sense of helplessness that comes with captivity.

Finally they reached the peak. Michael looked out over the view and saw the valley below. Though he'd seen this view before, he'd never seen it at this time of year, when the trees were still bare of leaves. It was a perspective quite different from the one to which he was accustomed. He saw the far end of the lake, where it narrowed to the river, which, he assumed, was its origin. The cell towers that jutted up over the treetops seemed to have had their arrangement altered. Some, the older ones, were bare metal—dark, ugly reminders of progress on its previous mad rampage. Others were disguised as pine trees so as not to offend the drivers of the Benzes and Beemers that once roared through their shadows, hurrying toward God-knows-what urgent meeting.

He listened for a moment. Again, it was birds and breezes—no cars, no trucks, no voices from a box, just the small sounds of nature.

Even in distress, he could not help but be soothed. His captor did not protest the momentary respite, and he imagined that she, too, craved that kind of peace, however brief it might be.

Eventually she said, "Let's go."

They began their descent. After a short distance, the woman said, "The path divides not too far ahead. Go to the left."

"All right," he said. He didn't tell her that he knew of the turnoff; this was the path he would have taken to get to the spot where they'd first collected the suspicious active bacterium that had brought him out here again. He thought it best to keep the nature of his own journey to himself until it became necessary to tell.

He turned backward as much as he could in the awkward suit. "Can I ask your name?"

She did not answer immediately.

"Lorraine," she said eventually. "Lany, for short."

"Lany," he echoed. "Last name?"

Another pause. "Dunbar."

"Ordinarily, Lany, I would say, 'Pleased to meet you,' but in truth, I think I'd rather not. In any case, my name is Michael Rosow."

She said nothing.

"My wife's name is Caroline."

Again she was silent.

"And we have a daughter, Sarah Jane. A lovely little redheaded—"

"That's enough chitchat," she said. "Just keep moving."

Keep engaging her, he thought. *Make yourself human to her.*

"And just when I thought we were getting—"

He heard a click of metal. "I said, *enough.* Maybe you better take that helmet all the way off so you can hear me better."

Once again he realized that she knew what she was doing.

For another hour they worked their way down the mountainside. At times the path was gently sloped; in some places, though, the going was so steep that Michael knew Lany Dunbar would have to look at the ground for balance, and those were moments when he considered bolting. If he were to ride off at a clip, would she shoot him? He had no way of knowing. What was it she wanted with him? Was she a single woman living by herself, in need of a man? If so, would he become her slave? How would she keep him captive if she needed him for labor—with leg chains?

All these questions, and dozens more, swirled through his consciousness. In the end, he knew that his most important goal was to stay alive so he could get back to his wife and child. The best means of doing that was compliance.

And so he did what he was told. Captor and captive progressed down the road. A few hundred yards along, they came to the small cluster of buildings, a modern-day ghost town, where Michael would have collected the new samples had his journey gone as planned. Despite the compromise of his suit, he reached up quietly and pulled down the plexi, hoping she wouldn't notice.

Not quietly enough.

"Why did you close your visor?"

He hesitated. "Allergies," he said, after a moment.

"Bull," she said. "Tell me why."

Finally he told her. "There's a hot spot near here."

She stiffened. "Where?"

"I don't know the full extent of it, but in that building up ahead there are live bacteria. Not DR SAM." He pointed toward a dilapidated mill town Victorian with peeling white paint and a sagging porch. "The whole area may be contaminated, but I can't say for sure."

He watched with mild amusement as she pulled a bandanna up over her nose and mouth.

He thought about saying, *It will just get in through your eyes*, but kept the remark to himself.

Her voice was now muffled by the bandanna, and his hearing was dampened by the closed helmet, but he understood that she said, "How do you know that?"

We almost slipped out, but he caught himself. "I took some samples there, a few months ago. I was coming back to take a repeat batch when we—met."

"Coming from where?"

Now it was his turn to smile and remain silent.

"We'll find out eventually."

She'd said *we*. She was not alone. It was almost exciting, until he began to wonder how *they* would get the information out of him.

They hurried through the rest of the town. After a torturously long time on the same road—Michael judged by the sun that it might be as much as three hours—they came to an intersection. The route sign was still there, but the once dark-blue color of the placard had faded to something that resembled stressed denim, and the pole was lurched to one side at a sharp angle. Remnants of the word *Orange* could barely be read; Michael recalled the former mill town that he'd once passed through with Caroline.

They'd been traveling roughly north since Lany Dunbar had taken him captive, and even though they were at a much lower elevation than the compound, there was snow on the ground still.

"Go right," she said.

"Okay," he said. "But may I please ask your permission to stop for a moment?"

"Why?"

"Because, Ms. Dunbar, I need to see a man about a horse, if you get my meaning."

"Aren't you wearing a CD?"

He was momentarily stunned. How would she know about the capture device? He regarded her quizzically; there was an *Oh, damn* look on her face.

There were two possible explanations: She had a close relationship with someone who'd worn the green suit, or—harder to fathom—she'd worn one herself.

After a few moments of consideration, she said, "You'll have to wait. But it's not far now."

Michael hadn't been in the midst of a crowd of strangers in a very long time. He found himself in the center of a large group of men, women, and children, all of whom stared at him as if he had recently arrived from Jupiter. The courtyard in which they were assembled was not unlike their own; a couple of buildings, tie-ups for the horses, stone pathways, patches of dead brush that would soon green up. Under the watchful eye and pointed gun of Lany Dunbar, the men helped him down off Galen. Their hands were friendly and careful, not at all rough. One of the men took Galen by the reins and led him off to a building that Michael assumed was a stable.

"He needs the outhouse," Lany said. She looked at one of the other women. "Linda, can you get him some clothes? He says he has just underwear underneath."

The woman she called Linda looked Michael over quickly and said, "I'll get something of Steve's." She ran off toward one of the buildings.

Then to another woman, Lany said, "He'll need some help getting that thing off."

The woman nodded and came forward. Her hands were practiced on the suit's fasteners; she asked no questions, but moved from snap to zipper to button without instruction.

"You've done this before," Michael observed.

She met his gaze but did not respond otherwise.

Just as the last snap came open, Linda returned with an armful of garments. He stepped out of the suit and took the offered pile. Modesty seemed inconsequential at the moment, but he blushed slightly at the notion of strange women seeing him nearly in the altogether and covered himself quickly.

His boots were still on the ground, but when he reached for them, Lany said, "No. Leave them off."

"My feet will be bare. The ground is still frozen."

"Don't worry. You won't be doing much walking."

He tiptoed to the outhouse with an escort and did his business under the watchful eye of one of the men, to whom Lany had given Michael's gun. Thoughts of escape screamed through his brain. *Bolt backward, knock the man down, wrestle the gun away from him and run . . .* but where would he go, shoeless and horseless in frigid March, in the time after, with bacteria waiting to eat his flesh?

Stay alive, he reminded himself. He would be theirs until a good opportunity presented itself.

.   .   .

When they heard the gate opening, the books for the children's reading lesson went down fast. Janie and Caroline followed them into the courtyard. Kristina wasn't far behind.

As she took Jellybean's reins, Janie looked up at Tom and said, "You're back a lot sooner than I figured."

He explained about the roadblock. "I guess it had to happen sooner or later. Nature's taking over again."

"What about Michael?"

Tom looked directly at Caroline. "He went up the rest of the way without me," he said. "Galen was doing better than Jellybean, so I turned back earlier than we'd planned. I didn't want to put too much strain on her ankle."

Caroline's brow tightened.

"He was fine," Tom reassured her. "He'll *be* fine."

There was nothing more to do than to go about the tasks of living, but a mist of uncertainty settled over the day.

Every few moments, as she and Janie prepared dinner, Caroline would glance out the window toward the gate, hoping for a sight of the neon-green suit. Sunset was no more than an hour away.

"He should have been back by now," she said.

Janie tried to put a hopeful cast on the situation. "Not necessarily. He might have found something worth bringing back."

"He's been down that route a number of times. If there was something worth scavenging, don't you think he would have found it before?"

"Maybe, maybe not. Try to relax—he'll be back any minute now."

She looked out the window once again. "I hope you're right."

The hour passed with painful slowness. The pork was done, and the sun left the sky. The children finished their lessons and came, with Kristina in tow, to the dinner table. The table was set and ready, but dinner had not been called.

What few smiles Caroline managed were forced and brief. She tried to put a good face on the situation for the sake of the little ones, but it was not an easy task. When Tom came in from the barn, Janie took him aside and asked quietly, "What should we do?"

"Wait" was all he could offer. "We eat dinner, just like we would if he was here. And we wait."

"Maybe someone should go out after him."

"It's too soon for that," he said. "Michael can take care of himself. Maybe he doesn't want to push Galen too much. He's probably just holed up somewhere in a barn for the night, and he'll be back in the morning."

"Could you sleep in that thing?"

Tom didn't answer that question. "I'm sure he's okay. He's a smart man."

Not very smart to let yourself get caught like this, Michael thought to himself. He paced angrily back and forth in a small room inside the largest of the buildings, a farmhouse that had, at some point in the time before, experienced a loving restoration to what he imagined was its original condition. The floors gleamed with lacquer, the walls were clean white and unblemished. One wall was lined with tall bookshelves stuffed with all manner of volumes; it pleased him, until he recalled that this library was his prison. There was a narrow window with lace curtains, through which the low rays of the sun streamed in; he considered smashing it until he looked out and saw the young man who stood guard outside. The fellow had shoes: a distinct advantage.

Not to mention youth and knowledge of the home ground.

But he'd seen no one in leg chains, and they'd treated him surprisingly well, so he began to think that he would not be hurt. Best to settle down and rest, he thought, while the opportunity presented itself. In his agitated state he wouldn't sleep, so he tilted his head to one side and read through the titles on the shelves until he came up with one of value: *The Dairyman's Guide to Cheese*.

He was halfway through a discussion of the various forms of rennet—not that he could concentrate—when the door opened. One of the men from the original greeting party came in with Michael's gun in his hand, followed by the woman Linda, who carried a tray of food. Michael could see steam rising, and the smell of food filled the air; he began, quite involuntarily, to salivate. On the plate were corn, chicken cut into small pieces, and something that had once been green—perhaps spinach. A plastic spoon rested to one side of the plate; its surface was dull with age.

Linda set the tray down, then backed out the door.

"We thought you might be hungry," the man said. He had a slight Southern drawl. "Go ahead and eat something."

Michael ignored the tray and stood up. "Who are you?" he demanded. "And why am I here?"

The man smiled and pointed at the food. "My wife doesn't take kindly to having her efforts wasted, so you best eat what she made for you." He backed away and stepped through the open library door. Before closing it, he said, "We'll be asking you the same questions in a little while."

Tom hung the lantern on the hook over the door and scraped the spring muck off his boots. As he undid the laces he heard the quiet voices of Janie and Caroline. He set his boots on the mat and padded into the main room in his socks. The two women stopped speaking and turned in his direction when they heard him, and he saw immediately that Caroline had been crying.

On most nights, when he and Michael and the other men came in after bedding down the animals, they would find the ladies sitting with their tea—thank God for the greenhouse—while working quietly at the vital chores of their new world. There was always a hole to be mended or a mitten to be replaced, a new pot scrubber to be crocheted, a doormat to be woven. Tom often marveled that his wife, a woman of immense education and accomplishment, seemed to find satisfaction—most days—in these simple tasks. She, who had touched the open brains of hundreds of human beings, now used her exquisitely sensitive fingertips to knit and weave and stitch the necessities that they all once took for granted. She never complained about what others might consider a diminished station in life. Often the men would play cards or Scrabble; if one was tired or under the weather, another would sub in.

Tom glanced around the room but did not see his daughter. "Where's Kristina?" he said.

"In the lab," Janie answered. "She has a couple of projects to check on."

It was her graceful excuse to escape the discomfort of waiting. He knew that his daughter had never been fond of emotional discomfort; it confused and upset her. The fret of Michael's delayed return hung in the air heavily, and it was visible on all the women's faces. The evening's conversation would not have been pleasant.

After a brief visit with his daughter, Tom came back to the main room and sat down next to Caroline. He put his hand gently on her forearm. "Maybe it's a little early for this."

"Easy for you to say," she said with a sniff.

"I know," he said. "I don't mean to belittle what you're feeling. But don't make yourself crazy, at least not yet."

"God," she said, hugging her own sides. "If we just had a radio or something..."

"Yeah, it would be a lot easier, I know."

For a few more minutes they all sat quietly, each with private thoughts of how they would cope with the change in their order, should it come to that. Caroline finally went off to bed, and shortly thereafter the room began to empty out. Janie and Tom found themselves alone.

Janie glanced toward Caroline's closed bedroom door before saying, "So. What now?"

"I don't know. I'm beginning to think maybe we shouldn't have sent Michael out there."

"He went for a good reason. We need to know about that bacterium. There's no other way to find out."

They were silent for a moment, then Tom said, "Even if he went a little farther than we'd planned—and I don't know why he would do that—he should still be able to leave wherever he is at daylight and get back here by noon tomorrow. The farthest gathering point was still easily within that time frame, even if he's walking."

Janie considered that for a moment, then said, "If we need to go out and find him, it should be me who goes."

Her husband's reaction was immediate and strong. "No way. I'll go. Or one of the other men."

"And if something happens to you and *you* don't come back, what are we going to do, with *two* less men? If Michael's hurt, I'm the one who can take the best care of him."

"You're not going. Don't even think about it. You don't have a suit—what about the hot spots? That's why he went, remember? The *hot* spots."

"No one else would have a suit either! He would have gone in and out as quickly as possible. Whatever happened to him is more likely to have happened en route." As if it would change his mind, she added, "I'll wear the mask."

Tom said nothing but sat at the table for a moment with a dark and unhappy look on his face. Then he rose and spoke calmly, hiding the agitation that Janie knew would have colored the voice of a lesser man. He was once again the lawyer, arguing his point from a stance of authority. "With all due respect, my love, we're getting way ahead of ourselves. He could still be out there for a *good* reason. For all we know, he found something fantastic that will change our lives and he's dragging it back here by the ankles."

Nine

Night was nearly upon de Chauliac's party. One soldier was lost, having taken an arrow to the heart, and the other, with the shaft now cut off barely a finger's width above the skin of his neck, lay horribly wounded on a quickly fashioned travois. The town of Digoin was still a good hour's ride farther. Alejandro was desperate to arrange a moment of private talk with de Chauliac, but the opportunity would not seem to present itself. Nor had he managed to speak with Philomène, the savior of the wounded man, since the fateful hour of battle earlier.

They were all drained and exhausted. Guillaume clung tightly to Alejandro's back, but he was nervous and fidgety, not at all the good rider he had been before.

The body of the slain soldier lay draped over his own horse. *We will bury him in Digoin*, de Chauliac had announced, and as they made their way, Alejandro could not help but think that the man's death had had no purpose. The free-company marauders had not taken so much as a *sou* from any of them.

Philomène rode toward the head of the guard; Alejandro could see her plainly, just behind de Chauliac, who now and again would glance in the woman's direction, as if to determine her condition. She was shaken, Alejandro knew; he had seen it in her face as the battle drew to a close. When she got up on her horse to resume the journey, her hands were trembling.

The captain of the guard now kept the party riding at an exhausting pace; they had used up an hour of their travel time in fighting, and their wounded comrade required shelter as soon as it could be found. As the group neared Digoin, they came upon the occasional farmhouse, and more than once Alejandro saw the captain look to de Chauliac for what he supposed might be permission to bring the party to a halt. But they headed onward, and soon the little town became visible in a valley before them. A tall steeple stood out among the trees; Alejandro supposed it was their destination.

But their arrival at the quaint and lovely abbey in Digoin lacked the pomp and ceremony of those they'd had in previous towns en route. De Chauliac himself saw to the care of the wounded man, who was carried into the abbey immediately by a troop of robed brothers under the Frenchman's watchful eye. The dead man was brought down from his unhappy horse and carried off as well, but with less haste. As he took Guillaume down from the saddle, Alejandro caught the boy staring at the man's body.

It struck him that this was the child's first sight of death. Alejandro let him watch as the body was taken into the abbey.

"Where are they taking him, *Grand-père*?"

"To be buried," Alejandro answered. "First they will wash his body and then put him in a shroud, and then he will be buried in the ground. Soon he will meet the angels in heaven."

For a moment, the boy said nothing, then he posed a difficult question. "Have you ever seen an angel?"

"No, Guillaume, they seem to keep to themselves."

"Then how do you know they are real?"

Alejandro paused. "I do not," he said quietly. "I only believe that they are. Knowing and believing can sometimes be two different things. I believe in God, but I have never seen Him either, so I cannot know that He is real. But I see His works all around me, so I must believe, logically, that He is. Do you understand what I mean?"

The child nodded, almost gravely. Alejandro knew that it was perhaps not the answer he wanted, but it would have to suffice.

"A fraction of its value," the cooper's wife called out the door as her neighbor stumbled off under the weight of a large iron pot. "A bargain!"

She stepped back into her home and walked through the small, empty rooms. The rest of her belongings were already dispersed among the Jews in the *ghetto;* the bargaining had been hard and protracted, but the weight of her purse had measurably increased. She would ride in a coach from Avignon to Paris and then on horseback in a traveling party to Calais—a far cry from the mule she rode, behind her walking husband, in the opposite direction more than a decade before. She would return to Eyam well dressed and well fed, and on seeing her apparent prosperity, all would be forgiven. They would welcome her back. She would buy their silence, if it was required, but it seemed doubtful to her that it would be necessary. After all this time, she reasoned, even a monarch with as long a memory as King Edward could not give a whit for the wife of a dead poacher.

Her bags were packed and ready at the door. The carriage would come for her at dawn. She opened her one remaining coverlet—so decrepit that no one would give her a *sou* for it—and spread the ratty thing out on the dirt floor of her empty house. It would be her last night of hard sleep in a long while, for tomorrow and all the nights of her journey would be spent in comfortable inns along the way—at least that was what the gentleman from the conveyance concern had assured her.

She pulled one side of the quilt over herself and settled in, hoping for sleep. It was only a matter of seconds before she felt the annoying bites of the fleas that had no place else to go for warmth but her own flesh. She leaped up from the floor and violently shook out the old coverlet, spewing curses as the dust flew around her.

One last night, she told herself. She slipped between the layers of the coverlet once again, vowing to herself that she would never spend another night in the company of fleas.

Philomène was nowhere to be seen; nor was de Chauliac. Alejandro had hoped to keep an eye on her movements and discover where she might be quartered, so that he could call upon her later as they had agreed. Supper passed, and then the hour of vespers, without any sign of either. Guillaume fell asleep on Alejandro's lap. He cradled the boy, who had experienced a sudden attack of homesickness. He was just tucking him into a blanket on the straw when he heard de Chauliac's voice behind him.

"Someone wishes to speak with you," the Frenchman said.

Alejandro rose and turned. "Someone," he said, pointing to his own chest, "also wishes to speak with *you*." He guided de Chauliac out of the small room in which Guillaume slept and pulled the door quietly closed. "Many events took place today that I do not understand. I would have an explanation."

De Chauliac remained quiet, saying at last, "You shall have one, in due time. All I can tell you right now is that things may not be what you think they are. Again, I ask for your trust. You have a long and grueling journey ahead of you, even after your time in Paris. Please, colleague, do not work yourself into a froth over things that should not concern you and have no influence upon you."

"The woman," Alejandro said. "Why does she travel with us?"

"I am taking her to Paris, for her own protection. There are those who would see her destroyed."

"For God's sake, why? Has she committed some heinous crime?"

"Some would say she has. If she is of a mind to do so, she will tell you why she is with us. If she is not of such a mind, well, I would challenge you or any man on this earth to make her speak."

"Tell me, and save me that effort! I have little time for such foolishness."

"None of us has any time for foolishness, my friend. Least of all me. But hers is not a foolish tale. Be patient. All will be revealed in time."

De Chauliac led him straight to Philomène's room, then departed. When Alejandro entered, she seemed to be waiting for him. With her hair loose, the breeches and loose-fitting soldier's shirt seemed out of place. Her boots were on the floor, still muddy from the day.

She showed him a chair and asked him to sit. He complied, but his agitation would not let him stay still, so he rose up again. "This was not precisely my intent when I requested your company this evening."

"Nor mine in agreeing," she said. "But after today, I understand there is much to be discussed. Please, sit. Your pacing will not accomplish anything, except to muddy the floors."

He flopped back into the chair. "A woman would think of such a consequence in times like these."

A perturbed look came onto her face, but in a moment it softened. "I will take that utterance as a compliment, and hope it was intended that way. Now, Father Guy said you wished to see me urgently, so—"

"He told me that *you* wished to speak with *me*," Alejandro interrupted.

"Did you tell him that we had made arrangements to meet tonight?"

"No, of course not. You asked for my discretion, which request I have honored."

"I said nothing to him either."

Alejandro rose again. "Then he did not know."

They looked at each other for a long moment; gradually, the tension began to resolve. Almost in unison, they each laughed softly. Their building suspicion evaporated, and they began to speak.

"All the physicians yet alive in Avignon were summoned to the papal palace at the onset of the Great Mortality," he told her. "It was 1348, and I had just arrived there. I wanted to prepare for my family to follow, so I had purchased a surgical practice from a widow. When I arrived to take possession, I found de Chauliac's summons on the door. It was supposed to have been for the other fellow.

"At first de Chauliac did not remember me," he told Philomène. "I stood in line with a dozen other men, and he walked before all of us. He did not recognize me as having been one of his students in Montpellier. Of course, being a Jew, I stayed as far toward the back of the study rooms there as I could, so as not to expose myself to the vitriol of the other students. But sometimes I had to come forward, for there were things taught that I was loath to miss. In my time there, it was de Chauliac himself who would dissect the one body that the pope would permit in each year."

After a thoughtful pause, he said, "I have always been grateful that de Chauliac was in such a close position to the pope, else we should have had no dissections at all in Montpellier."

For a few moments, Philomène was very quiet. "Myself as well. There is a part of me," she said finally, "that agrees with such restrictions against the dissection of the body. It is, after all, a divine temple that God has provided for our souls to dwell in while we are here on earth, and we must not desecrate it lightly."

He trod carefully on these waters. "Please forgive me—I do not wish to offend you, but how are we to care for the temple if we know nothing of its structure?"

"Some believe that God will guide us. I say that He does so by granting us the will and the intellect to discover the structure of the temple for ourselves. In that way we preserve it for His adoration."

"So we agree," Alejandro concluded. "In a manner of speaking."

"It would seem that we do." She smiled, and leaned toward him a bit. "Now, I would hear of what followed."

He found that his recollections were still clear, and she set him at such ease with her manner that the words seemed to flow effortlessly. "He trained me in ways of protecting against plague, mostly with isolation as he had done with the pope called Clement. I was sent to

Windsor Castle to protect King Edward and his family. My efforts were successful, despite some resistance, and when my work was done, I thought to remain in England."

This seemed to surprise her. "But your family was in Spain."

"No. They had been banished from our town and sent to Avignon."

"Why?"

He sat back, taking her measure one more time. Already there was a camaraderie growing between them; they had much in common, it seemed, beyond their shared protection by de Chauliac. To have a companion to whom he could speak from the deepest parts of his heart seemed an unattainable dream to him. He wanted so much to tell her what had happened in Cervere, he could fairly feel the words bursting forward.

But no matter how trustworthy Philomène seemed, the story of his crime and subsequent flight to Avignon would have to wait until he knew, first, that she would not betray him and, perhaps as important, that she would not reject him. He settled on what seemed the best explanation. "For the most part," he told her, "it was because we are Jews. There were other intrigues—my father was a moneylender; one Spaniard or the other was always trying to cheat him out of his legitimate profits."

Most especially, a Spaniard who happened to be a bishop.

She was respectfully quiet for a moment. "Yet, you thought to remain in England, despite their notable hatred for the Jews. . . ."

"Yes," he said, his voice quieter. "You see, there was a woman." He fell silent for a moment and lowered his gaze. "We were to be married. I thought perhaps I might find a way to locate my father and bring him there to live with us. But it was not to be."

When he looked up again, Philomène was gazing at him with a deeply sympathetic expression. He thought, for a brief second, that he saw tears in her eyes. "Thank you for your candor," she said. "I have heard of what followed in France from Father Guy. Your story fascinates him. He thinks you the most remarkable man and counts himself privileged to know you."

"That is my opinion of him as well." He straightened up a bit.

"Now I have spoken, and my tale is a sad one....I have great hope that yours will be more cheerful. But before anything else, you must tell me about de Chauliac's priesthood. It seems so *unlike* the man; he is rational to the point of annoyance."

"Faith and reason are not necessarily contradictory forces," she said. "You are a man of science and equally a man of faith. De Chauliac is no different. It is just that one thinks of a priest as someone who has given himself over to God entirely."

"I have known few priests who exhibit any signs of cogent thought."

"Not so Father Guy. We are from the same region in Provence," she told him. "I was a very small child when he came home to our parish, before he resumed his studies in Montpellier. He was beloved among us for his exuberance in tending to our spiritual needs, and yet we all feared him when it was time for confession. The penances he would dole out could wear one down. My mother told me many years later—after he went to Montpellier—that he seemed never to be satisfied with his life in the clergy, that his intelligence drove him to seek more."

She paused for a moment, then said, "In this way, Father Guy has guided my path. He protects me now, I think, because he feels responsible for what I did."

He waited for the confession, and when it did not come, he said, "And you did what, dear lady, that should inspire him to look after you?"

"I disguised myself as a boy and enrolled in Montpellier to study medicine."

"But it is forbidden for women to practice medicine. Now, I do not agree with that edict——"

Before he could finish, she interrupted him with a light laugh, though it was laden with bitterness. "I have heard those words a thousand times. They have become like gnats to me—I swat them away." Then her demeanor grew sober. "My mother and father were horrified," she said. "They refused to acknowledge me; many times I felt that I had no family at all. We were not wealthy but comfortable—my father was a silversmith, and he earned a good living. He had among his customers some of the best families in all of Provence. Of course, they had hopes for a strong marriage for me. 'You are virtuous and intelligent, graceful and polite,' my father would say, 'and you come from a family of decent means. Yet, no offers of marriage have come forth.' It was all he could think to do, to see me well married. He cared not one whit for my great accomplishment."

"But of course he cared for you. . . ."

"In his own way."

"I speak from some experience; it is not an easy task to father a spirited daughter. You might forgive him for wanting the best for you."

"Yes," she said softly. "He was a good and decent man, and I miss him terribly."

"He has passed over?"

"Some five years ago there was a terrible storm. A tree was uprooted and fell upon the roof of our house. I was not there at the time; I was attending to a woman in the depths of labor in our town. The hearth coals were thrown everywhere; the thatch caught fire, and he and my mother were burned to death. Every day I regret that we did not entirely make our peace with each other."

Alejandro reached out and touched her arm for comfort. "You might have perished yourself had you been there."

"I know," she said tearfully. "And for that I am grateful to God. But it was so—abrupt. And had I been there, things might have gone differently."

"You must bring this regret to God. You cannot carry such a burden on your soul. Surely de—I mean, Father Guy has told you this."

"He has, and I try to remember. But sometimes, in the middle of the night, I am neither awake nor asleep, yet I can hear my mother's screams as the fire engulfs her. . . ."

"As I, in the same hours, hear the cries of those whose plague deaths I could not prevent."

They looked at each other, two kindred souls, each having passed through a darkness, each with yet another passage to make before the sun shone.

In Nevers, they met again.

"Most of what I did in my practice was with women," she told him. "I had a few patients who were men, but many would not trust me, even the husbands whose wives I treated. Of course, I understood this somewhat, as it is often a difficult thing for a man to be touched by another woman, knowing that his wife is privy to it. But all went well, at least for a time; it was a small village, and my father did most of his business elsewhere, so I was able to continue without harassment. But one day, six months ago now, it all came to an end."

"How?"

"A nobleman from Italy was traveling through on his way to the Languedoc. Often we had travelers pass through, but because there was no abbey or tavern in our town, it was rare that anyone stopped. This man's wife was with child, perhaps six months on. Her pains began early, and she had started to bleed. One of the women in town told them of me, and they brought the noblewoman to my little cottage. It was clear to me that her time had come, however unfinished the child within might be. I told the husband so and that the infant was not likely to survive."

"Wise counsel," Alejandro said. "At six months, it is too early. . . ."

"He did not find the counsel wise," she said. "He begged me to take the child from her womb. He was much older than she and had no sons to follow him. I told him that I would not consider such a thing, that I am no surgeon. But he would not accept that."

"I do not understand. Refusal of treatment is always the right of the physician."

"There was a young girl with me when they arrived suddenly; I was teaching her to gather certain herbs that I needed. The man grabbed her and put a knife to her throat, and told me that if I did not put my own knife to his wife's belly, he would kill the girl."

"A beast," Alejandro said quietly.

"You cannot imagine what I wished to do to him. In any event, I gave the woman as much laudanum as she could stand and opened her womb. I had no choice. But I had no experience in such a thing; I cut too deeply, and the woman died. There was more blood than I have ever seen from any wound. The child was a male, and he took breath, though he was pitifully small. The nobleman seemed not to care much about his poor wife, but he was ecstatic about his son. Then the child began to gasp and his skin turned blue; it broke my heart to hear his helpless wheezing, but there was nothing I could do for him. Before he was an hour old, his life was over. It was all horrible enough, until the nobleman cast the dead infant onto the floor. He had no regard at all for his own child's soul and had not baptized him. And so I did it, in the hope that the child would be taken to God.

"In a while, men from the traveling party came to take away the bodies. The next day, different men came for me and took me to Avignon, where I was to be charged with the crime of practicing medicine as a woman. Of course, de Chauliac was advised of this notable event and came to see the criminal; he told me later that it was as much out of curiosity as official duty, for he considered the prohibition archaic. When he discovered that it was I, he arranged my immediate transfer to his custody, 'for inquisition,' he told everyone. He assured the cardinals who protested that he would see to my captivity, but he kept me among the nuns until it was time to leave."

A few moments of silence passed, during which she seemed to reflect on these painful events. Finally she said, "Now you must speak again."

"I kept a journal during my travels, at least until my time in England," Alejandro said, glad for the opportunity to break the discomfort. "It was a gift from my father, a sort of reconciliation over the matter of Montpellier. I met much the same resistance to my decision to go there as you did. 'Physician!' he roared when I told him. 'And what of our business? Who will follow me?' In the end, that did not matter, as his business perished when he was banished. I kept that journal faithfully for many years."

"What has become of it?"

"I lost it, in England. We left in such haste, and I was still weak from plague...."

"A pity to have lost it," she said. "What sort of things did you record?"

"Notes on my observations, of course, and sketches of things that intrigued me—organs, bones, other features of the body. I wrote the route of my journeys, described some of the people I met...I do not pretend that the writings could be of import to anyone but myself. But so many moments of my life are recorded within it, my travels, my triumphs—"

"Your love?"

"Indeed," he said quietly. He was about to say that he despaired of ever finding such a love again, but it came to him that that might no longer be true.

After three more days of hard travel in cold rain and wind, the party finally reached Paris, in late afternoon. Guillaume stared intently at the marvelous sights of the grand city as they made their way along the banks of the Seine. The river was full of boats and barges; the boy could not take his eyes off them.

When they came to the cathedral, Alejandro stopped the horse, though the others continued.

"*Grand-père*, we will lose them...."

"I know the route well from here. I would have you look for a moment, and listen."

They sat in the shadow of Notre Dame and let the haunting music of vespers fill their ears, the same captivating chant that had lived in Alejandro's head since he first heard it. Raindrops dripped from Alejandro's hat and the tip of Guillaume's nose. Nevertheless, the boy sat motionless and awestruck by what lay before him. After a few more moments, Alejandro heeled the horse and turned him around, for he was feeling chilled and he knew the boy would be as well.

They caught up with the others as they were turning onto the street where de Chauliac's *maison* was located. The building was just as

Alejandro remembered it, a solid brick edifice with an intricately peaked roof and a stout wall surrounding the courtyard. As they rode over the familiar cobblestones, Alejandro had a strange but comforting sense of homecoming. He knew the *maison* well, understood its secrets, and could find those places where whispers would not be heard. He looked up to the roofline and saw the small dormer where his room of eight years ago had been. The planks and corners of the small space came clear in his mind.

They entered the foyer in a flurry of activity; servants bustled about the arriving party to help with their belongings and to take away the dripping wet cloaks. The servants in the household were all different from his time here before, save one, the same elderly man who had served as his keeper. Alejandro said nothing to him when he came into the foyer but saw the old man's little wink of recognition.

As they made their way up the narrow stairway, Alejandro began to renew his acquaintance with the elderly man. "I congratulate you, fellow," he said, "on a remarkably long and vigorous life."

The old man turned stiffly and smiled. "I was waiting for your return, master, and I have followed carefully all the rules you gave me about proper living. One day soon I'll die happy!"

"Not on account of my return, I hope." At the top of the stairs, he gestured toward the boy and said, "Allow me to present my grandson, Guillaume."

The servant bowed to Guillaume and said, quite formally, "Welcome, young sir, to *la Maison de Chauliac*."

Guillaume did not seem to know what to do, so he thanked the servant, then bowed himself, mimicking his motion as closely as possible. This brought a laugh from the old man.

"We'll get along just fine, you and I. Now, come into your room and get settled."

He pushed open the door to the same small room Alejandro had occupied during his month of captivity in Paris eight years before. The bed was in the same position, to the side of the window, but the washstand and chair had been moved to accommodate an upholstered pallet that lay on the floor.

The servant placed their satchels in one corner. "If you are in need of anything, sir, you have only to ring the bell."

Alejandro thanked the man, and he left.

He turned to see Guillaume looking out the window at the activity on the Paris street below.

"So many people, *Grand-père*."

"Yes, Guillaume," he said. He knelt down next to the boy and joined him in his observations. Horses with riders passed, and students scurried by toward the university, the robes of their colleges billowing out behind them. A few of the guards from their retinue could be seen taking some ease outside the *maison*'s courtyard. It was a day in the life of Paris, nothing more or less. But it was fascinating.

As he stared out the pane of wavy glass, Alejandro let his mind drift back to the day, eight years before, when Kate and Guillaume Karle stood on the street below and tossed up a message tied to a rock. It was the beginning of their plot to free him, and it was also the first time he had noticed their mutual affection.

I should not have been surprised. They were kindred souls, both spirited and determined, handsome and well built. He thought of the kindred spirit he had found on this journey and marveled at how such things often came about by what seemed like sheer luck.

No, I should not have been surprised. Nor should I now.

He felt a tug on his sleeve and looked down at Guillaume.

"*Grand-père*, are you all right?"

The vision of Kate and her lover slipped away. "Yes, Guillaume."

The boy's voice was full of concern. "Are you certain?"

"*Yes*, child, but why do you ask?"

"It is just that, well ... you are *weeping*."

Ten

Three men came into the library, two of whom he'd seen before. Instinctively, Michael stood and faced them.

Southern Man—late middle age, plaid flannel shirt with patched elbows, neatly trimmed hair with a touch of gray at the temples— seemed to be the leader. At his side was the youth who'd been outside his window. The young man was tall and well muscled, with rosy cheeks and a haircut so short his head appeared nearly to have been shaved— the classic farm-bred American boy. The third stood back from the other two, with his feet spread slightly apart and his hands crossed over each other. Michael realized when he saw the weapon on his hip, *He's the sentry.*

He heard the hinges again; Lany Dunbar entered. Michael noticed a quick exchange of smiles between her and the youth.

Way too young for her, he thought, *but then, these are desperate times.*

"Sit down," Southern Man said.

Michael wasn't about to put himself below their level. "Only if you'll join me," he replied.

"All right, if that's how you want it."

Everyone but the sentry found a seat.

"Let's have some light in here," Southern Man said. "The daylight's fading." He reached toward a lamp; Michael, half-consciously, wondered where the igniter was. Then he heard the click and saw the flood of light.

"Bloody hell," he said. He stared at the lamp in awe.

"Generator," said Southern Man. "Electricity we've got. But lightbulbs," he said with a small laugh, "now, they're gonna be a problem one of these days."

Michael found himself wanting to say, *We have a closet full of lightbulbs that we aren't using at the moment,* but he kept the thought to himself.

"Okay, now that all this protocol silliness is out of the way, let me introduce myself. My name is Steven Roy, but everyone just calls me Steve." He extended his hand to Michael, who looked at it suspiciously.

"I don't have the plague," Steve added with a laugh.

Reluctantly, Michael gripped the offered hand.

"You already know Lany Dunbar. That fine-looking boy next to her is Evan."

"My son," Lany said.

Michael was instantly ashamed of his earlier thought. He said quietly, "Hello."

"And that's George back there." Steve pointed over his shoulder to the man with the weapon.

Despite his growing sense that he was trapped in a surrealistic dream, Michael nodded politely to the man with the gun, who returned the gesture with equal courtesy. Then he sat back in his chair, trying to absorb everything and failing miserably.

"Now, if you'd be kind enough to tell us who you are and where you come from, we'd be obliged."

He glanced once more at George, then let his eyes drift down to the gun. Steve smiled and said, "That's a formality for the moment. Don't pay it any mind. No one's going to shoot you unless you make a lot of trouble. I know Lany feels bad about having to be so tough on you this afternoon, but we've had a couple of unfortunate experiences with strangers here, and we like to be careful until we get to know our company a little better." He grinned again. "You seem like a pleasant-enough fellow. And you've got a bit of an accent. I know the feeling," he said, exaggerating his drawl as he spoke. "So, just like we were saying earlier, who are you and where do you come from? We'll tell you about us, but we want to know about you first, since you're the company."

Michael had prepared himself mentally for the new-era version of name, rank, and serial number, but somehow it didn't seem appropriate. They'd disarmed him with civility.

"Michael," he said. "Last name's Rosow. I'm originally from England. I came here just—well, before."

"The first pass or the second?"

"Second."

"So you were in England the first time around."

"Yes."

"How'd you get here, then?"

"It's a long story. I was on, uh, the crown's business."

"Where specifically do you live now?"

He looked from Steve to Lany to Evan, and then back at Steve again.

"Look, we're the good guys," Steve said. "There are lots of folks out there you have to worry about a great deal more than us."

Michael didn't know what to do; his tribe was alone on the other side of the mountain and therefore vulnerable, but here were potential allies just a few hours away, not to be undervalued.

"On the other side of the peak," he said finally.

Looks of confirmation passed between the people of Orange.

There were dozens more questions. Michael answered cautiously, trying not to give away too much information, just in case.

Yes, we have a generator, but we use wind for most of our power because there's lots of wind up there, and we have two cows but no bulls; you have a bull—that's fantastic. . . .

No, we don't grow wheat, we're too high up, but we've got wild rice and barley and lots of oats and plenty of blueberries. My wife cooks them down for jam; you have strawberries; the children will be very happy to hear that. . . .

Two, a boy and a girl, seven and eight, and a young woman about this lad's age, and among the adults we're all different ages, but mostly middle-aged . . .

And a lab with some fairly sophisticated equipment . . .

And a computer that still works . . .

And schoolbooks . . .

"What about weapons?"

Michael hadn't even noticed that he'd leaned forward in his excitement. On the mention of weapons, he leaned back again with his hands on his knees. "Mostly arrows," he said. "Everyone has a good knife, even the children, though we only let them carry theirs when they go outside our immediate area, which hasn't been for a while now."

Steve Roy nodded. "You have a gun."

"Had." He glanced in Lany's direction. "The lady relieved me of it when we met."

He waited for someone to say, *You'll get it back,* but no one did.

"You were wearing a suit," Lany said. "I'd be interested in knowing where you found it."

"I didn't, exactly," he told her.

"You stole it?"

"No," he said. "It was assigned to me."

"You were a biocop?"

"Here and on the other side of the pond." He looked her directly in the eye and said, "And I'm guessing someone here was too."

The silence was conspicuous, until Steve started asking questions again.

"What about the other adults? What do they do?"

"One accountant, a librarian, a few other useless things. But my wife's a research biologist," he said, "and we've got a chemist too. Our young lady's quite a whiz in the lab. And of course, we have the obligatory lawyer," Michael said. Then, almost reluctantly, he added, "And a doctor."

Everyone sat up straight.

"You've got a doctor? *Alive?*"

He cursed himself silently for the mistake—too much trust, too soon. *I should have known better.* "When I left she was."

Lany stood; Evan followed suit quickly, and then Steve. "We'll be back in a moment," he said to George. "You know what to do."

When they left the room, George repositioned himself in front of the door. He gave Michael a little smile; Michael nodded in return. After that, it was one long stare between the two, until Michael picked up the cheese book again.

True to their promise, the others returned in short order. This time Evan was not with them.

"You can lead us back to your place?"

It seemed a silly question. "Well, of course." He paused, then said, "But why would I?"

Steve ignored the question. "How much farther is it from where Lany found you?"

He stared at them both for a moment. "You don't really expect—"

"Please," Lany said, with marked urgency. "It's important. We're not going to hurt you or anyone in your group."

He made a leap of faith, one he hoped wouldn't backfire on him or those he loved. "About an hour or so on horseback, all downhill."

Steve and Lany looked at each other and nodded.

"One of our little girls is very sick," Lany said.

Michael stiffened.

"It's not DR SAM. It's something chronic. We think she might have diabetes. We'll take you back home tomorrow if your doctor will help her."

"I'm not sure she'll be able to help."

"If she could just try . . ."

"What about the suit and the weapon?"

They didn't reply immediately. Finally Steve said, "We'll give them back, but only after we get to your place."

"Agreed," Michael said. He stood and extended his hand, and Steve took it.

They left him alone to consider the ramifications of his first act of intercommunal diplomacy.

· · · ·

"You don't think I'm a monster, do you?"

Bruce opened the birdcage. His fingers—also scarred like his face—didn't work as well as they once had. He dropped a piece of raw meat into a flock of ravenous fledglings whose greedy little beaks bobbed up and down in a frantic hunger dance. Their wrinkled brown faces were even more grotesque-looking with the tongues wagging out and oversize nostrils flared in excitement.

"No, you can't say a thing," he cooed. "You're the ugliest damned things on earth. Not like your buddies next door. They got their pictures all over the quarters. They're so pretty, we give them little bracelets on their ankles and then we let them out. Yes, you'll be really ugly when you grow up."

The baby birds screeched at the tops of their little lungs and converged on the food in a fuzzy white huddle.

"*If* you grow up," he said. Some of the turkey vultures would be raised to adulthood, so they could make more baby turkey vultures. They'd feed them until they reached a certain point of maturity, when their droppings would be analyzed.

It was a far cry from what he'd done in London, where he'd studied humans—their bodies, not their droppings—as a researcher in a prestigious scientific institution. He didn't know if anything like that still existed. Here, in the abandoned campus of the Worcester Technical Institute, their growing group had everything they required to be fruitful and multiply. Once they were reorganized, Fredo had led a foray outside the enclosed walls of the campus and into the immediate countryside to gather in more people, hoping that those who came to join the community would be friendlies. The few nonfriendlies they'd imported were quickly banished, without the possibility of appeal—there were no legal rights of redress in the new world. Once, one of those nonfriendlies had come back with a gang of sorts to try to take over their little kingdom; all of them were buried in one of the athletic fields just outside the enclosed campus.

I am not a warrior, he'd told himself. But he'd led a successful resistance and in doing so established himself more firmly as the leader of the Worcester group, whether or not he wanted to be.

He'd led them to the realization—based on his own thoughts during his healing year, when all he could do was think—that the world, or at least their small part of it, could be rebuilt.

But first it had to be made safe for human occupation, and that meant finding a way to keep the bacterial monsters at bay. The baby birds now tearing at their food would become—he hoped—an integral part of that process. Their adult stomachs would be lined with enzymes that digested and at the same time destroyed bacteria and viruses; vultures ate carrion, nature's perfect reservoir for such creatures. Nature in her wisdom had given them the means to survive each virulent meal.

He glanced at a clutch of spotted eggs in a nearby incubator; they were the result of a mating between two birds with extraordinarily high levels of those substances. He was close to the goal of creating a super-race of antimicrobial birds. Soon enough, they'd know if the liquid gold that lined their stomachs would become the ultimate weapon in the war against disease, in the fight against the remnants of the Coalition, wherever and whenever they showed themselves again, which he was convinced they would do.

In the meantime, it was comforting to know that there were creatures on this earth more hideous-looking than himself.

Knife, bow, arrows, mask, the best pair of hiking boots she had left—all were laid out on a counter in the kitchen.

"This is nuts," she said to the assembled preparations, with the hope that they might rise up together and pummel some sense into her.

No, she told herself a moment later, *this is right*.

They'd all made an effort to go about the tasks of the day as if nothing had happened to Michael, but an undertone of anxiety tainted every act, word, and thought that took place in the compound. It wasn't yet noon, but the sun rose steadily, heralding the hour of departure. As Janie was packing the items in a knapsack, Tom came up behind her and folded her into his arms.

"Don't go," he pleaded, his head pressed against hers.

She turned herself around, still in his arms, and clutched him fiercely.

"I don't want to," she whispered. "I know it can be bad out there. But if Michael's hurt... Terry won't know what to do by himself. Ed won't either."

She hugged him closer, then brought her lips to his and kissed him deeply. When she pulled back, her eyes were wet. "Let's go talk to Alex."

Tom grabbed her by the wrist. "Maybe this would be a good time to tell him. About himself, I mean. It should be something we do together."

Maybe, Janie thought. But the time was too short, and she still wasn't properly prepared, despite all the years she'd had to think about how to speak to her son about his uniqueness—or, more accurately, his lack thereof. "Not now," she said. "There isn't time to do it right. And if anything happens to me out there, Kristina can help you... *talk* to him. But you won't need to, because everything will be *fine.*"

"All right," he said reluctantly. He pulled her into another embrace.

In the middle of it, Alex charged into the kitchen. "Mom! Dad!" he shouted. "Michael's back!"

Janie pulled herself out of Tom's arms in surprise.

"And he's got *people* with him!" He turned and ran out again before they could catch him.

Janie stood outside the door and saw Michael, in clothes she'd never seen before, lowering himself off Galen. Terry and Elaine came out shortly and stood together right next to her, their arms around each other as if in protection against the new arrivals. Janie turned to Elaine and said, in a quiet voice, "My God, they look friendly."

After Elaine's nod of agreement, Janie looked at the gate area again. Things were beginning to unfold—it was all happening very quickly, *too quickly,* she thought. She was stunned to see the ferocity with which

Caroline and Sarah attached themselves to their returned explorer. Janie glanced away, so as not to intrude on their moment, and looked at the newcomers more closely. She observed—waiting patiently for the reunion to be concluded—a small group of people on horseback.

People. My God.

Her eyes drank them in. There were three men and two women, and—to her great surprise—a child, a little girl who was almost completely enclosed in a cocoon of sheepskin. She looked very small indeed on the huge horse, and the woman on the saddle behind her didn't seem much larger.

Eventually, she saw Michael let go of Caroline and Sarah and watched with curiosity as he reached up to take the child out of the woman's arms. At that point, everyone dismounted. He was walking directly toward her with the child clutched tightly to his chest. The others followed him, quickly taking in the details of the compound as they approached. Janie started forward, and when she met up with Michael, he offered her the bundle in his arms.

"I brought you a new patient," he said.

Janie pulled aside the sheepskin and looked at the little girl's face briefly as Michael held her.

"Diabetes, they think," he said.

"Damn," she said under her breath. "Put her on my bed. I'll be right there."

She ran to the lab, surprising Kristina, and began to gather her equipment. "Come along," she said.

"But I'm right in the middle—"

"Leave it. You won't believe what's going on."

Michael made the quick and cursory introductions as he laid his precious cargo on Janie and Tom's bed. "Janie, Kristina, meet Lorraine Dunbar."

"Lany," the visitor corrected him. The small woman wasted no time on the usual pleasantries but got right to the point; as she unwrapped the child, she rattled off a list of the girl's symptoms. "For the last few days, it's been really bad. She's been so lethargic that we can hardly rouse her. We put her to bed yesterday morning; she's been in and out of consciousness since then."

Together the two women undressed the little girl.

"What about the last few months?"

"Tired, thirsty, irritable. Infection after infection. Any kind of cut or scrape just becomes a mess." Lany turned the child onto her back and carefully removed a dressing from one of her legs. Janie gasped when she saw the festering wound that ran from just below her knee to mid-shin.

"We've been treating it with soap and sterilized water. Five, six, seven times a day we wash it, but it just keeps getting worse. We boil the rags before we use them again, but it's just not healing."

The little girl's face was angelic, surrounded by a halo of curly blond hair, miraculously clean despite her condition; they had cared for her meticulously. When the eyes fluttered open momentarily, Janie saw that they were clear, light blue. But the child seemed all bones with barely any flesh at all, and when Janie smelled her skin, it had a sweetish, fruity odor.

"Bananas," she said. "I think you're right about diabetes." She placed her stethoscope on the child's chest; the little girl flinched from the touch of cold metal on her bare skin.

"Weak, but steady," she said as she pulled off the stethoscope.

"Kristina, there are some sugar test strips in the metal cabinet behind my desk. Can you bring them to me?"

As Kristina was passing through the bedroom door, Janie called out again, speaking each word very deliberately, "Sugar-test-strips."

Lany Dunbar gave her an odd look.

"I'll explain later." She ran quickly to the door and called to Caroline. Her friend appeared in just a second.

"Maggots," Janie said quietly.

Caroline glanced at the child's leg and winced, but nodded her accord. She ran off quickly.

When Janie returned to the bedside, Lany gave her a worried look. "Maggots?"

"They eat putrid flesh," Janie said, "and their droppings, for lack of a better word, contain an enzyme that actually promotes healing. With a little luck, we can save her leg. Now help me get this little one cleaned up."

In her delirium, the child had wet herself. They removed the remainder of her clothing and quickly cleaned her. "Ouch," Janie said when she saw the bedsore that had taken over the child's coccyx.

She placed a pillow in the small of her back to keep the sore from touching anything and wrapped the sides of the blanket up over her while they waited for Kristina and Caroline to return.

"These are old," she said when Kristina handed her the strips. "We brought them along when we came here, but we've never had occasion to use any. Let's hope they're still reactive."

Very little blood came out when Janie used the lancet on the tip of one small finger, but it was enough to smear on the test paper. It took just a moment for Janie to ascertain that Lany Dunbar's speculation had been correct.

"Off the chart. Diabetes, all right."

Caroline returned, bearing a small cup, a spoon, and a bundle of rags. Janie glanced into the cup, nodded her approval, and then looked away from the cup's contents, as if repulsed. Lany stepped back instinctively and let the other two women do their work. She watched as they spooned a long line of white, writhing maggots onto the leg wound, putting her hand over her mouth to contain her nausea when Caroline lifted the leg and Janie wrapped the rags around it to keep the larvae in place.

"What about the bedsore?" Caroline said quietly.

Janie turned the child onto her side and looked at it. In a whisper, she said, "I don't know. Maybe if we keep her on her side . . ."

Lany stepped forward at this point. "Aren't you going to put them on that too?"

Janie took the stethoscope off her neck and set it down on the bed. She stepped away from the bedside, drawing Lany along with her.

"Is this your little girl?" she asked.

"No. One of the men outside is her father. Her mother is gone."

Janie didn't have to ask the cause. "Can you bring him in here?"

"I'll go get him," Lany said, sounding agitated. "But before I do, what can you do for her? He's going to ask me."

Janie pulled in a long breath, then let it out slowly. "I can make her very comfortable."

"Is that all?"

Janie said nothing for a moment. Her thoughts went to a passage in Alejandro's journal.

It was all I could do, to watch with pain in my heart, as the child slipped away. Each day her body consumed more of its own flesh. And no matter what herbs or potions I administered to her, nothing revealed itself to be a cure. The frustration was evident in the medieval physician's writings, but Janie recalled how Alejandro had concluded that passage in his journal with a bit of hope: *But the mother was blessed and managed to get herself with child again quite soon, and everyone in her family rejoiced that there would be another daughter to help her.*

"She needs insulin," Janie said. Her words contained all of the same frustration but none of the hope. "We don't have any."

They put the child in one of the extra bedrooms and set out a cot for her father. All the excitement that should have accompanied the discovery of a friendly clan nearby was dampened by the matter that had brought them together. Janie's answers to the father's question were short and tender: *Watch and wait, keep her warm and clean. We have something that will take the edge away, but I don't think she's feeling much of anything right now. Days, probably, but it could happen at any time; she's very ill.*

The father sat down on the edge of his daughter's bed, in the first moment of what Janie knew would be a sad vigil. She touched his shoulder once and tried to revisit a few of the times she'd conveyed bad news in an intimate manner to people she'd met only hours before. A few moments of bonding and then she would walk away, leaving a family to shrink into itself for the duration.

She turned to leave and saw Alex and Sarah, with their heads peeking inside the door, their eyes fixed on the man at the side of the bed, whose shoulders were slumped forward as he cried over his daughter. When their eyes turned up to Janie, she gave them a little shrug and motioned with her hand for them to step back.

Alex waited until his mother was out of the room and the door fully closed to ask, "Will she be all right?"

"I don't know. We just have to wait and see."

"You can't help her?"

"She needs a certain medicine, and we don't have any."

The children exchanged worried looks, and Janie led them away, one hand on each of their shoulders, toward the main room of the lodge. There, they came upon an unusual sight: The huge, long table in its center was for once seated to its full capacity. Caroline had quickly put together a small feast of sorts—mostly consisting of breads and jams—and introductions were proceeding. Janie sent the awestruck children into the room with gentle pats on their shoulders and watched as they found places among the adults. She took one step forward and was about to enter but felt something clutching her arm. She turned and saw Kristina.

Her voice was all excitement. "I found a recipe for insulin on one of the DVDs."

Janie glanced into the main room, then back at Kristina. "Should we be revealing our capabilities to this degree?"

Kristina's eyes flashed in anger. "I can't believe you even asked that question."

Janie let herself be pulled to the lab.

"It's more of a process than a recipe," Janie said as she read through the file on the computer screen. She pulled off a pair of reading glasses that were three years too weak and faced Kristina. "And we'd have to give up a cow or a pig to do it."

"But we *can* do it."

"*You* can do it, Kristina. I don't have anywhere near the skills for this. And even if you succeed, it might already be too late."

"I want to try."

Three hours from now, Janie knew, the gangly *savante* might not remember this moment. But once started on the task, she would persevere until it was done or she was certain of failure, even if the initiating emotion had gone over some synaptic cliff in her brain.

"We'll have to talk to the others about the animal. You should be prepared to hear one of us say that we don't know these people well enough to put our own welfare at risk for one of their children." She lowered her voice. "It might even be me who says it."

She'd clawed her way through obstacles a thousand times to save a patient—one citizen—often in total disregard for the expense to society in a time when extravagant resources were deemed a right. Now resources were categorized by layers, stacked according to the effort of acquisition and the likelihood of replacement. *They married off their daughter for three pigs, a goat, and a buffalo; if her complexion had been better, they might have demanded a cow as well. But in the end, the family was satisfied with the bargain.* These tales no longer seemed so disgusting.

She stood and looked around the lab. Tom had equipped it thoroughly—mostly on his daughter's advice. They had everything they needed, according to what she'd just read, to work a miracle. Everything, possibly, but the will.

Kristina's face brightened when Janie said, "Let's go talk to the others."

She allowed herself to be introduced to the new folks she hadn't yet met and stayed connected with them just long enough to be polite and politic. Then Janie looked around the table and said, "If you folks wouldn't mind, we'll need a moment to talk about a few things." A couple of the visitors started to rise, but Janie motioned them to sit again. "Please, stay here and relax, finish your tea and bread. We won't be long."

She beckoned with her eyes to Tom, Caroline, and all the others. They all rose up with visible confusion and followed her back to the lab, where Kristina explained, at Janie's urging, what she thought she could do.

"A pig or a cow," Ed said quietly. "I don't know."

"I don't either," Janie said.

It was Michael, fresh off his earlier diplomatic success, who put forth the notion that it didn't have to be their *own* pig or cow.

"There won't be time to go back there for one of their animals. It'll have to be one of our own, with a promise of repayment. I don't know if we should trust them to make good on it."

"They made good on their word about the suit and the gun."

The discussion continued for several more minutes; at times the words were heated. In the end, they all agreed that these were decent people who could be trusted to do what they said they would do.

"Just one more thing," Janie said to the others as they made ready to return. "The woman Lany Dunbar—something about her is familiar. I can't help but think I've met her before, but I can't place where."

She might have been a patient, or a relative of a patient, or a fellow student at one time or another. Despite a round of prompts from her companions, she drew a blank.

"Ask her," Michael said. "She's friendly enough."

"Not yet," Janie said. "I want to think about it a little longer. Maybe she'll say something to me first."

They all settled around the table again in a few minutes. Michael, who'd already established his own credibility with the visitors, put the offer forward and explained the conditions. "We don't have an animal to spare, but there isn't time to go back for one of yours. We'll go ahead if you'll give us your promise that you'll replace the animal."

The newcomers didn't ask for privacy for their own discussion. It took place in front of their hosts, who listened carefully to the repartee, knowing that they would have a far better measure of these potential allies when the discourse was done.

They directed their first question to Kristina: Was there a greater likelihood of success for one animal or the other?

"Not that I can determine from what I've read," she said.

"Pigs have litters, cows have one," someone said. Then another person asked: "What do you have, males or females?"

"We have one of each," Tom told them. "The sow is pregnant, so it has to be the male if we use a pig."

"We have three male piglets in a new litter. We can give you one of those."

And so the second treaty was ratified.

All that remained was to enact its terms.

Eleven

Guillaume fell asleep quite easily when he was put to bed in the attic room of de Chauliac's manse, unlike the nights of travel, when he often tossed and turned in the unfamiliar straw. Alejandro watched over him in the candlelight for a while, savoring the child's apparent peace. But though the boy found easy rest, thoughts of the days ahead swirled through the physician's brain, banishing all hopes of tranquillity. There was so much he wanted to ask of de Chauliac; the questions would not let him sleep.

He rose from his own bed and looked out the window again. The street below was quiet and dark; no visions of days past presented themselves, no matter how desperately he craved them. He crept out of the room with careful footsteps so as not to wake the boy and went downstairs, candle in hand, not knowing if de Chauliac was about or abed. It was late, and the servants had all retired; the *maison* was disquietingly void of human presence. He wandered from the foyer to the dining room, then the salon, but found no one.

The library, he thought. If de Chauliac was still about, he would be there, among his beloved volumes.

He found, instead, Philomène. And for the first time since he'd met her, she was dressed entirely in woman's clothing—no mantle and breeches, no tall boots. Her hair hung down her back in shimmering chestnut waves. Her eyes met his when he entered; she greeted him with a warm smile.

Encouraged by the reception, he said, "May I sit, *Mademoiselle?*"

She nodded her accord with another smile, and he sat down beside her. Before her on the table was a book, open to a page that showed a drawing of a woman's organs of reproduction.

"Such exquisite detail!" Alejandro said as he ran his fingers over the detailed sketch. "Who made this drawing?"

"Father Guy, naturally," she said. "It is his library, is it not?"

"But he owns so many volumes, some of which I know have been made at the hands of others, or by copyists...."

"This," she said, touching the same sketch, "is his hand at work. I would know it anywhere."

"The womb," he said.

She nodded. "It tears at me, what I did. I have revisited that failure a thousand times, and I can see no way to a better outcome."

"Perhaps there *is* no way."

"I cannot believe that. Surely there will come a day when mother and child can be safely preserved, despite the earliness of the labor."

"If it is in God's plan," Alejandro said, "then it will come to pass. In the meantime, you must cease this self-reproach. It will do you no good."

"And you? Are you up and about to take air at this hour, when God Himself does not care to rise? Or have your own demons come for a visit?"

"You are both beautiful *and* wise," he said.

His fingertips brushed against hers as he withdrew them from the page. A surge of excitement coursed through his veins, something he had not felt for too many years. She did not pull her hand away but let it rest, looking straight into his eyes.

He saw in her expression those things that he had craved for so long: acceptance, understanding, perhaps even some admiration.

"*Mademoiselle,*" he said in a whisper, "may I have your permission to kiss you?"

A little smile came upon her. She drew very slightly closer to him. "You may, *Monsieur.*"

He brought his mouth to hers, lightly at first, and then with more conviction. When their lips touched, he lingered so the sensation could be savored. He covered her hand with his and let the warmth of her skin flood through him.

Later, as he returned to his bed, he ran his fingers over the place on his chest where he had been branded in Cervere. He could no longer feel anything on the surface of his skin, but there was the faintest hint of the circular shape where the iron had been pressed down. *It might have been my face*, he told himself. To be scarred in that manner would have been horrible. He fell asleep with the kiss still lingering. A dream came to him not long after; he was walking along a wooded path, and the spirit of Adele appeared to him.

Beloved, she called out to him. But it was not the plaintive cry of dreams past, when she reached out her arms beseechingly. Instead, it seemed to the sleeping Alejandro that she meant only to greet him, to pass a few pleasant moments in his company. After a time, she slipped quietly into the woods. When Alejandro awoke the next morning, his manservant was standing over him. He looked to the floor pallet and saw that Guillaume was still sleeping soundly.

"*Monsieur* de Chauliac wishes to see you," the man said.

He made his toilette, then dressed quickly. A last look in the glass gave evidence of new gray in his dark, wavy hair; he tied it back with a leather thong, and wondered what any woman could find attractive in an old man such as himself. He followed the manservant downstairs to where de Chauliac awaited him in the dining room.

In the middle of the table was a plate of fruit and breads. "Please, colleague, join me."

Alejandro sat across the table from his mentor and friend.

"You are refreshed, I hope."

"Hardly," he said. "I stayed awake far too late, thinking of the days to come." He said nothing of his encounter with Philomène.

"Ah," de Chauliac said. "Naturally you are anxious. I would be surprised were it not so."

"I came downstairs hoping to find you, but you must have already been abed."

"Yes," de Chauliac said. "The journey, you understand. It tired me greatly. And I feel a bit of rheumatism coming on. But do not worry; it is just my age."

Alejandro nodded. "It will claim us all, in one form or another."

"If something else does not claim us first. But you have another journey ahead of you," de Chauliac continued. "This is why I wished to speak with you."

"I assumed as much."

"I have had a message from one of my associates."

"Ah. Your 'associates.' They have always been a talented bunch."

"Beyond your ken, Physician," de Chauliac said with a wry grin. "The news they have delivered this time is especially useful. From Windsor."

"Windsor!"

"Yes. It seems that the king has sent his soldiers out for 'exercises.' He intimates that these exercises extend into France, which is curious indeed. One wonders at their true purpose, with his current need for accord between this country and his. There is a wedding on the horizon—why would he need such a show of force at this time? It seems odd, indeed."

"The man is given to oddity and recklessness; I have seen it firsthand," Alejandro said. "Perhaps he deems it necessary to remind de Coucy of what might await him should he fail to complete the proposed match. After all, it was not so long ago that de Coucy was allied with Navarre, against the French throne, to which Edward presses his claim!"

"Ah," de Chauliac sighed, "to be privy to the secrets of his exalted chamber! Well, we can only speculate. It is a dangerous waste of thought. We must let these events unfold as they will and make our plans accordingly. But regardless of how things progress, it will be dangerous for you to travel to England at the moment; you must stay here awhile, until these exercises cease—or at the very least diminish."

"But what of Kate?" he said anxiously.

"There is time yet to bring her out, as I have advised you already—please do not fret. The pope has not yet issued an approval for Isabella's match, let alone Kate's legitimacy, so there is time to plan a proper course of action. Perhaps it is a blessing that I brought you to Paris a bit early. I apologize for my miscalculations, but matters such as these do not always unfold predictably."

Alejandro said nothing for a few moments as his thoughts returned to Avignon and his ailing father. *Please, dear God, let him survive until I return.*

"And perhaps there is a blessing—beyond having time to plan—that comes of this development."

"How so?"

"I need your help."

"Always," Alejandro said. "But how, exactly?"

"The Cyrurgia I showed you in Avignon," de Chauliac said. "My reason, as far as the Holy Father is concerned, for this sudden journey to Paris. There is much work yet to be done before...before it is finished," he said in a low voice. "Your help would be a great blessing to me. As I began this work, I often thought of you, in the wish that you might be part of its creation. I have students aplenty, of course, but only two to whom I would trust this work—yourself and the lady who has caught your eye."

The man seemed to have an uncanny knowledge of everything that went on in his realm. Alejandro wondered for a moment if his own manservant was informing de Chauliac of his activities. There was nothing he could do if that was the case, save to accept the situation and behave accordingly.

"But I shall have to leave here soon."

"Then I will enjoy your help while it is available to me. Come, Alejandro, do not disappoint me."

"I do not know what to say to this honor."

"Then simply say *yes*. Now, I took the liberty of making arrangements for the boy; one of the manservants has a son of similar age. He will bring his child here each morning so the two can spend time together."

It was an undertaking the likes of which Alejandro might never know again. His heart soared, and then just as quickly fell, for he knew that at any moment he might be ripped away from it.

And when the time for leaving arrived, he would also be ripped away from Philomène. Too much loss.

"I must think on it," he said to de Chauliac.

On her return to the ladies' quarters after the long and distressing hunt, Nurse greeted Kate with a hushed announcement. "Master Chaucer awaits you again, lady. He seems very eager indeed to speak with you. He has paced a furrow in the stones of your balcony!"

She untied the bow at the neck of her cloak and dropped the garment on a bench as she crossed through the door to the balcony. On hearing her, Chaucer turned; he smiled broadly as she approached. She strode with purposeful steps over the stones and launched herself into his arms as the younger of her two guards reached the door. She looked back just in time to see Nurse's arm go out in front of the guard, who stopped short and looked at her in astonishment.

"Leave them be," she heard Nurse say to the guard. The old woman's voice was shrill and commanding. "Imagine having to court your sweetheart in front of the likes of yourself! And where do you think they will go, down the castle wall?"

The dumbfounded man stepped back as if he had been chided by his own mother.

God bless you, dear Nurse, Kate thought as she embraced her comrade in conspiracy. She kept one eye on the guard to be sure he was watching. When she released Chaucer from the embrace, she sat down on a bench and drew him to the seat next to her.

"A kiss," she said. She drew closer to him and closed her eyes.

Chaucer looked intently at her but did not lean in for the kiss. After a few moments, Kate opened her eyes.

Only then did he kiss her. Their lips stayed together longer than necessary.

"Your eyes," he said as he pulled away from her. "They are wondrous blue."

She blushed as she had on their first kiss, the heat of it rising up into her cheeks. "We have given them a convincing performance," she said. "Soon the king will be asking you questions. What will you tell him?"

"That I find you most alluring, and quite admirable."

"Then we must make our plan before he forbids you to see me, which he may well do, and soon, if our 'courtship' threatens his plans." She shifted her position on the bench slightly. "All this long and horrible day, I have done little else but try to think of ways in which I might leave here. I can come up with no way to elude my keepers, except one. There is a passageway I used once, when I was a little girl, to leave the castle."

He stared at her for a moment. "Good heavens, lady, why have you not tried it before now?"

"Because, in part, I don't know if it is still there. It was a flaw in the castle's structure; it may well have been repaired in the interim. And," she added, "because it was just barely large enough for me to pass through as a child. I am many hands taller now. And there is another reason," she said. "My son. They threaten to take him if I flee." She grabbed his hands and squeezed hard. "But I cannot endure this confinement any longer! I shall perish if I must remain here—more quickly if I must marry that beast Benoit!"

"You have seen him?"

"I have, and far too close for my liking," she said with a shudder. "At first I was not sure, but as the hunt went on, I noted that there was a good deal of intrigue between him and his cousin de Coucy. Even de Coucy must find that tie of kinship a tenuous one! I should not admit relation to him were he even my brother. Dear God, he is vile! As God is my witness, Chaucer, I shall cut his lips from his face with a shard of glass if he ever tries to put them on me."

For a few moments, Kate seemed lost in imagining that horror; Chaucer did not disturb her until she seemed to relax a bit.

"Dear lady, there is something I must tell you. And for once, it is news you will welcome."

She looked at him quickly. "Good news is indeed rare," she said. "Speak it, please!"

"I do not believe that the king knows where your son is," he said. "Only last week he sent out a party to France, supposedly on 'exercises.' There is no need for any kind of war practice at this time, especially not in France; I can only assume that he sent them in search of your son, so that when they find him, they can use him to make you bend to their will."

A strange calm came over Kate. She sat in silence and considered what Chaucer had just told her.

"For all this time I have believed them," she said finally. "For seven years, I have lived with the notion that if I attempted to escape, they would kill my son."

After a pause, Chaucer said, "And now you are freed from that belief. It is only your own fate you need to consider."

Tears streaked down Kate's cheeks. Chaucer reached up and brushed them away with his fingertips.

"I shall investigate this passageway for you," he offered.

"Oh, Chaucer . . . would you? I shall kneel before you in gratitude!"

He blushed slightly. "Save that for God, lady, who will determine if it all works out as we hope and pray it will. Now, where, approximately, is it to be found?"

"Near one of the kitchens below," she said, "against the north wall. I wish I could describe its location better, but it has been many years since I went there. I cannot even think of a reason why I should request to go, unless it is to cook. And then my guards will follow. It seems impossible!"

"Do not fret about that now; it may well be usable still. Of more serious concern is what you will do if you manage to depart through that passage. You will be alone and on foot. And," he added, "there are not many women who look as you do, so you will easily be found."

"A disguise can be arranged," she said, "perhaps some peasants' clothing left in the brush near the point of departure. But a horse is essential. I cannot outrun a man on horseback, but with a good mount and a preconceived destination, I can perhaps outride him."

Chaucer echoed her words. "A preconceived destination."

"I cannot simply ride out. I must have someplace to go, to gather my wits and make a reasonable plan! I know so little of what passes in England now that I should surely stand out as odd among the people by my behaviors alone. There is a place that might serve me well, but again, I am unsure of its condition, so many years later."

"Where?"

She glanced quickly at her guards before speaking, this time in a near whisper. "There is a stone cottage near Charing Cross; it lies at the end of a narrow road, which itself passes between two massive oaks. They have grown together as one tree, despite their awesome size. They sit on the edge of a meadow. We crossed that meadow in our escape many years ago. *Père* buried his clothing there before we fled; he was afraid that someone might steal it from the cottage and contract plague from wearing it."

"But—how should anyone contract plague from his clothing?"

She sat back slightly and said, "He was himself afflicted."

Chaucer gasped in surprise.

Her mind drifted to the terrifying days of Alejandro's illness. A darkness descended upon her as the physician's words came back.

You must not let me spit out the medicine. Do you understand this, child?

"I was only a small child," she said. "I do not recall all the details, but I remember the place itself well, for there seemed to be a magic quality about it. . . ."

Seeing that her distress was further deepening, Chaucer moved a bit closer and put his arm around her shoulder. "To further the notion of our romance," he said as an explanation. "This place near the oaks, will your *père* remember it?"

"Without doubt," she answered.

"Then let us arrange for you both to go there."

"But how can we get a message to him?"

"Through de Chauliac! His position is such that he has the means to see it delivered, no matter where your *père* may be. The king sends envoys to Paris often, weekly these days, with so much to attend to; the pouches are always full of messages and letters for the various French royals and ministers."

"But our message must be clandestine. If we send it with the king's courier, someone will surely break the seal and read it."

"If they can."

"Well, of course they can! The seals are only wax, and—"

"You misunderstand me, lady. Of course the seal can be broken. But if the message cannot be read, then there is no need for concern."

Kate stood, quite abruptly. "Your riddles are not amusing, sir." She glanced at her guards, who took notice of her sudden movement and followed her with their eyes.

"Please," Chaucer said, offering a hand. "I did not mean to confuse or upset you. Please sit again."

She sat, though her expression showed uncertainty.

"If we send this message in a sort of code, then no one will be able to read it."

"Including *Père*, unless you can magically implant the key to this code within his head from afar."

Chaucer smiled. "That will not be necessary, for it is already implanted there."

Twelve

The pig was slaughtered with one precious bullet to the brain; the bloody business that followed was contained entirely within the barn. Janie stood over the slit-open gut and identified the animal's pancreas, using an old farm text. She carried the steaming organ in a covered metal pan, going from the barn through the house and then into the lab, each step placed with exactitude. Thereafter Kristina literally installed herself in the small room, allowing only the occasional forced interruption for sustenance.

Or the occasional visits—purportedly to check her progress—of Evan Dunbar.

The harvest of the animal's parts and pieces kept everyone busy, visitors included, for the remainder of that day. Lany Dunbar decided to stay on with the child's father. Her son, whose fascination with Kristina was sweetly obvious, needed little convincing to remain as well. The others, realizing they would be fretted over by those they left behind as Michael had been in his protracted absence, paraded out the front gate early the next morning in a flurry of waves, with vows of animal husbandry to their new best friends and pleas to hurry back to those they left behind. No one was fooled by the pageantry; they faced a rough ride, dangerous in ways no one could fully anticipate, and long explanations when they got home. Sleep would be late but deep for the travelers that night.

The father remained at the child's bedside, leaving Lany Dunbar in the company of her hosts. She fell in by default with Janie. With Kristina constantly in the lab, Caroline took over her usual role with the children. Lany drifted into the kitchen after the others went back and found Janie setting a roast into a large metal pan.

"Too bad they couldn't stay for dinner," Janie said. "We have a special on pork today."

"And tomorrow and the day after that, and so on," Lany said with a little smile. "Been there, done that. Just once, I'd love to sink my teeth into a nice big piece of salmon."

"With lemon," Janie added dreamily. "Hey, maybe someone will start a salmon farm around here one of these days, and they'll be friendly to boot."

"Wouldn't that be nice." Then Lany's tone softened. "Listen, I've been meaning to tell you—all this other stuff was in the way—I think what you're doing is amazing. I can't tell you how much we all appreciate it."

"It was Kristina, really, but hey, we all have to stick together in the brave new world, right?" Janie said. She pulled open the oven door and set the roasting pan in the center, then fooled around with the damper and checked the fuel box.

"Is this thing going all the time?" Lany asked. She pointed to the vent pipe. "I don't remember seeing any smoke outside."

"We run the hot air into the basement in the winter, to reclaim the heat," she said. "Tom put in a scrubber that takes out most of the particles."

"What a great idea."

"Yeah, my husband is a real waste-not-want-not kind of guy. But it's a misery to clean the scrubbers. We have to make the filters last."

"You have so much more technology than we do. The lab—I haven't seen anything like that since—"

She stopped short, then re-formed her sentence. "It's incredible that you can make insulin here."

"*Maybe* we can make insulin. There's no guarantee it'll work. But if anyone can do it, Kristina can. That girl is a brilliant technician." She leaned back against the counter and crossed her arms over her chest. "I hope I made it clear that there was no guarantee when we started. She may actually succeed in creating the insulin, but it might already be too late. We'll get enough for a few weeks, but then we have to contend with making it all the time—for the rest of her life. This will keep happening to her if she doesn't get it regularly. I checked on her a little while ago; she's very, very sick. And she won't get any better until we give her an injection."

"You've got the syringes and everything?"

"We do."

Lany said pensively, "How much insulin can you get out of one pig? I'd hate to think we're going to have to keep slaughtering them."

"I don't know. But Kristina's already talking about turning some of the cells she harvests from this one into little factories, with the help of a couple of viruses."

Lany stiffened. "You have those viruses?"

"You'd be amazed what you can find by looking down at the ground."

"Maybe not."

"Hey, listen," Janie said, "this roast will be a while, and I have to go out to our powerhouse and check on a couple of things. Tom usually does it, but he's, uh, a little busy today." She smiled. "Feel like taking a walk?"

"Love to."

"Good. Get your coat; it's windy along the path. I'm just going to take a quick peek at my patient, then we'll go."

She came back shortly. "Still no change."

"That's good, I suppose," Lany said. She pointed to the bow slung over Janie's right shoulder. "Should I be worried about this walk?"

As Janie pulled the quiver of arrows out of a cabinet near the door, she shrugged and said, "You never know what you might meet out there." She smiled and winked. "Just ask Michael."

"Hey, it worked out okay," Lany said. She pointed to the bow and arrows. "Got any more of those?"

Janie obliged her with a set from the cabinet. They left the warmth and safety of the house and set out into the cold woods.

The path was strangled on either side with stands of brush and the boulder formations that New England farmers had cursed for centuries. They made their way over the roots and rocks, always wary and respectful of what might be waiting to pounce from a branch. Soon they came to the same open view that had captivated Tom and Janie just a few nights before, and stopped to look out. In the bright daylight from their elevated vantage point, they could see about forty miles east. Sunlight danced on the lake; the tops of the trees were tinted with bits of green, especially in the valley below, where spring came sooner than on the mountainside. Small plumes of smoke rose from three separate locations within the vista.

"They're out there," Janie said pensively as she scanned the valley. "We've talked about connecting with other groups a hundred times, but we haven't gone yet."

"That's probably smart. We've gone out a number of times. Early on, we found some friendlies, but none of those groups seemed to want to team up. In retrospect, I think it was still too early at the time; it was the second spring. So we waited a year and went out again. Went to an encampment that we thought had possibilities, from the amount of smoke they were putting out. We figured they had to be pretty advanced." Lany shaded her eyes and pointed to the northeast. "There," she said, "do you see that cell tower, the one that looks like a tree, just past that hill?"

Janie strained in the bright sun. "I think so. One branch is hanging down?"

With a nod, Lany said, "That's where they are, or at least where they used to be. God alone knows what became of them. It was a disaster. Their camp was like some kind of wild Appalachian nightmare. Tents and boxes, blankets hanging in the doorways, filth everywhere. There was one house, but it was a real mess, just falling down around them. Everyone we saw looked sick."

Janie watched as Lany spoke, knowing by the tension on her face that the memories she recounted were not pleasant.

"They saw us coming—must have had some lookouts—and ambushed us as soon as we got there."

"God," Janie said. Images of her own last trip from the world before into the compound flashed through her brain. She could still feel her finger pulling the trigger back; her attacker's wide eyes stared back from dreams on more nights than she cared to count. "What did you do?"

"Fought back," Lany said. "What else could we do?"

"Did they have weapons?"

"A couple of guns. They got off several rounds, but they were pretty bad shots." She lowered her eyes. "We took out two of them, and the rest just ran."

Took out. It sounded so military, and the expression Lany wore hinted that she herself might have been the one who did the taking out. Janie let a few moments of silence pass. "I spent my whole adult life trying to save lives," she said. "I never dreamed I would ever take a life. But when it was him or me, I did."

Lany stayed very quiet herself for a brief time, then said, "I wish I could say I've only taken one. It's been a lot more than that."

"Were you a soldier?"

Lany's laugh was tinged with bitterness.

"No," she said. "I was a cop." A big sigh followed; her shoulders seemed to slump a bit.

There was a fallen log on the edge of the path. "You look a little tired." She gestured toward the log. "Let's sit down for a moment," Janie said.

.   .   .

As her eyes rested on Lany's face, Janie let her mind drift, hoping that with this new information the memory floating just beneath the surface of her consciousness would come forward into the light. Finally, it flooded out—she saw Jameson Memorial Hospital, and after that Betsy's school, surrounded by a chain-link fence and people in green suits. The image of a helmet being removed came to her. And then, miraculously, she saw Lany Dunbar's face as she had seen it the first time, a bit younger, the expression intense and worried. Helmet in hand, the woman shook out her hair. It was longer and blond-streaked, but the face was the same.

Janie had tried, unsuccessfully, to sneak past her.

She remembered the feel of Lany's vinyl glove on her arm, the pressure of her grip as she stopped her, and then the voice. *I'm sorry, ma'am, you can't go in there. . . .*

"Were you a biocop . . . in Northampton?"

Lany nodded.

Janie wiped away a small tear. "There was a lockdown at a school . . ." she said.

Lany lowered her gaze and stared at the dirt, as if she knew what would follow.

"My first husband, and my daughter . . ."

Janie could not finish the sentence. After a few moments of painful silence, Lany Dunbar put a hand gently on her arm. "I'm sorry," she said. "I know this probably isn't much consolation to you, but we had no choice, the building had to be isolated. So many more people would have died if we hadn't."

So many died anyway, Janie thought. "I know that. And you're right," she said, her voice barely a whisper. "It's no consolation."

The ensuing silence was beyond awkward until Lany said, "I probably don't have to tell you how many times we did the same thing in other places."

"No, you don't."

As Janie wrestled with her memories, her new acquaintance maintained the light, soothing touch on her arm. Finally Janie wiped one hand over her face. "Well. Enough of that." After a deep breath, she said, "How did you end up in Orange?"

"Long story."

Janie gestured toward the beautiful vista. "We've got time."

"We do, don't we? One of the good things about the new world—plenty of time to think." She managed a smile. "Well, it was a pretty circuitous route. I was actually a detective in Los Angeles. I had a big case that . . . had an effect on me and my family, and they put me on administrative duty for a while. I don't know if you remember the case of Wilbur Durand, the pedophile who murdered—"

Janie's jaw dropped. "You were *that* detective?"

Lany Dunbar, former Los Angeles detective specializing in crimes against children, gave a small nod of her head.

"Oh, my God. That case was all over the newspapers and TV." Janie's brow wrinkled as she worked to recall. "Wait a minute, it was your son's friend who he . . ."

"Maimed," Lany said, finishing the sentence for her. "Yeah, Jeff was Evan's best friend."

"I'm afraid to ask how things turned out for him."

Lany shook her head. "He didn't make it. I think he might have otherwise, but his body was so weak after what Durand did to him that when DR SAM came along, he didn't have a chance. Evan was devastated. But we all had to get over that stuff pretty quickly. He lost his two sisters right about the same time."

Now it was Janie who offered the reassuring touch.

But Lany Dunbar whizzed right by her own tragedy as if it were something she'd trained for. "They took me off administrative duty when DR SAM first started surfacing and sent me out to biocop school. I worked on the crew that went out first to set things up for the follow-up units. They told us we were the A team. In retrospect, I know it was really an honor and that they were throwing me a bone for the job I did on Durand. They put all of what I would consider to be the best people in that group."

The words flowed out of her as if she'd rehearsed them in her mind a thousand times.

"It came across the border from Tijuana, but very few people know that. Drug-resistant *Staphylococcus aureus mexicalis*—DR SAM." She gave a cynical chuckle. "The folks in Washington didn't want to make a stink, because they had some intense diplomatic stuff going on with Mexico, mostly over trade and immigration issues, and there was pressure from some pretty big corporations to keep the origin quiet so it could be business as usual, at least that's what the speculation in our unit was. God forbid anyone should be offended by the truth: That border was basically an open sewer trough. Every disease under the sun came in through there. Even after 9/11.

"But what they really didn't want anyone to know—maybe to avoid a 9/11 type of hysteria—is that DR SAM's arrival wasn't exactly a natural event. All that stuff about not being able to pinpoint the origin—it was bull."

Quietly, Jamie said, "We've always wondered."

"Well, wonder no more. The bacterium didn't just 'emerge' by mutation. It was engineered—cleverly, so it would *look* like a natural occurrence. But there were signs. The CDC kept pretty close tabs on active strains of bacteria from that region, even with the budget limitations they had toward the end, because the region was such a mess. There was only one strain that had the potential to give rise to DR SAM, and it would have taken three mutations to get there. Some whiz kid in our support unit did the math—the probability of three natural mutations taking place like that without any kind of an interim trail was off the charts of negative probability. Something like fifty *trillion* to one against it happening that way."

"So someone cooked it. My God." Janie paused. "I—I couldn't even imagine who could do such a thing."

"The same kinds of people who fly planes into buildings. It's no different."

"The scale was a little larger."

"I don't know if they understood that."

After a brief pause, Janie said, "But all along, everyone said it was natural—scientists, medical experts; why didn't anyone else come up with the same conclusion?"

"I don't have an answer for that. I think someone probably did. There were some pretty prominent scientists who died in the first outbreak. You'd think most of them would have known how to stay safe."

The implications of what Lany had just told her were huge; Janie sat on the log in silence and let the weight of it settle. Finally she said, "Does anyone know specifically who was responsible?"

Lany shifted her position slightly. "There were no public claims of responsibility, but rumors got around in our unit that it was a fundamentalist group: religious zealots who called themselves the Coalition. Supposedly they were a mix of assorted hard-liners—various sects of Muslims and fanatic Christians who figured out that they could bring the world back to the Dark Ages a lot more easily if they cooperated and then divided the spoils."

Or the Middle Ages, Janie thought. *What more appropriate way than with a plague?* "Where were they from?"

"All over the world. Pakistan, Saudi Arabia, some of the rogue former-Soviet states. We heard that displaced Russian scientists provided the raw materials; lots of microbe samples went missing from the Russian equivalent of the CDC when the Soviet Union fell apart. We were too busy tracking down stray nukes to worry about a few little bugs."

"Which proved to be the larger threat," Janie mused. "Did anyone ever go after this 'Coalition'?"

Lany shrugged. "I don't know. If anyone did, it had to be well after the first outbreak. But who would go? The army, the CIA? Everything was so confused. If I had to bet, I'd say they're still out there, working hard to create more chaos."

The sound of rustling leaves, louder than the mountain breeze could generate, shocked them out of their concentration. Janie turned toward the noise and saw a small flock of turkeys not far into the brush. She sat upright and pulled an arrow out of her quiver, nocked it into the bow, and let it fly. On hearing the snap of the bow, the birds took off into the woods. Janie's arrow went high and missed.

Lany's did not.

"That's a big hen," Janie said as she stood over the quivering bird.

Lany bent over and pulled up one pants leg. She drew a knife from a scabbard strapped to her lower leg, then stood and offered it to Janie. "You want to do the honors?"

Janie reached down and pulled up her own pants leg, revealing the same arrangement. "It's your bird."

"Okay." Lany reached down and sawed her knife through the bird's neck. The quivering stopped. They watched as the blood spurted out of the stump. When the flow diminished to a trickle, Janie said, "We should each take one leg. It'll be heavy for either one of us."

They carried the headless bird between them out to the power-house. After a cursory check, everything seemed in order, so they made their way back along the path, more quickly than they'd come out; a trail of fresh blood had the nasty tendency to attract larger predators. As they hurried by the same vista, Janie looked off into the distance at the cell towers, and said with a sigh, "Wouldn't it be great if we could just get them working?"

"What the hell, I'm already a bloody mess." Tom took the big bird out to the barn and gutted it, tossing the unusable innards into the growing pile of pig remnants, stuffing the rest into the cavity.

They went inside to check on the little girl, who seemed, miraculously, to be holding her own. The father maintained his tearful vigil at the bedside. Janie touched his shoulder lightly for reassurance, but said nothing. When they were back in the kitchen, she said, "I don't want to give him any false hope, but I didn't think she'd make it this far. That infection on her leg—it's bad. But maybe the maggots are taking some of the strain off her system in general. Once that infection is under control..."

Lany watched Janie put a large pot of water on the cast-iron stove. "Where's everyone else?" she asked.

"Chores," Janie said. "This time of year, there's so much to do to get ready for the planting. All those innards Tom had piled up? Trust me when I tell you he's dreaming of fertilizer. He'll grind it all up and make this kind of disgusting soup—Ed thinks it's some kind of gold.

The others are out there getting the ground ready—the greens and carrots can go in pretty soon. We have a tractor; Tom and Terry managed to convert it to ethanol, so we can use it for planting. We plowed behind the horses for a while, but it was a nightmare with the rocky soil up here. That nice stone wall along the edge of the courtyard is made up of rocks we pulled out just in the first two years."

The water was boiling by the time Tom came in with the turkey. As they yanked the feathers out of the bird's dimpled skin, Lany continued the interrupted story of her migration eastward. "I worked with a detective in Boston on the Durand case. Old Wilbur was originally from Southie. Well, the detective was happily married when we first met, but his wife died in the first round. We'd stayed in touch. When they were reassigning biocops across the country, I got myself transferred to Boston. Pete and I, uh, got together pretty quickly after that." Almost with embarrassment, she added, "Tends to speed things up when the world is falling apart all around you."

"Don't I know it," Janie said, her empathy genuine. "The way I got together with Tom was similar, although we've known each other almost all our lives. You get focused when . . . you *need* to."

She said nothing about Bruce.

Lany smiled again, but sadly this time. "I wish I could say my situation had as happy an ending." She heaved in a somber breath.

A dark look came over her; Janie watched in sympathetic quiet as Lany pulled feather after feather out of the bird, until she recovered her calm and began to speak again.

"So when they started transferring people out of the immediate Boston area, I told them I wouldn't mind being sent out, someplace where there weren't so many memories. Evan came along with me. They were so desperate for volunteers that they agreed to pretty much anything I asked. We went to Hamp for a while; Steve Roy's brother-in-law was a sheriff, and I had some dealings with him there. Just before things really went wild, he got in touch with me and asked if I'd like to come out to Orange."

"An offer you couldn't refuse."

She nodded soberly. "Evan and I came out just as the second wave was getting really bad. I probably don't have to tell you much about what happened after that."

"No," Janie said. "You don't."

Kristina shook Janie out of a dark dream in the predawn hours. She sat up quickly; Tom stirred at her side.

"I think it's done," the girl said.

Janie threw off the covers and sat on the side of the bed. "Already?"

Even in the thin light she could see the sparkle in Kristina's eyes.

"Come on," Kristina said, pulling her along.

Janie stood in front of the computer screen and looked at the results of the biospectrometer reading. The sounds of other people stirring throughout the lodge were a distant accompaniment. The lines and bars and numerals didn't mean much to her. "This is what it's supposed to be? You're sure?"

Kristina pointed to a line of text on the screen. "That's the formula for synthetic insulin," she said.

Still in her nightgown, Janie sat on the edge of the little girl's bed. She washed a small section of the thin thigh with soap and water, then rinsed it clean. She guided the needle into the flesh of the muscle—what was left of it—and gently pushed on the plunger until the syringe was empty.

The father gave her a pleading look.

"If it works, it won't be long. We'll know pretty quickly." She patted his arm with as much reassurance as she could manage, then left them alone.

The others were already assembled in the main room. Only Sarah and Alex were still asleep.

"So?" Michael said.

"We wait. And pray."

A short while later, the father came into the room. Everyone turned toward him, but no one said a word.

"She wants water," he said. His face was streaked with tears. A rousing cheer went through the room; everyone rushed to surround him with hugs of joy and congratulations. The father broke free and took Kristina into his arms, and nearly crushed her in his embrace. Janie went to the kitchen for a glass of water, then walked, her steps light and happy, to the vigil room.

"I guess it really was the greatest invention of the twentieth century," Michael said as he examined the duct-tape patch on the leg of the green suit. The mud from his fall had all been washed away by the people of Orange, who'd donated a bit of their precious supply of tape to repair it. "Inside and out," he said. He looked up at Caroline. "I can't imagine this won't hold."

"It'd better hold," she said. "Right now, I don't even care about those hot spots."

"We still need to know," he reminded her gently. "We got distracted by . . ." He paused, searching for words. "By everything else," he said finally. "Hopefully there won't be any additional adventures. No panicking, promise me."

She did, but he knew that the minute he was outside the gate, her panic would set in, and it would not abate until he returned. There was nothing more he could do to soothe her. He carried the suit, because this time he was accompanied by people who could help him get in and out of it when he was near the gathering point.

Lany and Michael went out the gate first, then the father and child on their one horse. Janie and Evan brought up the rear. As the gates on the safe world closed behind her, Janie looked back and hoped she would pass back through them, at least once again.

Thirteen

"Ah, Chaucer, come in," King Edward said.

The youth raised himself up from his deep bow and crossed the audience room, noting with interest as he approached the king that none of the usual sycophants were about.

"I am in need of your skills again."

"Of course, Your Majesty, I am delighted to be—"

"Yes," the king interrupted. He stood to his full and impressive height. "One understands *quite* well that you are."

Feeling a bit chastened, Chaucer stood straight and still on the ornate red carpet; he remained uncharacteristically silent while the king walked slowly around him. When the circumnavigation was complete, Edward said, "You have matured into a handsome young man. Your mother and father always speak well of your progress with letters. Of course, we are the beneficiaries of your expertise and see that progress firsthand while our scribe is otherwise occupied."

"Thank you, Your Majesty."

"I am told by those who have observed the two of you together that my daughter is equally appreciative of you."

So, he thought, *as Kate predicted, here is the warning*. Chaucer cleared his throat nervously, then said, "It would be an honor of unspeakable proportions to be admired by such a lady as herself."

The king smiled in amusement. "She is lovely, is she not? She puts me to mind of my own mother, even more so than Isabella. Of course, she bears some resemblance to me, would you not agree?"

"Beyond a doubt, sire. And if I may be so bold as to say again, for I have said it many times before, she bears a striking resemblance to my lord Lionel."

"Ah, yes, she wears the Plantagenet blood as handsomely as her brother." He sat down again on his favorite carved wooden chair and stretched out his legs. "I have plans for my daughter's future, Chaucer, that are important to the welfare of our kingdom. One day soon she shall be married—well married, I can promise. Therefore I must insist that any affection between the two of you remain a playful flirtation only, a *passe-temps*, if you will, and that you not profess any kind of love or other such nonsense to her."

Before replying, Chaucer reflected a moment. "Of course, sire," he said, "I shall comply with your request." He paused again, as if in reflection. "Begging your indulgence, my liege, do you truly consider love nonsense?"

"Young man, now is not an ideal time for such a discussion."

"I understand, Your Majesty, but I pose this question philosophically and with all due respect, for I would not displease you. I only ask because it is easily seen that you and our beloved queen, your wife, still show—on most occasions—a wondrous affection for each other."

The king laughed. "Boldly said! You are young yet, Chaucer. Someday you will understand the many forms that love takes. I would not recommend royal love as a model for emulation." Then he became quite serious again. "And for the moment, I must insist that you refrain from any serious entanglement with my daughter. It is a good and kind thing for her to have the occasional attentions of a worthy gentleman such as yourself. But we should not raise false hopes in her heart, for any romance between you will not have my sanction, despite your fine qualities."

Chaucer kept his face as emotionless as possible. He responded in a flat tone. "I understand completely, sire. But allow me to take my leave of her gently—she is a sensitive young woman, as you no doubt realize."

"Of course. Be kind and sweet to her; God alone knows that she deserves some sweetness after the horror of her time in Europa. Had I only known . . . Well, we shall not speak of the unhappy past right now; we cannot change it, much as one would like to do so. I am glad that we have come to this understanding. Now, if you will kindly take up the pen, I would dictate some letters. The rider will depart on the morrow and there is much to be written."

For several hours, Chaucer wrote as the king spoke; once or twice he asked the king to pause so he could stretch his hand and relieve the stiffness. It was very late when they finished the last letter, a particularly long one; this would be his last opportunity to set the plan he and Kate had formulated in motion. He looked up to see if the king was watching and saw that the monarch was rubbing his eyes in fatigue. Chaucer tipped the ink pot deliberately, causing a puddle of ink on the page.

He leaped to his feet and scooped up the parchment to contain the spill. The king turned around at the sudden noise.

"My apologies, Your Majesty," Chaucer said. "My hand has become quite cramped—please forgive me for my oafish spasm!" He showed the king the gathered mess. "I will rewrite the letter this evening and bring it around for your seal when it is done."

The king looked at the spoiled parchment and scowled. "Very well, but bring it back before the hour of terce tomorrow. We do not wish to delay the courier's departure."

"I will, sire," Chaucer said. He went to the secretary, grabbed two pieces of fresh parchment and another pot of ink, and bowed his way out of the king's study.

.   .   .

Two different guards stood outside Kate's door, having relieved those who were with her most of the time. Neither one of the brutes said anything to Chaucer as he stood waiting for the knock to be answered.

Kate opened the door herself.

"Your writing lesson, lady," Chaucer said, displaying the parchment and pot. "I have corrected the errors. His Majesty is quite chagrined and suggests that we review them."

To her confused look, he said, *"Immediately."*

She looked to the guards; they showed no interest whatsoever in Chaucer, who had acquired a reputation for exaggerated mannerisms.

"Oh, very well, if the king insists," she said, having finally understood Chaucer's feint. She closed the door behind him after he entered.

Chaucer took her by the arm and led her to the far side of the room, and spoke in a whisper. "The courier leaves tomorrow morning, so there is little time." He held out the parchment and ink. "You need only tell me what you wish to say to your *père*."

There was no hesitation, for the formation of a plan had occupied all her thoughts. "Tell him that we will meet beyond the oaks. On May Day."

Chaucer sat down at her writing table and put himself to the task of the message, pausing now and then to consider his words, once or twice scratching out what had been written to substitute a new word. A few times he asked questions about her intent and her destination. When the work was complete, he handed the sheet to Kate. Her eyes fairly devoured the lines on the page.

She looked up when she was finished reading. "A poem. I would not have thought of it."

"I have tried to disguise my hand," he said. "My apologies for the scrawl."

"I could not have done half as well myself," she said, "and he will understand! This is all that matters. You are a marvel, Chaucer. A true marvel." She handed the page back to him, her face afire with excitement.

He rolled it neatly and tucked it into his sleeve. "It will go to the courier on the morrow." He took her hand in his. "But before I go there is another matter to be addressed." He hesitated for a few seconds, then said, "We were, it seems, quite convincing in our portrayal of lovers. The king has, as you predicted, taken note, with disapproval."

"Ah, well," she said, "this is what we expected—indeed, what we hoped for."

Chaucer let out a sigh and glanced downward.

Kate reached out and placed her fingers lightly under his chin, then lifted his face until their eyes met. "It was not entirely a portrayal," she said softly.

"Ah, my dearest Kate, to hear you say these words...my blood quickens! You have become my heart's desire."

Now it was Kate whose sigh was long and heavy. "We knew this might happen, but that foreknowledge does not lessen my sadness by one bit. My admiration for your courage and your loyalty to me are boundless."

"You honor me with this sentiment," Chaucer said quietly. "One does not expect to win the admiration of a lady such as yourself."

"You have won mine handily, and shall have it always, my dearest friend and companion."

Chaucer allowed her praise to ripen in his heart, but his pleasure in it was brief. "I am to let you down gently," he said, "so as not to bring you pain. We can meet once or twice more to finalize the details of our plan. But we must be careful, lest he ban me altogether from your presence."

She remained silent for a moment, then said, with sadness in her voice, "When I am gone from here, I shall perhaps never see you again."

Chaucer stepped closer to her and put his hands upon her waist. "When you are away from here and safely with your son again, you will not feel such a deep need for my companionship as you do now. It brings me both joy and sorrow to realize this."

"Joy and sorrow often mingle," she said, "and in a life away from these confines, I would still *desire* your company. You bring a smile to my lips, even here. Imagine how I would smile with no chains upon my heart."

"I shall make that imagination my mission," he said. "Now, give me the inspiration I need to fuel it." He drew her closer and kissed her on the lips. And, feeling no resistance, pulled her into a deep embrace.

The sun poured in through the narrow window, putting the king in silhouette when Chaucer entered his private audience chamber the next morning. Against the light, the monarch's protruding belly and slouched posture were starkly unflattering. The young man cleared his throat to make his presence known.

Without looking up, the king said, "Good morning, Chaucer."

"Good morning to you as well, Your Majesty. I have copied the spoiled letter exactly. Shall I affix the seal for you?"

Before the king lay two piles of official papers. The pile still to be read was significantly higher than the pile of those he had finished. "You have not inserted a declaration of war into the text, I hope."

"No, sire," the young man said. He laughed, too nervously for his own liking.

"Very well, you know where it is."

Chaucer hurried to the secretary before the king could think better of it. "Permit me to bring this to the courier immediately. After all, the delay in its completion is a result of my clumsiness."

"Very generous of you, Master Chaucer. My manservant will thank you for the rest you have afforded him."

"Delighted to be of service, sire."

He sprinted away, with one letter in his hand, another in his sleeve, both sealed.

Cauldrons and beakers and measuring devices stood in a neat row along the back of a wood bench. A complete human skeleton hung from a wooden stand in one corner. Drawings of internal organs lay about everywhere, made by de Chauliac's own hand like those Philomène had shown him in the library. Alejandro stood in the middle of it all and let its magnificence soak into him.

Philomène entered, all smiles. She wore a simple dress of blue, over which she had tied an apron with many deep pockets. "A glorious morning," she said. "Thanks be to God for that."

He took hold of her hand. "Thanks be to God for your sweet lips."

"And yours." She stood on tiptoe and kissed him lightly, lingering for a moment. "Such pleasure I thought I might never know! And now we will know the pleasure of working together at our craft."

"My good fortune continues to astonish me." He looked around the room, and was once again amazed by what he saw. "It is even more well fitted than I could imagine."

"I know. I fear that if I am ever forced to do my work elsewhere, that place will fall far short of what is here."

"We lack only the master himself to begin."

"Ah," she said. "De Chauliac will not join us today; he is still abed, resting."

A moment of disappointment gave way to the realization that he would have Philomène all to himself for this day. "Then let us begin," he said.

The first of the pages that wanted correction and verification lay before them on a table. They fell into a certain rhythm; Alejandro would read from the text, one paragraph at a time, and then the two would discuss the exactitude of the wording. Philomène would then write the corrections on the pages for de Chauliac's later scrutiny. From time to time, they would engage in discussions over what might seem irrelevancies to anyone who did not know de Chauliac as well as they. Often, the discussions revolved around a single word that one found satisfactory, the other lacking.

Of elephancies, of variciles and middle vein swellings, and greatnesses without kind . . .

Greatnesses, largenesses, immensities . . . They went back and forth, finally settling on the first.

Now and again, Alejandro would leave the surgery and visit with Guillaume, whose new companion appeared to be quite amiable. Alejandro suffered a small bit of hurt in seeing that the boy did not seem to miss his grandfather. But it freed him to pay attention to the work; they continued well into the night, sharing their supper in the surgery itself, when the rest of the household, de Chauliac included, was already abed.

Each day when their work was finished, they shared the tasks of caring for the instruments, working side by side in quiet joy. One evening as he was washing instruments prior to storing them, he caught a glance of Philomène as she arranged in proper order the papers on which they had worked that day. She was not aware of his observation, for the sound of clanging metal continued as he stole the look. He realized, as he watched her, that he had come to know this woman nearly as well as he had any other to whom he was not related.

This is how a wife and husband ought to share their time, he found himself thinking. For a moment, his thoughts went to Rachel and her service to his family in Avignon. How many times had his own father urged him, nearly ordered him, to marry her? He could not count. In his heart, he knew that she would have been a good and dutiful wife to him. In time he would have come to cherish her, as his father had said. And he knew, without doubt, that this was what the woman herself hoped for.

But he would never have truly loved her, not in a way that would allow him to ask her to share the fractured life that lay before him. He had loved Adele with a part of his heart that he had never before known to exist. That feeling, he knew, was lost forever to him; the danger of their time, the urgency of their courtship, his own youthful innocence—those conditions could never be revisited. But Philomène was a comrade of his mind, indeed, his very soul. He had come to treasure their hours together in a way that he could not describe.

She looked up from her papers and saw him staring at her. She smiled, and for one brief moment, Alejandro did not miss his daughter.

．　　．　　．

When he was called to de Chauliac's chamber the next evening, Alejandro assumed it was to discuss the progress of their work on the Cyrurgia. But soon he understood, by the expression on his mentor's face, that this was not his purpose.

On a gilt and enameled tray at the foot of the bed lay a letter. The seal was broken. De Chauliac gestured toward it with a slight lift of his chin. "Go ahead," he said. "You may read it."

Alejandro reached out and took the letter in his hand. He looked at the seal, then quickly looked at de Chauliac again.

"This came in 1349, at midsummer. Open it, and read what the King of England had to say on the matter of your escape with Kate."

Alejandro unrolled the parchment and began to read the letter. It was written in court French in an elegant hand and began with the usual ornate greetings, which he ignored completely. The tone of the letter was not friendly, but neither was it laden with outrage. He paced nervously as his eyes moved down the page.

We find it curious indeed that the physician selected by you to attend to our court should be a man of what we can only describe as questionable descent.

"Questionable descent," he said aloud. He looked at de Chauliac. "How delicately phrased." He turned his attention back to the page and read on.

We shall, of course, remember these events, but it is our sincere hope that an occasion on which we feel compelled to address the matter with the Holy Father shall never arise.

"In other words, he would use this against you by informing the pope when it was to his advantage to do so."

"It was a trump card," de Chauliac said, "but he never made use of it. Clement died before he could make his play."

"But why should he not raise this matter with the pope who followed, if your actions were so despicable?"

"Jesus Christ said, 'Render unto Caesar that which is Caesar's,' and the same principle applies here. Being of a different faith, you perhaps would not know this."

"As it happens," Alejandro said, "I have read this passage with Guillaume in his study of your Bible."

"You are to be commended, colleague, on your broad-mindedness in educating the boy. I daresay I would not do so myself, were the situation reversed. In any case, a new pope is seldom interested in addressing the problems of the one he replaced. He is more eager to create his own, if history is any prediction. When Clement died, Edward missed his chance."

Alejandro read the rest of the letter quickly. There were vague threats of revenge if the girl child was not returned, but as a whole, it was far less vitriolic than he would have expected. He handed back the parchment. "One gets the impression that at the time he was glad to be rid of her, and his protests were more a means of pressing his influence with the pope."

"One does, indeed," de Chauliac said. "But the circumstances have changed, as they have a nasty habit of doing."

"And now, when she might be useful to him, he has her."

"Yes, but not for long, one hopes." De Chauliac lifted his coverlet and fished around beneath it, producing after a moment another parchment. He placed it carefully on the tray.

"This came by courier earlier this evening, while you were still absorbed in your work with Philomène. Naturally, I was loath to interrupt you. I believe the letter is intended for you," he said, "though it bears my name on the outside. Again, it is from England, and, quite curiously, under the king's own seal."

Alejandro picked up the parchment that lay on the tray and held it in his hands, his fingers barely touching it. He turned it over and examined it, as if trying to determine if it was real or simply an invention of his imagination.

De Chauliac resolved the dilemma for him. "Open it," the Frenchman commanded. "Read."

Alejandro lowered himself into a tall-backed chair at de Chauliac's bedside, all the while keeping his eyes on the parchment. He slowly unfolded the single page, but after a quick glance, he looked up at de Chauliac. "English!" he said, in surprise. "But who—how ..."

"I do not know, since I do not read that language myself. And though the letter came under his seal, I do not believe Edward knows how to write it. Perhaps he has developed an academic bent in his advancing years and an interest in the language spoken by the lower classes of his kingdom, but I would be hard-pressed to believe that. Therefore, I assume it is intended for you—and if it is not, if it is indeed meant for me, I shall depend on you still, for I am unable to decipher it. So read on, colleague, and then tell me what it says—I am beyond curious!"

ᶠourteen

Michael could hear his own breathing in the suit but none of the *whoosh*ing sounds that would indicate a leak. The rest of the traveling party remained a good distance behind as he walked slowly down the cracked sidewalk toward the first of three collection points, side-stepping when he could the dried tufts of weeds that reached up through the concrete and crunched under his heavy boots.

As he trod heavily up the wooden front steps of the abandoned Victorian, slowly lifting one foot in front of the other, he looked from side to side and wondered what spirits of occupants past might be lurking there in some other dimension, watching as he invaded their erstwhile homes in his alien suit. What they might think of him, he couldn't imagine. Would there be a little boy in knee pants, with a hoop and stick, or a Victorian lady in starched linen, her arms demurely lace-covered even on the most sweltering summer day? Or perhaps there would be a black-clad widow, a pearl brooch at the tight throat of her high-collared blouse, clutching her shawl around herself, as if to keep the advancing green demon at bay.

He found himself in front of the kitchen counter—he was supposed to run the swab across its surface, just to the right of the sink. He did his job quickly and then stowed the swabs in their containers. When he'd tucked them away, he took a quick look around.

The place seemed empty, but evidence of minute life was everywhere. He pushed his way through a lacy network of cobwebs that connected a few pieces of furniture so dilapidated as to be unworthy of pilfering. Petrified insects, small black droppings—he followed them with his eyes to the sound of his own breath inside the helmet. Along the windowsill behind the sink, he saw paw prints. Cats roamed wild around the countryside—those that managed to escape their predatory feline cousins. They could be nasty when provoked or hungry, and a series of claw rips would render his suit worthless. He heightened his guard even more.

An open door at one end of the kitchen beckoned to him; he peered cautiously around the doorjamb. Nestled in a pile of rags was a mother cat and a litter of kittens. In one corner, as if they had been arranged there, lay a pile of rodent remains, some skeletal, others covered with maggots.

The mother cat rose to her feet, and all the nursing kittens dropped from her teats to the rag pile. She was scrawny and mean-looking, and she hissed at him with bared teeth. Watching her closely, he backed off. He hastened out of the house, stepping quickly down the rotting steps, hoping he wouldn't crash through a bad board.

The others boosted him up onto Galen's back. He pulled up his visor and took a long, deep breath.

"I'm seeing evidence of lots more mice and rats than the last time I was here," he said. "I don't know what it means, but I know I'm not imagining it." He cast a quick glance at Janie, who took out her precious notebook and made a few quick scribbles. They made their way as quickly as possible to the next two collection points; Michael was swift and efficient in acquiring the needed swipes and, once again, commented on the increase in the rodent population.

The sun was nearly at its highest point when he was finally able to climb out of the suit and back into his regular clothing. With the samples safely stowed in their respective toothbrush cases, the travelers gratefully left the known hot zone and continued onward.

The descent to Orange was easier this time, as most of the ice had been banished by the onset of spring. They arrived late in the afternoon to the great relief of the rest of their clan, who welcomed them in with helping hands. Janie's patient was carried, once again by her father, straight to her own room, surrounded by the other children of Orange, all curious about her great adventure to the outside world. None of them knew how close her adventure had come to ending in tragedy.

When her patient was situated comfortably, Janie took another blood-sugar test and then administered an appropriate dose of insulin, worrying briefly about how they would determine the proper dosage when the sugar test strips ran out. When the child was in reasonably good spirits, Jamie left her in the care of her father and went out into the settlement. She explored shamelessly, the excitement she felt akin to that of being in a foreign country. She counted thirty-two people in Orange, including six children—a small town by their own standard. The adults possessed a marvelous assortment of skills with time-after value: carpentry, stonemasonry, engineering, farming, electronics— things they lacked in their own world. What was left of the afternoon passed quickly in discovery.

"An advanced society," Michael whispered to her as they settled into places at the dinner table. "They have us beat by a mile."

It was an odd thing to say, Janie thought. She leaned closer and said, "I'm not sure this is a competition, Michael. We're all just trying to stay afloat."

"Ah," he said. "I would argue that point. Claiming or conjuring a selective survival advantage is the biggest competition of all." He glanced around quickly at the Orange folks settling in for their dinners. "Just like politics, social evolution is local. They have the people to do the things they need so easily—things we struggle with."

"You seem to be forgetting that the reason we're here is because of something Kristina did. There's one little girl who wouldn't have survived without the advantage she provided."

"Of course, that's a gap in their assets. But I'm talking more about the physical skills they have. Wouldn't it be lovely not to have to tinker our way through every breakdown?"

Janie thought about the time that one of the windmills jammed and wouldn't turn. Tom had gone up the pole by himself, with Janie standing on the ground below him, to find that one of the bearings was damaged. She'd climbed up with more tools, and the two of them had spent the better part of an hour forty feet above the ground in a January wind. Gloves were too cumbersome, and their fingers were nearly frostbitten by the time they finished. Janie's thighs ached for days from the constant strain of balancing against the wind on a narrow strut. The process wore them down in ways she couldn't have imagined. But she knew—better than most—that parts wear out on machines and people; there was no getting around it. "I suppose it *would* be lovely," she admitted.

He pulled his chair in to the table's edge. As if he'd been reading her thoughts, he said, "This is how trade starts. They repair windmills, we make insulin. Engineering," he said as he flipped one palm, "and pharmaceuticals." He flipped the other palm with a grin. "Look around," he said, his eyes traveling over the friendly, energetic people who were taking their places. He leaned closer to Janie. "Tonight we're a trade delegation. Let's see what happens."

"Hey, boss, we got incoming!"

Bruce set aside his lab instruments and followed Fredo to the communications center. When they got there, Fredo sat down in front of the computer and typed in a few command lines while Bruce stood behind him, watching the lines of code scroll down the screen.

"Give me a second," Fredo said. "I have to scroll through all this header junk to get to the text of the message. When you get through reading it, I want to show you something. It might take a moment."

Without some of the essential pathways in place, the electronic route each message had to take after it was hijacked was long. "The machines that house the connection points are probably out of commission," Fredo explained. "I can't be the only guy who went out looking for parts."

The spyware Fredo had projected out into the digital cosmos had found a home somewhere, but as yet he hadn't been able to precisely locate that home. There were no more domain registries to tell them where the machine on which a particular URL lived was located.

The scrolling lines of code finally came to an end. The cursor blinked at the beginning of a block of text.

"About time," Fredo said. "Take a look."

He got up and let Bruce have the seat in front of the screen, and stood behind him as he read through a long list of cities.

After a while, Bruce sat back. "Just like we picked up the last time. It's got to be a list of locations where the next round of meetings will be held." He pointed to a few lines of text. "Worcester's on the list. No dates yet, though. Let's hope that comes soon." He got up from the chair in front of the screen and gestured to Fredo to sit again. "Okay, what did you want to show me?"

Fredo started the code again but pressed the pause key several times as it progressed, stopping and starting the message until he came to a particular point.

"Right there," he said, pointing to the screen. "A copy of the message takes a left."

"What do you mean, 'takes a left'?"

"It copies itself and sends itself out again, to a different recipient. I can pinpoint the server that it happens on." He recited the URL aloud. "I just don't know where that server is physically located."

"Could it be . . . I mean, could the Coalition—"

"They could be intercepting all the same messages we are."

"Can they find us through this?"

"They probably don't have any more access to URL locations than we do. But if there's going to be a delta meeting in Worcester, and we've picked up positives all around here . . ."

·   ·   ·

It was Steve Roy who assumed the role of foreign minister. He astonished both of his guests by bringing out wineglasses and a small wooden keg.

"Homemade from wild grapes," he said with a grin. "We found them not too far from here." He turned the tap on the side of the keg; a deep-red liquid flowed out into the waiting glasses. When everyone had been served, he raised his own glass and said, "We want to welcome you both to Orange, and in the future we hope to welcome more members of your community as well. We've been saving this wine for a special occasion, and we all agree it's pretty special to have you here. This has been a crazy few days for all of us, I know, but the outcome has been just wonderful. Nevertheless, we'd like to apologize to Michael for the incident of, uh, false arrest—"

Michael actually laughed. "You can lock me up in your library anytime," he said.

"We understand that. So we've taken the liberty of making a library card for you."

Steve handed over a small flat piece of wood with the letters ORANGE PUBLIC LIBRARY burned into the surface.

Everyone clapped; Michael beamed. Steve turned toward Janie. "And we want to thank you for saving one of our daughters." This produced reverential murmurs of agreement all around the table. He handed a small package to her, wrapped in pretty blue cloth and tied with a linen-looking ribbon. Janie undid the small bow and opened the folds of the cloth to reveal a carved wooden heart suspended from a leather strap. She tied it around her neck and showed it off.

"Thank you," Janie said, "but it wasn't only me. Kristina deserves more of the credit than I do. She was the one who came up with the means of making insulin. I wouldn't have known where to start."

"Nevertheless," Steve said, "you knew what to do with it, how much to give her—we haven't had a medical person here in a very long time. Lany has had some training and does what she can, but having a doctor now and then would just be wonderful."

And then the offer came, more quickly than either Michael or Janie would have expected.

"Let's just get right to the point here," Steve said. "We'd like to propose an exchange of sorts. To our mutual benefit. We'll send our tradesmen to your place if you'll send your doctor and, uh, I guess we could call her a pharmacist, here. For short periods of time, of course." He looked back and forth from Janie to Michael. "We need each other. It's a cruel world out there."

After a brief silence, Michael said, "We've noticed."

"So . . . what are your thoughts?"

Janie and Michael looked at each other.

"Give us a moment," Janie said. They rose up from the table and went to the library.

Michael spoke first. "I'm not even sure why we're discussing this. It's immensely sensible."

"Of course it is," Janie said, "but I'd have to be away from my family for stretches of time."

"Some of them would as well," Michael countered. "Look, Janie, this doesn't have to be a weekly event. A few days, once every couple of months, you know, like the traveling physicians of old." He added an image he knew she could not ignore. "Like that chap Alejandro's daughter did, in the journal."

He was not playing fair by bringing that up; she made no comment. "What do we really have to gain?"

He said simply, "An easier life."

Try as she might, she couldn't come up with an argument against that frank logic. "No more than once a month," she said. "I do a little clinic tonight and tomorrow morning, then we go back."

"I think that's reasonable."

They returned to the table and presented their response, which, as they expected, was heartily accepted.

"Well," Janie said to the middle-aged man seated before her, "you appear to be healthy as a horse."

He was their carpenter. "Must be all that clean outdoor work I do," he said.

"You're probably right. Your only real problem seems to be that bit of tendonitis." She took hold of his wrist again and prodded lightly. The carpenter reacted with a wince.

"I can splint it for you, if you want."

"It's not too bad."

"Not too bad is how very bad starts."

"How long would I have to leave the splint on?"

"That's up to you. A few days, then you can take it off and see how it feels."

"I can still work, right? I have a couple of projects going on."

"If you're careful. But it would be better to rest it. Let the inflammation subside. Heat and moisture will help. If you have pain, dip a towel in some hot water and wrap it around your wrist."

"Anything else I can take—some herb, maybe?"

"White willow bark helps. It has salicins, which are similar in chemical content to aspirin." She was about to add, *I'll bring back some aspirin on our next trip*, but stopped herself. On inspection, she found that the Orange medicine chest was dismal overall, and there were only twelve aspirin tablets—ancient, crumbling, grayed specimens tenderly put away for the proverbial rainy day. Janie doubted that they'd have much efficacy in their chemical dotage; compounds had an annoying habit of disintegrating over time, aspirin included. But even though the materials required for synthesis of aspirin did in fact grow on trees, it would take Kristina's effort and lab time to produce it. How much they should be willing to donate to the cause could only be determined as the alliance developed over time.

The previous night, before they turned in, she and Michael had talked more deeply on the matter of their new alliance.

We should take it slow, she'd said. *We have to be careful about making sure we have what we need before we give anything up.*

They're having the same discussion right now, you know, he'd countered. *You're right, of course; we have to take small steps. It will all work itself out in time.*

"I think I'll forgo the splint," the carpenter said as he rose up. "But I'll be careful with it."

"Please do," Janie told him. "We've got a gate you have to fix when you come to our place."

The children of Orange all seemed remarkably healthy. She questioned the adults in detail about immunizations—their own and those of the children born in the time before. Everyone over fifty had been immunized against smallpox. Most had survived the common childhood illnesses—measles, mumps, rubella, chicken pox—and the older children had all received the proper injections. It was the younger ones, those born after, who were most vulnerable. But they were not living in the sort of open, integrated society where the risk of infection from such diseases was high; they were sheltered by virtue of their isolation. That said, they still needed tetanus, at the very least, and an exposure to cow pox to protect them from smallpox, should it manage through some dark miracle to find its way out of storage in Atlanta or Kiev.

"Kristina's going to be very busy for a while," she told Lany as they prepared to depart.

The electrician, a lanky black man named James, was the first of the visiting "delegates." The group—Janie, Michael, James, Lany, and Evan—set out on their journey early the next morning, with an extra horse for all their equipment. They made the trip in a little more than half the time required for the ride out.

Alex and Sarah came running when they heard the commotion of arrival. Both stopped short when they saw James.

They'd seen photos and films, but neither of them had ever seen a real human being with dark skin before.

Oh, dear God, please, Janie prayed as she got down off her horse, *let them be polite.* Blessedly they were, saying only "Hi" when the introductions were made.

"Where's Dad?" Janie asked Alex when she finished hugging him.

"In the barn. I'll go get him."

The little boy ran off; a few moments later, Tom came out of the barn, and when he saw his wife home safely, he dropped the bale of hay he'd been carrying and ran toward them.

"Excuse us for a moment," Janie said. She drew Tom into her arms and held him close, until courtesy demanded release. It didn't take long to explain James's presence.

"Well, I guess my wife's not the only person I'm really glad to see," Tom said as he shook James's hand. He looked up at the sky. "Not that I mean to rush you, but there's still light enough; why don't we take a walk out to the powerhouse after you get settled?"

A short while later, as he and James passed through the vista, Tom said, "It's frustrating to look down there and see all those towers. So useless."

"They wouldn't be useless if there was a signal," James said, almost casually. "Something out there has to be emitting, somewhere."

Tom stopped and turned around.

"You mean they could be made to work?"

"Sure. They're just relay points. They don't really 'work' in the true sense. They just pass along a signal that originates from somewhere else. Thing is, they have to be pointed in the right direction. You remember the dead spots, where the cell phones just wouldn't work?"

"Who doesn't?"

"That happened when the cells had obstructed paths between them. You know, buildings—"

"Mountains?"

James smiled and glanced up the side of the mountain toward the peak. "Yeah, a mountain might get in the way."

They moved along the remainder of the path to the powerhouse. James made a quick but seemingly thorough inspection of the equipment. "Looks pretty sound to me," he said. "But there are things you need to do on a regular basis to keep it that way." He went through a list of lubrications and calibrations, with Tom paying close attention.

They stepped out into the fading daylight. James looked up at the windmill tower, then back at Tom again. "Do we have time for me to take a little climb?"

"I think so," Tom said. "Just be careful. You're the only electrician around here."

"Always."

He made his way up the side of the tower like an overgrown spider, his long legs and arms working in a rhythmic vertical dance. In half the time it usually took Tom to make the same climb, James was at the top. He strapped himself to one of the supports at the back side of the rotation unit and looked out over the valley. He gazed around for a minute or two with his hand shading his eyes, then released his safety strap and climbed back down.

"There's room enough up there for a cell," he said. "There are two cells down there that we can see from Orange. If we could position them properly, and if there are still cell units on them, we could set up a network between us."

"You're kidding."

"I'm not."

"So let me ask the stupid question. Why not before now?"

James shouldered his sack of equipment. "I'm not sure any of us wanted to be communicating with anyone out there. They're not all friendlies."

Tom nodded his accord. "But it could be done?"

"There are a lot of problems to work out—and I mean a lot—but if we had the right stuff, we could make it happen."

The night was clear and the half-moon cast a soft light on the clearing outside the lodge. Stars blazed above as Kristina and Evan Dunbar sat on a bench near a maple tree. A mercifully light breeze blew the previous fall's shed leaves around their ankles. Kristina reached down and brushed leaves into a pile atop her boots.

"Why'd you do that?" Evan said.

"My feet are cold," she explained. "I wish it would get warmer, *fast*."

"Me too," Evan said. "I lived in California all my life until Mom and I came out here," he said. "I'm still not used to it."

"What's it like in California?"

"Now?" he said. "I don't really know. It was nice before, though. Crowded, but nice. We lived in a good neighborhood, I had a lot of friends...."

"I never got out there...*before*. I wish I had. I probably won't ever get out there now."

"You don't know that. There's always the chance you will. Maybe things will get a lot better."

"It's going to take a long time before the world is anything like it used to be."

"It probably won't ever be what it used to be," Evan said. A brief gust of wind made him shiver. "But that's not entirely bad. There were some ugly things about the other world. Some of them I don't miss at all."

"Do you miss your friends?"

For a few moments he was very quiet, as if he were remembering something specific. Finally he said, "Yeah. I do miss my friends. A lot. And I miss my little sisters."

"DR SAM?"

"Yeah."

"I never had a sister or a brother," Kristina said.

Evan looked at her in surprise. "What about Alex?"

"Oh," she said, catching her breath. "I mean when I was younger. Like you had. Your sisters—were they a lot younger than you?"

"Julia was eight years younger—practically a baby. Frannie—she was four years behind me—was just old enough to be a pain sometimes. But she was fun, and she was really smart." He chuckled a little. "She used to help me with my English homework when I was in junior high school and she was still in grade school. She could spell anything. And she was a whiz at *Wheel of Fortune*. She could get the puzzles without any letters sometimes." He smiled at the memory.

Kristina brightened as well. "I used to love that show."

A spring breeze came up suddenly; Kristina shivered. Very slowly, Evan slipped one arm around her shoulder. She turned to face him and smiled. "Thanks," she said.

"Hey, no problem," he said. Then, bravely, he pulled a bit closer to her. "There," he said. "How's that?"

She snuggled into his warmth. "It's nice. Really nice. I'm really glad I met you, Evan."

"I'm glad I met you too."

They looked up at the stars for a few minutes before Evan spoke again. "So," he said, "what do you want to do if things ever get normal again?"

Dreamily, she answered, "Just to *live*. You know, a real life."

"Me too, I guess."

She leaned her head on his shoulder. He leaned his head on hers. They sat quietly and contemplated their individual futures. A meteor slashed through the sky above the clearing.

"Maybe it's a sign," Kristina said, pointing upward.

"A sign of what?"

"That we'll live."

Fifteen

Partway through the reading, Alejandro looked up from the page and said to de Chauliac, "One can hardly call this a letter. It is a poem."

He read it aloud from the beginning, in English, as de Chauliac listened.

> There lives a lady fair with hair of gold,
> Imprisoned in a castle built of old.
> Her captors, filled with enmity and hate,
> Now plot to make cold misery her fate.
> They'll wed her to a man so dark and vile
> That sight of him could thwart an angel's smile.
> But on the eve before the first of May,
> She'll garb in drapes of flowers and slip away
> To ride all night and in the morning pass
> Between two loving oaks, one lad, one lass
> Who cling together in a bold embrace
> And guard the entry to an ancient place
> Where sounds and sights ethereal are the norm

And sun shines bright, while all the world's in storm.
Safe there, she will await her father dear,
With desperate hope that he'll anon appear.

"Dear God," he said. The page trembled in his hands.

"Colleague?" de Chauliac said, his voice full of concern. "What is it?"

"She calls for me to rescue her, at *last*." Alejandro then looked directly at his mentor and asked, "What is today's date?"

"The sixth—no, wait—the seventh of April."

Alejandro set the page down on the bed and sat frozen in the chair.

"Do not keep me in suspense!"

His confused thoughts finally gelled. "Chaucer is there in Windsor, is he not?"

"I have told you that he is. But what does that matter?"

"I believe," the Jew said with increasing agitation, "that he wrote this. We spoke in English many times and he knows that I can read it as well. I daresay, de Chauliac, that you are right. When I was there, the king himself knew little of the language and could not decipher it written. In France, even fewer; you yourself, an educated man, are incapable. Chaucer knows this and wrote it as a code that few but I could understand! Listen," he said. "I will tell you what it means, in French."

The translation was not exact, but de Chauliac clearly understood the meaning. "The first of May," he said. He sat up straighter in his bed. "She has chosen the date wisely. It would be unnatural for the king's soldiers to be afield on that night and quite ordinary for a woman to be out and about. Depending on how she dresses, she might be taken for a celebrant, perhaps even a witch. But she will not be bothered. Clever, very clever."

"I do not understand."

"The peasants have not always been Christian there," his mentor explained. "Long ago, there were priests of a different nature, pagans, who worshipped things of this earth, not of the heavens. They have passed into history for the most part, but their traditions are deeply ingrained in the people. On the night of April thirtieth, the maidens will dance around a tall pole holding ribbons by the light of the fire; a Queen of the May is chosen from among them. The king casts a blind eye upon them, for they keep his people happy—at least for that night."

"Three weeks," Alejandro said, his voice almost a whisper. He looked straight at de Chauliac. "I must leave immediately."

"Yes," de Chauliac said quietly. "And we have only just gotten you back."

Alejandro found Guillaume in their turret room, sitting on the chair by the window. The afternoon light cast a warm glow through the windowpane, and the little boy's hair gleamed in its rays.

"What so absorbs your attention, young man?"

"I am reading the *Biblios* that *Monsieur* de Chauliac lent me."

"Ah. Yes. I will be sure to thank him again for granting you that privilege."

The Bible that de Chauliac had sent to him many years before, a simple Latin volume, was the book Alejandro had used in teaching Guillaume to read. The first part of the tome was familiar, for it was the teachings and history of his own people, but the second part was new to him. On reading those parts for the first time, he recalled his own instruction in Christianity at the hands of a mad priest in England and how he had nearly howled aloud at the man's insistence that Jesus was born to a virgin.

Impossible. Beyond belief, and yet they believed, fervently—some so fervently that they devoted their entire lives to her glorification.

But he would not keep this history from the boy, however inane he considered it to be, for his mother—at least in heritage—was a Christian, and though in their travels together she had not regularly practiced the rituals of that religion, she would often invoke this Virgin Mary for protection, or as part of a quickly said prayer. In honor of that, he allowed, even encouraged, Guillaume to learn of Jesus.

"Look, *Grand-père*, there are pictures!" De Chauliac's own Bible was beautifully illustrated, with colorful paintings and wonderful exaggerated letters written in gold ink. It was the paintings more than the pennings that held Guillaume's fascination. They admired together the delicate strokes that the artist had laid upon the parchment. "I must interrupt you, I fear, for there are other important matters requiring discussion between you and me."

"Yes, *Grand-père*." The little boy closed the book dutifully, but not without first placing the ribbon marker in the crevice between the pages.

Alejandro pulled his own stool close to Guillaume's and sat down. Guillaume stared up at him, his eyes wide, wearing an expression of solemn curiosity.

"I must make a journey beyond Paris without you, to someplace very far away. I will be gone for quite some time, perhaps a full season."

Guillaume looked troubled. His voice became smaller. "But why?"

"My voyage concerns your mother. And I alone can do it; no one else can go in my stead."

The boy sat up taller. "Will you bring her with you when you return?"

"I hope so. If God grants it."

A look of excitement came over the boy's face as he pondered the news. Then he made a bold announcement of his own. "I shall go with you, *Grand-père*. I will help you."

It was a sweet surprise; Alejandro had feared that the boy would whine or cry or make some other kind of distressing fuss. Instead, quite unexpectedly, he had offered to help.

"Guillaume," Alejandro said respectfully, "you will someday be a very fine man. Generosity such as yours is a fine quality and I thank you, but in this case I must refuse it."

The look of hope faded to one of woe. Alejandro tried to soothe him with a hug. "Now, before I leave, I need to tell you some things and you must listen very carefully."

Guillaume nodded soberly.

Where to begin? *I murdered a man in Spain and was forced to flee, and*

I found myself in England, where your mother was enslaved by her shrewish older sister, who now once again holds her captive and would marry her off to the foul underling of an even more foul fiend. . . .

No; it must be said in a way that would not frighten him.

"I have told you about England. . . ."

"*Oui, Grand-père,* many times, that it is far to the north, and that we are at war with them. . . ."

We, Guillaume had said; the child considered himself to be French. Of course—his father had been French, and his mother was unknown to him. Still, it was something of a surprise to the nationless Jew to hear it said that way.

"Well, yes, we are at war, and have been for some time, though right now there is relative peace. England is ruled by a king, as are we. His name is Edward. Many years ago, I served as his physician."

"*Grand-père!*"

"Yes, I know, it seems an impossibility, but it is true. It was not my choice to do so; I was sent there because de Chauliac thought I could protect the English royals from plague."

"But de Chauliac is your friend—why would he want you to go to our enemy?"

"Because it was important for all of the English royals to be kept alive during the Great Mortality, or so de Chauliac told me. And at the time our friendship was . . ." He struggled to find the proper words. "It was not as well formed as it is now."

"You didn't like each other?"

"That was not really the case—I have admired de Chauliac greatly since the day I met him, for his remarkable intellect and his dedication to learning. It was more accurate to say that we didn't trust each other. He did not know as much about me then as he does now, nor I about him. I believe I can safely say that for a good while, de Chauliac considered me a scoundrel. But over time we have come to respect and even enjoy each other. We are blessed now with a loyal friendship."

Guillaume digested what he had been told for a few moments before asking, "But why must you go there again?"

"I am getting to that. Now, King Edward had many children, most of them by his queen. But as many royals do, he had other liaisons, some of which resulted in children."

Guillaume made no comment except to giggle.

"One of those children is your mother."

The boy nearly leapt off the chair, then climbed up into Alejandro's lap. "My mother is the English king's daughter?"

"Shhh! Keep your voice down. You will give up our secret to the servants! But, yes, it is true. She is a grown woman now, a wonderful woman, but when I first fostered her she was a young child. I have always called her 'daughter,' but in truth, she is the daughter of King Edward. I stole her away."

"Then he is my *grand-père*, not you."

Alejandro caught his breath on hearing that blunt truth from the child. "That is correct."

The child looked upset and said, "You stole me from my mother as well."

Alejandro explained quickly. "Of course, she wanted to be stolen—begged me to take her, in fact. As she begged me to take you so you would not be taken by the English royals."

He saw some relief in Guillaume's expression, but the child was not yet calm. Alejandro prepared himself for the flurry of difficult questions that would surely follow. He was surprised to hear a simple statement:

"King Edward must have been sorely vexed."

He reflected for a moment on the harrowing succession of events; anger hardly began to describe Edward's reaction to their flight, though you would not know it from his carefully worded letter to de Chauliac. Someday Alejandro would tell Guillaume of the wild rides, the hiding, and his own battle with plague.

Or, God willing, his mother could tell him.

"He was past the point of mere vexation, child; he was enraged beyond all decency. He sent out his best warriors to capture us, but we were very fortunate, and we evaded them."

"But—why did *Mère* want to leave England, if it was her home?"

"Because her sister Isabella had her shut up in a castle and would have harmed her in order to make me suffer, for she hated me."

"How could anyone hate you?"

Sweet innocence, Alejandro thought. "Someday I will also explain to you about hatred, young man, but for now you will just have to believe that she did. She was convinced that I stole the affection of one of her ladies. That lady—Adele was her name—might have been my wife had she not died."

With great seriousness, Guillaume said, "What of Rachel, then? *Arrière-grand-père* says that you should marry *her*."

Alejandro forced a smile, knowing how Guillaume adored Rachel and that a marriage between them would please the boy immensely. "People of great age often have opinions that they deem worthy of expression," he said. "Those opinions sometimes relate to matters that are the private business of other people. He means well, of course, but the question of marriage between Rachel and me should rest between Rachel and me, should it not? When I am of advanced age, I hope you will remind me to tether my own opinions, lest they annoy other people. Now, where was I?"

"You were speaking of *Mère*'s sister."

"Yes. Isabella." He recounted the events at Canterbury as accurately as possible and explained that Isabella once again held his mother.

"A cruel sister!" the boy said.

"Yes, and more. I know this will be difficult for you to understand, Guillaume, but royals often hurt their own family members, even kill them, in order to steal their power and holdings or to keep control over them. It is the same everywhere—Spain, France, England—and so we had no choice but to flee. We crossed to France on a boat of cargo. I paid the captain handsomely to keep our secret, and as far as I know he did, because we were not pursued or discovered for a very long time, and only then by odd coincidence. We traveled around the whole of Europa, until we found a place that seemed safe, not far north of Paris. It was there that your father came into our lives."

Guillaume went very quiet. Little had been said of his father, and he had not asked, as if somehow Guillaume Karle did not figure into his life at all.

"My father," he said, almost imperceptibly. The boy sat very still in Alejandro's lap, saying nothing for a moment. When he spoke again, his voice was very serious. "*Mère* was not a virgin, then."

Alejandro sat back slightly and put a hand to his mouth to stifle the laugh that threatened to break free. "No," he said finally, "she was not. Such births happen only in the Christian stories. You have a father and a mother, both from *terra firma*. And though your mother looks like I imagine an angel might look, she is very much a human being, an exquisite one. It is time you came to know her."

The little boy threw himself happily into Alejandro's arms, and they clung together for a few moments. When they released each other, both faces were wet with tears.

It did not surprise Alejandro to find Philomène in de Chauliac's surgery, for it was where he himself would have been, had he not been called away so urgently.

"Good morning," she said gaily as he entered. And then, seeing his dark expression, the gaiety left her voice. "You wear the look of a troubled man," she said. "What ails you?"

He stood still in the doorway for a moment, regarding the work in progress. He looked in her direction and said, "You know me too well for such a short acquaintance."

"A stranger could detect the uncertainty in your face." She paused. "There has been news from England, I take it."

"There has," he said. "I am troubled, and I am transported in the same moment. I may soon have my daughter back—a joy I cannot even fathom—but in order to save her, I must leave all this behind." He gestured to the pages that lay on the table, then looked into her eyes. "And, to my greatest regret, you."

"How long will you be gone, if you can say..."

There was no certainty that he would return at all, but he did not tell her that. "It may be as little as five or six weeks, but I suspect it will be much longer than that."

She set down her instruments and took one of his hands in her own. "The work will suffer for your absence."

"Perhaps. But I think not. I leave it in the hands of a capable physician, and I do not refer to the Frenchman upstairs."

She smiled, and then blushed. "You have paid me a fair compliment, Alejandro."

"It is well deserved. You will make wonderful progress while I am gone. De Chauliac will rise up from his sickbed and partake once again in the work. Only then," he said with a little smile, "when he is standing over you with his invisible whip, will you understand how deeply you miss *me*."

She laughed lightly and stepped even closer to him. "It is *I* who will suffer most for your absence."

With his heart racing, Alejandro put his arms around Philomène and drew her close. "Well said, *Mademoiselle*," he whispered into her ear. "That would be my confession too."

A prayer, nearly an accusation, formed in his mind as the warmth of Philomène's body flowed through him.

Why, Dear God, have You set a mountain in my path at this time, when there is another mountain for me to climb, also according to Your plan? You presented this good woman to me, and now You compel me to leave her.

Thy will be done. But perhaps for once You will take pity on this lonely Jew, and soften Your will.

He sent it off to his God with an internal shake of his fist.

His boots were polished to a shine so perfect that Alejandro could pick his own teeth in the reflection they afforded. What clothing he would take was clean and folded into a satchel. Guillaume was asleep on the straw, as if the morning would bring nothing special. Alejandro was as ready as he could be; all that remained was to sleep through his last night in Paris, to prepare himself for the journey ahead. It seemed an impossible task, with his heart so torn.

He was drawn to the surgery by the work he was about to leave behind—and the woman with whom he'd shared it. He hoped, as he pushed the door open, to find Philomène there, but the room was empty. On the table lay the pages they had recently completed, and as he gazed upon them, he felt a pride that could hardly be described.

May it please God that I shall have the privilege of working on these pages once more.

He heard soft steps behind him.

"I say again, Physician, the work will suffer for your absence."

He turned and saw Philomène standing in the doorway. The way she looked took his breath away. Her hair fell in waves around the shoulders of her white nightdress. She carried a single candle in her hand; its light cast a warm glow on her face.

"I see that sleep eluded you as well," he said.

"I think perhaps I shall not sleep well again until you return safely," she said. "My mind races . . . in one minute, reason rules, with thoughts of our progress on the manuscript, but in the next, I am overwhelmed with emotions. I do not want you to leave. I have only just found you." She looked into his eyes and said, "Is there no other way for this task to be accomplished save you going there yourself?"

"Had there been," he said quietly, "my daughter would be here now. But consider this: If this journey had not taken place, we would not have met."

"I cannot consider such a thing. It would be a mistake on God's part."

"He does not make mistakes."

He walked over to the table where the sheaf of pages lay. "This," he said with a sweep of his hand, "is God's plan. He has made it possible for me to leave a portion of myself on this earth that will resonate long after I am gone. It is the child of de Chauliac's mind, but in many ways, I am his child as well. I am a far better physician than I would have been had he not put his touch upon me. When I am long dead, a part of me will live on in this masterpiece." He paused, then said, "It is a vanity, I know, but I cannot deny my own desire to leave a good footprint on this world, so that others who follow will find the path easier."

She approached and stopped directly in front of him. "This is not a vain aspiration," she said. "All men should have such a desire. The world would be far better for it."

They were quiet for a few moments, until Philomène said, "I will miss being able to speak with you."

"And I with you."

"You spoke of your journal. . . . You have inspired me. I shall keep one of my own, and when you return, you can know what transpired in my heart in your absence."

He smiled. "You must write down all of your day's progress as well, so I can be envious when I return."

She searched for words for a minute, and finally said, "You have spoken with Guillaume. . . ."

"Earlier. He has taken the news of my departure as well as can be expected; having a playmate will be helpful. I suspect that a few days hence the true weight of my absence will descend on him, and he may be quite sorrowful."

"I will watch over him, for he and I will share that malady." She came closer to him and, with no shame or hesitancy, wrapped her arms around his waist. She turned her head sideways and pressed it against his chest. "Please," she whispered, "will you speak to me, as you did Guillaume, to calm my fears of your leaving?"

Alejandro put his arms around her as well and rested his chin on the top of her head. "All will be well," he said, barely believing it himself. "There will be so much more time for us."

He touched the side of her face, then gently took hold of her chin and guided her mouth toward his. "This is my promise to you," he said as he pulled away. "That I will return, that I will hold you in my arms again, that I will place a thousand kisses on your sweet lips."

She pulled him back into her arms. "Then place a hundred tonight," she whispered. "In promise of the rest."

She took his hand and led him out of the surgery, up the stairs, and into her room. There, in the light of a single candle, she let her night-dress slide from her shoulders, then undid his buttons with her delicate fingers. When their bodies came together, he wept, in the joy of having her, and the dread of never having her again.

Sixteen

Speaking to the entire group, James listed the requirements and then gave a brief explanation of how it would work. "We'd have to plot out a series of cells that would connect us directly, since we can't depend on other cells for relaying. One can go on top of your windmill, and you've got electricity right there. There's a direct line from the top of the windmill to a cell just south of where we are. We can angle that cell so it points toward us and put one on something tall near us. We might have to put one in between, but we won't know that until we try it. Then we just have to hope there's a signal somewhere. And if we get one but it's weak or intermittent, we'll need another relay point. But we've got some pretty high trees on the edge of the woods, without much obstruction."

"Can the cells in between work without electricity?"

"That depends on what type they are. Just before the last round they started putting in models that had internal solar power sources. Maybe we can find a couple that are in good shape."

"Where are we going to find them?" Caroline asked.

James smiled. "On top of those towers in the valley," he said. "Hopefully no one got there before us."

"Someone will have to climb?"

"Unless someone can fly."

Janie stared into the microscope. The first of the repeat samples that Michael brought back showed the same level of bacterial activity. She sighed deeply, then set about the task of loading the second set. She heard a voice from near the door.

"Mom?"

Her son was there, keeping his distance from the equipment until he had permission to come closer, as he had been taught to do.

"Come in, honey," she said. "Just don't touch any of the slides."

He came directly to her side but kept his hands to himself. "What are you doing?" he asked.

"Checking the samples that Michael brought back."

"How's it going?"

So adult, she thought. *Too adult.* She pulled off her gloves and set them down, then wheeled her chair away from the scope.

"I guess well. The samples are very usable, but I'm not sure I'm going to like what they tell me. There's a lot of bacteria out there."

"Everywhere?"

"I don't know. Probably not, but we can't be sure where it is, so we have to be careful."

"Oh."

She judged, from his somber expression, that he was unhappy to hear that for a very specific reason.

"What is it, Alex?"

"I hoped the samples would say there wasn't any bacteria."

"So did I." He had no idea how deep that hope ran.

He remained quiet for a moment, then said, "I want to go with Dad when they go out to get the cells."

Cold day in hell was Janie's first thought, but she forced herself not to voice it.

He's not an infant, he can ride a horse as well as I can. This is his world; he deserves to see it.

But it's so dangerous out there!

She thought about the original Alejandro, of his journeys, and the perils he survived.

"I'll talk to your father," she said, "but I can't promise that we'll decide it's a good idea."

"Okay!" He bounced up and down with excitement. "I'll go do my math now," he said when he'd calmed down. He ran off looking happier than she'd seen him in a long time.

They agreed to ride out to the nearest of the cell towers in the valley. Tom, Lany, and James would go, as would Alex. Evan would stay behind.

They set out on foot with just one horse for their supplies, tools, and gear; it was too steep, at least at the start, for horses to negotiate with riders. The ground was spring-wet and the footing occasionally slippery, so it took most of the morning just to reach the point where the pitch became tolerable. Alex nimbly climbed circles around the adults until the going became easier. They reached the lake in mid-afternoon and made it to the base of the cell tower just before sunset.

The first thing Tom did was to take out his binoculars and hand them to James, who trained them on the top of the tower.

"Hot diggity dog, they're solar," he said with a broad smile. "I guess we go up."

Alex stood near the crumbled cement footing and looked upward, shading his eyes against the sun.

"Up *there*?" he said.

"Yep," James answered.

"Who?"

"You. Isn't that why we let you come along?" He grinned at Alex's look of surprise. "April fool," he said.

"What?"

"It's April first. April Fool's Day. You know—we get to play jokes on each other and no one can get mad about it."

Alex stared blankly at him.

"I guess you don't know."

As James was explaining further, Tom crawled out of one of the small tents. "Food!" he announced. He spread out a mat and laid out several cloth-wrapped bundles. They ate grainy bread with preserves and cold pork.

"Guess we better figure out what we're going to do tomorrow morning," James said as he stowed his utensils away.

The three adults looked up the tower as Alex had done before.

"We already discussed this," Tom said. "I climb, you stay on the ground. If we lose you, there's no point to any of this."

James reiterated his displeasure with that notion.

Lany said, "You're sure you want to do the climb?"

He drew in a breath, wondering just how sure he was. "I am," he said. "You'll have to talk me through it from down here. With the binoculars, I mean."

Until the light faded, they went through the steps Tom would follow to remove and lower the cells. When the sun finally snuck below the horizon, they all bedded down. The next day would be full and trying at best.

With rope strapped to his waist and assorted tools in his belt, Tom began the seventy-five-foot climb to the top of the tower. He hitched up the safety rope as he went, slipping it over and around the foot pegs as he moved upward. He stopped every few feet to rest, but not for too long, being mindful of the time pressure they faced. It took him almost half an hour to reach the top.

He looked down the tower to the ground; fear shot down the back of his legs. A wave of vertigo passed through him, and he clutched on to the pole with all his might.

Don't look down, don't look down, he told himself. *Just do what you have to do and get back on solid ground.* When he'd found his calm again, he looked up at the assembly of cells. They spoked out from the center of the pole in three layers, six to each layer. He was surprised to see, wedged between the top two layers, a nest of some kind. From his vantage point, he couldn't see if it was occupied.

He uncoiled a section of rope from his belt and tied it around a loop on one of the cell units, then went to work on the bolts that held it in place. One by one, they gave way, but not without some strength on his part; eight years without maintenance had taken their toll.

He lowered the first cell unit to the ground slowly; Alex, so eager to be helpful in any small way, was there to pull it in. He untied the rope while James held the cell unit, then gave a small tug on the rope, signaling that it was okay to pull it up again.

Tom drew the rope in carefully and secured it at his waist again, then went to work on the second cell unit. A wind came up; he steadied himself against the pole as it pushed on his back. The sound of the air rushing past him, combined with the grating sound the wrench made as he loosened the bolts, was just enough to mask the frantic warning cry of the eagle that winged its way back to feed its young. Tom had the second cell unit lowered so it was about twenty feet from the ground; below it he saw the rest of the party looking up, their eyes shaded against the sun as they watched the dangling cell unit inch downward.

It was Alex who saw the bird first, when she was only a few seconds away from his father. He'd never seen a bird that large before—except a turkey, and they didn't really fly. He screamed, "Dad! Look out!" and waved his arms frantically in warning.

But Tom didn't seem to hear him. He was still focused on lowering the cell unit when the eagle came at him with its claws extended and beak open. Alex watched in horror as his father let go of the rope and flailed at the bird. The cell unit fell rapidly downward with the rope snaking behind it. James reached out in an attempt to catch it as Alex rushed toward him to help. A sharp metal edge glanced across James's left wrist and hand; blood pulsed out in spurts, all over Alex's jacket.

Mom will be mad flashed through his brain, and then just as quickly disappeared when he looked up and saw his father dangling from his safety rope. Then Lany was there, pushing him aside as she pressed the hem of her jacket against James's wounded wrist.

Alex stepped back and looked up again. He saw Tom, still under attack from the enormous bird, working his way down the pole one agonized step at a time, slipping the strap of his belt around the footholds with one hand, beating away the bird with the other.

"Alex!" He heard Lany's voice through the haze of confusion. "Come here! I need you to hold the rag on James's cut."

"But my dad—the bird is still—"

"I'll help your dad, but you have to help James...."

He went to her. She took his small hand in one of hers, then placed it firmly on the blood-soaked rag. "Keep pressure on it," he heard her say.

He did as he was told. He stood motionless at the base of the pole with his hand pressed against James's wrist as Lany sent arrow after arrow in a counterattack against the bird.

Stop fluttering, his mind screamed. *Let my father come down!*

But Lany's arrows all went wide.

"Hug the pole, Dad!" he screamed.

Tom clung to the pole with both arms. Lany aimed carefully and let another arrow fly. This one hit its mark; the determined mother spiraled to the ground, one wing flapping frantically, the other immobilized by the arrow.

Alex looked pleadingly to James, who understood immediately. He pressed his own good hand to the rag on his injured wrist. "Go," he said through his teeth.

Alex ran to the very base of the pole. "Dad?" he called out.

"I'm coming down, Alex...."

"Be careful!"

"I'll be okay, son," he shouted down. "I'm coming—get away from the bottom of the pole in case I have to jump the last few feet."

He did as his father told him to do and rushed away to where Lany was working on James's wrist, not far from where the eagle had landed.

He glanced back at his father and saw that he had come a few steps down. His fear began to abate.

The bird was still thrashing around, trying to lift herself up into flight again. Alex stood over her and stared down with a hatred so deep that it frightened him.

"Don't get too close," Lany warned. "She might try to hurt you." She tightened a bandage around James's wrist, then rushed to where Alex was standing over the bird.

True to her prediction, the eagle made one last upward heave with wild eyes and searching beak. Alex jumped back, and Lany came forward, pulling the ax off her belt as she advanced. With one swift chop at the neck, she stilled the raptor.

They stood panting over the carcass of the magnificent bird for a moment. Alex bent down and pointed to a small metal box attached to one of the eagle's legs. "What's this thing?"

"I don't know."

He began to reach for it. Lany quickly grabbed his hand.

"Don't touch that," she said.

He looked up at her. "Why not?"

"Because we don't know what it is."

"We should find out," the boy said. "Can't we take it off and bring it back with us?"

It was then that they heard the sharp crack. They turned and watched, horrified, as the pole to which Tom was strapped came down in a sideways arc, as if in slow motion. Tom's body weight turned the pole so that he was underneath when it hit the ground. When the debris settled, Tom lay still under the pole, one leg savagely twisted.

Alex ran toward his father.

"Dad? *Dad?*"

Tom moved one hand slightly toward his son. Alex took hold of his hand and squeezed. Lany stood above them, frantically undoing the buckle of Tom's safety belt, which still tethered him to the pole.

His voice was barely a whisper. "I love you, son."

"I love you, Dad."

"Tell your mother and Kristina I love them too."

He did not hear the chopping in the background. "You—you—can tell them yourself!"

"Yeah," Tom whispered. Then he closed his eyes.

"Alex, you have to help me now," Lany said urgently. "We need to move the pole." She handed him the thick branch she'd just removed from a maple tree. "I'm going to lift up the pole with one stick and I want you to use this one to push it away."

She positioned her own stout branch under the pole just past Tom's head. "Get on the other side of me," she said. She placed the smaller stick under the pole a bit farther down than her own. "I'm going to lift, and you're going to push," she said. "Ready?"

The boy nodded quickly.

"Okay, don't push until I tell you to." She tightened her grip. "All right, here we go."

She used all of her compact strength to pull up on her own stick. The veins on her temples bulged with her effort. The pole rose up minutely.

"Now!"

Alex dug in his feet and shoved with all his might. The pole rolled forward, and Lany was able to raise her own stick-lever more.

"More!" Lany said.

With all the strength his body could manage, Alex shoved his stick. The pole slid away and landed on the ground, about a foot past Tom's head.

One of his feet was still pinned under it. Lany clawed in the earth with her hands to create a channel until she was able to pull the foot free.

"Okay," she panted, "it's you and me now. We have to take care of your father and James. We need to get them back up the hill, and your father won't be able to walk, so we have to make a stretcher," she said. "James can't do anything because his hand is really badly hurt, and he's weak from losing so much blood. So you're going to have to help me to help them."

Alex looked down at his father, whose eyes were still closed. His voice quivered when he asked, "Is he going to be all right?"

"When we get him back home, your mom will be able to help him, I'm sure of it."

They cut the necessary branches and laid them out on the ground in a rectangular pattern, then lashed the corners together with the rope Tom had used to lower the cells. They folded one of the tents so it fit neatly into the rectangle, then secured it with the tie-downs.

"Let's bring it next to him," Lany said.

With as much tenderness as possible, Lany and Alex rolled Tom onto the makeshift carrier, then covered him with another blanket. Using the rest of the rope, they secured the travois to the back of the saddle and raised it up so Tom would not be dragged along the ground.

"We'll have to take turns riding the horse," she said. "She'll do better if there's weight on her front, not just in the back. I want to make sure everything works okay, so I'll start."

Lany hastily assembled the rest of their gear and stowed what wouldn't fit in the saddlebags at the base of the travois.

"James?" she said.

"*Uhn*" was the reply.

"I know you're weak, but you have to walk now, just for a little bit."

James rose up stiffly from his seat on a log and stood, swaying slightly until he found his balance.

"Okay, let's go," Lany said. "We have to go as quickly as we can, and it's all uphill."

They headed off into the woods. About fifty feet into the journey, Lany came to an abrupt halt. After a look back at their campsite, she jumped off the horse and ran back to retrieve the canvas bag that held the cells.

"The ax," Lany said to Alex. "I left it by the pole. Go get it, but be careful."

Alex ran back and found the ax. The carcass of the eagle, forgotten in the confusion, lay on the ground only a few feet away.

The metal box called out to him like a siren song. All the lessons of respect for living things that Janie and Tom had tried to instill in him disappeared from his consciousness in an instant. There, within reach, was the creature that had felled his father. Anger he didn't understand and couldn't contain welled up within him. He released it with a chop of the ax.

The bird's foot fell off. He reached down and pulled on the metal box. It wouldn't come off, so he pulled harder. A small amount of the bird's coagulating blood oozed onto his hand as the box came free; he wiped it off on his pants. Then he picked up the small metal box and shoved the trophy of his dark victory into his pocket.

As soon as she had a feel for how the travois would work, Lany got down and put James in her place, and for another three hours they struggled up the slope, working their way through the mud and twigs. Alex walked alongside the travois whenever possible and talked to Tom, though he got little response; sometimes he ran ahead to pull away branches that he thought might snap back on his father. But when the sun was only half an hour from setting, they still had the better part of a mile to go to reach the vista, the most strenuous part of the journey. James was slumped forward on the horse in visible distress. Tom was conscious, but in such pain that he could barely express himself. The horse plodded along valiantly at Lany's urging, but each step seemed a little slower.

She brought the horse to a stop when the last of the sun was glinting through the trees.

"Alex," she called out.

He ran back from his self-assumed point position.

"We aren't going to be able to make it to the compound before the sun sets, so we're going to have to spend the night out here. I remember a spot that's a little more level not too far ahead; when we get there, I think we should stop."

"What about my father?"

"I don't know," she said. "But we can't go any farther. It's too dangerous."

"My mom can help him."

"As soon as we get back. But we won't be able to travel without light. It's too risky. If the horse stumbles, we'll be in big trouble."

For a few moments, Alex remained silent. Then he said, "I can go get her."

"No" came the stern reply.

The boy stood there, frozen for a moment as his mind worked through the situation, then said, "I can do it."

"No," Lany said again.

But the boy was already off at a run, all alone, in the direction of the compound. He stopped only briefly to turn toward her and call back, "Light a fire so we can find you."

Lions and tigers and bears . . .

"Oh, my . . ." Alex said aloud. "Oh, my, oh, my, oh, my . . ."

He wanted his mother. He wanted his father to be okay. Neither of those things would happen until he reached the compound.

Straight up, he told himself, this time silently. *If I just keep going straight up, I'll come out somewhere near the powerhouse.*

The sun was down; darkness came sooner to this side of the mountain, the eastern face, than it did on the other. Each step forward made his small legs ache more than the last, but if he didn't continue, he knew he would have to spend the night by himself in the dark woods.

And Alex was old enough to understand that in these dark woods, he was prey.

The sounds of dusk enveloped him. The birds went quiet while the bugs screamed. Even in the early spring, there were already mosquitoes, and they buzzed around his ears, biting him viciously. Moths fluttered by, but the gnats were not so polite—they dive-bombed his eyes and nose, driving him to distraction. His face was stinging and welted from the twig-whipping it took as he charged through the brush toward the ridge path.

Don't cry, don't cry, he commanded himself. But as he brushed the insects away from his face, he knew the moisture he felt was not sweat. Finally, after a full hour of frightened lurching, Alex saw what he thought might be the clearing of the path up ahead. He pressed on-ward, and tears be damned.

Janie worked her way along the path from the powerhouse. She didn't know why she felt compelled to check it out; Tom and James, an expert in such matters, had just inspected it the day before and found every-thing in order. Surely one day's use wouldn't break it.

It was the habit that comforted her. This was something Tom had done almost every night since they'd taken up residence in the com-pound. And when they returned—any minute now, she hoped—they would emerge from the woods at the vista point that lay along the route to the powerhouse. When she came to that spot, she looked out over the valley. Stars were just beginning to appear, and she tried to envision where her husband and son might be at that moment. In her prayers they were on the verge of breaking out of the forest below, making their way up the narrow rocky path with their mission accomplished and all sorts of wonderful discoveries to report. Perhaps the world out there was not as threatening as they'd all reasoned it would be. Perhaps they'd stumbled upon another established community and they'd been welcomed heartily. Perhaps there were no lions and tigers and bears at all.

She stood in front of the log seat for a moment, wondering if she should sit and wait, just in case....A swarm of gnats assaulted her; she shooed them away with her hands and decided that it would be bet-ter to wait in the house. God alone knew when they would return; she might sit there all night waiting.

Alex crashed through the woods, gulping air as he plowed forward. He scrambled up the last incline like a monkey, using his cut and bleeding hands, for his legs were so weak and rubbery that he could barely move them anymore. His wet face was smeared dark with dirt, and all of his fingernails were torn.

One more minute, he told himself, *before I reach the path. One more minute.*

Janie was about fifty feet past the vista when she heard the sounds in the brush.

She stopped and turned back. "Tom?"

There was no answer. She remained still and listened more intently.

"Anyone there?" she said, a bit louder.

She heard only the crackling of twigs and a deep panting. Against all wisdom, she started walking, her steps very measured and quiet, toward the sound.

"Tom?"

Alex heard her voice, but he had no wind left for speaking; all of his breath was consumed in simply reaching the path. He struggled through the last clump of brush and put his hands on the rock outcropping that marked the edge of the path. One foot after the other, he forced himself to continue, though he had little substance left.

Mom will be so mad so mad so mad. . . .

I am so scared so scared so scared. . . .

He used all of his remaining strength to pull himself upward and heave himself over the rocks onto the dirt path.

"Strange," Bruce said as he watched the monitor. "Fredo," he said, loud enough to be heard in the next room.

The biker-geek appeared in the doorway a few seconds later. "Yeah, boss?"

"Take a look at this."

He pointed to the dot on the screen. It moved but so slightly that it was nearly imperceptible.

"What do you make of that?"

"I don't know," Fredo said. "Which bird is it?"

"908."

Fredo stared at the screen for a few more seconds, then said, "Hard to say, but if I had to venture a guess, I'd say she was—*walking.*"

Janie crouched behind the trunk of a large tree. One hand gripped the hilt of the knife she kept hidden in her ankle strap. The sounds that came out of the brush were louder now, but no more human than they'd seemed before. She saw the brush part and pulled out the knife. A dark creature crawled onto the path on all fours; in the thin light it looked like a small dog. She readied the knife but stayed hidden.

Then suddenly the creature flopped down on the ground in the middle of the path.

Seventeen

De Chauliac was sitting in a chair in the foyer when Alejandro came down the stairs in the morning.

"I did not expect to see you before leaving," Alejandro said in surprise.

"I feel reasonably well, though I am still quite fatigued," the Frenchman replied.

Alejandro opened his mouth as if to speak, but de Chauliac waved him to silence. "I should have to be on my deathbed not to be here," he said. And then he smiled. "I would fail in my duty as your host and teacher if I did not give you one last lesson."

Alejandro smiled as well. "Get on with it, then, for the day is wasting, and I have many hard miles before me."

"Indeed, you do." De Chauliac rose stiffly from his seat. "Remember that you must be a simple traveler, so your appearance must not betray you as anything more." He regarded Alejandro's brown breeches, the plain mantle of gray wool that he wore over a linen shirt, the woven belt, his common-man's hat. He nodded his approval. "If someone should ask you why you travel, it is wise to give a reason that does not involve money, say, as a messenger or a tutor. Otherwise, they will wait in secret for you and rob you. Do you carry much gold?"

"Enough to see me through, I hope," he said, "but hardly an excessive amount."

"Good. That is wise. But in the event that it is not enough, you can go to a certain banker in London for additional funds." He reached into a pocket and extracted a folded parchment bearing his seal. On one of the outside folds was written the man's name and the street in London where he could be found.

Alejandro took it, then examined it briefly. "No," he said. "I cannot put you at such risk. If I am captured and this letter is found, your complicity will be revealed. I will not have that on my conscience." He held out the letter.

But de Chauliac would not take it. "I am counting on your success, more than you are yourself, it would seem." He sat back down in the chair, again somewhat stiffly. "I have been too long abed, I fear. My joints protest." He put his hand into a deeper pocket in his robe and pulled out a parchment that had been folded in quarters. "Here," he said. "This is a gift, on the occasion of your great northern journey."

Alejandro opened it and saw the lines and letters, the curves of the coastlines.

"A map . . . colleague . . . this is priceless!"

"I have been assured that the markings in England are accurate. The route from here to Calais, of course, is well marked and easily navigated. We cannot have you riding aimlessly all over France and England—there is much for you to do here."

"I will return as quickly as I can, I swear it."

"I will hold you to that oath. And one more thing, above all else—I feel almost foolish in telling you this: Do not reveal yourself as a physician! To do so will place you in grave jeopardy. And I would have you back here again, so I can be the cause of all your deepest troubles by working you to the point of insanity."

Alejandro saw in de Chauliac's eyes the smallest hint of a twinkle.

They embraced, somewhat awkwardly, after which Alejandro took up his satchel. He walked quickly out of the foyer and into the court-yard, where his horse was already waiting.

He turned back to face de Chauliac after mounting the horse. "Look after my grandson," he said. "And Philomène."

De Chauliac nodded. Alejandro slapped the reins on the horse's neck, and the animal headed for the gate.

As he disappeared onto the street, de Chauliac called after him, "Godspeed."

He rode, and rode, and then rode some more, for he had a long dis-tance to travel and not much time. The desperate loneliness of his ride and the dread that grew within him were lessened to a small degree by the great beauty of the French spring. The earth seemed to be bursting out in wanton fruitfulness. The sun shone brightly in a brilliant blue sky as Alejandro worked his way steadily north and west.

On the fourth day, when the solitude was beginning to take its toll on his psyche, Alejandro was fortunate enough to fall in with an affable lot of tradesmen, with the fruits of their labor jingling in their pockets and a great spirit of camaraderie. The despair he felt in his heart abated somewhat as he rode in their jovial company.

The walls of the river-bound city were nowhere near as stout as those that enclosed Paris, but the fortifications were in superior condi-tion, for Calais was a city well accustomed to siege. At the moment it was King Edward's territory, but it was inhabited—and surrounded— by a French-allied citizenry that would throw him off in a heartbeat, had they but the means to do so. English bowmen lined the top of the southwest wall; Alejandro had seen their acumen for himself and knew that each one had a sharp eye and a ready hand. He stayed in the lee of other riders as they neared the bridge that crossed to the fortress, but when a small group of English foot soldiers approached, the entire party moved to the side of the narrow road to let them pass. His com-panions, it seemed, were every bit as edgy as he regarding the occupy-ing English force.

When the soldiers were safely past, he took a cordial leave of the others and rode ahead a bit. A crowd was gathered on the bridge, awaiting the midday opening of the gate. It was different—far better fortified— than it was when he had last passed through it in 1348. Now it had a de- cidedly English look, more like the outer gate at Windsor. Soon enough, he would ride through that gate, if all went as he hoped it would; the thought of it sent a shudder down his spine.

Soon enough, he knew, he would have to ride between the oaks.

Think of something pleasant, he commanded himself. *There will be time for fear later.* He thought of Philomène and remembered the feel of her arms around his waist, of her lips pressed to his own. Memories of their night of love, after so many years of solitude, absorbed his mind. The thought of her skin, her arms, her lips, the eagerness with which she had received him into her body—all kept him entirely distracted until he heard a sudden commotion near to where the tradesmen had settled, a few meters away on the other side of a stand of brush. The leaves were not yet fully opened, so he squinted through the twigs, hoping to see better. A number of men, including members of his own party, had gathered around something on the ground. He wrapped the horse's reins around a slim young tree and walked around the brush, then pushed his way through the crowd.

On the ground in the center of those gathered lay a large man whose enormous belly rose up like *le Massif Central* itself. His face was red, and his tongue protruded from his mouth; frothy saliva ran down the sides of his cheeks, puddling at his tight collar. There was fear in his bulging eyes, which darted around to the eyes of those surrounding him in a desperate plea for help.

De Chauliac's warning rang in his ears: *Above all else, do not reveal yourself as a physician.* He watched in agonizing frustration, doing noth- ing as the man on the ground gasped for breath and turned redder. His eyes met those of the frantic man, and he watched, feeling deep shame, as the man's life slipped out of him. There was a moment of silence, af- ter they were sure he was dead, in which no one dared to speak; the spirit of the dead man was taking its leave. Alejandro saw on the faces of those in the crowd the shock and fear that are the natural companions of an unexpected death. They made the sign of the cross, and lips moved in silent prayer all around, until one of the soldiers from the group that had passed before spoke up.

"Does anyone know this man?"

There was silence in the crowd.

The soldier looked at one of his comrades. "Gather his belongings." The other soldier nodded and came forward to remove the dead man's traveling bag and money belt. That done, the leader looked among the crowd, his gaze finally settling on Alejandro.

"You," he said.

Alejandro remained still, saying nothing, while everyone around him shifted slightly away. The soldier pointed to the ground. "Bury him."

A spade was brought; as he plunged it over and over again into the soft earth of the forest floor, he consoled himself with thoughts of what might have happened had he stepped forward to offer treatment. The dead man was not terribly old, nor had he a sickly appearance; he was just a man whose time had come.

He brushed the dirt from his hands when he was finished, vowing silently that he would cling ferociously to this life, if only for the gain of an hour. As he tamped the dirt in place with his foot, he thought of his aged father and wondered with deep self-reproach how the old man was faring with Rachel. He considered Rachel herself, whose heart would be his for the asking. Then he thought of Guillaume, whose whole future, however molded it might be by the circumstances of his times, lay before him still. He let his mind wander again to Philomène, whose life he would share, given the opportunity. He longed for Kate, whose life was not her own at the moment. As he glanced up at the walls of Calais, his resolve strengthened anew to bring her out of England and return to those he loved. For at any moment, God might reach down and take him, in a bitter red-faced fit, into eternity.

Kate entered the king's private salon with her eyes cast downward, while her guards waited outside.

"Ah, my lovely daughter," King Edward said. He walked toward her, his hand extended. She looked away as he approached and clasped her hands together in front of her. Almost as an afterthought, she made a slight curtsy.

"How very sweet," the king said. "But unnecessary—you are my child, after all, a princess of royal lineage. Your sister and brothers only make such gestures when there is someone present to see it. I see no reason why you should be required to behave any better than they do."

She did not acknowledge the sentiment, but said simply, "You wished to speak with me, Your Majesty."

"Yes, indeed. Please," he said, gesturing to a finely carved chair, "sit."

"I prefer to stand."

"Very well, then. I *command* you to sit."

Kate did so. She folded her hands together in her lap and stared at them.

The king held a plate of dried apricots sprinkled with sugar in front of her. "Will you have one?"

"No, thank you. I have no stomach for food at the moment."

The king ate a few before putting the plate down again, keeping his eyes on Kate all the while. He brushed the sugar off his hands and said, "Have you chosen a suitable costume for the masque?"

She lied. "I was not aware that I was expected to attend. I received no invitation."

"Well, of course this is an oversight," he said. "Your sister is so bound up in preparations for her wedding that it must have slipped her mind. It is in her honor, of course, and we intend to announce her engagement formally. I have decided, though it is against my better judgment, to honor her request for a dance at the Maypole. You being one of our family, and a young woman of appropriate age, why, she would naturally assume that you would know yourself to be included."

On hearing this, Kate looked up. "I am not a member of your family. And despite the taint you imbued to my blood, I am no royal princess."

Remarkably, through all her insults, the king kept control of his temper. "I beg to differ," he said. "We have received this just yesterday from Avignon." He pulled a scroll out of one sleeve and offered it to Kate.

She eyed the scroll but did not take it from his hand.

"I would advise you to read it," he said.

She finally accepted it and struggled to control the shaking in her hands as she unrolled it to its full length. Her eyes widened as they moved down the page. When she was finished reading what the pope had written, she let the scroll roll back on itself again, then dropped it to the floor.

The king smiled. "That bit of rebellion will not mitigate its contents. You are now my legitimate daughter, by virtue of this papal bull. After your sister's engagement is acclaimed, we will also announce yours, to Count Benoit, a cousin of the Baron de Coucy, whom I believe you already know."

Rage boiled up within her; she kept it at bay by concentrating on thoughts of her son.

The king did not seem to notice. "His lands are in Bretagne, and his allegiance will be most helpful to me. The *famille de Rais* is too powerful in that realm; they own far too much land for my liking, but they refuse to ally themselves to me."

He smiled, though it was not a pleasant gesture. "So. I will make an ally of their rival. You will play your part in that alliance, as befits your lineage." He stepped closer and spoke directly into her ear. "You will smile at Count Benoit and act the proper lady. You will accept him as a princess of England should accept the husband her father chooses for her. At the masque, you will receive the congratulations and gifts of well-wishers, and you will stand next to your betrothed, smiling as the happy fiancée. When you and the other maidens are finished with your May dance, you will dance with him. I have gone to considerable lengths, not only with the Holy Father, but with my queen as well, to arrange all of this, and you will comport yourself accordingly."

"You might have asked the bride before going to all this trouble."

"It matters not what the bride thinks. This is a diplomatic match. And she," he said, touching the side of her cheek, "is no diplomat. Her thoughts on the matter are inconsequential."

He waited for a moment to let that thought settle into her. "In time, if you are a good and proper wife, your new husband may accept your child, and he can come to live with you. We should very much like to see this happen, as he, too, is of royal blood, and his future—"

As the king spoke, Kate did all she could to keep herself from saying, *You will never set eyes on him.* When she could stand no more, she blurted, "And what if the bride refuses the groom?"

The king did not appreciate this interruption and let her know with a scowl. "Then she will find herself childless." He stared intently into her eyes. "Is my meaning clear?"

"Very much so," Kate said. She rose up without asking permission, giving no indication that she knew he was still blind to Guillaume's whereabouts.

The king remained seated, but his eyes were upon her. "Good," he said. "But your leaving is too hasty! Now that we have reached this understanding, it is only proper for you to meet your groom."

As the king rang the summoning bell, Kate stood in place, staring downward in speechless horror. She heard the chamber door open but could not look, heard the footsteps across the room but could not turn her head to the sound. She heard the king say, *Arise,* to his visitor, and squeezed her eyes tightly shut.

"Count Benoit," King Edward said, "allow me to present my daughter, Katherine Plantagenet."

Alejandro stayed in a modest inn, waiting for a vessel that might accept him as a passenger. For several days, no ships appeared except one vessel filled with supplies for the English army, and he wondered anxiously if the war between the French and the English had escalated to the point where no passages were being made, save those of the military. If so, he knew, there would be no passage at all, and his mission would be doomed. Finally, in desperation, he asked the innkeeper why the port was so quiet.

Why, 'tis on account of Les Pax. Have you been so long at travel that you do not know that tomorrow is Good Friday?

Ah, yes, I had forgotten!

He knew he would have to observe the holiest of Christian days along with everyone else, lest he reveal himself to be a Jew. The next morning, on rising, he made no request for food but instead fasted as everyone else did. And when the innkeeper left with his family just before noon to join the procession through the streets of Calais toward their church, he followed in silence, trying hard to lose himself within the crowd. All around him he heard tearful prayers as the column of Christians mourned their way through the narrow streets.

The crowd of worshippers wound its way into a small square; hundreds of people were already gathered there. They seemed to have a collective anger over something in their center, though he could not see what it was. He pushed through the mass of people, politely so as not to attract too much notice, until he came to the center.

There, in a small clearing, he saw something that made his growling stomach want to give up what little it held. Three men were nailed to crosses; they wore white cloths around their loins and crowns of thorn around their heads. Blood dripped from their hands, feet, and foreheads.

He had seen these crosses in this marketplace during his meanderings through Calais as he awaited passage. But he had taken them to be symbols of Christianity, rather than the tools of torture and execution.

All around him, people were making the sign of the cross and then pressing their hands together; he did so himself, lest he stand out. After a short time, the temperament of the crowd began to change, making a gradual shift from lamentation to indignation. The moans and cries of misery were replaced by angry shouts, until finally one man stepped forward and shook his fist at the man on the center cross.

"Killer of Christ! Die now, as you made our Savior die!"

Alejandro looked quickly to the man on the center cross and then to the two who flanked him. They were all dark and bearded. He looked to the ground and saw long locks of hair that had been cut away lying in the dirt beneath their feet.

Beneath those loincloths, he came to realize, all three would be circumcised.

The same man who had shouted out the accusation threw a rock, which hit the man in the center squarely in the chest; Alejandro saw the man's head raise up in a grimace of pain and then flop back down again. Soon more rocks were hurled by others as well.

With a heart breaking and bitter, he turned and slipped through the throng of people as quietly as possible. He could not, as he had done once before, put an arrow through the heart of the sufferer to end his misery. No soldier would come forward with a sword of mercy to pierce the side of any of the men on the crosses. These Jews would die a slow and painful death, alone and afraid.

The expression on Kate's face was intended to leave no doubt in Benoit's mind that she would never willingly submit herself to him.

He bowed low to her, showing his greasy scalp under thinning black hair. She closed her eyes until she sensed that he was fully erect again.

"*Mademoiselle,*" he said. He looked her up and down, quite lewdly. "I am exceedingly pleased by your loveliness."

She thought, *Not half as much as I am disgusted by your beastliness.*

She curtsied so slightly that it was almost imperceptible, but said nothing, and would not look him in the eye.

The king let the insult go without reprimand. "You shall make your first appearance together as a happy couple at the masque." He turned to Kate. "Tell me again, for I have forgotten what you said earlier—what sort of costume will you wear? It ought to be something fetching, to show your beauty. No doubt your fiancé will appreciate seeing you in glamorous attire, as will his admirers."

Finally Kate turned to face Benoit, though she was speaking more to the king. "One cannot imagine that he has any." She rose up from her chair. "Will that be all, Your Majesty? I am feeling faint with all this excitement and would retire to my chamber."

"Yes," he told her. "I shall not keep you any longer."

"Indeed not."

She turned and walked out, quite calmly, leaving her fiancé bewildered and the king with an odd sense of discomfort.

The holy days came to an end, and life in Calais began to return to normal. Finally, Alejandro found a captain willing to take him across—for an exorbitant price. On the morning of departure, there were many people waiting to board, as vessels had not departed in the time of the holiday. He stood on the pier and looked out at the gray sea. The chill of the ocean crept into his bones and made him shiver, or perhaps it was the natural fear that came from knowing what lay on the other side of these harsh waters. Twice before he had crossed; neither time was it enjoyable. It would be no more pleasant this time, from the look of the sky.

The vessel was of a good size, and he realized, as a small crowd gathered on the dock, that he would not be alone in his passage. He watched as a flock of groomsmen led horses up a wide plank that reached from the dock to the starboard side of the boat. His own horse was among the group; the animal pranced wildly as a stranger drew him by the reins up the wood boards. Bit by bit, the rest of the luggage was brought aboard, and, finally, the passengers. The best of those who waited went aboard first, followed thereafter by commoners who were still prosperous-looking, far more so than the ragged crowd in which he himself waited.

A figure on the plank caught his eye. He leaned forward and peered closely at the squat woman in a fancy red hat who boarded among the commoners with means.

He shook his head to clear it, not believing what his eyes saw: It was Emily Cooper.

Impossible! But she turned as he was watching her, and the face came into full view. It was the same woman he had known in Avignon; there was no mistaking it. He quickly ducked behind a pylon.

But something about her was different; she had always had a pink and rosy complexion, even in the darkest hours of her husband's decline. Now she was pale and shivering, with her shawl wrapped tightly around her. The fashionable red-plumed hat she sported did nothing to improve her ashen look. She struggled to carry a small satchel and would not give it up to the deckhand; draped over it, folded in a small square, was the same blanket that Alejandro had seen on her dying husband. A sense of terrible foreboding overtook him when he saw it.

She had somehow acquired the means to return to England. There had been no money in that family, even before the man took ill. She had little to sell of value—

A terrible realization came over him as he saw her nod politely to an English soldier, who smiled back as if they knew each other.

She had sold him out.

Alejandro would have turned around to wait for the next ship, had his horse not already been brought up the plank. When it was his turn to board, he pulled his hat down over his face as much as he could. He stepped off the plank and onto the deck while the boat strained up and down against its moorings. He quickly handed his billet of passage to the steward, then slipped into a throng of passengers. The cooper's wife stood not thirty paces from him, looking out to sea. He pulled his cowl up around his neck and watched her as the ropes were untied and the ship put to water.

All that day he kept his eyes on her; she stayed in one place, with her back leaned against the side of a wood stairway that led up to a platform at the stern of the craft. As the hours progressed, she grew ever more pale, and toward sunset she lowered herself to a sitting position. Though the sailors who crewed the ship went up and down that steep staircase all day, no one paid her much attention, and Alejandro realized that those whose trade was to ride the seas would not find it even slightly odd for a passenger to seem sick.

But they didn't know what he knew, that she'd already been unwell when she set foot on the ship, long before the wicked, lurching waves of *la Manche* had taken hold of it. The waters were still glassy when he first noticed her malaise.

Would she recognize him, without his beard, wearing European attire instead of the robes of his people? Perhaps. But if what he suspected of her current condition proved to be true, she would not be thinking clearly.

In his mind, he heard the voice of an old man telling the tale of a plague ship at the start of the Great Mortality, a thousand lifetimes ago on his journey from Spain to Avignon:

It stood a month in the harbor before anyone dared set foot upon it.

He would have to risk her recognition. *Pestis secunda* had not the savagery of the Great Mortality, but it held its own, and if the ship arrived in London with a plagued passenger, they would surely be sent back to the mouth of the Thames. There they would be forced to wait at some mooring until everyone on board had died or all danger of spreading the disease was past—weeks, at the very least.

He did not have weeks to wait.

The physician moved slowly along the rail, holding it tightly against the strong wind, and made his way from his position at the fore-end of the ship to one farther astern, which afforded him a closer view of Emily Cooper. He was perhaps only fifteen feet away from her when she glanced up with her glazed eyes and stared directly at him.

He froze where he was and waited, doing nothing at all. She held his gaze for a few moments, and then her head dropped so her chin rested on her chest. He moved a bit closer; she did not react. He moved closer still, now only about five feet from where she sat.

For a full hour, as the sun slipped below the horizon, he kept a silent and motionless vigil over Emily Cooper. Her condition deteriorated rapidly; whatever aberration had spared her husband for so long was not at work in her. She began to cough, and her shivering became plainly visible. Someone would notice that she was more than seasick, soon enough; he placed himself directly in front of her and glanced around quickly to see if anyone was looking in their direction.

The wind picked up, and the boat began to toss even more violently than before. The other passengers gathered at the front of the boat. After a few moments of confusion and fright, they seemed to form a kind of circle. Alejandro stood up on his toes and saw in their midst a priest in a brown robe, whose hands were outstretched as if in blessing.

While the others were distracted, Alejandro bent over and lifted Emily Cooper's chin with one hand. She seemed unaware that he was doing it. On her neck he saw a cluster of dark buboes.

The wind grew stronger still. The people in the circle of blessing clutched on to each other, forming a tight ring against the wind. They huddled closer as the priest railed against the sudden storm.

With the gale raging and the salt water spraying up onto him, Alejandro bent down and picked up Emily Cooper. For one second she opened her eyes, and by her expression he thought she knew him. He looked away from her and out to the sea. In two quick steps he was at the rail.

"Forgive me," he said to her. He glanced back to the circle of passengers; no one seemed to be looking. Then he closed his eyes again and dropped her into the sea. The splash could hardly be heard in the whistling wind, and she made no cries of protest. Clinging to the rail, he looked down and watched as Emily Cooper sank slowly out of sight. All that remained of her—the red hat—floated on the surface for a few seconds, until it, too, was sucked into the deep by a sudden swell.

He moved forward, holding on to the rail, and finally reached the circle of passengers. He grabbed the wrists of two on the outer edge and separated them. He was pulled into their midst, almost welcomed. He listened as the priest in the center continued to shout above the howling wind.

The Latin words flowed over him—*kyrie eleison*—a thousand times, or so it seemed. He prayed for mercy, hoping that any God would hear him, for he was as much in need of forgiveness then as in any moment of his life.

In time, the heavily laden craft proved worthy of its burden, though the winds continued to be unfavorable. It was morning of the following day before they rounded Ramsgate and entered the Thames. Alejandro stood at the rail, still stiff from a sleepless night of self-accusation spent on the hard deck. He watched the scenery through tired eyes as the boat drifted down the Thames, driven in large part by the incoming tide.

To the south, he knew, lay Canterbury. He envisioned the tall spires of the cathedral gleaming in the first rays of dawn. Hours passed and the river narrowed; the sun rose to its height and began its decline again. Those who had made this journey before—and were familiar with the route—began to stir in excitement at nearing London. With each turn in the river, the water grew more foul; rotted planks, assorted garbage, and the occasional clump of feces floated by.

But no bodies that he could see; it was a relief.

When the boat was finally moored at the dock in London, only a short distance from the Tower, the sun was quite low in the sky. Alejandro stood among the lower classes and waited his turn to debark. Here, Emily Cooper would have lifted her skirts and stepped down the plank and onto the soil of London, looking every bit the fortunate housewife. She would have disappeared into the throng of people on the muddy street that ran along the banks of the Thames. A bitter taste rose up in Alejandro's mouth; he had given so much of his time and care to her husband, only to be sold away. He had had his revenge, but in its excess it would be far more of a burden to him than the relief it ought to have been.

She would have died anyway, he told himself. *She might have brought plague to many other passengers and to the heart of London. I did only what was right. It was a good thing that I—*

He could not finish the thought. Now Emily Cooper would join the young soldier Matthews, the old warrior Hernandez, the blacksmith Carlos Alderon, and the innocent Adele de Throxwood in haunting his dreams. It was a bitter company, from which he would never find an escape. His turn to debark came; he walked down the plank himself, his satchel over one shoulder. Halfway down its length, he stopped, for there on the dock was Emily Cooper's satchel with the blanket still folded neatly under the handle. Someone must have brought it along, thinking it forgotten. The thing stared back at him in accusation. He steeled himself to the screams of guilt inside his head and forced himself to move forward. After a few more steps, he placed his foot once again on the soil of England.

The physician did not need to consult de Chauliac's map to know that there was no other route from the river; he would be forced to pass the Tower in order to leave London. He soon found himself surrounded by a sea of beggars, all of whom grasped at him with dark and blotchy hands, pleading for alms and mercy. Though he could not help but feel great pity for those whom fate had treated so shamefully, he pushed their grabbing hands away, for it would not do to reveal himself as a man of any sort of means. When he finally reached the open street again, he felt unclean. He washed his hands at a pump, and as he took a drink, he thought about the old man in the tavern who had warned him of the Jew-tainted water.

But there were no Jews in London anymore, save perhaps himself.

He watched as stevedores led the horses over the plank and onto the embankment; his own horse was among the last. As he waited, he saw the cargo being dragged from the hold. Bundles and crates were hoisted onto flat-planked pallets and tied in place, and then hoisted with pulleys over the boat's edge and onto the pier.

Dark little bodies scampered out of the clouds of dust that rose up when the pallets thudded onto the surface of the pier.

Alejandro retrieved his horse and pulled the animal behind him as he walked through the London streets. He felt as if he were in a horrible dream and stayed well in the shadows. He could not bring himself to speak to anyone.

Several times he was passed by soldiers of the king; once he had to pull his horse out of the path of a group of bowmen as they thundered past him. There seemed an inordinate amount of activity with a supposed "peace" through the land.

But with a wedding on the horizon, and a peace that is tenuous . . .

His senses told him to be careful. When he was finally past the

Tower, Alejandro looked back at the strong, forbidding edifice and walked through its labyrinthine passages in his mind. What few English words he had when he came to the Tower in 1348 were learned from a man who knew little French; his first attempts at speaking the language, in the dining room of the Tower castellan, were laughable at best.

But not so now.

> *There lives a lady fair with hair of gold,*
> *Imprisoned in a castle built of old.*

He spoke, for the first time in England, to a passerby.

"Can you tell me, kind sir, what is today's date?"

The man answered with no show of alarm or undue interest.

"April twenty-eighth, I believe."

He thanked the man for the information, then broke himself free of the Tower's spell and led the horse farther down the road.

Fatigue overtook him as the sun slipped lower. *April 28.* He could allow himself a night of badly needed rest. He came upon a small tavern; cooking smells wafted out the open door. He tied his horse to a post outside and entered.

The landlord was a short, thin man with stark white hair under a dark cap. He welcomed Alejandro into his establishment with a sweep of his hand. Alejandro removed his hat and said, in English, "Have you a room to let for a weary traveler? I will stay but one night."

The landlord nodded and called out to his daughter, who appeared in short order from the kitchen. She wiped her hands on a filthy brown apron that Alejandro thought at one time might have been white.

Alejandro wondered if she had washed it in the Thames.

"Prepare the front room," he said. The girl, every bit as skinny as her father, curtsied quickly, then hurried off.

"A draught for your thirst?" the landlord asked.

"Aye, and some porridge, if you have it."

"I've a fine leg of mutton, just roasted yesterday."

"That instead, then," Alejandro said.

He sat, waiting for his meal to be brought, thinking how good it would feel to remove his boots when he was finally upstairs. By now his feet would be swollen and sore; air and light would do them good after such a long confinement.

He began to hear, in the distance, the sound of riders approaching. The noise increased, and soon the landlord came out of the kitchen and hurried to the window. The pounding of hooves became nearly deafening, and the whole house shook as a large retinue of soldiers thundered by. Glass tinkled in a cabinet; the landlord put one hand on either side, in the hope of stilling it. Finally, when the caravan was well past, the tinkling stopped.

The landlord wiped his brow and turned away from the window. "Nothing broken, *this* time, thank the Lord," he said nervously.

It was a natural opportunity for Alejandro to speak of the concern that had been lurking in his mind. "There seems to be much activity among the king's soldiers," he said. "I have been traveling for a very long time; please, tell me, is there a war to come?"

"Not a war," the landlord told him, "but even worse: a wedding! The princess Isabella is to be married, God save her groom! There will be a masque on the eve of May at Windsor, and the whole world's turned upside down in getting ready for it."

The man went to the window again and looked out. His movements were quick and tight, betraying his anxiety. "Still," he said nervously, "it does seem a bit much."

He went back into the kitchen and returned with a pitcher and a plate. Alejandro ate and drank, sitting comfortably for the first time since departing Paris. He paid the landlord for his own keep and that of the horse, after which the daughter showed him the way up the stairs to a small room that overlooked the street. In one corner, there was an empty tub.

"I will have a bath," he said. He pulled out another coin and handed it to her. The girl gave him a curious look but pocketed the coin. She curtsied once again and ran off to set the water heating.

Alejandro pulled a small chair to the window, then sat there as he waited for the water to be brought, watching the goings-on below. London was a thriving city, not unlike Paris—still crowded, though plague had taken half its citizens not too many years prior. He saw many children; nature was working her magic in filling the void left by the scourge.

Merchants hurried, carrying baskets and satchels; a woman pulled a small boy along by the hand, turning to scold him once or twice in the time it took them to pass. A lone soldier rode by, with his lance held upright.

The girl returned with the first bucket of water. Alejandro turned to see the steam rising out of the tub, thinking how wonderful it would feel to sink into the soothing warmth of the water. When he turned back to the window, something far to the west caught his attention: a dot of bright red in a sea of brown and gray. He looked more closely and saw that it was a woman in a red shawl, and by the way she was bouncing up and down, it was a donkey she rode, not a horse. He rose up quickly from the chair and leaned out the window for a better look, but by the time he'd positioned himself, the figure was gone. He closed his eyes hard and then opened them quickly and looked into the distance again, but there was no sight of her.

Eighteen

Janie heard crying.

Familiar crying.

Oh, dear God . . . "Alex?"

She jumped out from behind the tree and ran to where he'd collapsed on the path. She dropped instantly to her knees beside him and pulled him into her arms. "Alex, oh, my God, what happened? Where is your father?"

"Dad—fell," he managed to say.

"But where is he?"

"Down there still," he panted, "with the others."

"Then why . . . how—"

"James is hurt too. Lany is taking care of them."

She felt instant rage toward the woman who would send a small child out into the darkness alone.

As if he could read her thoughts, Alex said quickly, "She didn't want me to go. I ran away from her."

"How bad, I mean, he's not—"

His voice was weak and small. "Dad's alive," he said, "but his leg is really hurt."

"Was he awake when you left?"

"No."

Unconscious from a fall; the news stabbed her in the heart. "What about James?"

Alex struggled up on one elbow. "He cut his hand. The cell thing dropped on him. He bled a lot where the metal part cut him."

Janie supported her son with one arm and helped him get to his feet. "Can you walk okay?" she said.

He tried a few steps but stumbled.

Janie stood in front of him and hunched down. She reached her hands back over her shoulders and said, "Grab on. I'll piggyback you."

Alex did as he was told, and his mother drew him up onto her back. As she hurried toward the lodge, he slumped against her back and fell into a deep and desperate sleep.

Lany went as far as light and fatigue would allow. She found a fairly flat piece of ground and covered it with fallen leaves for cushioning. She laid out one of the blankets—the tents were folded under Tom—and arranged it so they would all be somewhat dry.

"Come on, cowboy," she said as she helped the dazed James down off the horse. "You can't be too comfortable like that."

It was a test of strength for a small woman, but she got James to the blanket without any damage and made him lie down. He groaned as he lowered himself. When he was settled onto the blanket he nodded toward Tom. "How's he doing?"

"I don't know. I wanted to get you down before I check him. Not good, I'm guessing. I think he must have passed out from the pain."

She walked over to the travois and knelt down beside Tom. There were leaf flakes and bits of dirt on his face; she brushed them off, then swiped at the black bugs that were gathering around his exhalations. "Tom?" she said quietly.

He didn't respond.

"Can you hear me?"

Still nothing. She spoke to him nevertheless, assuming that he could.

"We're going to have to stay here for the night," she said. "I'll make us a fire." She tucked the blanket around his neck and made what she hoped would be comforting small talk. "I think it might be chilly tonight, so let's get you covered."

He stirred and murmured, "Alex…"

Lany wondered if he'd been aware of his son's departure. She put a hand on his arm and squeezed. "All right," she said. She rose up, whispering a silent prayer to the God she hoped was still out there that Alex would indeed be all right.

The fire crackled reassuringly, but Lany didn't sleep. She was the only one capable of fighting something off, should the need arise. Before she'd settled herself in, she'd seen red eyes on the edge of the clearing, small and close-set, probably a curious raccoon or ferret. She hoped it wasn't a fisher; they were unpredictable at best and mean when aroused.

Nine hours until daylight—it would be an eternity.

Janie and Evan stood on the edge of the path and looked down into the forest. Evan searched through the brush with binoculars, making sweep after sweep of the darkness, looking for the light of a fire. From what Alex had said, they judged that the encampment, if they'd made one, was at least a mile into the woods.

"I don't see anything," he said. "I think we should just go ahead down and keep looking as we go. They may be on the other side of some outcropping, out of our line of vision. I know Mom would make a fire, especially after what Alex said. She'll be thinking we'd expect it."

"Okay," Janie said. "Let's go."

With lanterns in hand, they worked their way down the first rocky section to the steeply sloped path below. The going was treacherous; their steps were small and careful, inches rather than feet. In her backpack, Janie carried the medical equipment she thought she would need, based on what Alex had told her about the accident. Its weight affected her already darkness-impaired balance. Once she slipped but caught herself on a tree branch. The lantern swung wildly in her hand, and she nearly dropped it.

"Careful," Evan said. He held her arm to steady her. "Mom and I can't bring three of you back."

The eyes on the edge of the clearing were bigger this time, slanted in the way of cats, and wide-set. They were focused directly on Lany, who stared back, gun in hand.

"Come on, one step closer," she said evenly. "I could use a nice new coat."

The mountain lion made a low growling sound.

"You must be really hungry to be so bold around this fire," she said quietly. "Come on in, why don't you."

The glowing eyes moved forward.

Lany pulled the trigger back just far enough to hear the click.

The cat leaped into the clearing.

Lany fired one shot, jolting the cat in midair. Its forward momentum continued, but instead of landing on its feet with bared fangs at Tom's side, it fell in a crumpled heap about a yard short of him. Lany saw Tom's head, in silhouette against the fire, rise up and then quickly lower again. She crept over to him.

"It's okay," she said, "I got it. It's all right."

"Good," he groaned. Then he said simply, "Alex," and fell back into unconsciousness.

"That was a gunshot," Evan said.

They reoriented themselves in the direction of the distant sound. Evan put the binoculars to his face and searched the vista below.

"I see something," he said. "A fire!"

They lurched through the night in a direct line toward it.

Twenty minutes later, Lany looked up the mountainside and saw the dancing light of the two lanterns as the searchers neared them. She stood and cupped her hands around her mouth, shouting, "Over here!"

Evan signaled to his mother by waving the lantern back and forth.

She slumped to her knees and clutched at her sides. For a few brief moments, Lany wept in relief. As the lanterns approached the edge of the clearing, she wiped her wet face on her dirty sleeve, then got up and brushed herself off.

The lanterns hung from a branch above Tom's makeshift bed. Janie examined him as well as she could without moving him.

"Tom?" she said softly. There was no reply.

"Tom!" she repeated, louder and firmer.

He opened his eyes and looked up at her.

"Hi," he whispered. The hint of a smile came onto his face. "I fell," he said.

"So they told me. I love you."

"I love you too."

"Tell me where it hurts."

"My nose doesn't hurt."

She sat up on her haunches at his side and wiped her forehead with the cuff of her jacket. Despite the seriousness of their situation, she made a small chuckle in response to his attempt at humor. She reached down and pulled up the pants on his injured leg and pinched the skin inside his sock. He didn't react. She pinched harder still. He didn't seem to know she was doing it.

It took all of Janie's will and strength to remain calm. As she examined him further, it became agonizingly clear that her husband had no sensation in his injured leg. She pinched the skin on his other leg, in the same place, and the leg twitched in reaction.

"*Ouch,*" he said.

"Sorry. I didn't mean for it to hurt." She put her hand in his. "Can you try to squeeze my hand?"

Tom looked into her eyes. "Do I have to? It seems like it would be too much work right now."

"Yeah, you do," she said.

He squeezed, with enough success to convince her that he did not have a spinal injury.

"Felt that," she whispered. "You stay right here. I'll be back."

He gave her a wan smile. She rose up and hurried over to where James lay. "Give me your wrist," she said. He obliged her by raising it. She undid the wrapping and saw the deep gash in his arm, straight across the large surface vein. Blood oozed from the wound still, though not in spurts as it had before.

"You I can definitely fix," she said, "but not out here." She poured sterilized water over the wound to wash it and pressed a clean bandage against the gash, then tied the bandage tightly around the wound. "That'll hold you until we get back to the compound."

She rose up slowly and turned to look in Tom's direction. Lany was hunched down next to him. When she saw Janie, she stood and came over to her.

"I heard what you said to James." She placed one hand on Janie's arm. "What about Tom?"

"I don't know," she said. "He's got no feeling in the injured leg. The other one seems to have sensation. Was he able to move it at all when he first fell?"

"A little," Lany told her. "He was able to use the other leg to help us get him on the travois. He didn't feel completely leaden."

The tone in Janie's voice betrayed her uncertainty. "Then I don't think he has a spinal injury."

"Should we be moving him?"

"In a better world, probably not," Janie answered. "But I can't do anything for him out here in the woods. He needs to be warm and dry and clean."

"Do we need to go now?"

Janie heard the anxiety in Lany's voice. "We'll go as soon as the light comes back. It won't be long now. In the meantime, though, we should get some blood into our other patient. I'll need to type him and see if there's anyone here who can be a donor."

Lany stuck out her arm. "Type A positive," she said.

"You're certain?"

Lany nodded. "Absolutely."

"Then let's hope he is too—it'll save us a lot of trouble."

Janie went to James again. "Believe it or not, I'm going to take some of your blood."

She unwrapped the bandage and smeared some of the oozing blood onto a paper.

"A positive," she said. "Great luck."

Lany stood, while James sat. Janie hooked a direct line from one to the other. As Lany's blood was dripping into him, Janie looked up at her and said, "Got any diseases I should know about?"

"Nice time to ask," Lany said, "but no. I'm clean as a whistle. God alone knows how, with everything I've been exposed to."

The mountain was simply too steep for the horse to pull up the stretcher, so Evan, his mother, and Janie all worked together to carry it up the incline. When they reached the path, they hitched it to the horse again and Janie ran ahead. She found Kristina and Alex in the main room of the lodge, sitting on a sofa together. Kristina was cradling Alex in a blanket and staring blank-faced at the roaring fire. His face was red with scratches; one eye was slightly swollen.

They sat up instantly when they saw Janie.

"Dad?" Alex said. His face was a mix of fear and hope.

"They're bringing him along."

"Is he—is he..."

"He's not dead. But his leg is very badly hurt."

They huddled and held each other and wept. Finally, Janie whispered, "No matter what happens, we'll be okay. We'll find a way to make it all work."

As she tried to pull away, Alex clung tightly to her. She let him cling for a few more moments, then pulled his arms away from her neck. "I have to go get ready for Dad," she said. Then she kissed her young son on the forehead. "You did an amazing thing last night. Your father will be very proud of you."

"He won't yell at me?"

He would if he could, Janie thought. "No, Alex, he won't. What you did was very brave."

As she walked out of the room, Alex struggled out of the blanket and ran after her. He caught her hand, and she turned.

"I want to help you make Dad get better."

"Alex, it's going to be a lot of work, doing lots of hard things—"

"You can teach me, Mom. I'll study really hard, I promise."

His face was so hopeful. She didn't have the heart to tell him that his father's road to recovery would be very long, with or without his help.

"Please."

"Okay, Alex, I'll teach you. But maybe we should wait until your dad is feeling a little better."

"I want to learn now."

She looked down at her beautiful son, the boy she'd stolen from another time and place. She'd brought him forward as a means of satisfying some selfish craving in her own heart to know about the man he'd once been, and rarely, if ever, had she wondered if it was something Alejandro or those who loved him would have wanted, had he and they been given the choice.

"Okay," she said softly. "We should get started, then. Go wash your hands. It's the first thing a doctor has to do."

The small boy nodded solemnly and ran off. His mother watched, wondering why, all of a sudden, he seemed inexplicably taller.

Nineteen

—⚜—

This April day, though touched with a slight chill, was balmy in comparison to the day—a thousand bitter winters ago—when Alejandro had first traversed the length of the Charing Cross road. He rode then to the same destination; by his side was Adele, who would, a short time after that, become the only lover he had ever had, until Philomène. On that windy November day, in a cold downpour, they rode with wild urgency to find the midwife known as Mother Sarah. Now, for an entirely different reason, he traveled to the same place. The road looked so much the same that Alejandro thought he must have gone back in time, but the place had a way of working its magic on the intellect, fooling it with mists and glamours. He had long since given up trying to understand the strange and seemingly impossible things that happened to Adele and him while they were there.

Yet, familiar or not, he could not seem to find the road that led east to the meadow. He stopped his horse along a stretch of road that tweaked a moment of recognition, but it dissipated within his confused brain, leading nowhere. The road, the open clearing, two tall oaks that had grown into a leafy embrace—all seemed to have disappeared. The meadow might well be overgrown; he could not imagine that anyone would dare to disturb the bones of the plague dead who had been so hastily buried there in the dark days of 1349. To do so would surely invite the wrath of God! Somewhere, just beneath the surface of the soil, lay buried a shirt that he had worn in the throes of his own disease. That insignificant bit of cloth could not begin to enshroud the thousands of Londoners who had given up their souls in the Great Mortality.

He glanced up through the trees to check the position of the sun. By its lay, he knew the direction he'd chosen was correct. He could not seem to make his memory work properly; could it be that the spell of the place had extended this far out and was already warping his thoughts?

He turned his mount into the woods and urged him forward through the thickening brush. A pheasant ran in front of their path, startling the horse, who reared up and neighed. Alejandro calmed the animal with soothing words and urged him forward again. And then there was a doe who came almost within touching distance and stood there as still as a statue, staring at him from within a pair of deep-brown eyes.

She is here, among these animals.... An owl hooted somewhere off in the distance; he turned his head toward the sound just in time to see the winged creature lift off a branch and disappear into the shadows of the forest. When he turned back to the doe again, she was gone.

Logic yielded to fantasy in his weary mind. "Run," he whispered to all the beasts of the woods. "Tell your mistress I am here."

No sooner were the words out of his mouth than a needling rain began to fall. The horse picked its way carefully through the underbrush and finally stepped into the clearing. The rain ceased, and as he traversed the high grass of the meadow, the sun's rays began to shine.

A stand of flowers now covered the spot where he had clawed at the earth with his bare hands to bury his clothing as the hounds barked in the distance. He stopped the horse and stared, transfixed, at the colorful cluster of blossoms, and wondered what Sir John Chandos—a man he had befriended—must have thought when his king commanded him to hunt the fugitives down. A Jew and a little girl—not his customary prey, certainly, for Chandos was a warrior of great skill who had survived many battles, including the bloodbath that had later occurred at Poitiers. Edward had sent him and his finest men out to find and capture them, a simple enough task. And yet, he had failed; Alejandro knew in his heart that the failure must have been intentional. It would not have been unlike the man, who fairly dripped with honor, to let Alejandro and Kate escape, despite his loyalty to the king. There would have been no honor for such a good man in such a vile capture.

Insects buzzed lazily through the air, landing at will. The horse fluttered his ears to rid himself of the interlopers. Time slowed, just as it had in 1349 when he and Adele crossed this meadow. Ahead were the two ancient oaks, old lovers entwined in a desperate embrace.

Poor gentle beast, he thought, patting the horse's neck, *you have no notion of what faces you*. Alejandro stared at the space between the trees, gathering courage, until finally he heeled the horse. The animal bolted forward through the arch and into the forest beyond.

They plunged into air so warm that it felt like the waters of a bath. On the other side of the oaks there was a sweet, musky scent; rays of sunlight, confounding all reason, seemed to turn corners. Step by step, they proceeded along the root-snarled trail. Alejandro could barely breathe; he looked from side to side constantly, waiting for the shade of the warrior Eduardo Hernandez to rise up out of the earth. Would he be greeted again by Matthews, the young soldier who died at the hands of comrades who feared he had brought plague into Windsor, or even Carlos Alderon, the Cervere blacksmith whose fish-belly-white corpse Alejandro had exhumed, thus beginning his forced journey through the whole of Europa?

Would Adele come, and speak to him in her sweet voice?

"Time still runs here at an unfathomable pace," he said quietly.

Of course, the woman he'd found in the stone cottage on his first visit would be long dead; at that time, she was already white-haired and bent. By now, Alejandro was certain, her bones and a drift of dust would be all that remained of her on this earth. Her cottage might well be deserted and uninhabitable.

Yet, in his memory, Mother Sarah was as alive as she might ever have been. Her riddles, which prompted him to think beyond what he assumed to be the limits of his own mind, all came back to him. It was she who had shown him the curative qualities of the sulfurous water that welled up from the depths of the earth to present itself as foul-smelling ooze. Had she stumbled upon its chemical nature through a fortunate accident, or had someone before her made a serendipitous association through repeated observation? He regretted that he had not thought to ask her when he had the chance.

He recalled the words of the Talmud: *When we face our Creator in our last hours, we must answer for all those pleasures we have not tasted.* So, too, he assumed, would God hold him responsible for all the knowledge he had not managed to acquire.

Why, he lamented silently as he rode, *could I not have another lifetime, that I might know and understand all that escapes me in this one?*

Suddenly he was at the edge of an open space; in its center was the small cottage in which Mother Sarah had lived. He pulled back on the reins to bring the horse to a stop and sat silently astride the big animal, with all his senses tuned and taut. The sound of insects seemed almost thunderous, the rustle of leaves like a clarion. The shadow of a bird might well have been a bolt of lightning. When a rabbit ran out from under a thick stand of brush, Alejandro started. He was reminded, on seeing it, how hungry he was. But food would have to wait until he was sure his body and this place were indeed real.

A voice came out of the thicket from his right.

"Welcome back, Physician."

The horse turned a full circle around as Alejandro struggled to control him. When the animal was calm again, he turned him to the right and found himself facing what he thought must be another apparition.

"It cannot be," he said, almost under his breath. "Surely—"

"Surely I am dead by now?"

For a moment Alejandro could not speak. Finally he breathed, "Yes."

The old woman who stood before him laughed, and when she did, the birds began to sing, as if in chorus to her chant. A stronger breeze came up in further accompaniment. "Take ease," she said. She pulled on her chin as if to demonstrate her own reality. "I am not a specter, if that is what you fear. But I am not the woman you imagine me to be; I am her daughter."

Alejandro stared, as if his eyes were lying to him. "But—you might be her twin! The likeness is uncanny."

"So I am told, but I eschew the glass, so I cannot say whether 'tis true."

Alejandro said, "It is said that witches make no reflection in the glass."

The woman laughed again, with the same lilt. "I am no witch, Physician—leastwise, no more witch than yourself, though it was rumored after your leaving hereabouts that you are the Devil himself. I am merely an old woman who cares not to examine the lines that have overtaken her face."

A moment of silence passed as the two regarded each other. Finally, the woman spoke. "She told me you would come again."

"She" could only mean Mother Sarah. "That seems a rather bold prediction. Your mother was a woman of great substance, but I daresay even she could not have known what was to happen in the future."

"You are here, are you not?"

"Only because the twists of fate have compelled it."

"The reason matters not. You have come back to us, as she said you would."

She turned and lifted her skirts slightly, then waddled off toward the cottage. After a few steps, she turned back to him and motioned with her hand. "Well, come along. You did not travel here for pleasure, so let us be about your business."

He dismounted and tied up the horse, then walked along the stone path toward the cottage. With each step he felt lighter, as if, one by one, his burdens were being lifted from his shoulders.

My Dear Companion,
April 29—how slowly time passes since you left here. It is as if each second is a minute, each minute an hour, each hour a day. I miss

your comforting voice more than I can say. Each day as I enter the surgery, my heart hopes to hear you greet me, but always I am disappointed.

Father Guy's health and stamina continue to improve, though he wears a look of melancholy often, I think from worrying about you. Rats and plague, he says, how bold the thought! This led us to a discussion of contagion today as part of our work; he is absolute in his belief that some invisible vapor lives in the air, some poisonous humor that floats unseen from one man to the next. It is a daring concept, brilliant in its simplicity, and I am hard-pressed to come up with a reason to doubt it. When I tell him so, however, he reminds me that one cannot absolutely disprove any theory and that we must not be concerned with reasons for doubt, but instead should concentrate our thoughts on finding sound reasons to believe it true. Those reasons, he insists, must be demonstrated, for only in that way will others embrace his theory. He deprecates himself because he cannot come up with the means to do so.

Save your daughter, and hurry back, so you can save our poor teacher from himself!

Chaucer walked by the entry to the kitchen with quiet steps, hoping not to be detected. He glanced in through the door, and in just that moment, a scullery maid looked up from the work on the board before her. He smiled at her and made a little wave, not knowing what else to do; the young girl blushed and looked away. He continued past the kitchen, reasonably sure that she would not make much of his presence as he skulked around in search of the fault Kate had described.

Shaped like a pine tree, she had told him—*wide at the base, narrow at the top.*

He continued following the passageway, looking for the narrow tributary that would branch off a few paces beyond the kitchen. He found it where she said it would be.

His heart quickened with excitement as he turned into the narrower passage. He had to strain to see, for there was no torch, and he had not brought one, knowing that it would attract attention. He felt along the wall with his hands—*the top of the passage will be near to the level of your eyes*, she had said, *on the left side.*

His hands came upon an indentation in the stones. "May it please God," he whispered as his hands moved up, down, and around, "that there be no dragons lurking in these rocks."

But the passageway was obstructed. He found an indentation in the surface and pushed with some force. Sand and pebbles tumbled down, creating a pile around his feet, but when he reached forward again, his hands found only a solid wall. He stepped back and brushed the debris from his hands, his heart heavy with the discovery that Kate's passageway had been filled in.

His shoes and stockings were caked with dirt and sand. *They will ask me how that came about.* He hurried to his own quarters, to clean them in privacy.

On his door was a note.

"Quickly," Nurse said when she saw Chaucer at the door. She pulled him in and then closed the door immediately. "Isabella is much about today, in a proper tizzy over her costume for the masque or some other such nonsense. Do your business as fast as you can and then be off, or there'll be whatnot to pay." She gestured with her hand toward Kate's bedchamber.

Chaucer nodded and went to the door. When she saw him enter, Kate rose up from her chair, blushing, one stocking on, the other in her hand.

"Forgive me," Chaucer said hurriedly. "I came as quickly as I could, because we must make another plan. I found the passageway easily, but it is filled!"

"Oh, no . . ." she cried.

"But that is not all—there are additional complications." He held up the king's summons. "I am called for transcription at sunset tomorrow. There are official papers to be signed regarding the engagement, and the terms have only just been negotiated. The papers must be ready before the masque begins."

"So even if I can find another way out, there is no one to bring the horse...."

"I can bring it out in the morning," Chaucer said, "for I am not required until late in the afternoon."

"No, it will likely be stolen or, worse, taken away for stabling." She looked into his eyes and said, with great defiance, "I will go on foot."

"If you do, they will put the hounds on your scent, and you will be discovered before you are out of shouting distance. But no amount of time will keep them from your trail if you do not ride."

She sank down hard on the bed. "*Père* may already be at Mother Sarah's cottage!" she said frantically. "We must get word to him!" She stood again and gripped the lapels of Chaucer's mantle. "Please," she begged, "if you have any heart in you at all, help me. Ride out today and tell him that our plan must change!"

"I will gladly do so, lady," he said, his voice full of frustration. "But before I can tell him of a change in the plan, there must exist a new one! What shall I say, that he should charge up to the gates of Windsor on his horse, slash his way through with a gleaming sword, scoop you up into the saddle with him, and then ride off into the night?"

She stood, wordless, as her mind raced with notions of how she might escape. "I can think of only one other way," she said. "You and I are of a size, Chaucer; tomorrow at the masque, we can have two identical costumes, both so fully covering that no one will see what stands beneath. If you can keep yourself aside for a while, you can come forward at an opportune moment—perhaps in the May dance—and I can slip off. When I am safely away, you can step into cover and remove the costume that is a twin to mine, underneath which you will wear another!"

Chaucer let out a bitter laugh. "How shall I convince someone that I am a light-footed lady?"

"Use that marvelous imagination of yours to think of how it feels, and then make your body do what your mind tells it to do. You can do this, I know you can!"

He considered her suggestion, and though it was born of desperation, he knew it might work if everything went off without a flaw. "And what of your *père*? How shall you *rendezvous* with him after this bold escape?"

She struggled over his question for a few moments, then finally said, "Tell him that he must wait outside with a sturdy horse, and I will find him. When you ride out to speak to him, find a place that we can both easily recognize."

When Chaucer did not respond immediately, Kate pleaded with him anew. "Please, for the love of all that is good, help me get away! That ogre will take me to God knows where in France and I shall never see my son again!"

It was another very long moment before Chaucer whispered, "All right. We will have need of the costumes and masks as soon as possible. Can your nurse prepare them?"

"I have no doubt of it."

"Then set her to the task, and I shall ride out at dawn."

Kate threw herself into his arms in gratitude. After a long and desperate embrace, she let him go. "It is not too far," she said. She described the route to the meadow in detail. "At the southernmost end of it, you will see a pair of tall oaks that have grown together to form an arch. Go through the arch and follow the path to a cottage. If God loves me, you will find my father there." Then she finished with a warning: "Beware of the passage through the oaks, for there is witchcraft within, and it can play dark tricks on your mind!"

"I shall take that advice to heart," he said, making light of it. "But I have no fear of witches, for I am a rational man." He then rose. "I must depart; the hour is far too late for decency."

He made as if to leave but then turned back again, with a wild and hungry look in his eyes. He gripped her by the shoulders and pulled her close and kissed her hard on the lips.

When finally he let go, he said, "By God, Kate, you are everything I have ever dreamed of in a woman and a wife. What a life we could have together!" He stepped backward toward the door. "But it is not to be. I can only beg you to remember me well, wherever you are."

She reached out for his hand and pulled him back toward her. She brought his hand to her lips and kissed it. "My dearest Geoffrey," she breathed, "that is one thing in this world you may count on. You will be in every prayer I speak for the rest of my life."

Sorrow was all over his face. "That will have to suffice, I suppose," he said quietly. He pulled his hand free and hurried away.

My dearest love,

You are gone now three weeks.

Guillaume has become quite melancholy in the last day or so; I think he has taken on my mood, for I miss you with all my heart. I have spoken with him, hoping to discover the cause of his distress, but he will not confide in me. I will watch him carefully to see that he does not sink too deeply into the pain of your absence.

But now I will speak of joy, not melancholy. I expected my menses several days ago; they have not come.

Chaucer found the clearing with far more ease than Alejandro had the day before. With no knowledge of what lay beneath the soil, he rode hard across the meadow and straight toward the oaken gate.

Witchcraft, indeed, he thought as he approached the passage between the oaks. He slowed his horse but did not stop him completely. No sooner had they plunged through the passageway than the horse reared up, nearly throwing him. When his hooves hit the ground again, the animal pranced about wildly.

"*Whoa,*" Chaucer said as he pulled in the reins. "Steady!"

But as soon as this command left his lips, he began to feel as if all his normal senses had taken leave of him. The horse's legs seemed to drift to the ground, ever so slowly, and made no sound when they touched. He got down off the horse and stood on the path with the reins in his hands, though he could not say why he felt compelled to do so at a time when moments were precious. He stared at his forest surroundings as if he were in a daze. Somehow he found the will to move forward, though his steps were slow and measured, and as he progressed through the underbrush, pulling the horse behind him, he glanced from side to side, expecting to see a gremlin or a fairy. Even in the thin and rarefied air, he began to sweat. With each step, his wonder increased, until he finally stopped and stood still.

He had no notion of time having passed until—out of the corner of one eye—he saw a movement. He turned his head in the perceived direction and saw to his great surprise a figure that appeared to be a woman. She approached him with steps so light that he thought she must be floating. The folds of her gossamer gown lifted and fell in the light forest breeze. She was young and quite lovely, with deep-red hair and fine, pale skin.

She stopped a few paces away. When she spoke, her voice was soft and refined; wisps of her remarkable hair blew playfully around her face. "He is within," she said. She waved with her hand in the direction of the cottage.

"The physician?"

She did not answer his question but said only, "Tell him that he must take care of himself."

And with that, the woman began to drift backward. After a few seconds, she began to fade, and then she was gone.

Chaucer stood, entranced, in the same spot for some time, though he would not be able to say just how long. Only the horse's quiet nickering brought him out of what seemed to him an enchantment. He took the reins and led the animal forward again, thanking God with each step for the solid earth under his feet.

Before him, Alejandro saw a meal of plums, cheese, and hard bread. Sarah sat with him, and together they broke their fast, washing down the simple food with an ale of her own brewing. Its taste was bitter, but the fullness it gave was more than welcome; there would be little time for tabling until he and Kate were safely out of England.

All that was left to do was wait. Sometime in the night, if all went according to the code poem, she would come here.

"This day will pass with the speed of a century," he said.

"You must calm your anxiety, Physician," Sarah told him. "When you are back out among the English, you will give yourself away."

"Is my fear so obvious?"

"Obvious enough, at least to me. Now, if you would be useful, go outside and bring in some herbs—nightshade, monkshood, whatever else you find that seems useful." She pointed to the thatched ceiling. "Hang them to dry up there. You are taller than I; it is not such a strain for you."

She handed him a woven willow basket.

He took it from her hand but paid it little notice. In the daylight, the little details he could not have seen in the dim light were plainly visible. He searched the place with his eyes, then said, "I would ask you of something that I left behind when I was here before."

"In my mother's time?"

"Yes. I know that it was many years ago, but still, I must ask. I left behind my journal, a leather-bound book. I wrote my observations in it, recorded the paths of my journeys. It was a gift from my father and it means a great deal to me."

"One wonders, then, why you would leave behind an item of such importance."

"I have often pondered that question myself. We departed so quickly, I was not thinking clearly.... The plague had taken all my strength and cunning."

"You were thinking clearly enough to bury your soiled clothing."

He looked down, as if ashamed, though he should not have been. "That task was driven by my heart, not my intellect. I would not have passed my contagion on—the clothing surely would have been found and taken, for it was quite serviceable."

"Ah, yes. Then it was a commendable act. But I regret to tell you, Physician, that I am not aware of such a journal being here."

"What might have become of it, then? You and your mother have been the only occupants of this place."

"We venture out on occasion, as you know," she said. Her eyes went to the red shawl hanging on a peg near the door. "And besides that, my mother in her last years was not entirely—competent. She did things that seemed—*rash*. Even I began to think her mad. God alone knows what she might have done with such a treasure."

Alejandro took up the basket again, his shoulders sagging with disappointment. "I had hoped you might know something of it." He tapped the basket idly on the table. "Well, to the herbs, then. I suppose a task will keep me occupied until the time comes."

She smiled and nodded. "Yes. Until the time comes."

He went outside into the sun and marveled at its position—he had slept through most of the morning. He walked through the gardens that surrounded the cottage in something of a fog, thinking of how the night ahead might unfold. As possibilities surged through his brain, he knelt down now and then to cut free a handful of herbs, not liking the slight stiffness he felt in his knees on rising again. Soon enough his basket was full of green medicinal marvels, so he stopped for a moment to gaze at the warm pool of water that oozed up out of the ground in the midst of one of the gardens.

My salvation, and Kate's, he thought. *But not Adele's.* The familiar stab of frustration ran through him. Every few moments a bubble drifted slowly to the surface and broke. Insects buzzed lazily above the water, now and then alighting. He set down his basket and knelt again, and touched his finger to the surface of the water, creating a circle of ripples. He put his finger to his tongue, prepared for the foul metallic bitterness he remembered.

Instead, the water tasted completely ordinary. He stared in bewilderment at his fingertip for a moment, then dipped it further into the water. The taste was the same, bland and unremarkable. It was plain water.

"By all the gods..." he whispered to himself. Could the medicinal qualities of this water, which had so approached magic in his eyes, have dissipated since he had last been here?

Once before he had knelt over this very place with an expectation of one thing and had found another. He had leapt off his frothing horse after the furious ride from Canterbury and found only a muddy ooze, not the warm, fragrant water that had saved Kate's life only a few months before. The desperate frustration he had felt in that dark moment had been beyond description.

Could it be that the magic had served its purpose? Had it lost strength with each use, until its strength could no longer be perceived?

Had he used it properly? There might, he knew, come a time when it would be needed again.

And if it was not there because he had used it up...

Alejandro slapped the surface of the water in anger; it splashed up onto his garments and face. He stood and wiped the drops from his cheeks and chin and watched with a heavy heart as the ripples lapped at the reedy edges of the pool. They had nearly disappeared when he heard a sound that was neither bird nor insect. He grabbed his basket and stepped away from the edge of the water, turning his gaze toward the path that led from the oaks.

Kate.

His heart began to pound. Could it be... had she come already?

Leaves rustled under the horse's feet, and branches parted as a rider emerged from the shadows of the wooded path. Alejandro saw to his great disappointment that it was not his daughter who emerged from the trees but instead a well-dressed young man, perhaps in his early twenties. He seemed confused and shaded his eyes against the high sun so Alejandro could not see his face clearly. The young man was walking slowly, as if in a daze, and pulling a horse behind him. Though he sensed no real danger from the unknown visitor, Alejandro ducked behind a nearby tree and watched for a moment as the stranger looked around.

Then the stranger spoke. "Physician?" he said.

Alejandro did not respond but peered more closely at the young man.

Dearest God. His eyes would not believe what his brain told them, so he came out from behind the tree and called out, in amazement, "Is that you, Chaucer?"

Chaucer looked in his direction and, seeing him at last, made a wave of his hand. He let go of his horse and came forward in a rush. "Thank God," he said. "This place... it is uncanny!"

"I hardly think you know the half of that," Alejandro said quickly. "But—why are *you* here? What of Kate?"

"Do not fret, she is well, but—she cannot escape as we had originally planned. The fault in the wall has been filled, so—"

"I had thought you more mannerly, Alejandro."

They turned in unison to see Sarah standing there, smiling broadly. "We so rarely have visitors. Please, invite our guest inside."

Sarah gave him a tankard of ale, which Chaucer drank in one long pull. He wiped the drips from his face with one hand. "I am in the land of the fairies and elves, and God alone knows what else! What thing of old rules this place?"

"All in due time," Alejandro said anxiously. He leaned closer. "But what of Kate?"

Chaucer delivered his news. "The masque is tonight," he told them. "The maidens will dance at a Maypole. We have devised a new plan—Kate and I will trade positions long enough for her to slip away. I must accomplish the task of fooling her guards long enough to allow her to escape."

Both Sarah and Alejandro stared at him in disbelief.

"We are of a height with each other," the young man explained. "Her nurse will provide two identical costumes, both with headpieces and masks. She is certain it can be done, though I have less faith than she."

Sarah spoke first. " 'Tis a good fortune that you are already clean-shaven," she said, "or such an ill-advised plan would have no chance of working."

"Let me be certain that I understand you," Alejandro said. "When the exchange is made, she will simply walk out?"

"It is a masque, Physician. No one will know it is she who departs. She plans to leave the castle and meet up with you somewhere outside. Bring a sturdy horse, for there is no way we can bring one around, as I am required by the king in the afternoon."

"What if she should happen to be discovered as she is leaving the castle?"

"She does not believe she will be noticed."

Alejandro rubbed his chin as he went over the proposed plan in his own mind.

"I do not care for this scheme. There is no accommodation for the unhappy event of her discovery." He stood. "We must decide in advance what shall be done if that happens." He thought for another minute, then said, "I will go to this masque and make certain that she comes out unharmed."

"That would be even more ill-advised, for I suspect through my observations that they are seeking you now."

"As you say, it is a masque! Can I not go in disguise as well? She will stand a much better chance of getting away if she is accompanied by someone who can protect her."

Chaucer said, "You underestimate her, Physician. I have seen her work a bow, and more than once since she was taken to Windsor, she has handily wielded a knife, when one was within reach."

With hope in his voice, Alejandro said, "Her spirit remains, then."

"Stronger than ever, I daresay." Chaucer glanced downward sadly. "She is a woman of great and wondrous heart, the best of the Plantagenets. It is a pity that she cannot someday be queen, for she of all his progeny is the best suited to rule after him."

Alejandro understood, when he saw the young man's expression, that Kate's departure was not something he wanted. And yet, he seemed a willing participant. "You are a good man, Chaucer, and brave. I know that if you could, you would protect her." He stood abruptly. "Nevertheless, you can only do one thing at a time, so I will come to Windsor. I have not come this far to leave without her."

Chaucer made no argument.

"Well, then," Sarah said, "since that is decided, time is short. We must devise a disguise for you, and Master Chaucer must be off so he can play his part in this intrigue." She turned to Chaucer. "Before you go, lad—you know the nature of these events; what is expected?"

"Deception, madam," he said. "One is to make oneself into something that one cannot otherwise be. That is the purpose, to come as what you are not, and to then meet with others who are also similarly antithetical to their true selves."

He turned to Alejandro. "Regardless of what your costume is, you should cover yourself as fully as possible, as we plan to do. And now I must be off, to do the king's—" He rose, and then said abruptly, "I nearly forgot!" he said. "An invitation. You will require one to enter the hall." His brow furrowed as he considered how it might be accomplished. "I have it," he said. "I shall already be within the castle, so I will have no need of mine; I will secret it outside for you. But where… where…" He thought for a long moment. "Ah! I know. There is an alms box outside the old chapel. I will tuck it behind the box. Now, the chapel is—"

It was within the chapel that Alejandro had quarantined Matthews and Isabella's tailor. "I know where it is," he interrupted. "Only too well."

They conspired quickly thereafter on the nature of Alejandro's costume; it was Sarah who came up with the ideal disguise—one easily accomplished with the things at hand.

"Then my mission here is done. And now, finally, I am off. There is much yet to do! Good-bye—for now."

As Chaucer was turning to leave the cottage, Alejandro grabbed his wrist. "I will not forget this," he said. "I can never repay your kindness, but I am forever in your debt."

"When I see you and Kate reunited, that will be payment enough for me. Mine is but a small part in it."

Alejandro squeezed Chaucer's wrist once more, then let it go. He smiled and nodded, and the young man left. Sarah remained behind in the cottage, but Alejandro went out after him and watched as the poet mounted his horse. He had the horse turned toward the path, but before he heeled him forward, he turned back to Alejandro.

"A curious thing happened as I came through these woods before," he said, pointing in the direction of the path. "A vision, perhaps. I should have told you before now, but with all that transpired within…"

Alejandro had known many "visions" on that pathway. He stepped closer. "Tell me now."

"There was a lady with pale skin and red hair," Chaucer said. "She came to me with—a message for you, I believe."

Alejandro's heart was in his throat. "What did she say?"

"That you should take care...."

Of what? "She said nothing more specific?"

"No."

After a moment of silence, Alejandro said, "Thank you."

The poet nodded, then spurred the horse and disappeared into the forest. The physician watched until he was out of sight, with the sure knowledge that he had just put his fate and Kate's into the hands of an Englishman who, if Alejandro had read him right, would weep for joy should the plan fail.

Sarah wrapped a riding cloak around Alejandro's shoulders and tied it at the throat. "Thank God there will be a chill tonight," she said. "No one will find it the least bit odd that you are wearing such a cover."

He turned and faced her for inspection, wearing an uncertain expression.

"No one will know you, once you don the hood," she said.

"When I leave tonight, I can never return here," he said. He waited for a moment, then added, "Once again, I must ask you—are you certain you do not know the whereabouts of the journal?"

"As far as I know, it is not here," she said. "This is the God's truth. But I will give you another gift, one you might find useful." She turned away and went to a cupboard, from which she took a small flask with a cork stopper.

"Laudanum," she said as she handed it to him. "A most useful substance. There are many beneficial things that can be obtained by simply looking at the ground—but not this."

"Let us hope it will not be needed, but if it is, I thank you now."

He stowed the flask in a pouch and tied it to his belt. They went out into the late day sunlight. Alejandro filled his water flask from her barrel, then brought his horse around from behind the cottage.

As he mounted, Sarah said, "You remember the road to Windsor?"

"Too well."

She stood in the yard, clutching her red shawl to herself as he disappeared into the path that led out of her private enclave, toward the twisted oaks, through which he would pass back into the harshness that was England.

As the dust of his departure settled, Sarah whispered, "May the gods watch over you." She turned and tottered toward the cottage. As she passed through the door, her eyes touched on the small chest her mother had left behind. It tore at her heart to look upon it.

He will come back, her mother had told her. *He will ask you to return that which he left behind. Do not give it to him. If you do, he will take it away from here. There will come a time when it is needed for a greater purpose.*

But if he asks, the daughter had wanted to know, *then what am I to say—that it is not here? He is a good man, you have said so yourself. How am I to look him in the eye and tell a blatant falsehood about something that has such great import to him? How shall I do so without his knowledge, by the shame on my face, that I am keeping it from him?*

Her mother had simply smiled. And so the chest had remained closed, secured with a silver padlock. In one of her cupboards, there was a chalice that she herself had used long ago as Queen of the May, before she had come to serve in this place. Inside that chalice was a silver key. Someday, though she could not say when, she would take it out and open the chest, and finally, so long after the old woman's death, she would have a look at the treasures she left behind.

She wished her mother had been more specific! *I am not so skilled as you, Mother, in knowing when things ought to be done.*

There would come a time when she would have to decide on her own. Certainly it would have to be before she herself left that chest to her own daughter.

She was now, after all, Mother Sarah.

.   .   .

Alejandro felt only a small chill as he passed between the oaks. He wondered if the place's magic had dissipated with the change in proprietress. He was a rational man with a fine education, and yet he believed with all his heart that there was some inexplicable mystery to this place, so close to the seat of England's power yet a world unto itself. He would never unravel it, for he could not envision any circumstance under which he would return after this departure.

As he rode toward Windsor, he considered how his life might have evolved if he had followed the path his father would have set him upon: to establish himself within the trade, to enter into an arranged marriage, to procreate—joyfully—and raise well-mannered, industrious, and piously faithful children, to the eternal joy of himself and his wife, as well as the children's grandparents.

Physician? Avram had roared the word when Alejandro first spoke of his dreams. Yet, somehow this dream had come to pass. Now he was thundering along a forest path in a faraway land, dreaming yet again of something that seemed impossible to achieve. These next few hours would determine the course of the rest of his years.

He passed familiar landmarks along the route—the abbey where he had taken his instruction in Christianity, to win the hand of Adele; the fork in the road, where he could choose Windsor to the west, or to the north the estate King Edward had given him in reward. A small roadway came into view ahead on his left. As he neared it, he slowed the horse, finally bringing the animal to a full stop as painful memories overtook him. He felt a sadness he could not describe, as if there lay a great weight upon his chest. Here he had spent a sweet fortnight with Adele and Kate, only to be tortured by its end. Within these walls, Kate had struggled against her own illness, and his devotion to her had solidified.

Adele's warning to Chaucer echoed in his mind.

Take care.

The horse wanted to move; he let the animal wander forward on the road. His hands trembled so badly that he had to grip the sides of his saddle as they entered the open courtyard. When at last he found the strength to look at the manor house, he saw with a nearly shameful sense of relief that the place was poorly kept, perhaps even abandoned. Though it saddened him to see such a fine estate in a state of disrepair, he gave a few silent words of thanks to God that their sacred place had not been despoiled by another occupant.

Then he turned the horse around. Windsor awaited.

More familiar landmarks came into view: a house he remembered, though now it had a barn where none had existed before; a rise in the road, beyond which he knew he would have his first clear view of the castle itself. He rode to the crest of the hill and came to a stop.

Once before he had sat on a horse and contemplated what lay below, only then he had been allowed to enter Windsor freely. In the distance, he saw the throngs of celebrants, all making their way toward the night's festivities. He tethered the horse in a well-hidden spot and began his own descent, wondering how legs so gelid could step one foot in front of the other. The answer, he realized, was simple: It was these legs that would carry him to Kate.

On this night of things-as-they-are-not, after so many years of separation, they would be reunited, and his heart soared to think of having her by his side again. He had allies in Chaucer and the old nurse, but beyond that he had only his wits and the sharp knife that lay snugly against his calf, in the top of his maligned boots—which, after Sarah's costuming, might never be restored to their previous fine condition. But if he could be restored to his daughter, that was all that mattered.

Behind the alms box, he repeated in his own mind. He looked around to see if anyone was watching, and, finding himself quite alone, Chaucer tucked the invitation in the crevice, as promised. Then he hurried off, hoping he would not be late. He arrived at the audience room just as the parties were assembling. Outside the door, he smoothed his garments and tried to compose himself. When he strode into the room, he hoped that the disarray he felt within his heart would not show on his face. The king greeted him with great joviality and introduced his guests, the names of which Chaucer promptly forgot—with one notable exception.

He eyed Benoit with cold hatred for the briefest moment, just long enough for the man to understand his disdain. Then he turned back to the king, all smiles and readiness. With despair in his heart, he wrote the documents, which were signed and sealed by all the parties. Copies would be made and given to each one in turn after the festivities—Chaucer had no doubt that the task of their creation would fall to him again, due to their sensitive nature. He would be forced to swallow the bitter pill many more times.

He handed the completed contract to the king and bowed low. "With your leave, Your Majesty, I shall depart to complete my own costume."

"At the eleventh hour, eh, Chaucer? Very well, you may leave."

He walked out of the audience room with as much dignity as he could manage, while the parties to the agreement raised their glasses in a toast to their future success. Only when he was out of hearing range did he begin to run, as fast as he could, toward Kate's quarters.

When he found her, she was standing on her balcony and looking down at the gathering crowds. "At last!" she said when she saw him.

"I am sorry, but my delay could not be helped—the dowry was not entirely negotiated! They stood over me for the better part of an hour, voicing their demands."

"What of *Père*? Was he there? Did you see—"

"He was, and I did."

She clutched his mantle breathlessly. "Tell me—"

"He is well, have no fears, and as bold as ever. He insists that he will come into the masque himself. I have already left my own invitation for him, outside the chapel." He described the costume Alejandro would be wearing.

"Then all is arranged," she said quietly. She gathered up the costume Nurse had fashioned for Chaucer and handed it to him. "We will be so alike as to be twins tonight."

Chaucer took the costume and held it up, comparing it to the one she wore. "So it seems, lady."

"I have dreamed of this moment for every minute of my imprisonment," Kate said. She turned to face the gathering throng of celebrants below. "*Père* hates crowds. He always feels so captured within one, with people all around him; it disturbs his fastidious nature. But he will come for me, as I have said all along. I would rather die than go to what awaits me here. And he would rather see me dead, knowing what such a fate would do to me."

"Lady, what dark imaginings! Your *père* would never harm a hair on your head!" He took her face in his hands and kissed her cheek. "I am the poet, you may recall—you should leave such drama to me."

She laughed nervously, trying to dispel the dark cloud she had created with those words. "I know; I am certain that neither will come to pass. Tonight, I shall be free, at long last." She looked into Chaucer's brown eyes. "I know not whether I ought to be wild with joy or terrified of what is to come."

"Of what is there to be fearful? As you have said, tonight you shall be free."

"Unholiness," she breathed. "Evil. *Père* and I have encountered an inordinate amount of it in this world."

"And now, attired as a holy abbess, you seek the very personification of evil as your savior."

"Yes," she said, her eyes still on the crowd. "One of those devils who poisoned the wells."

Chaucer let her bitter utterance pass without comment. "It is time," he said. He held up the white costume and regarded it for another moment, then tossed it aside. He took Kate's face in his hands and kissed her tenderly. "Remember me in your prayers."

"I shall, I promise." She pressed a small pencil portrait of herself, one he had admired, into his hands. "To remember me," she said.

"Thank you," he said. He closed his eyes and pressed his forehead to hers, and then, with his heart breaking, let go.

Twenty

They had no X-ray machine, but Janie knew that she would soon be facing yet another surgery outside her own narrow specialty. Tom's leg was a pulpy mess of torn tissue wrapped around the jagged pieces of what had been the bones of his lower right leg. She had no titanium or ceramic replacement parts. When she opened the leg up—as soon as his condition stabilized—she would decide on the spot whether or not the leg would have to be removed, based on what she saw there.

For the first few days, he went in and out of consciousness; when he was awake, his limbs seemed endlessly restless. Finally, knowing that he would never heal if he didn't stay still, Janie sent Kristina to the lab in search of recipes for something that would keep her father in a state of near-sleep, so his leg could mend.

May it please the Force that it mends, Janie thought, every time she looked in on him.

She wondered, as she and Alex did their daily work of caring for Tom, if he could hear the conversations that transpired between his wife and the boy he'd raised as his son.

Hold Dad's wrist like this, and press your finger against this spot. There's a vein right there. Do you feel it pulsing?

Yes, I feel it!

Listen to your own heart first, then listen to Dad's. Is it the same?

His is slower. But mine is louder.

That's because there isn't as much muscle and flesh in between the stethoscope and your heart. Dad has bigger muscles.

She didn't mention that his father's muscles, once hard and smooth, were rapidly shrinking as his body remained in the same position.

Look at the color of his urine in the tube. What do you see?

It's darker than it was last time.

He needs more liquid, then. Let's turn up the drip.

They cleaned him together, checked his vital signs together, rolled him to one side to change his linens together. Every little thing Janie did in caring for Tom became a lesson for her eager son, who, through some force of will that his mother couldn't fathom, managed to keep his own sorrow and worry at bay in his father's presence. Had he learned that from watching her? If so, it would be sheer mimicry, for she hadn't specifically instructed him in that kind of bedside manner. Had her sweet and innocent son somehow garnered through his "mother" the steel and drive that guided her through dark hours but sometimes made it hard to recognize the light?

In one moment, she hoped so; in the next, she hoped not.

As soon as he left the room, he became the little boy again, as prone to crying about his father's plight as any other child might be under the same circumstances. But in Tom's presence, no matter what his state of awareness, Alex wore his hopeful face.

Can he hear us?

I don't know. But I think we have to assume that he can.

One night, two weeks after they brought Tom home, Janie rose up sleepless from her cot and went to Tom's bedside. She felt his pulse; it seemed a bit rapid. His arm had the familiar warmth and twitched in response to her touch. She leaned over and kissed him lightly on the cheek. The skin at his temple had the same Tom smell. But when she lifted the covers to look at his leg, a new odor arose, one that brought bad news.

In the dim light of her candle, she saw the darkening areas. Maggots could not reach into the depths of his flesh to root out the gangrene as they had done with the flesh of the little girl whose diabetes they had conquered. The infection was not of the kind that rose to the surface and festered visibly, like a boil; it permeated the muscle and bone, hiding deep within each cell, eating it to death from within.

She draped her arms over him and rested her head on his chest.

"Oh, lover," she whispered. "What are we going to do...."

There would be no surgical repair, only an amputation, now that an infection had taken hold. There was nothing she could do until the morning light came, so with her heart leaden, Janie went back to her own cot. The sheets were like ice, and she shivered under the quilt. And after a long while, she drifted into an uneasy slumber.

In the last cold moments before dawn, she awoke to find Alex touching her arm.

"Mom—you have to wake up."

She rose up on one elbow. "What is it?"

"It's Dad—he's really hot," he said quietly.

Without a word, Janie threw off her covers. Before going to Tom's bedside, she drew Alex into her arms and held him close for a few moments. "Go get Kristina," she said. "We need to be together as a family."

"Is he going to die?"

The voice was so childlike; it broke her heart to understand that his childhood would be way too short. "No," she said. "But we need to make a decision about his leg."

She realized, as she watched him run out of the room, that on this day her son's medical education would advance at warp speed. She sat down in a chair next to Tom's bed and just stared at him while she waited for Alex to come back with Kristina.

It's only a leg, she told herself. *We can make him a prosthesis.*

But even the best prosthesis did not allow for the exquisite variations in balance and spring that were part of the miracle of an intact, functioning limb. And what about his pain—would he spend the rest of his life in a stupor just so he could bear to be alive?

No! Of course not. And it's not his mind, she told herself. *He'll still be the same Tom I married. I'll still love him just as much as before.*

But will I?

Too many thoughts coursed through her brain.

Do I love him enough to overcome this trial?

Is my love for him too centered on what he does for me—providing, protecting, cherishing, all those manly things that make me understand how fine it is that there are two sexes . . .

The possibility that her heart would fail to do the right thing—to adore her husband as before even though he would not be whole—so terrified her that Janie could not continue to think about it. When Alex came through the door with a still-sleepy Kristina in tow, she was immensely relieved that she could turn her thoughts to something less frightening—telling these two children that she was going to cut off a piece of their father.

As she had done before, Janie set up the lab as the surgical suite. No one wore gloves; there simply weren't any that Janie felt she could trust to be clean enough. Boiling the ones she still had would certainly degrade them to the point where they would be useless anyway, so it was bare fingers for everyone.

She called upon Caroline, as she had done during previous surgeries, to monitor Tom's vital signs. To Kristina she assigned the task of hovering over the instruments, to pass what was needed when Janie asked. For Alex, she found a small step stool, and now he stood by his mother's side, doing whatever she told him to do. When prompted—to her amazement—he pinched a vein while Janie cauterized it. He suctioned off blood with a basting syringe and squeezed it into a bucket. From time to time she would hand him small pieces of his father's flesh, which he would reverently place in a tray—for later burial—with no visible signs of revulsion.

Once, between slices, Janie took a moment to rest her hands so they would not cramp up during the two or more hours it would take to complete the procedure. She looked around the lab; with its bucket of blood and tray of flesh and ungloved attendants, it looked for all the world like a medieval surgery. And when it was all over—a resounding success by their minimized standards—Janie oversaw the scrubbing of hands. *My kingdom for something antibacterial,* she thought as she directed the three other members of her "surgical team" to get into every crevice and crack of their hands, to scrape under each fingernail, to wash and rinse and wash and rinse, and then to do it all over again. Now, when everyone had gone off to recover, Janie sat on the edge of the bed she normally shared with Tom and let her gaze drift along the wood grain of the floor until it met up with the bureau. There, tucked underneath, she saw a pair of his boots. She got up silently and took one away to the closet, where she stowed it behind a box of summer clothing.

No one seemed to have any notion of what to do, beyond wandering through the compound in search of something to banish the deep and terrible worry that marked the first few days after the amputation. Kristina was the only one who seemed to have a sense of purpose—she had thrown herself immediately into the task of conjuring up a batch of corticosteroids, which might, she believed, have saved Tom's leg, if they'd been administered quickly.

It broke Janie's heart when Kristina berated herself for not having done the work sooner. She said anything she could think of to help ease the girl's burden of pain and remorse.

He would have needed them within minutes of the injury to keep the inflammation down. Please, don't torture yourself like this! We were all so used to working miracles with our medicine in the time before; now the miracles are much fewer and farther between.

"*I'm* a goddamned miracle," she'd cried. "So is Alex!"

"A different kind," Janie said.

She would be in the lab now, Janie knew. It was her asylum.

•   •   •

Tears dripped off the end of Kristina's nose and into the petri dish she'd set out on the lab counter. She sniffed and wiped her nose on a handkerchief, then put the dish in the sink for washing. She brought out another one and set it in place. As she was removing the cover, she heard a soft knock on the door.

Evan Dunbar stood at the edge of the threshold with a tray in his hands.

"I hope I'm not disturbing you," he said. "I thought you might like some lunch."

Kristina brushed tears off her cheek. "I'm not really hungry. But you're not disturbing me. Come in, if you want."

"Okay," he said.

He brought in the tray and set it down. "If you're not going to eat it, would you mind..."

"No, please go ahead. I—I'm just not very hungry."

Evan sat on one of the stools and began eating the soup and bread he'd brought for Kristina. "It's good," he said. "Sure you don't want some?"

"Maybe later."

"What are you doing?"

She wiped her hands on her apron in frustration. "Trying to make some steroids. They reduce inflammation."

"My friend Jeff had to take them for a while," he said, "after Will Durand hurt him." And then, as if it might console her, Evan added, "He said they were pretty awful."

"But they might have helped my father's leg."

"Do you really believe that?"

Kristina turned away, saying nothing.

Evan remained respectfully silent for a moment. Then, in a quiet voice, he said, "It was supposed to be me, you know. Durand thought he had me. Jeff looked a little like me, and we were always together."

Kristina thought for a moment, as if she were trying to recall something. Then the light of remembrance of what he'd told her about Jeff came into her eyes. "What a terrible thing to have to live with," she said quietly.

Evan set down the soup bowl. "Every day I think about it. Some days more than others. But it's always there, that awful thought: It was supposed to be me." He hung his head. "I'm so glad that it wasn't and I'm ashamed to feel that way, in the same moment."

"It wasn't your fault, Evan. I mean, really, from what I read, he was a complete monster...."

"I know. But I felt guilty as hell. I still do."

"I'm really sorry."

"And I'm sorry about what's happened to your father. An eagle, for God's sake. And your brother saw the whole thing. He's so little to see something like that, and then going through the woods in the dark..."

"Yeah. But I think he's doing okay. He gets a lot of strength from his—from Janie."

"My mother was really helpful after Jeff got taken. I don't know what I would have done if it hadn't been for her."

Kristina didn't say anything immediately. After a deep breath, she looked at Evan and said, "Janie's not really his mother."

Evan, too, hesitated before speaking. "Is he adopted?"

"Sort of." She looked directly into his eyes. "So am I. In kind of the same way," she said. "And I guess now is as good a time as any to tell you about it. Just promise me one thing."

"What?"

"Promise me that you won't stop liking me because of what I tell you."

"Why would I stop liking you because you're adopted?"

"Just promise."

"Okay. I promise," he said. He moved closer and took hold of one of her hands. "I like you a lot, Kristina. It's going to take something really terrible to make that stop."

"I like you too, Evan." She squeezed his hand and said, "But just remember, you promised."

Twenty-one

Nurse had been called away to attend to Isabella, so Kate was alone in her bedchamber when Benoit opened the outer door. Her thoughts were dominated by the last-minute details of her planned escape, so she did not hear him as he crept in stealth across the carpet of her salon.

He stood in the doorway and watched as she set down the white robe that she would wear to greet her freedom; she turned in surprise on hearing his laugh.

He stared at her as she stood there in her undergarments. Her traveling breeches—which would surely have aroused suspicion—still lay on the bed. She quickly grabbed up the white abbess robe and held it in front of her.

"No," Benoit said, "lay it down again. I rather enjoy the sight of you sparsely clad." He strode forward and touched her hair, pushing one errant strand behind her ear. "I look forward to seeing you in this condition every day when we are married. Perhaps more than once a day."

Though all of her instincts told her to lash out at him, she forced herself to remain calm.

"I am a man of appetites, as you will soon learn. And I do not speak of food."

She glanced downward, saying nothing, with the robe still clutched before her.

"I think it quite appropriate," he whispered into her ear, "that I should have a small taste now." He took the white robe from her hands and tossed it on the bed, blessedly covering the breeches. He pulled her close; she could smell his foul breath and turned her head away. He grabbed her chin and forced her to face him again. She closed her eyes and remained rigidly still, trying not to breathe as his stench filled the air around her.

"After all, we are to be married soon enough," he cooed. He took hold of the bow that tied the lacings on her bodice and undid it with one rough tug.

The urge to kill him swelled up inside her. A silent scream went through her as he pulled down the shoulder of her camisole. The dagger was only inches away, under the breeches.

She envisioned the motions—grab the knife, lunge at him, rip it across his throat. It would be over in a matter of seconds.

But she would be covered in his blood, and it would not be long before he was missed. Had he told anyone of his intention to visit her? If so, her chambers would be the first place de Coucy would look for his cousin.

He had freed one of her breasts, and in the chill air, the nipple stood erect.

"Ah," he said as he brought his mouth to it. "Your acceptance pleases me."

Tears streaked down her cheeks as Benoit put his putrid self upon her. She prayed to God that it would be quick and that no child would result, for should that come to pass, she would rip it from her womb with her own hands.

My Dear One,

Today is the last day of April. By now, if all has gone well, you are nearing Windsor Castle and will soon be reunited with your daughter. My heart soars to think of the joy you will know when this happy event takes place.

Can it be only weeks that we have known each other? I feel in my heart as though you have been with me far longer. Perhaps you have always been hovering somewhere nearby, waiting for God and fate to cast us together so you might show me the way to happiness. Every day I pray that there will come a time of safety, when you and I can share our lives without fear of losing them. The child that grows inside my belly will be born of love and will bind us together with an unbreakable bond.

And now to a more mundane subject, though it hardly seems so when I am at it: The work proceeds. This morning de Chauliac and I refined his chapter on dyspepsia, while the subject was fresh in his memory from his own bout. He insists on doing this work, though he is still abed and rests too little, but this is what one has come to expect from him. He speaks of you often, always with praise, and I think sometimes that he is as eager for me to know you as I am myself. "Philomène," he says, "Jew or not, there is no man more worthy than he in all of Europa." One thing is sure: His admiration for you will never expire.

Nor will mine. I have said nothing to him yet of my condition, but I know in my heart that de Chauliac will be filled with joy when he learns of the happy event that will come to pass.

The last time Alejandro had crossed through the forbidding gate, it was to go in the opposite direction, out into England, in the freedom and prosperity he'd secured through his long winter of service. He rode proudly under an arch of swords en route to a new life, his own estate, the hope of marriage, family, happiness—best of all, there would be endless opportunities for study and learning. Those dreams had evaporated, disappearing like a cloud of mist on the whim of an angry princess. On this eve of May, she would be principal among the revelers, when her engagement to the man who had shattered his daughter's dreams would be made known to the world. How delicious it would feel to plunge a knife deep into the chest of each one! Such a thing, he knew, could never come to pass without resulting in his own death, perhaps by a method so horrible that he dared not even consider it. The king would surely unburden his executioners from any and all restraints and send him to his Creator in pieces.

And so he would have to satisfy himself with the joy of simply imagining such an act. But tonight he would have the sweetest revenge—he would slip in beneath their notice and escape into the night with one of their prizes.

The massive stone lintel loomed overhead as he passed under the raised portcullis. He saw before him the central keep, its tower festooned with standards. Torches were lit throughout the courtyard, though it was not yet full dark. Celebrants poured through the gate in a dazzling assortment of costumes; he found himself engulfed in a sea of fairies and butterflies, bears and beasts, giants and jesters. As more arrived, the crowd began to close in on him; he pushed his way to one side and leaned against a wall for a moment, his heart pounding, to catch his breath.

He watched for a short time as England's finest citizens presented their invitations and were ushered into the main hall of the central keep. *Dear Chaucer,* he said in his own mind, *God grant that you were able to hide that precious paper already!* Keeping close to the wall, he made his way into the courtyard around the lower keep, where he saw the familiar structure, then a small chapel in which he'd quarantined the soldier Matthews and Isabella's poor tailor.

He stopped before the chapel and stood very still while he let the memories of what happened there have their way with him. He saw, in his mind's eye, the body of the tailor slumped over a stack of Isabella's drawings, and the terror in Matthews's eyes to be enclosed with a plagued cellmate. He let his gaze drift to the spot where the young soldier's arrow-ridden body had fallen. He closed his eyes to banish the sight, but he could not shut his ears to the hard rush of air as each missile spun toward its mark, the thud of each piercing, the crackling of the pyre twigs as Matthews fell upon them. The smell of the man's flesh burning away from the bones would linger in his memory for all eternity. The shame and waste of a good and brave man would forever burden his soul.

"Sir."

He quickly positioned his mask, then turned and saw a soldier, perhaps of an age with what Matthews had been at the time, standing not ten paces behind him. There was a haunting and uncanny resemblance between the two—as Matthews had been, this soldier was tall and strong-looking, with a ruddy complexion, a man full of the juice of youth.

The soldier moved a few paces closer. "You have lost your way, sir." He pointed in the direction of the central keep. "The celebration will take place yonder."

Alejandro had not been aware of the man's approach; the memories of his horror in Windsor had overtaken his senses and left him vulnerable. "No," he said quickly. "I meant to be here." His eyes went to the alms box. He saw the slightest hint of ivory-colored parchment peeking out from behind it. "I just wished to make a charity here in honor of the princess's engagement."

"Ah. Indeed," the soldier said. "You may do so, then. You will have the thanks of the king, I am sure. And then please go yonder to the great hall." He pointed again toward the central keep.

Alejandro nodded, then turned back to the box. As he dropped in a coin, a pleasing thought entered his mind: *This is payment for what I take from you. This time, it cannot be called a theft.*

He left the chapel with the precious invitation and rejoined the entering crowd. Soon he found himself being driven toward the main hall as if on the command of some greater will. He let the throng carry him, though the closeness made him more anxious with each minute that passed. When he reached the door, he presented his invitation in turn and hoped that the sentry could not hear his heart pounding right through his cloak. The sentry gave it the most cursory glance, then waved him through.

Music, layered with laughter, echoed in the cavernous hall. Candles and torches blazed everywhere, making the bright colors of the costumes seem even more vivid. Memories overwhelmed him as he moved about the room in a dream, hearing his own heartbeat.

Somewhere in this crowd would be his daughter.

He felt her presence as surely as if she were standing right next to him. Through the slits in his hood, he peered at person after person, judging each one's height and carriage, passing over those who were clearly not Kate, lingering on those with possibilities. Panic crept into his heart; there were so many people, and there was so little time to find the one his heart craved.

At the front of the room he saw a raised dais. Several ornate chairs were lined up in a row along its length. Off to one side, there was a long table; servants scurried around it, arranging plates and items of service. He glanced up at the ceiling and saw the huge hanging candelabra, and he began to feel very small, as if he could not possibly accomplish his task under the scrutiny of all this grandeur. He began to feel as if Windsor would swallow him once again as it had nearly done before. . . .

He felt something brush against him and froze where he stood. *Please, dear God in heaven, let this not be a soldier or a guard or, worse, someone who would recognize my face were I to be unmasked.* He turned with as much grace as he could muster and saw before him, a mere arm's length away, a person—he assumed a woman—dressed in the garb of an abbess.

The abbess stood very still for a few seconds, as if she were assessing him. And then the woman in the white flowing robes greeted him with a precise bow— not the curtsy that would be expected.

A voice came from behind the mask. "This is how a proper bow is made."

He stood, stunned; once again, he let his mind drift back to his time before in Windsor.

This is how a proper bow is made, the little girl told him. And then, as neatly as any well-bred young squire might do, the child he knew as Kate executed a perfect bow at the waist, one arm before her belly, one behind her back. And then came her grin, with teeth just beginning to bud through her upper gum.

But the voice—could it be hers? The voice he'd just heard seemed lower than what he remembered.

She would be a woman in full bloom now. In his mind, she was still the hopeful girl with a simple wreath of flowers in her hair as she gave her vows of marriage to Guillaume Karle. Sorrow and time would have set their hands upon her in ways he could not anticipate. He pulled in an anxious breath and stepped forward, leaning in so only the abbess could hear, and said, "Thank you for the excellent instruction. One senses that you might have taught someone before this."

The abbess stepped closer to him. "I have," she said. "A traveler who came here, many years ago."

The voice was hers. He reached out and took her hand.

"Daughter," he whispered.

"*Père.*"

They stood quietly together.

"You are here, at last," she said.

Alejandro whispered, "I am. And so are you." He found that he could barely breathe. "Let me take you in my arms and hold you...."

"No," she said quickly, "we cannot, for my guards are nearby—their eyes are upon us now."

So they stood together in quiet peace, a black devil and an abbess in white, with their hands entwined, as bears and lions and jesters and brides danced all around them. They were enclosed in a bubble of bliss, and nothing could reach them through its rainbow surface. Neither one could move, for fear of losing the other. Finally, Alejandro said, "We must act according to your plan. Tell me what you will do."

Kate nodded quickly. "Do not look away, but twenty paces toward the rear of the room are my guards. They are two, not costumed, but in their ordinary garb. Large fellows, and brutal if provoked, so we must do nothing to anger them." She glanced to her left briefly and then looked into his eyes again. "Chaucer waits in the shadows. When he hears the music of the king's entry, he will get his white robes and mask and stand by the privy, over there." She pointed low, so only Alejandro could see. "When the dance begins, I will join in, and while it is still early in the dance, he will come through the crowd and take up my ribbon, and I will slip away, on the opposite side, so the guards will not have a clear view. When the king and others enter, my guards will stand with their fellows, for a very brief moment. It will be just long enough for Chaucer to throw off the white robes. He will be differently costumed underneath and will move to the other side of the room. They will find the white robes in the privy."

"Then you will go through the gate—"

"No. There is a stairway on the south wall, the Hundred Steps. It is in some disrepair; no one takes much notice of it, without enemies on the hillsides. It will be difficult going, a steep downward climb."

"I remember it," he said immediately. "But it is very treacherous...."

"I have had plenty of time to memorize its peculiarities." The tempo of her words quickened. "The fifteenth step is badly broken; take care to place your foot very close to the right side. And the forty-second step is barely there. Try to step right over it, or you will surely tumble! When you reach the bottom, turn right, and just a few paces ahead, there is a low spot in the outer wall; the drop from there is only about twice our height. I will await you on the crest of the hill, under the apple tree. Do you recall it? We looked over the wall when I was a child; you said we might put a swing there when the plague was past. I have looked upon that tree every day with such longing. It is in full flower now; the petals drift down, almost like snow, so you can find it, even in darkness. We can meet there."

A clarion sounded, startling them both.

"I will make sure that I am but a few steps behind you."

She nodded, her eyes tearing. "I must leave you now, *Père*."

He gripped her hand even harder. "Too soon!"

"Please," she said in a desperate whisper, "Isabella and de Coucy will be presented after the dance. I am to be called forward thereafter, and the king will speak again to claim me as his own child. I must be well away before then!"

He squeezed her hand one last time. "Take care, daughter of my heart," he said, and then, with terror in his soul that he would never claim her again, he let her go.

.   .   .

A contingent of soldiers in ornate regalia parted the crowd as the king and queen entered. Loathing rose up within him when he saw the king, but he felt genuine pity for the queen, for she seemed a shrunken woman in comparison to what she had been. Her hand was placed lightly on her husband's arm as he strode down the short staircase with his chin in the air. She made two steps to each one of his, and though her steps were still graceful, their entry was nearly comical. Alejandro might have found it all quite amusing, were his hatred for the man not so cavernous.

As the royal couple moved forward in their glittering garb, the sea of guests moved aside in a synchronized wave of bows and curtsies on both sides of the hall. Kate stood at the outer edge of the viewers, just a few feet in front of Alejandro. He saw the king nod very slightly as he passed his white-robed daughter, though Alejandro could not be sure if he knew who she was. The queen seemed not to recognize her and made no specific gesture. Kate dipped slightly in the same manner as all those around her, as would be expected. Alejandro knew it was a bitter moment for her, but this would not be the proper time for an act of overt rebellion. Her disgust for the man who had sired her would become plain soon enough.

When the king and queen were seated on the dais, there was another bright fanfare. In swept Isabella, gloriously attired as a princess of Arabie. All heads turned to watch her glide down the stairs with silks and gossamers floating all about her. She stopped on the bottom step for a moment of admiration; the crowd buzzed in approval of her costume. She brought a fan out from behind one of her veils and fluttered it a few times in front of her face, which brought a round of hearty applause from the observers. A bevy of attendants, each similarly though less dramatically costumed, rushed forward to pick up the silk veils that trailed out behind her.

Her turbaned prince, complete with his gilded scimitar, awaited her at the foot of the dais. For one short moment, Alejandro stood on his toes and saw de Coucy reach out to take the hand of his fiancée and then lead her up the steps onto the platform. The resplendent pair then turned to face the crowd, to yet more applause.

Alejandro's hand twitched for want of a sword.

The king rose and spoke—interminably, it seemed—of the fine qualities of Enguerrand de Coucy, of the suitability of the match between him and Isabella, of the joy it all brought to him and his queen. Would they feel that way, he wondered, if they had known de Coucy as he and Kate had, eight years before?

Alejandro recalled the very young man who stood with sword in hand and made it clear that the physician had a choice: He would sew up the ruined sword arm of Charles of Navarre, or watch Kate die. And though Navarre had probably been the one who ordered the death of Guillaume Karle, Alejandro had done what was asked of him.

Liars, both; no sooner had Alejandro finished with Navarre's arm than de Coucy made it known he would have his way with Kate. But before he could take her, she had pulled the knife from her stocking and thrust it between his legs, against his manhood. What kept her from plunging it home, he would never know. De Coucy had been forced to let her go. He had hated her, and she him, ever since.

Alejandro kept his eyes on Kate as he listened to the vile lies that poured out of the king's mouth; she remained on the edge of the crowd of guests, never moving or reacting. When the speech was finally finished, pipes and drums and lutes sounded again, and Isabella stepped forward to take her own ribbon for the dance. As soon as she had it in her hand, dozens of other gaily clad ladies came forward to find their own strands. A white abbess was among them, as bright and pure as a dove in the midst of a flock of parrots.

It begins at last, he thought.

He looked behind to the place where the guards would be. A few paces away, he saw a figure in a white robe well back of them with the mask full on. Though Alejandro could not be sure it was Chaucer, his heart told him that it was; the young man played his part perfectly, never casting so much as a glance in Alejandro's direction.

The tempo of the music quickened, and with it the pace of the dancers who made their way around the pole holding ribbons in their raised hands. The crowd dispersed somewhat and became less defined as the king's guests greeted one another and began to socialize while the ribbons twirled in the center of the room.

Soon the ribbons were a blur, so frenzied was the May dance. Alejandro's heart raced as he watched Chaucer make his way through the crowd. He glanced at the guards; they had relaxed their vigil, lulled perhaps by the immensity of the festivities and some notion that their charge was contained within it.

Alejandro saw a flash of white, and in the blink of an eye, Chaucer's hand reached over Kate's head and took the ribbon from her. She slipped low into the crowd and through it, and finally disappeared from view.

Alejandro felt a stab of panic; it was all according to the plan, but he was desperate not to lose sight of her. He worked his way through the celebrants as quickly as he could, heading toward one of the corridors that ran along the side of the hall. He approached two large gentlemen who seemed rooted in their position; the crowd was thick, and there would be no going around them. He made a polite bow and gestured with his hand in a request that they part. They nodded in return and stepped aside. Alejandro passed between them and found himself face-to-face with Elizabeth of Ulster.

He came to a stop and stood staring into the hard, violet eyes of the woman whose venomous disdain for him might be even greater, he imagined, than that which Isabella felt. Elizabeth was as coldly beautiful as he remembered when he had pursued her—with his own escape in mind—in Paris.

She was attired as a gem-studded butterfly on this night, but he saw no evidence of metamorphosis in her hateful expression. Alejandro had used her shamelessly as an unwitting player in his attempt to flee from de Chauliac, and with the help of Guillaume Karle and Kate, he had managed to get away, leaving his guards and a bewildered young Geoffrey Chaucer in a state of disarrayed confusion.

In truth, he had found her enticing; she was an educated woman, and he had found her company delightful. But always in the back of his mind was the guilty knowledge of his own duplicity; there could never be a love between them, not even the courtly sort of love that men and women of nobility seemed to find so convenient. Even so, he could not help but recall that she—the wife of a prince, the mother of children who might grow one day to rule England— had brought herself willingly to the flirtation.

Their escape from Paris had felt like a victory of sorts, until her son fell ill with plague. De Chauliac had convinced Alejandro to return to help save the child. Through his and Kate's efforts, the boy had recovered, but Elizabeth had repaid him with only viciousness. It was in the attic of her Paris estate that he had last seen Kate, before this evening.

Elizabeth's eyes opened wider and then narrowed again. Had she recognized him, though only a small portion of his face was visible?

She was a woman scorned, jilted, and duped, and, as such, would know her tormenter anywhere. He glanced back quickly at the dancers, then rushed past her as she began to speak. He looked back again and saw that the white abbess was just stepping away from the pole. He looked once more in the direction of the guards; they seemed completely unperturbed. A few paces later, he looked back one last time and saw a young man wearing the traditional red robes of a physician emerging from the shadows. Alejandro squinted to get a better look at him.

The mask came down, and Chaucer smiled.

There was no doubt in his mind that Elizabeth would sound the alarm for him to be caught. Alejandro damned the luck that had put her in his pathway, when he needed the advantage of every moment! He hurried, faster than he thought wise. The shadow of the wall along which he crept provided decent cover, but the torches were bright and damnably plentiful, so Alejandro stayed low as he made his way in the darkness toward the Hundred Steps. Up ahead was Kate, the white robes of her costume flowing out behind her as she hurried toward her freedom. He lost sight of her momentarily in the curvature of the wall; when she came into view again, it was because she had bolted away from the wall across the courtyard, toward the place where the Hundred Steps began.

She was halfway across the open expanse when he heard a voice call out, "Stop!" A figure approached from the opposite direction and followed Kate's path. She did not stop but ran even faster. She seemed to be fumbling with the front of her robe as she ran, though he could not see clearly. The follower began to catch up to her; Alejandro moved faster through the shadow of the wall in their direction.

The figure spoke again. "Katherine Plantagenet!"

He saw the silhouette of his daughter freeze in place, then slowly turn.

And then the voice came again. "Where goes my bride-to-be? I thought we were getting along so famously!"

With that, Alejandro saw her turn again and dash toward the entry to the Hundred Steps. Her pursuer lunged forward and grabbed her by the hem of the white cloak, and she lurched backward, stumbling into him.

"No!" she cried. She turned and hit at him with her fists. "You shall not have me again!"

Alejandro saw her reach down and pull something from her ankle; he was still too many steps away when she began to stab at Benoit. He saw Benoit clutch briefly at his arm. And then Alejandro heard the scrape of the sword against its scabbard.

He pulled off his devil's cloak and rushed forward, throwing the massive garment over Benoit from behind. It settled over him like a shroud. Benoit struggled to throw it off but was soon completely entangled in the folds. He fell to the ground, thrashing and writhing. Alejandro bent over him for one moment and spit on him.

Then he turned and ran toward the Hundred Steps; Kate was already well on her way down when he finally reached the entry. He counted each touch of his toes in the darkness as he made his way down, but quickly lost count in his effort not to trip. It seemed an hour before he placed his foot down and felt level ground.

He ran to the right, as Kate had told him to do; panic began to take hold when he did not see her. The dip in the wall was where she said it would be; he put one leg over the jagged rocks and seated himself on them. Down below he could see the white cloak, which she had left behind; it made a target toward which he could leap.

Twice my height! It sounded easier when spoken than it seemed on seeing it. Nevertheless, Alejandro leaped; it seemed an eternity before his feet hit the earth again. He tumbled forward in a hard somersault. Somehow he managed to pick himself up off the ground, and he ran forward into the night, hoping that God had not set any trees in his immediate path, for he would be hard-pressed to see them. He was ten steps beyond his landing place when he heard a commotion from above. As the noise grew louder, he turned and looked back. He saw no soldiers but knew it would only be a matter of seconds until they were there. He plunged through the darkness; soon he was running up the hill toward the apple tree; in the dark, in silhouette against the tree trunk, he saw Kate.

They clutched each other in a short embrace, and then Alejandro took hold of her hand. "Follow me," he said. "The horse is not far."

They ran again, both panting hard, until they reached the horse. Alejandro quickly mounted, then reached down and pulled Kate up behind him. With her arms around his waist, he heeled the horse hard, and they rode off into the night.

Twenty-two

James found Janie in the kitchen early the next morning.

"Breakfast will be in just a few minutes," she said. "I made oatmeal."

"That'll be great. Thanks." He let a moment pass. "How are you doing today?"

"Getting by," Janie said. "But just barely."

"I expect that's all you'll do for a while, at least until Tom's up and around," he said.

"That situation will present a few challenges too," she said. "He'll have to learn to live in a whole new way."

James was quiet for a moment before saying, "I want you to know how sorry I am. It all happened so fast, there wasn't anything anyone could do."

She looked directly at him. "I know that. I mean, it was all just an unfortunate series of events...nature's way." She pointed at his wrist. "If that cut had been just a little bit deeper, nature might have had her way even worse with you, you know."

He raised his wrist and regarded it for a moment. "Gravity still works, I guess. Wish everything else did too. I was hoping you could take a look at it. It's a little sore today."

She set down the wood spoon she'd been using to stir the oatmeal. "No time like the present. I'll be right back."

She returned in a few moments with a bottle of home-distilled grain alcohol and a pair of small scissors.

"Give me your arm."

He complied. She removed the wrapping from his injury. It was red along the stitch line but otherwise clean and healing. "Looks great," she said. "It would probably look neater if I hadn't been so upset when I sewed you up."

"I don't think my prospects will be ruined."

Janie managed a smile. "Probably not. This might smart a little." She swabbed the scab on James's arm with alcohol to clean off the coagulated blood; he winced as the liquid penetrated his skin. She examined the wound closely. "No infection, thank God. I think we can take out the stitches."

"Good. It's really starting to itch."

"That's a good sign. It means it's healing well."

"When can I start to use it again—I mean, for something other than holding a spoon?"

"Anytime now. But if you're going to do something strenuous, we should put some sort of a brace on it to hold the seam together. It's pretty well healed, but if you pull too much on it, it might split. What were you thinking of doing?"

"I was going to go up on your windmill and see if I can put one of the cells in place." He paused, and then said, "That's why we went out there in the first place. It wouldn't be fitting not to see it through. After what happened to Tom, I mean."

For a moment, Janie looked at him without saying anything. Then, "You're right. It wouldn't be fitting," she agreed.

James rubbed the scar on his wrist and then held out his arm again. "So I guess you better brace me up."

·   ·   ·

Janie, Evan, and Alex stood at the base of the windmill and watched with their hearts in their throats as James attached and positioned one of the cell units. He wired it into the windmill's power and then made the climb back down, slowly and carefully, favoring his injured arm as he descended.

Alex stood with his back against his mother's legs; she could feel him trembling and wondered if he was reliving what happened with Tom.

He has to live in the world, she told herself. *Bad things happen, just like they happened in Alejandro's first world.*

As James set his foot back on terra firma, there was an audible sigh of relief. Evan took his equipment bag and said, "Mission accomplished?"

"Yes, sir," James answered. "At least on this end. Now let's just hope we can line it up with the one at the end of the lake. I got a pretty good view of it from up there and I think it's pointed correctly. But we won't be able to tell until we get the other cells in place."

They walked back along the path to the compound. Lany was tightening the string on her bow in the main room when Janie found her.

"You have a fine son," Janie said to her. "He's terrific." She sat down on the bench. "I don't know if you noticed, but Kristina seems to think so too. It's so good for her right now to have someone to talk to."

"It's good for Evan too," Lany said. She chuckled a little and said, "Maybe we should just arrange a marriage."

"Sounds like a plan," Janie said. "I know you're joking, but it's not so far-fetched these days, is it? I'm guessing her father will approve."

Lany set down her bow and looked at Janie. "Speaking of which . . . Evan said he had a pretty serious talk with her the other night."

"Oh? About anything in particular?"

In a calm and even voice, Lany replied, "About how she was, uh, 'adopted.' "

Somehow Janie managed to maintain her composure. "Ah. Yes. Adopted."

"Quite a story. Almost sounds like it couldn't be true."

Quietly, Janie said, "It does, doesn't it?" She let out a long breath. "But it's real, all right."

"You repeated yourself to her when you sent her for the sugar test strips. That was so she wouldn't forget, wasn't it?"

"Yes."

"So there were some—ramifications, I guess, with the process."

Janie did not speak immediately; she spent a few moments considering Lany's statement so she could give a completely accurate response. "There might be, but we don't know that for sure. The one ramification I can be sure about is that every genetic problem the original suffered from, the copy will also suffer. Her original had an aneurysm when she was just a girl—and died in surgery. The same blood-vessel flaw showed up in the second coming. Kristina underwent surgery to correct it before it could become a problem again. It was the surgery—not the process of creating her all over again—that caused her problem. So there may be ramifications, but we haven't seen them yet."

"Hmm," Lany said. She paused for a second, and then said, almost casually, "She also told him about Alex."

Janie felt herself stiffen. Anger at Kristina surged through her but passed when she thought about how it must feel to be different in that way. Evan, and now Lany, were the first ones outside their "family" to know.

"Were you already pregnant when you got here?"

"No."

"So you did the entire process here?"

"We did. But please," she said, "don't say anything to anyone else. Alex doesn't know yet."

Lany's eyebrows arched, creating an expression that said *Don't you think it's about time to tell him?* "To have that capability..." She leaned the restrung bow against the table. "Very exciting, but also pretty scary. Lots of responsibility. And lots of possibilities. For instance, why haven't you cloned one of the cows who lived through DR SAM, or whatever the cow version was?"

"We've talked about it, but you know what—the process is so

complicated that with animals it's just easier to let them do it the natural way."

"Too much bother?" Lany said, almost snidely.

Janie stared at her for a moment. After a while she said, "We haven't misused it."

The look she got back said *Oh, haven't you?* The words were less damning. "I won't say anything. I'm not sure anyone would believe it, anyway."

"But you do."

"Yes, I do. But only because I can't imagine why anyone would make up something like that."

The night before they were to depart to return to Orange, Evan sought out his mother. He found her in the barn, checking the shoes on one of their horses.

Lany recognized the look on his face instantly. "You want to talk about something?" she said.

"Yeah. But promise you won't get upset."

"I can't promise that until you say what you have to say."

"Well, at least try."

"Out with it, Evan."

He complied. "I think I should stay here for a while." On seeing her sharp look, he added, "You know, to help them until they get used to Tom's situation."

Lany set down the horse's foot. "That's very admirable."

"You can get by without me for a while in Orange, right?"

"Of course we can, but everyone else will have to pick up some of your responsibilities. And I'll miss you. How long were you thinking of staying here?"

"I don't know. I guess I could just see how things go."

"It might be a long time until everything falls into place, son. Things will probably never be the same here again."

She set down her shoeing hammer and faced her son full-on with her arms crossed in front of her. "This is about Kristina, isn't it?"

He lowered his gaze and nodded. "I really like her, Mom. I want to spend more time with her. I never had a *real* girlfriend."

"How does she feel about you?"

"The same, I think."

Lany faced her son—a man, all of a sudden. "You know something?" she said. "Before we moved east I used to worry about girls—they always seemed to be all over you, you're so cute and smart and nice. I was so afraid some girl would entice you and I'd be a grandmother before my time. But since we came to Orange, well... I worried that you'd never find someone at all, because there just wasn't anyone available. I think it's really sweet that you like each other so much."

He beamed. "It really makes me feel good to be around her."

"That's great. That's just how it should start."

She slipped her arm inside his and led him out into the starry night "But I need to say something, before you get too involved. Take it really slow, for both of your sakes. Back in the world before, it was a lot easier to get into and out of a relationship, because we didn't have to depend on continuity as much as we do now. Things were much more mutable then. If someone went out of your life, it was painful for a while, but no big deal in the long run—there were other people to depend on, other prospects for romance. Just think for a minute about how much everyone here depended on Tom. His injury leaves a big hole. If you enter into a relationship with Kristina, you're essentially forming an alliance with her, and that implies interdependence. It's a big responsibility, especially in view of what she's been through recently."

"I know that."

"I'm just saying don't do anything like this lightly."

He stopped walking and turned to her. "Mom, I don't think I'll ever do anything lightly again."

It made Lany sad to hear that. She took Evan's blunt statement of his truth as her cue to say nothing more.

.   .   .

They all met the next morning in the main room over a breakfast of bacon, eggs, and flat bread.

"Well," Michael said, "it's been quite a visit, I should say. Not what you expected when you agreed to this exchange, I'm guessing."

"To tell you the truth, we had no idea what to expect," Lany said. "But we really hope that when you come to see us, things will go a little smoother."

"Amen to that," Janie said. She put her arm around Alex's shoulder and pulled him closer, then glanced at Lany. "I can't thank you enough for the way you took care of Tom."

"I wish I could have done better."

"You did as well as anyone could have."

Everyone was quiet for a moment. James finally broke the melancholy. "So," he said, "when should we expect you?"

Janie hesitated at first. "Two weeks or thereabouts," she said finally. "That'll give us some time to reorganize things around here so Tom can be without me while I'm there." She looked at Evan and smiled. "Having Evan is going to help a lot."

"That timing should work out well," James said. "It'll give me a chance to get out to the other cell tower at the end of the lake after we get back. I'll make the adjustments in the positioning and try to get a small network up and running between us and that tower."

"Be careful," Janie said.

"I will, I promise. Now, I don't want to get anyone's hopes up too much, but you should probably set up your computer and leave it on all the time. Make sure the wireless receiver is enabled. We have an old server; I'll set it up as *orangecommunity.net*. What do you want for your e-mail name?"

She thought for a moment. "How about *doc@orangecommunity.net*?"

"You got it. Set up your e-mail client for that address and for automatic receiving. Once in a while you should check it to see if a message has come in."

"I'll set it to chime."

"Perfect."

"You really think this can work?"

James smiled. "Send out your most hopeful vibes. Maybe that's all it'll take." He pushed away from the table and stood. "Well, we should head out."

"I'll be right along," Lany said. Everyone else drifted out of the room, leaving Janie and Lany alone together.

"I don't suppose you happen to have any condoms here," Lany said.

"Fresh out."

"Damn."

"I could probably put together something that would act like a diaphragm, but I don't know how effective it would be. I did tops, not bottoms, in my practice. But I'll have the talk with Kristina, and I'll make sure she starts taking her temperature, so she'll at least have an idea of when she's fertile."

The two women sat quietly for a few moments, each one experiencing her private concerns.

Kristina isn't even my own daughter. But she's Tom's daughter, and I'm Tom's wife. There was a sacred trust, one she would never willingly violate.

Alejandro had taken on someone else's daughter and raised her brilliantly in times that were just as hostile, if not more so.

Janie looked at Lany and said, "Who knows, we may end up being related."

Lany smiled. "Hey, we already rhyme, so why not?" She stood and gave Janie a surprising hug. "Take good care of my son, will you?"

"Count on it."

That afternoon Janie set her e-mail client for the recipient *doc@orange community.net*. It seemed an exercise in futility. *I suppose we can all dream*, she thought sadly.

It was four nights before Evan made his way into Kristina's bed. Janie went to sleep that night wondering how Tom would feel about such an event when he learned. She did not allow herself to consider that if Tom hadn't been injured, Evan would not be here and there would be no issue about a young man sharing his daughter. The people of

Orange would have left days ago, Evan among them, to await the exchange visit from Janie and Kristina. But things had not worked out that way.

She floated in and out of thin sleep, trying as she did every night but failing as always to adjust to sleeping on the small cot while Tom's stump healed. Her husband was morose, which was only to be expected, but his withdrawal still stung her torn heart like the alcohol she'd poured on James's wrist. The sanctuary of their shared bed seemed so distant; in its place was a cold void, a teasing reminder of what had been. She dreamed, half awake, half asleep, of eagles in perfect soaring flight, of nests silhouetted against a dark and angry sky. What if Tom had turned in time to see the bird approach and had managed to climb down, maybe only a few feet, so the bird hadn't felt so threatened. . . .

What if, what if, what if . . .

She was interrupted in mid-dream by the sound of a chime.

To: doc@orangecommunity.net

From: cop@orangecommunity.net

This is a test. Greetings from the People's Republic of Orange. And when you see my handsome son, tell him his mother loves him.

Janie turned around and saw everyone in the compound assembled at the door of the lab. They'd all awakened at the beloved and sorely missed electronic sound. Janie smiled at everyone, then looked at Evan and said, "Your mother loves you."

Michael was the first to step forward. He stood behind Janie and looked at the computer screen in disbelief. "Bloody hell," he said. "Is that really an e-mail message?"

"Unless we're all dreaming," Janie said.

She wanted to go wake Tom and say, *See? You did it.*

"Can we send one back?" Caroline asked.

"I don't see why not," Janie said. "That's the whole point."

She opened a new message window and typed in the address.

"Wow, this feels so good. . . . I forgot what it was like to do this. What do you all want to say?"

No one said anything for a moment, until Alex said, "Tell them we can't wait to visit them."

Janie dutifully typed his sentiment. "Anyone else?"

Caroline said, "Ask them if we can borrow that book about cheese that Michael told me about."

Janie's fingers clicked away. "Done."

Evan said, "Tell my mother I love her too."

The text was many lines long by the time they'd all made their contributions. Janie queued the message and then clicked *Send*. In an instant, the message disappeared. A small window came up on the screen: *Message sent successfully.*

Everyone cheered. Over the next few days, jokes and recipes climbed down and around the mountain as if e-mail had never been interrupted. Aches and pains were described, to prepare the traveling doctor for the patients she would see when she arrived in Orange. A new rhythm took hold in their lives; the pace seemed to quicken.

Now and again, an e-mail came from an unknown address. When Janie dared to open them, they all seemed to contain one version or another of the same basic message:

Is anyone out there? We're friendly.

There was no doubt about it, humanity was reorganizing after the plague. These random messages from would-be allies became the subject of heated dinner-table debates. Michael was all for going out into the world to explore. Carolyn wanted to hunker down in the safety of their compound. Terry and Elaine were eager to see if anyone had any remedies for the Alzheimer's disease that had so ravaged her mother, so they were all for reaching out.

But Janie wasn't ready for anything beyond Orange until Tom was up and around and beginning to function again. Michael had made him a good pair of crutches, and he was doing well with them, but it would be a very long time before she would feel comfortable leaving him for more than the few days of her "rotation."

So she threw herself into Alex's medical education, much in the way that Alejandro had thrown himself into a translation of the alchemy manuscript while he was separated from Kate the first time. It passed the time productively as the day of their departure for Orange approached. One afternoon, as they were going over a section on the skeleton in *Gray's Anatomy*, the chime sounded.

Alex looked up from the text. "Can I open it, Mom?"

The excitement in his voice was heartening.

"Go ahead," she said.

He ran off, smiling, and came back very shortly with his report. "It's from Lany," he told his mother. "It's pretty long."

Janie got up from her seat and went into the lab.

If you can think of any questions you need to ask before you visit, please let us know. You know what medicines we have....

The rest of the message was filled with administrative minutiae, until the last line:

And, Janie, remember to tell Alex how special he is!

Innocent enough; even Alex could read it without understanding the meaning behind it.

She sat back in the chair and considered what she ought to do.

Tom always maintained that Alex should be older before they told him of how he came about. It would be a strange conversation at best, perhaps quite difficult, depending on his reaction.

Now the time had come. She would leave the compound to go to Orange and Alex would stay behind. Tom was doing well, but the possibility of an infection in his stump was something they would have to live with forever. If something were to happen to her on the journey, Tom would have to tell Alex. And if for some reason he didn't, and the worst came to pass . . .

"Mom?" he said, interrupting her thoughts. "Are we done?"

He'd recognized her distraction.

"Yeah, for the moment."

He ran off to play.

. . .

Tom was in the kitchen, removing the boot from his left foot after a walk around the courtyard, when she found him.

"How's it feeling?"

He sighed. "The stump? Pretty good. But the leg you took off hurts like hell."

The leg you took off. She wished he wouldn't say it that way. "Phantom pain," she said. "A common aftereffect of an amputation. I'm sorry."

"Not your fault," he said. There was a bitterness in his voice. She understood that he probably thought it was a little bit her fault, but she forgave him. Forgiveness was becoming a daily exercise in their relationship for her, just as walking around the courtyard was for Tom.

"Will you be okay while I'm in Orange?"

"Yeah, I think so."

"You're doing really well, Tom. I admire the way you're working at it."

"Do I have a choice?"

She didn't answer that question. After a moment to gather her strength, she said, "I want to tell Alex before I go."

She didn't have to explain what she wanted to tell the boy. She steeled herself for an argument as Tom mulled over her announcement. She was surprised when he said, "Okay. But you do it. I don't think I can handle it right now."

"Fair enough," she said. She came over to Tom's chair and kissed him on the forehead. He didn't react.

Janie stepped back and looked at her husband. "Please," she said after a moment, "don't push me away. I'm your best friend, and you're mine. We need each other."

Tom would not meet her eyes. "You need me like you need a hole in the head," he said. "I'm perfectly useless."

"Only until you're healed."

"Right. And then I'll be half useless."

"Stop it."

Now he looked at her. "Stop what? Thinking about what a burden I'm going to be to you and the others for the rest of my life?"

"Tom, don't—"

He stared hard at her. "I wish I'd had the chance to tell you the same thing."

She was confused. "I don't understand what you mean...."

"I wish I could have told you *don't* before you took off my leg."

For a moment, Janie was speechless. "You would have died if I hadn't taken it off."

"That should have been my choice."

"Oh, for the love of God..."

"You should have left it all in God's hands, where it belonged." He gestured at his stump. "Look at me. I can't walk, I can't carry anything, I can't even take a piss without making a mess because I can't balance."

"And you're blaming me for all this?"

"I'm just saying, maybe my leg would have healed."

"You don't know what you're talking about. I'm the doctor here—"

"And the Indian chief, the way you're making decisions. I guess I'm just the lawyer."

She was so hurt she could barely speak. She lashed out in anger. "Yeah. And right about now, you're acting like one. Arguing a ridiculous case, knowing full well that everything you're putting forth is bullshit. But you're putting it forth anyway, because it's all you've got to justify the way you're acting."

"It's not bullshit. And you had my *son* help you do it. What was *that* all about?"

"He's my son too, and I didn't *have* him help, I *let* him, because he asked to. And that was a good thing, because now he has a stake in your recovery. Just like I do." She turned and stomped off to the door, but before leaving the room, she turned back. "*You're* the only one now who doesn't."

Janie dashed past everyone in the house and went outside to the barn. She stood between the two cows, one hand on each of their tall shoulders, and watched them chew their cud peacefully, hoping some of that peace would rub off on her tattered psyche. After a while, the smell of the straw and the warmth of the cows worked a kind of magic on her, and she was able to focus again on what lay before her. The most important thing she had to do before leaving for Orange—which was now looking like a vacation to paradise—was to speak with Alex.

She found him a few minutes later playing his one permitted weekly game of Civilization on the computer, at a time when the children would ordinarily have been working on math. He gave her a curious look when she entered his room, and she realized that the vestige of hurt must still be on her face.

She willed it away. "Where's Kristina?"

"I don't know, but I think she's probably with Evan."

"Ah. I see."

"She *likes* him."

That matter-of-fact assessment brought Janie a much-needed bit of amusement. "You think so, huh?"

"Yeah. Since he got here, she's been with him whenever she can."

Janie sat down next to Alex. "You and Sarah are used to having her all to yourselves," she said. "Does it bother you that Evan's here?"

Alex thought about it for a moment. "Not really."

"You're sure? If you want, I could talk to her about it."

He tapped a couple of keys and answered absently, as if he were barely hearing what she had to say. "You don't have to. It's okay."

A face popped up on the game screen.

Monitoring Alex's computer games had been Tom's responsibility. Until he was ready to take that on again, she would have to pay attention.

"Who's that?" she asked.

"My military adviser."

Janie looked closer; the digital figure appeared to have stepped out of the Middle Ages. He wore a silver-colored close-fitting helmet, and said, in a British accent, *"France is now cautious of you."*

"Oh, great," Alex said unhappily. "A few minutes ago they were polite."

"Does this adviser tell you every time there's a change in attitude?"

"Yeah. They can be gracious, polite, cautious, annoyed, or furious." He clicked on the adviser's image; the head shrank rapidly and disappeared.

"What makes them change how they feel about you?"

"I don't know what it is each time. But it could be that one of my battleships met up with one of their submarines, so I wouldn't see them, but they'd see me and get mad."

DEFCON 2 to DEFCON 3, she thought. *None of us ever knew when it happened, but it did regularly in the time before. At least in this game, they give you a hint.* "Do you have spies that tell you what's happening?"

"Yeah, if I pay them. It costs a lot of gold to have a spy."

No surprise there. "What kind of information do they get for you?"

"Oh," he said absently as he tapped the keys, "they tell me about how many soldiers they have, where they are, and what kinds of weapons the other guys have...."

"Wow, that's a lot to absorb."

"Lots of times I forget what they have and then I get in trouble. I wish I could write it down." He glanced at his chalkboard longingly.

"We're leaving in a couple of days for Orange," she said.

Alex turned away from the screen and gave her his attention. "Can I go, *please*?"

"No."

"But I won't be able to have any doctor lessons."

"We'll double up when I get back. And I'll be checking on your progress by e-mail. I'm going to leave you some homework. And you'll be very safe here with everyone until then."

"Will *you* be safe out there?" he asked. His voice seemed suddenly small. She saw the worried look on his face. A few scabs remained from his night of running through the forest, but they were healing well, and Janie doubted he would have any scars.

At least none on the outside.

She hugged his shoulders. "Yes, I will. This is a different kind of trip than the one you went on to get the cells. All roads, no forest. Much safer. We can make it in less than one day."

And now, she thought, *I guess it's time to let him know how special he is.*

She let go of him and said, "There's something I want to talk to you about, something about you that's really neat."

He perked up instantly. "What?"

All the careful phrases she'd stored up for the occasion simply vanished. She'd come up with hundreds of psychologically correct euphemisms for *clone* in the seven years she'd had to think about it, but now, with the child in front of her, eager to learn and understand, she'd forgotten every one.

She swallowed hard and said, "This isn't the first time you've lived."

Alex saved his Civilization game and moved completely away from the computer. Janie welcomed him into her arms as he climbed, unbidden, onto her lap.

"I lived before?"

She took a deep breath and plunged feetfirst into the treacherous waters of truth. "Yes. You did. You were brought into *this* world by means of nuclear transference, which means that the nucleus from a cell in your first body—which carries all the genetic material that makes you who you are—was transferred into one of my egg cells. The nucleus was already removed from that egg cell. Then all of it was implanted in my body so I could be your mother, because I wanted to be."

For a moment, Alex remained silent as he considered the implications of this news. Janie bit her lower lip to keep quiet. *Let him ask questions*, she reminded herself. There were bound to be plenty of them.

The first was startlingly simple and insightful. "How long ago, I mean, did I live, before?"

"Almost seven hundred years ago."

He didn't say *cool* or *wow* or *really*; he just let out a long *whew* before asking, "How old was I?"

That one proved more difficult to answer. At what point in his life? Did he want to know how long he'd lived the first time around, or something less finite? She did not want to reveal the age or manner of the first iteration's death to the second iteration. "Well," she began, "of course you were a little boy for the normal time that people are little. And then you were a teenager, but I think in those days it meant something different to be a teenager than it does now. After that, you grew up to be a man. A very good man."

Somehow, the skewed reply satisfied him. "How was I good?"

"In the same way you're good now. You were kind and generous and brave and smart and ... well, you were just very, very decent."

His face began to brighten, and Janie felt encouraged. She continued her explanation with some of her own fears resolved. "You were born sometime around 1325 in Spain," she said, "in a little town called Cervere. Your name was Alejandro Canches."

"Alejandro Canches," he whispered reverently. "Is that why you named me Alex?"

"Yes."

"Who were my mother and father?"

"Your father's name was Avram. Your mother ..." For a moment, Janie was stumped. "I don't know," she finally admitted. "You never—I mean, there was nothing about her in what I read."

Alex looked as if he were about to speak, then he abruptly stopped. "Where did you read about me?"

Janie knew she couldn't tell him the whole truth; he would want to read the journal. He was still too young to learn all the details of his previous life—his hardships and losses, the long separations from loved ones that he suffered, the terrible crimes he committed in order to preserve himself and the people he loved. She simply said, "In an old book. I thought you were a fascinating person. Someone I knew in the time before had a piece of your hair and a flake of your skin. She gave them to me and I used them to get the material I needed for the nuclear transference."

He brightened with excitement. "What did I do when I grew up?"

"You were a physician."

He clapped his hands spontaneously. "Like I'm going to be again!"

"Yes." She was gladdened by his exuberance. "But medicine was different then than it is now. You went to medical school in France, in a city called Montpellier. You studied under some very famous teachers, one named de Chauliac. He was the physician to two popes, and he lived in Avignon, as you did for a while. He eventually became your best friend, like Sarah is now."

As you did, as you do, as you are, as you were... Phrasing was suddenly an immense challenge.

But not to Alex; he was crystal clear on the matter of his own continuity.

"Did *I* know the popes too?"

"Not really, I don't think." She was about to say, *You didn't write anything about meeting with them directly,* but contained it.

Alex jumped off her lap and went straight to the computer. He brought up a mapping program and went to the section for Europe.

"How do you spell Cervere?" he asked.

Janie spelled it aloud, and Alex searched the program for that town.

"Here it is!" he proclaimed enthusiastically. They looked at the map together for a few moments. "What was the other place?"

"Avignon," she said, after which she spelled it. She traced a path between the two places with the tip of her finger. "You made a journey along this route, from Cervere to Avignon."

"It's in France," he said.

"Yes. You spoke French. But you also spoke a lot of other languages. In those days people had to do that because they traded with people in other countries."

"What languages did I speak?"

"Latin, because that was the language people learned in—you spent a lot of your life learning. And Hebrew, because that was the language your parents spoke. You spoke English at a time when it was just becoming popular as a language. It's different than it is now, but it's the same language."

"Different, how?"

"Well, languages change over time."

"Why?"

Oh, God, why indeed? "Here, let me show you an example. Where's the CD that has the classics of literature on it?"

He stood on his chair and poked around on the shelf above the computer, eventually drawing out the requested disk. When it was up and running, Janie searched out *The Canterbury Tales.*

"Here, take a look at this," she said.

With us ther was a doctour of phisik; In al this world ne was the noon hym lik, To speke of phisik and of surgerye . . .

He struggled to read the unfamiliar words aloud.

"That's English, from Alejandro's time. The writer is talking about a doctor."

He thought but did not say: *Who tells a tale about a knight who kills his daughter rather than allow her to be married to a man who would destroy her spirit. . . .*

"It doesn't sound like English."

"It is. Languages grow over time. And you know what else? You knew the man who wrote these words. His name was Geoffrey Chaucer."

"No way!"

"It's true."

Alex disappeared into himself for a few moments, as if he were considering the ramifications of what his mother had just told him. When he spoke again, his tone was more somber. "Why don't I remember anything about it?"

This was a question she hadn't considered.

"I don't really know, Alex. You're still very young." She thought about Kristina, who had no memories of her previous iteration at all.

But her son didn't seem unhappy with her vague answer. His face brightened. "Wow," he said. "I lived *before.*"

They'd watered the animals well before departing for Orange and expected they would make the trip without having to stop, but the day was warm for spring, and when they passed close to a stream about two hours into the journey, Jellybean headed straight for it.

"Let's make a quick stop," Janie suggested. "I could use a minute in the bushes, anyway."

James and Evan brought the horses to the edge of the water; Janie and Kristina went into the brush in separate directions.

Janie found a secluded spot and looked around carefully. As she was undoing her button she thought, *What an idiot you are, Crowe. Like anyone would be out here to see you pee.* She dropped her drawers and assumed the position.

A twig cracked as she did her business. The sound came from her left; the horses and the others were off to her right. She froze with her pants still down. Her spine began to tingle, but she remained motionless. After a minute, her thighs began to ache and she rose up.

The zipper made too much noise; she'd just finished rebuttoning when there was another crack, closer, still to the left. She turned and faced in that direction. Crouching down—*It's harder to hit a small target,* Michael had once told her—she peered through the brush. Slowly and carefully, she inched up her pants leg and grasped the knife, though her hand was trembling.

She heard a hiss and hoped that the others had heard it, but knew they were probably out of earshot. Knife in hand, she stood, easing her way to vertical over the course of many seconds. *Now turn, walk away slowly, escape....*

But it was too late. She was alone, separated from the herd for the inconsequential reason of modesty. The cougar made a throaty, almost monkey-sounding howl and bounded in her direction, with claws outstretched and teeth bared. The velocity with which the cat soared through the air astonished her as she watched, nearly frozen. Janie shrieked once in fear, then instinct took over. She thrust out her arm as far and as firmly as she could as the cat closed the last few feet between them. Her knife caught the leaping feline in the throat; it gurgled in wild pain, but its momentum was barely lessened. When the leaden weight of the animal landed on her chest, its claws ripped right through her jacket and shirt, tearing open the skin of her shoulder. She felt the pain and understood in some deeply primal place that she was wounded, though probably not badly. The weight of the cat dragged her arm down and the rest of her with it; as she tumbled to the ground, she turned her head just enough to see Evan and Kristina tearing through the woods in her direction. Evan had something in his hand, though she couldn't see what. She heard a sharp, loud crack and saw the cat go totally limp.

Through the haze of her shock, she heard Kristina asking, *Janie, are you all right?* Evan's voice, also in a thick fog, was spewing out vilifications to the dead cat. Off in the distance she heard the nervous whinnies of their horses as they pranced in fear. Janie was aware of breathing, then exhaling, then trembling. Welcome hands drew her upright.

As if in a trance, she walked through the woods with Evan and Kristina on either side supporting her by the arms. Three steps shy of Jellybean, she doubled over and vomited.

"That's good," Kristina said, rubbing circles on Janie's back. "You'll feel better now."

Evan held an open canteen in front of her. "Here. Take a drink."

She drank and then spat out the bitter taste of terror that coated the inside of her mouth. Then she pulled her shirt aside and looked at the cat-scratch wound. "I'm all right," she said. She touched the red rips in her skin; they didn't hurt much yet. Later would be another matter. "At least I think I am." She looked back into the woods in the direction of the incident. "Let's get out of here."

Once she was up on Jellybean's back, she pulled back her clothes and tried to look at her shoulder again. Blood oozed from the scratches; she opened their medical-supply case and took out the bottle of alcohol. With the hem of her shirt, she dabbed the stinging disinfectant on the rips in her flesh, wincing as the cold alcohol hit the cuts.

To Evan's and Kristina's worried looks, she said, "I'll live." She pointed to the carcass draped over the back of Evan's saddle. "But that guy's my next hat."

"Big cat," Kristina said. "My God, Janie, he could have really hurt you."

"Or worse," Janie said. She looked closer; the cat was a female, with pendulous teats. Somewhere in the forest, cougar kittens would starve, but that was the natural order of things.

Without that knife, Janie thought, *I would be cat food right now.* "Maybe we should just leave her here."

"That's up to you," Evan said. "But it's a nice piece of fur. I'll skin her for you."

She reached for the reins and winced at the pain it caused. "I think I'd probably enjoy doing that myself," Janie said. "But, okay, you can skin her."

They went back out to the dirt shoulder and were quickly on their way to Orange again. Their pace was quite a bit faster.

That afternoon, as Janie tended to her wound, Kristina set up her small pharmacy and began taking blood samples from everyone in Orange.

When Janie found her, she was just finishing the task of organizing the vials in a leather case.

"You'll have some lab work to do when we get back," Janie said.

Assuming you go back with me, Janie thought as she watched Kristina leave the room in search of Evan. Once again, she wondered what Tom was thinking of all this. They hadn't spoken much before she left; the effects of their heated exchange lingered. And when they did speak, he hadn't mentioned Evan.

"You'll get over it," she whispered aloud. "And everything else too."

"What?"

She turned to see Lany standing in the doorway.

"Oh, I was just muttering to myself."

"You do that too, huh?"

"It's age," Janie said to the woman, who was younger than she, but not by all that much. "This is what you have to look forward to."

"As long as I keep having *something* to look forward to," Lany said. They chatted amicably for a few moments about this and that, until one of the Orange children interrupted them.

"There's e-mail," the little boy said.

"Probably from Alex," Janie said. "I told him he could write to me while I'm here."

But when they got to the computer, the return address was not the familiar *doc@orangecommunity.net*.

From: director@doubledelta32.org

Janie looked closer, her eyes narrowing as she read the message address.

To: cop@orangecommunity.net

"How did he—they—whoever—get this address?"

Evan arrived with Kristina, just in time to hear the question. "They send out electronic feelers, basically," he said. "They mine addresses, literally from the airwaves. We're wireless, so anyone who can hone in on the signal can pick up what's being said, if we don't encrypt it."

"Maybe we shouldn't read any of them," Kristina said. "If we just ignore them..."

"I think we should read them," Lany said. "*Know thine enemy* still means something. But if I had to guess, I'd say these aren't enemies. So..."

She clicked on the message with the mouse; it opened. She leaned closer and read each word carefully. Everyone waited eagerly for her report on the content, to see if it was, as they all feared, an electronic version of Pandora's box.

"This is really strange," she said when she finished reading. "We're being invited to a meeting of 'double deltas,' whatever that means."

She turned and looked at the gathered listeners. "Does anyone know what double deltas are?"

For a moment no one said anything, until Kristina said, "I do."

All eyes were upon her, expectantly.

"I think I'd like to sit down for this," she said.

Twenty-three

Elizabeth of Ulster bypassed her ineffectual husband, Prince Lionel, and went straight to her father-in-law with a report of what she saw. With a few graciously tendered excuses, the king slipped away and retired to his private chamber, where he flew into a raging diatribe. The brunt of this verbiage was heaped on Sir John Chandos, who now kneeled before his liege, having just delivered the news of Benoit's embarrassment and de Coucy's resulting outrage.

"He made such vile threats against your daughter, sire, as one cannot imagine."

"He has only spoken what is in my own heart!" the king roared. "Find them!" He pounded his fist on the table; the windows rattled.

Sir John rose up. "A thorough job of searching the grounds has already been done, my lord. We did not find your daughter here."

The king shot him a hard glance in response to the unwelcome reminder that he was now legally Kate's parent. "As you suspected?"

"I believe, sire," Chandos continued, "that she has gone into the countryside with the Jew. She knows the grounds well, and she is far too clever to remain here."

The king said nothing, but with terrifying quickness he picked up a carved ornamental figure and threw it through the window. As glass tinkled to the ground outside, he boomed, "De Coucy must not have a reason to sever ties with us! An ally with such lands must be retained at all costs."

With astonishing calm, Sir John said, "It would be a foolish move on his part to do such a thing. To forgo a kingdom over a relative's embarrassment—a vile and revolting relative at that—it is simply not sensible. He may use this incident, however, to extract a better dowry from you. One ought to consider that perhaps he has even set these events in place himself in order to—"

"He's been given dowry enough for twelve brides! And he is not clever enough to think of such a convoluted plot. No, it is all her doing—she must be found and brought back. Then I shall deliver her to *de Coucy* instead of Benoit—to be a scullery maid for her sister's kitchen. Now go, and bring her back."

"We will not find her tonight, sire. Tomorrow we can take out a proper party and—"

"Gather the best trackers in the kingdom and set them on her trail. The dogs can search in the night!"

"But we without keen noses cannot follow. We will find her tomorrow, of that I am sure."

"Those who keep the May might have seen them—you can enlist their help. Go out into the villages and roust out everyone who spent this night in Maying. Threaten them all with troubles if they do not cooperate."

"Begging your pardon, sire, but I must disabuse you of the notion that those who keep the May will make themselves your allies."

The king glared at him. "All Englishmen are my allies, if they wish to prosper."

Sir John nodded. "That said, sire, I am sure you realize that among your guests tonight are a number of lords—all of whom profess sincere loyalty to you, one cannot help but say—who would much prefer to be out in the countryside, ensuring the survival of humankind by coupling with each and every Maid of the May he could find, were he not obliged to be here tonight to celebrate your daughter's eventual coupling." He made a sly smile. "Their wives, however, are forever your allies for commanding their husbands into unwilling faithfulness, which may prove to be more beneficial."

The king uttered an obscene curse under his breath. "Very well, go at first light. Take de Coucy and Benoit with you. I would not have either of them here to annoy me until this matter is resolved. Though I cannot fathom why de Coucy has such venom against her, perhaps it will satisfy his lust for retribution to join in the hunt."

He waved his knight off.

Sir John bowed, wondering in echo of his king why de Coucy should hate the young woman so. He told himself that it did not matter in the end, as he hurried out of the audience chamber to wake the master of the hounds.

North, she told him. *They will expect us to go south.* Reunited father and daughter hastened through the darkness, as fast as the horse would run. The lights of May bonfires could be seen here and there along the route; they rode past the pagan revelries and never stopped until finally they came to a small stream in a wooded place where the horse could rest and be watered. Alejandro dismounted first, then brought Kate down off their mount. With the immediate threat of capture behind them, they were free at last to embrace each other in the joy of their reunion.

When at last Alejandro was able to let her go, he said, "Did he harm you, daughter?"

She could not tell him the full extent of her encounter with Benoit; there would be time enough later. "My spirit was wounded," she said, "but you have restored it." Tears welled up in her eyes. "I am still not convinced that you are real," she said. "Can all this time have passed in separation, and now we are together again?"

Alejandro laughed with genuine joy. "I am real enough, and time has indeed passed. Very much time. I shall prove it to you tomorrow by showing you the gray in my hair."

"It will become you, I am sure."

"As womanhood becomes you." He lifted her off the ground, then spun her around, grinning with joy, until they were both dizzy and laughing.

When he set her down again, the youngest daughter of Edward Plantagenet looked into the eyes of the man who had lovingly raised her as his own child. "Seven years," she said.

"Nearly eight!"

"And now that we are together again I feel as if I saw you only yesterday and that we have never been apart! How can that be possible?"

Alejandro embraced her again, this time a ferocity that bordered on desperation. "I regret every day that we have missed. I should have come sooner. . . ."

She clung tightly to him. "I know you would have come sooner if you circumstances permitted." She pulled away slightly and said, "I fear almost to ask—what of my son? Is he sound and hale?"

"Oh, yes!" Alejandro cried. "Far more than that—I cannot properly describe his excellence. He has brought me nothing but joy and pride. He is quick-witted and polite, handsome, fair in his coloring, just like you and—"

He stopped abruptly. After a moment of silence, Kate finished the utterance for him.

"Like Guillaume Karle?" she said.

"Yes," Alejandro said, under his breath. "Like his father, whose name he bears. I thought it the proper name for him."

They stood in quiet remembrance of the good man who had touched their lives so deeply. When the time seemed proper, Kate glanced up at the sky and said, "Dawn is coming. We must ride now. There will be time to speak of my son later, when we are safe."

Alejandro nodded. They remounted and started off again. This time Alejandro turned the horse in an easterly direction. Kate stopped him.

"*Père*, I say again, it is not wise to head to the south or the east just now."

He brought the horse up short. "But we must go to Dover to cross."

"That is what they will expect us to do. Of course we should go that way eventually, but right now it would serve us well to be a bit more unpredictable. They will never think to look for us to the north."

"Why not?"

"Because we have no reason to go that way. There is plague in the north, and Chandos knows that I know it."

"Chandos..."

She hesitated slightly, then said, "The king trusts no other man more than Chandos. It will be he who comes out after us."

She saw the disappointment in Alejandro's expression and understood. Softly, she said, "His heart will not be in it, *Père*. But he is a loyal knight and will do what is asked of him."

"And your brother? Will he take part in the chase?"

"Perhaps," she said. "Not because he cares whether I am found or not—he has no great fondness for the affairs of state. But he is a warrior, albeit a bloated one of late. If he comes along, it will be for the thrill of the hunt itself, not because he has any great wish for me to return."

She said nothing for a moment. "But de Coucy is another matter. He will want vengeance for Benoit's humiliation, and if the feel of the tip of my knife remains in his memory, he will want to punish me, simply to satisfy his own pride."

With great defiance in his voice, Alejandro said, "Let him come. I will take his head, as he took Guillaume Karle's."

For a moment, each one wrestled with the memory of Karle's helmet tumbling to the ground with the head still inside it, while the body remained astride the horse.

Then Alejandro said, "The time for settling scores will come. Now is the time to be away from here."

They rode north through the woods at the swiftest pace they could manage. After a good stint of hard riding through the forest, they ventured out onto a road, which, by its width and wear, seemed relatively well traveled. Yet, as they continued, they saw that weeds and brush were beginning to encroach. After a time, they came upon a signpost.

The board was cracked and dry; all the lettering seemed to have been worn away.

At the bottom of the sign hung a tattered, faded flag. When they reached it, Alejandro took hold of the cloth and pulled it toward him, spreading it wide open. Within the folds, where it was not bleached by the sun, the cloth was dark gray.

Both knew what a black flag meant.

Alejandro said quietly, "Shall we proceed?"

"Yes," Kate replied.

Farther along, they came to a small abandoned village.

"They cannot all be gone to the celebrations," Kate said bitterly.

"No, daughter, I think not."

Alejandro dismounted in the village square and took the horse's reins in his hand. He walked about, leading the horse with Kate still astride. He stopped in front of a small cottage; its door was wide open, but no one was within.

He examined it quickly, then came back outside. "There should be peace in solitude of this sort, but my heart shivers with wondering what happened to the people who once lived here."

"I feel as though we are trespassing, though against whom, I cannot say," Kate said. "Let us be off again, *Père*; I care not for this place."

They continued on the same road out of the village; its condition worsened. Perhaps a half hour's ride farther, a small manor house came into view.

Alejandro dismounted again and wrapped the horse's reins around a low tree branch. "If it is unoccupied, it will be easier to hide here than in a cottage. Certainly it will be more comfortable than sleeping in the forest. Stay here," he said. "I'll look within."

Halfway to the manse, he turned and looked back at her, as if for re-assurance. She read his expression and said, "Go. But hurry back."

Outside the planked wood door was a bell; he rang it loudly, then waited with nervous anticipation. After a short while he rang again, but as before, no one appeared to greet him. He tried the door, and to his surprise it opened without difficulty.

Inside, the furnishings were sparse and of lesser quality than he would expect to find in such a manor. He walked quickly through a few of the rooms but saw little evidence of occupation. There was a small room with its own hearth, which opened into a room with a door to the rear gardens. A narrow window afforded a decent view; the horse could be tethered within sight. At the back of the gardens there was a brook, perhaps fifty paces back, so they would have water.

"This will do," Alejandro said when he returned to Kate's side. He glanced back wistfully. "I am put to mind of the place given to me after I first left Windsor," he said. "Too grand for a simple man like me."

His daughter touched him tenderly on the shoulder, knowing that his memories of that place would be bittersweet. "In the light of morning, this place will seem positively small, and you will be thinking of our escape to France."

"No doubt," he agreed. "But before we sleep, we should do what we can to confuse our pursuers."

They rode back to the village square on the same trail he had followed into the woods. He guided the horse in an ever-widening series of circles in the dirt, and though the animal seemed somewhat confused, he responded to Alejandro's tugging on the reins precisely as Alejandro had hoped he would. After leaving a concentrated scent in one place, they rode to the east, knowing that in the morning they would ride north again. Then he spurred the animal back into the woods and cut a switch, which Kate dragged behind them until they entered the stream. Alejandro guided the horse through the stream's twisting path until the rear gardens of the abandoned estate came into view.

They tied the horse to a tree that they knew would be visible from the window and went inside with their few belongings. When they had settled into the chosen room, Kate began to look about, displaying to Alejandro's delight the grown-woman version of the curiosity that had defined her childhood. With a grin, he offered his daughter the support of his arm. "My lady . . . shall we?"

She slipped her hand through the crook of his elbow. "Indeed, sir."

As he led his daughter through the rooms, Alejandro knew that the shock and struggle of their escape could not have worn off her any more than it had himself, but there was a calm in having each other's presence that put off all fears, however temporarily. Glancing up into the heights of the main hall, Alejandro said, "What ghosts are watching? Surely there must be some."

"Let us hope they keep to themselves tonight."

They followed a stone staircase to the upstairs. One of the rooms appeared to have been used by ladies for sewing and embroidery. There was a handsome wood frame on which a cloth might be stretched for decoration, left in disconsolate solitude. Yet another room had many shelves. Alejandro ran one finger through the dust, leaving a line in its path. "This room might have been a library. How forlorn..." he said, his voice echoing in the room's emptiness. "Not one volume remains."

They worked their way back to the other side of the landing and came upon another series of rooms that had likely been bedchambers. Just as they were leaving the last one, Kate hesitated; she knelt down and put her hand under one of the beds, left sadly naked of straw or feather mattress. She pulled out a single small shoe, its laces untied. It looked to have been worn by a child of perhaps six or seven years of age. She stood slowly and turned to Alejandro.

He saw tears threatening in her eyes and wondered that it had taken so long for them to come to the surface.

They found straw enough in one of the stables to mattress two of the beds, though the padding was thinner than either of them would have liked. Kate arranged the straw for herself and her father, saying, "It will not be a featherbed.... I'm afraid I've grown lazy, *Père*. Even the most rebellious royal child is accorded a certain level of comfort." She looked into his eyes and smiled. "But the freedom I feel in this moment erases all cravings for that comfort."

She pulled off her boots before slipping under the thin blanket but set them down next to the bed, so if the baying of hounds should awaken them, she could recover her garments quickly for their escape. Then she turned on one side and gazed at Alejandro. "Now, while we are safely at rest, tell me more of my son."

After a deep breath, Alejandro began. "There is so much to tell. He favors you strongly, though often I think he looks very much like his father, as I remember him to look. He is tall for his age—at least he appears to be so among the Jews of Avignon—and strong, in his own small way! His hair is the same gold as yours, and his eyes are blue." He smiled when he said, "He calls me *Grand-père*."

That seemed to please her; she smiled as well. "Is he quick-witted?"

"Remarkably so! He is reading Latin already and has acquired a bit of Greek, and he loves to stay by my side as I do my work. Often he mimics what I do, and it touches my heart. His hands are clever—he is very fond of whittling in wood. He seems almost to have a magic touch with the knife, as if it is just an extension of his own hand. He makes the most remarkable little things."

He continued to speak of the wonders of Kate's son, until finally she said, "God bless you, *Père*, for taking such good care of him. It seems a dream to me that I will see him again!" She closed her eyes and said quietly, "I have never felt such fatigue as I do now. I long so for the time when I can go to sleep without fear and awake to see my son smiling at me."

"Those days will come, sooner than you think." He reached over and tucked a stray wisp of her hair behind her ear. "Sleep now, daughter, and I will watch."

"Just as before, when I was a child."

"Always in my heart, you will be my child. Now, go to sleep."

"You must promise to wake me when you grow tired of the watch, *Père*. I will take my turn."

Alejandro nodded, though it was fully his intent to lie on the opposite bed and stare at his beloved Kate for the rest of the night, so no one could take her away from him, ever again.

When Kate awoke, the dawn was just about to break. Alejandro was standing at the small window, looking out into the gardens behind. He was already fully dressed in the same common clothing he'd worn on his ride from Paris; his dark hair was tied into a tail at his neck. When he heard his daughter stirring, he bade her good morning. "These gardens—they must have been lovely," he observed quietly.

Kate rose up on her elbows. "We should depart immediately."

She smoothed the wrinkles out of the clothing she'd worn to bed, then put on her boots. Once again, she tucked her wondrous hair into a cap to hide it.

The gesture reminded him of Philomène. He grabbed the small satchel that contained his few belongings, and they headed toward the door that led out into the garden. As always, the horse seemed glad to see him; the animal had chewed down all the grass within his reach. Alejandro mounted with one strong step, then pulled Kate up behind him. They set out into the forest, just as the sun was making its first peek through the trees.

Sir John Chandos chose ten of his best fellows, all of whom he knew to be loyal and brave, to accompany him on the hunt for the Jew physician and the young woman. The rugged group assembled in the lower keep near the gate, all fully armed and ready to depart. The master of the hounds struggled to keep hold of the leathers against which his fine animals strained; they danced about with their tails wagging and dewlaps frothing. As the group saw to the last details of armor and weapons, a young woman came running through the cobbled yard, holding a bundle out in front of her as she ran. She came up to Sir John and dipped low in respect, still panting, and handed him the bundle.

"Her bedsheet, m'lord."

He brought the sheet to his nose and sniffed; the scent of Kate was detectable even to him. "Very good. Thank you."

The girl curtsied again, then ran off quickly. When she was well away, Sir John called out to his men. "Gather 'round," he said. The entire lot of them formed a circle near the old warrior, who surveyed them with a certain pride, despite his distaste for their mission.

"We are given an honorable quest by our king," he said. "We will ride out immediately and bring back his daughter. She has been stolen away from him again by the same Jew who took her from Canterbury so many years ago, when she was but a child. Now her sister, our princess Isabella, mourns the loss of her kin and is nearly inconsolable."

He heard the sound of hooves and stopped speaking to look in that direction. He saw de Coucy approaching, with Benoit trailing close behind.

"Look, it is the bridegrooms." His voice, through the entire recitation, was flat and completely void of enthusiasm.

There fell a pronounced silence among the men; Chandos understood why, without having to be told. Each one of them knew of the young woman in question, and all had admired her from afar. It was no secret that had she gone to the altar, it would have been against her will. She was a lush, ripe beauty who could command a man of the highest caliber, had her life not taken so many savage twists and turns. The dark and beastly Benoit had made an ass of himself time and again during the armsplay; no one looked forward to his continued presence during the jousting season, which was not far off. His humiliation at the masque had brought upset to no one but himself and de Coucy.

Chandos hated the task the king had set before him, but he knew only too well that if another knight led the hunt, the treatment the fugitives would receive when captured might well be far less generous than what he himself would afford them.

De Coucy brought his horse to a halt next to Chandos. He looked at the troops, inspecting their readiness. They were perfectly uniformed and armed almost to excess. "Well," he said to Chandos, "you have assembled a handsome lot. One hopes their skills in hunting are equally attractive."

"Only time will tell," Chandos said. He turned to his troops. "Assemble!"

The men lined up in proper order.

"Our quarry are bound for France," Chandos said as he drew on his gloves. "They will head east or south, with the notion of finding passage."

The standard of King Edward waved in a light wind as they thundered over the planks with the hounds baying hungrily in the lead. Once outside the gates, the hounds lowered their heads to the ground, shifting left and right in unpredictable jerks as they followed the scent from the bed linens.

"Follow," Sir John shouted to his troops. "We must bring back the king's daughter."

And her Jew captor. The words bore a sinister innuendo, and therein lay part of the shame. Chandos knew Alejandro to be a man of honor and spirit, who treasured truth beyond almost anything else in this world. But in the end, none of that would matter, for he had sworn to serve his liege until the day when his services were no longer required.

May it please God, he prayed silently, *that such a day will never come.*

"Sir John," he heard. It was the master of the hounds who spoke. "The trail leads north."

"Not east?"

"No, sir. North."

She was baiting them, the knight realized, tempting them into a direction that seemed illogical. He had played chess with her many times; she was a brilliant player, and now they were engaged in a match of the finest sort. Regardless of the outcome, he thought to himself, it would be a hunt worthy of remembrance.

It went against all his inclinations, but he said, "North, then. And God help us if we are wrong."

When the sun was directly overhead, Alejandro and Kate stopped by a brook to rest and eat. Alejandro tied the horse to a tree and rubbed him down with a chamois as Kate went into a nearby field in search of greens and roots. She returned with the tail of her shirt full to the brim with things edible—all of them green, all of them in need of washing. She bent to the stream and put them in the water and rubbed her treasures clean.

"Lamb's-quarters," she said to Alejandro. " 'Tis too bad we have no means to cook them."

"Then we shall eat them raw and ignore our bellies when they complain later."

They ate in the still of the woods, with thin streams of sunlight touching the ground all around them. Kate sat with her back against a tree and watched as her beloved *Père* fell into a light slumber. She rose up and walked quietly away, but stayed in sight of him. She searched among the branches of the trees until she found a suitable one, then cut it away with her knife and went back to where Alejandro was sleeping.

As she removed the bark from the branch with her knife, he twitched now and then; *What dreams visit your mind in this brief rest?* she wondered silently. *Do you dream of a woman?* She resolved to ask him when the moment seemed right. Her own dreams were often of Guillaume Karle, of his tender touch on her skin. Her husband had not been a laborer but a man of numbers, whose knowledge of his overlord's duplicity led to the revolt that cost him his life—while Kate was ripe with their only son. He would come to her in the deepest parts of her sleep and smother her with his kisses— such sweet, warm kisses as could not be described. Guillaume had been a common man with many uncommon qualities and a vision that served his fellows well beyond their own understanding. For as the Great Mortality had changed the life of each human being who had witnessed it, so had it also changed the course of history; serfs who would never have dared to rise up against their masters now understood their value, and the power that came with it. Without their labor, there could be no agriculture, no commerce, no trade or travel. They could, for the first time, command a wage on which they might prosper. Guillaume Karle, a man of numbers, had understood this and had gathered them into a fighting force. He led them—with undeniable bravery—in their first failed steps toward freedom. How long, Kate wondered, would it be before the common folk of France and Bretagne rose up against their rulers again and set a course toward independence?

Centuries, she told herself. It was a sad realization.

She felt her own chin nodding onto her chest. She forced herself to remain awake; the sun was just beginning its downward arc.

"*Père*," she said as she gently touched his shoulder.

Alejandro came awake with a start.

"It is time to be off again," she said.

He rose without a word and shook off his sleep.

"I was dreaming," he said.

"We must go," she said. "They will surely have the hounds after us by now."

"What is that?" Alejandro said, pointing to the denuded branch.

"The start of a bow," she said. "We have need of weapons beyond our knives. Arrows are easily made. Now we must keep our eyes open for something suitable."

He nodded. "To the north," he said.

"North," Kate concurred. They mounted the horse and rode out of the woods, with the sun now to their left.

"They have stepped in and out of the stream," the houndsman reported to Chandos. "Are you sure this man she travels with is a Jew?"

"Yes, and he is very clever and cunning, like all his race. But it is just as likely she who would think to do that," Chandos said. "You must behave as if you were tracking two men. In this way, we may stand a chance of catching up with them."

He saw the doubt in the eyes of his men. "She is, after all, the daughter of our king. As his offspring, she possesses many of his attributes. Our king is an intelligent man, is he not?"

There was an immediate chorus of agreement.

"He possesses many skills in war, would you not agree?"

There were enthusiastic *ayes* all around.

"Then so is his daughter skilled, certainly far more so than her sister, perhaps even in a league with her brothers." He cast a glance at de Coucy and Benoit, neither of whom made comment.

Surely, Chandos thought as he regarded the pathetic little count, *the lands in Bretagne cannot be so important that King Edward would give his own daughter to him. . . .*

Murmurs of doubt could be heard among the troops, for the Black Prince was a genius at combat; Chandos's assertion that Kate was alike in that regard bordered on blasphemy.

"Oh, come now, my fellows—many a good Englishwoman has taken up the sword and made a splendid job of it." He glanced from man to man. "Many of you may recall the Countess of Salisbury, who held off a siege of her husband's lands for more than a fortnight while he fought in France. And some of you, if my memory serves me, were there to see it."

One and all went silent with shame. Chandos did not need to remind them that the brave and beautiful countess had successfully held off the attacking forces of the man who would take over her husband's land and wealth—King Edward himself—until her food and water were finally exhausted.

Quiet *aye*s went through the lot of them. Chandos gave the signal to proceed. "North," he murmured to himself. "Though God knows why."

Twenty-four

Kristina tucked a wisp of hair behind one ear and cleared her throat nervously. "Double delta is a genetic mutation," she said. "A very specific one."

"That does what?" Steve asked.

"A lot," she said. "I'll explain as well as I can. There are some details I don't know. But there's a story behind it. There's a town called Eyam in northern England. You know about the Black Death in the Middle Ages—well, plague showed up there too, around the same time as all the other outbreaks, theoretically from fleas in a bolt of fabric from London."

Janie sat up straight on hearing this, and thought to herself, *Fabric from London is a perilous substance.*

"It could just as easily have come from a different source. But the historical records say that a shipment of fabric bolts arrived just before the outbreak began. Well, they'd managed to keep plague out before then and they felt very blessed, so in return for what they called 'God's good grace,' the people of Eyam did something incredibly right

and moral—they quarantined themselves so plague wouldn't go beyond their own town. They didn't really understand the mechanism of
it, but they knew that it spread geographically. They all agreed that no
one should go in or out of Eyam until the plague was over. When
someone took ill within the town, that person and all his or her family
were put into complete isolation, in a jail or something. I don't know
where they specifically put them—it was a really small town and I can't
imagine that they had a jail that big. Maybe they used a church or some
other public building."

"Dear God," Steve whispered. "I wonder how many people who
might otherwise have lived ended up dying of plague because they were
shut in with people who had it."

"A lot, for sure," Kristina said. "But that's where it gets interesting.
You'd think that pretty much everyone would contract plague under
those circumstances. There are hundreds of recorded cases where
everyone was infected in a closed system—monasteries and abbeys, the
colleges..."

Janie tuned out momentarily; she recalled a passage from Alejandro's
journal about a monastery he'd come upon in his first journey to
England. Only one priest among dozens remained alive, and when
Alejandro found him—insane and babbling—the man had just buried
the last of his brothers. But he was alive.

She recalled as well a passage about a place called Eyam, and when
she heard Kristina say the name of the town again, it brought her back.

"There were a significant number of people in town who didn't *ever*
get plague."

Janie felt Kristina's eyes linger on her for the briefest moment before she continued speaking. "And considering how it's transmitted—
which they of course didn't understand at the time—that was pretty
amazing. And then there were a lot of people who got plague and lived
through it, a much higher percentage than what it seemed to have been
in most other places. They recorded everything, so it would seem
strange that they wouldn't have recorded something as significant as a
cure. There was one woman who was so delirious with thirst that she
thought a jar of bacon grease was water, and she drank it. She lived, so

a whole bunch of other people tried it too, thinking it was a cure, had there been one. They thought a lot of strange things were cures—bats' eyes, ground-up bones, all sorts of icky stuff. The one thing that actually might have worked—the 'dust of the dead,' with the power to prompt an immune response—was never mentioned. Some of the people who drank the bacon grease *did* live, but that wasn't what kept them alive. It was something else."

Lany's cop nature surfaced. "How did anyone figure it all out? It doesn't seem like there was much real evidence beyond hearsay."

"It's not hearsay at all," Kristina countered. "They were maniacs for records—births and deaths, and pretty much every event of significance. But none of this would have ever come to light if it hadn't been for something that happened in San Francisco in the nineties. There was a gay man into the scene there for years, way back into the late seventies and early eighties, when no one really understood AIDS. He did the bathhouse thing for a long time, had—according to himself— 'multiple' contacts. He was at huge risk for AIDS, but he never got it. He was tested dozens of times but he's never been HIV positive. His lovers and friends were dying all around him, men with whom he'd exchanged body fluids, but as far as anyone knows, he's still alive."

Everyone leaned in as if to hear her better, though she was not speaking softly. "So eventually, someone in the medical community in San Francisco decided it might be worth knowing what it was about this guy that protected him. They did all kinds of tests, including a DNA workup. And blammo, right away they saw something unusual on CCR5. He had two copies of a genetic mutation called delta thirty-two."

"Double delta," Janie whispered.

"Yes," Kristina said, looking at Janie once again. This time her eyes stayed even longer. But before Janie could say anything, Kristina continued speaking.

"So they did some DNA dating and were able to determine that the original mutation surfaced abruptly about seven hundred years ago, shortly before the first plague pandemic in the 1300s."

Murmurs of excitement went through the group.

"And then they tested a whole bunch of people, including patients with end-stage AIDS, patients who had AIDS but were doing pretty well, and people who should have been at risk but never got it. The results were pretty exciting—a lot of the high-risk people who never got AIDS had the same double mutation as the original guy. None of the people who were very sick had a copy of that mutation. But what was really interesting is that the people who had one copy, even though they did get AIDS, responded really well to medications and stayed healthy for a much longer time than people who had no copies. That's one reason why nonwhite people seemed to get AIDS at a higher rate within their ethnic group—the original mutation arose in the northern European population. With further testing of large groups, the researchers were able to determine that the mutation doesn't exist in blacks, Asians, and South American Hispanics. They have absolutely no genetic protection. But it runs at a rate of fourteen percent in people of Celtic and Scandinavian origin."

Evan asked, "But what does this have to do with plague?"

"It turns out that the infection mechanism is the same in plague and in AIDS. HIV and *Yersinia pestis* both attach themselves to immune cells in the same receptors, and both of them trick the immune system into carrying the microbe throughout the body. *Yersinia pestis* rides right into the lymph nodes, which is why people with plague get swellings and bruising around the neck and in the groin. Then it goes everywhere else. In double deltas, the microbe can't get a lock on the receptor, so it can't fool the immune system. The person is essentially immune to plague and highly resistant to HIV."

It was a large amount of information to process, and the listeners were all understandably quiet for a few moments. Finally, Steve asked, "So why would these folks be wanting to know if we have any double deltas now?"

"I don't know for sure," Kristina said, "but I think I can guess. DR SAM is a receptor-based microbe, so maybe if you have a double copy of the mutation, you're immune to DR SAM too."

It was a long moment before Steve said, "Boy, wouldn't it be nice to know who is and who isn't?"

There was another pause before Kristina said, "There's one that I know of."

All eyes turned to her.

"And how do you know?" Lany asked.

"I've done genetic profiles on the people in our compound." She looked straight at Janie, as if in apology. "We've all given blood for one reason or another in the time we've been there. We have the equipment for me to do polymerase chain reaction, so I can get a very small amount of DNA to reproduce itself, enough for me to prompt a readable sample. I figured it might come in handy someday to know what each one of us is carting around in terms of genes."

"Kristina," Janie said, "why haven't you said something about this before?"

She dropped her head and stared at her own lap. "I don't know. I didn't think it meant anything. And I guess I probably forgot."

No one commented but Steve Roy. "So," he said, "you're keeping us in mystery. Who is it?"

Her eyes went straight to Janie. This time they stayed there.

The conversation narrowed to Janie and Kristina; everyone else just listened in awe.

"I don't get it," Janie said. "Both of my parents died. How could I have inherited complete immunity?"

"They had to have been single deltas. You had to have gotten one copy of the mutation from each of them. Was either of them of Celtic or Scandinavian background?"

"My mother was German and Swedish, my father was Irish."

"Well, there you go. They fit the profile. Having one copy doesn't protect you completely, but . . ." She hesitated. "It'll keep you alive longer."

"You mean it prolongs the agony."

Kristina hung her head, as if she were more than just the bearer of news, as if she were responsible for its content. "I hate to ask you this stuff, but did your folks die quickly or did they last awhile?"

What was "awhile," in DR SAM terms? "Three days each," she said.

"That *was* a long time for DR SAM. Now, I hate to ask this even more—what about your daughter?"

"Not quite four days."

"And her father?"

"Healthy one morning, dead before midnight," Janie said. "He went to the school where Betsy was in quarantine." She glanced at Lany, who let out a sigh as she revisited her own involvement in that incident. Janie's voice began to tremble and there were tears in her eyes. "He talked his way in, but he never came out."

Kristina remained respectfully quiet for a brief moment, as did everyone else in the surrounding circle of listeners. Then she said, "Well, this is all speculation, but I'd venture an educated guess that if we had their profiles, we'd find that each of your parents had one copy, which is how you ended up with two. And that your daughter had one from you, and none from her father, who probably had none himself."

Steve Roy rose up and pointed to the hard drive. "So, what does all this mean to us?"

"I think," Kristina said, "that we should check all the blood samples I took and determine everyone's status."

Janie sat straight up and looked around the room. "Anyone object? It's your right, at least in the country we used to live in, to refuse."

A stark moment of silence ensued.

"Well," Kristina said, "I'll take that for a no."

Kristina and Evan went back over the mountain much sooner than planned so Kristina could do her work. Janie did not relax again until she received the e-mail that they had safely reached the compound and that Tom was doing well. Coming from his daughter, she took the report as truth; Caroline or Michael might have sugarcoated it.

On the morning they left with the cheek swabs from everyone in Orange, Janie began the process of working up complete medical histories on all the people who lived there. There was an urgency to her work that she had not felt before the double-delta revelation. It was a relief, after the CCR5 revelation, to discover that with minor exceptions they were a spectacularly healthy lot. She removed a few suspicious-looking moles, shaved off a few corns, and cataloged the aches and pains of all the adults and children. Her diabetic patient was doing very well indeed.

Two days later the news about delta status came, in a cryptic message:

> J and L do more than rhyme
> The son shines every single day
> The king's book is half readable

Janie and Lany were doubles, Evan a single.
" 'The king's book'? What does that mean?" Steve said in confusion.
For a moment, no one had an answer.
"The King James Bible," James finally said.
"But I thought . . ." Lany did not finish the sentence.
"My mother was white," James said.

The argument over the invitation to go to the double-delta Web site was heated, and lasted long into the night. Eventually, it was decided that Lany's assertion that they ought to know their enemies made sense—if these folks turned out to be enemies. With a little bit of luck, they would be friendly, and a whole new world would open up to both communities, a world they all hungered after.

But going onto the Internet again was like sailing to the edge of the world—a confusing mix of terror over the unknown and excitement over what might be found. The browser worked and worked; the hourglass hung on the screen for what seemed an eternity, until finally the page unfolded. Everyone gasped as the images rolled open, as if they were seeing the Internet for the first time.

The date in the corner of the page was correct.
"Well," Steve said, "I guess it's current."
The same information that had arrived in the e-mail was posted on

the page itself, stating the date, time, and location of the gathering of deltas.

"This is scary," Janie said. "I thought I'd be so delirious if we got the Internet back again. Now I don't know if I want it."

"I want it if it's friendly," Steve said.

"It wasn't entirely friendly in the time before," Janie reminded him. "Pedophiles, identity thieves, all sorts of scams—a lot of those bad guys will probably have survived. They were sitting in front of their computers, isolated from everything, while the rest of us were breathing airplane air and touching door handles."

"Look, there's a mission statement," Lany said. She grabbed the mouse from Janie's hand and—before she could protest—clicked on the link. She began to read aloud.

> We believe that we have been set apart by our Creator's hand and He has blessed us all with

"Oh, no," someone groaned from the back of the group. "Religious fanatics—"

"Wait a minute," Lany said. "Give it a chance." She read on.

> an unearned ability to withstand certain ravages of nature, which He also created, in which He placed us to live. We believe that this blessing calls us to a higher purpose, and we aspire to rise to that calling. To that end, we set this goal: to spread throughout the entire human population, by benign means, the genetic code that enabled us to survive when so many died.

Lany sat back in her chair when she finished reading the short paragraph. "That's it," she said.

Those who'd gathered around were silent for a moment. Finally Steve said, "Seems pretty simple, doesn't it? At least on the surface. But what's this?"

He pointed to a link in one corner of the page. It said, *The Story of Mecklenville.*

"Go there," he said.

Lany was reluctant, but finally she clicked on the link.

http://www.mecklenville.in.us.gov

The site unfolded before them.

Mecklenville, Indiana, United States of America. Population as of this writing, 1. Population as of three months ago, estimated to be 62, all survivors of DR SAM.

There was a link that said *Photo Gallery*. Lany clicked on it. It took a few moments for the page to unfold; when it did, those gathered around the computer saw a group of people who looked pretty much as they did. The caption under the first photo read, *Mecklenville gathers to celebrate the renovation of the power plant*. Behind the smiling folks was a Quonset hut of rippled steel, painted in camouflage colors.

The next photo showed a smaller crowd. The faces of the people were sad and bewildered. The caption was disturbing: *Mecklenville buries three of its own.*

The one below that showed an even smaller group, who by their expressions were all in a state of something like shock. *Mecklenville buries twelve more.*

There were no more photos on that page, only a link to another. That page contained a personal letter, with a photo of a young man who looked to be in his mid-twenties, sitting in front of his computer.

As I write this letter, I know that I am already sick; I can feel it taking over me. I don't know why I was left here to document all these deaths; God must have it in His plan for me. At least that's what I'm hoping, because I would never have chosen this for myself.

If you are reading this now, I am dead; I set up my computer to automatically load this last page if I didn't initiate a certain command; I'm at the computer every day if I'm well, because it's all I have left.

Like all of you who may stumble on this page, we were afraid to
go out and make contact. We didn't know what we'd find; we had a
good little community here and we were getting by. But DR SAM
came back again and took us all, only this time it was very slow. In
the time before, it swooped in like lightning and took out so many
of the people we loved, but this time it was long and agonizing.
I've watched every one of the townspeople take ill and die over
the period of a month.

I liked it better when it was quick. Not that I like it at all.

In the last few days, I've read about the deltas. Please, if you are
reading this, support what they are trying to do. It's our only hope.

As everyone around her was silent in response to what they'd just
seen, Lany went into the quiet, stern discipline of cop mode. She wrote
down all the information about the New England gathering—there
were apparently meetings all over the country, if what the delta Web
site purported was true. She studied the map of the route to the
Worcester Armory that the delta group had placed on the site and marveled that it was so close to the campus of Worcester Technical
Institute. "I think I've been there for training," she said.

As soon as she stopped scribbling the details on the slate, she went
after Janie as if no one else were there. "We should go and hear what
they have to say. Worcester's about forty miles from here," she said.
"Especially after what we just saw. A day and a half on horseback." She
looked directly at Janie. "What do you say?"

Janie didn't respond immediately. "I don't know," she said.

"What would hold you back?" It was almost an accusation.

"I have my son's future to consider."

"As do I," Lanie said. "And they both deserve long lives. If we go
out there and find out what's going on in the world, they might have a
chance at that."

Janie pointed to her shoulder. "DR SAM's not the only danger out
there."

She didn't need to say a word about Tom.

"I know there are all sorts of hazards, but with two of us—both theoretically immune—we stand a chance of getting there and back again safely. We can continue to look for signs of renewed infection in places we haven't looked before. And if what we're seeing on the Net is true, there's a developing world out there, and we can find a way to connect with it. Someone might have one of those crazy natural cures for DR SAM for the people who aren't double deltas. Maybe there's some kind of vaccine!"

Janie stood. "There isn't going to be a vaccine," she said. "We've tried since the day we locked ourselves into the compound to develop something that would work, and even if we or someone else could come up with one, DR SAM is a bacterium—a vaccine isn't going to confer longtime immunity like it would if it was a virus. Six months to a year, at best. Then you need a whole new immunization, *if* it doesn't mutate in that period."

"But there are still lots of good reasons to go," Lany said. "There are other groups out there—we've seen their smoke. They can't all be bad."

"So why haven't any of them tried to contact us?"

"Same reason we haven't tried to contact them. They're afraid. They don't know we're all friendly any more than we know they're friendly. But this . . . With that mission statement, they've got to be friendly. But we'll never know if we don't try. Look, I'm not saying we should rush right out tomorrow. But for God's sake, let's give it some thought."

All eyes were on Janie. When the hot seat became intolerable, she got up and left.

"An exploration," Lany said when she caught up to her. "Think of it that way. And I'm sorry, I didn't mean to put you on the spot like that."

Janie stopped walking and turned. "It wasn't pleasant."

"I know. I am sorry."

"I'm too old to be an explorer."

"No you're not. You're healthy and strong. And you're smart."

"Right about now I should have been thinking about retirement.

My husband and I should be planning a trip to China or a safari in Africa. He was a lawyer, I was a doctor, for God's sake."

"Now he's an amputee, and you're just a human being."

Janie ignored the rebuke. "I'm a mother who has a young son to raise."

Lany gave her a hard look. "A son you borrowed from another time. You brought him into this world for reasons of your own, not because nature made it happen. It was as much an act of selfishness as anything else. You brought someone from another time into this mess without asking him if he wanted it. If you'd cooked him up in the time before, it might be different. But now I think you owe him a world that he can actually live in. You have something inside you, just like I do, that can make a difference. Not everyone can say that."

"Why does it have to be me?" Janie lamented. "Why can't it all just be taken care of, like it was before?"

After a pause, Lany said, "That's a question I can't answer. If I was a believer, I'd say it was all part of some greater plan. Trouble with the greater plans is that when you're one of the parts, it's hard to see or understand the whole."

Janie turned away again. She thought about Tom and the hurt that was between them. Maybe it would be good to go out and see the hurt in the rest of the world, to understand her own good fortune better. Maybe then she could inspire him to understand for himself that there was good fortune in living, even if his life was limited. She tried to clear her head; everything was suddenly even more confusing.

The larger part of her wanted to get back on her horse and return to the other side of the mountain, to snuggle into the oblivion that could be found there. So what if she turned into a recluse—so what if she kept Alex at her side until her dying day. Her son would live to pass on his genes.

But it was the smaller part of her that had the louder voice. More than six hundred years after his death, the spirit of Alejandro still resonated.

Six hundred years from now, her own genes and their uncanny resilience might resonate too.

"Two days out, two days back, right?"

"That's it. A total of four days. Five at most if we stay in Worcester one day for the meeting. Assuming we leave from here. From your place, it would be longer."

"If we left from here, I wouldn't see Tom or Alex before we go."

The tone of Lany's voice was softer now. "You can e-mail them that you're going. You won't be gone much longer than you would have been here, anyway. Just a couple of days."

"Tom's working through a lot of stuff right now," Janie said. "Truth is, he could probably use an even longer break from me. He'll have more time to sort through the things that are depressing him. But Alex will be upset."

Lany could not help but smile. "I saw what he did that night on the way back from the cell tower. I think he'll be upset, all right, but more that you're not taking him than that you're going in the first place."

Lany was right.

I wish I could go with you. Tell me where you're going so I can look for it on the map.

We're not exactly sure yet. I'll tell you all about it when we get back.

Be careful.

I will. I love you.

I love you too, Mom.

As she clicked the message closed, Janie wondered if Alejandro had ever told his mother that he loved her. Probably not, she decided. Those were different times, and she was a different mother.

That evening at dinner, Steve Roy came to the table with a book in his hand. He handed it to Janie.

She looked at the title, then up at Steve. "The Lewis and Clark Expedition? I thought we were going into known territory."

He laughed a little. "Known to a degree," he said. "We don't know what you'll find for supplies and tools. These guys made it through an incredibly long journey with just what they had and what they could gather." He pointed to the book. "There's a chapter in there about how they prepared, what they brought, all that. I thought it might be helpful."

Janie thanked him for his kindness. As she ate her dinner, she perused the summary of the items the pair had taken along:

> *Their arms & accouterments, some instruments of observation, & light & cheap presents for the Indians would be all the apparatus they could carry, and with an expectation of a soldier's portion of land on their return would constitute the whole expense. "Portable soup," medicine, special uniforms made of drab cloth, tents, tools, kettles, tobacco, corn mills, wine, gunpowder in lead canisters, medical and surgical supplies, and presents.*

Great. she thought. *But we aren't going eight thousand miles.* It would only seem that way.

She found Lany stowing clothes in her saddlebag.

"I think I'm all set," Janie said. "As set as I can be under the circumstances. I just wish there was some way we could communicate with the folks here. I would feel so much better about going. It was bad enough when Michael was out of touch for a day."

"Smoke signals."

Janie frowned. "Yes, it would be *so* wise to show a visible trail of our progress."

"Too bad the Palms don't work anymore," Lany said. "I got so used to mine."

For a moment, Janie said nothing. Then, "Don't they?"

"Of course they don't."

"If we have wireless that works with the computers, why wouldn't the same wireless work for a Palm?"

"Good question," Lany said. "Its receivers would have to be reset...."

James was in the kitchen doing his turn at cleanup when they located him a few minutes later.

"You know, I never even thought about that," he said. "I have one in a box somewhere. Thought it might make a good paperweight. Hang on a moment, let me see if I can find it."

He left them in the kitchen; Janie dried dishes and Lany put them away while they waited for him to return. He came back with a small black object in one hand and something Janie couldn't quite make out in the other.

"Here it is," he said, handing the black box to Janie.

"Does it still have power?"

"I didn't try it, but it's been stored in a cool, dry place, that's for sure. Eight years, though—that's a long time. Open up the back and look at the batteries. If they aren't corroded, they might work. It's a long shot."

There was no corrosion that anyone could see. Janie removed the batteries and rubbed the contact points briskly on the denim of her jeans, then replaced them in the unit.

"Here goes," she said. She pressed the power button. Miraculously, the screen began to glow.

"Son of a gun," James said. "Gotta love those nicads. And guess what else I found in the box."

Grinning widely, he held up a battery charger. The two women nearly cheered.

"Now, don't get too excited just yet," he admonished them. "I still have a lot of setting up to do for this to work. No point in taking the thing along unless it'll talk."

For the next couple of hours, he tweaked, and eventually it talked.

"Okay, now just a couple more settings to create an account...and by the way, what do you want the account to be called?" he asked.

Janie didn't hesitate. "Lewis and Clark," she said.

By noon the next day, they were already eight miles to the southeast, in a journey that proved remarkably uneventful at the start. They followed a small reedy river in the hopes of avoiding those remnants of civilization that were likely to be unsavory; according to their map, it paralleled the road that led to Worcester. Despite the thick brush and uncertain footing, neither woman wanted to brave the road.

As they progressed, the river widened, swollen by the meltings of spring. The reeds disappeared, and the water swirled in fast-moving eddies around fallen trees and frothed white over submerged rocks. In summer, Janie suspected, it would be a trickle in comparison. They rode against the current; the river's origin was close to their final destination, and they hoped to be able to follow it almost all the way.

Somewhere along the way, Janie let her guard down long enough to experience her surroundings. She found a sense of peace in their sheer natural beauty. After a night rain, the trunks of the trees were starkly blackened with moisture, except the birches, which were blazingly white. The budding leaves were nearly fluorescent. Here and there on the forest floor there were small still pools rimmed with bright green sprouting things. A chorus of peeper frogs screamed out advertisements for their own virility; birds chirped to announce their territory. The light was bright but indirect, diffused as it was by the new leaves of the canopy. It was lovely.

" 'Whose woods these are,' " Janie said pensively.

Lany turned back and faced her. " 'Miles to go before I sleep.' "

"Spoilsport."

Up ahead, the water seemed to swirl in a more pronounced manner, as if its flow were blocked by something. Janie shaded her eyes and focused.

"There's a canoe up there, on the edge of the river."

Lany took out a pair of binoculars. "A sad-looking one," she said. "I don't see anyone near it."

Nevertheless, she undid the strap on her saddle holster.

"Let's check it out."

They moved forward and brought the horses alongside it. The canoe lay against the bank, sad and forlorn. The floor was completely rotted through.

"Made of wood," Lany said. "Usually they're some kind of resin. Haven't seen one of these for a while."

Janie pointed to a cluster of small green shoots sprouting out from between the shrunken side boards. "It's got a new career as a planter." She glanced up at the sky, judging the time. "This is nothing to be concerned about. We should keep moving."

Lany did not disagree. They urged the horses along, still following the water's edge. Here the water flowed smoothly along the bank; Janie's calm returned.

It was short-lived.

"What's that?" she said, pointing to a mounded area a short distance ahead. "It doesn't look like it should be there."

"Don't know, but nothing's moving. Maybe a beaver hut."

"Not the right shape."

A few yards short of the mound, they dismounted.

The pile of leaves was odd-shaped and seemed out of place, though it didn't look as if the leaves had been put there but rather had accumulated naturally. Janie rooted around on the ground and came up with a stick. She poked into the leaves repeatedly; it went in easily, the first few times.

"*Whoa,*" she said.

"What?"

"Something's in there. It has a strange feel to it."

"Strange like what?"

"Not mushy, but not firm either. Spongy."

She handed the stick to Lany, who probed on her own.

Janie found another stick, and between them they worked at the leaves. When a blackened hand appeared, they jumped backward in unison.

With her heart pounding, Lany said, "You'd think it wouldn't be such a big thing for a cop and a doctor to come across a dead body."

"That's just a hand. We don't know that there's a body attached to it."

"There usually is," Lany said.

As the body was revealed, Lany seemed to slip back into the practiced personality of her former profession. She leaned over the body, analyzing it with her eyes while ignoring the smell.

"Thirty-five to forty years old," Lany said. "Caucasian male, no blatant signs of trauma."

Janie squatted down beside the bloated body. "I wonder how long he's been here."

"Hard to tell," Lany said, "coming out of winter." She shoved aside a small piece of ice that had emerged from beneath the leaves. "He might have actually died sometime in the last three or four months, and his body is just now thawing."

"I don't know," Janie said. "The clothes look awfully good for being out here all winter, and he's not wearing a coat."

She used the tip of the stick to push up the collar on the man's shirt.

"Oh, my," she said quietly.

"What?" Lany said.

"His neck."

Lany looked closer. "It's bloated and discolored," Lany said. "That's normal in decomposition."

"But he's not really all that decomposed."

Lany gave her an odd look, then moved closer to examine the discoloration. She pushed the collar away with her own stick.

"I'm not getting what you mean."

"I mean that his neck is darker and more swollen that any other part of him."

"We can't see anything but his hands."

"Then we need to take his clothes off him."

"Are you kidding? We're already too close."

"Please," Janie said, her voice hushed. "It's important."

They had no gloves for this sort of task; Lany stood up and looked around, and found a large dark leaf that was still intact enough to use as a barrier. It became her pot holder as she undid the buttons of the corpse's shirt and pulled down the zipper on his pants. She spread apart the front of the shirt and then, with Janie's help, pulled off the man's pants and underwear.

The naked corpse lay before them, in all its terrible glory.

"My God," Janie said. "I don't believe this."

"Don't believe what?" Lany said. "That another one bit the dust from DR SAM?"

"This isn't DR SAM," Janie said. "The discolorations on the neck and groin aren't from decomposition. The rest of him would show at least something of it too." She swallowed hard. "This looks like plague. Or something very much like it."

Twenty-five

As Alejandro and Kate went farther north, the conditions improved and the path widened to the point where a cart might pass unimpeded, and it became clear to both of them that they were nearing some sort of town. The trees thinned, and they came upon a wall that ran along the side of the path. Beams of sunlight touched the forest floor at the long angle mandated by the low position of the sun.

"In Spain, the shadows seemed shorter," Alejandro said.

"I should like to go to Spain one day, *Père*," Kate said.

For a moment he did not know what to say; it had been so many years since he left his country of birth that he had to stretch his mind to bring it back. His memories of the place were not entirely fond. Still, it was his first home. "It was always warm there," he said, rather pensively. "Not like England, where a third of the year is spent in shivering. Sometimes in that winter when I was here, I felt as if I would never get warm again, so deep was the chill that penetrated my bones."

"Had you spent more time here, you might have become accustomed to it."

"Not likely," he said. But had Adele lived, he might now still reside in England, as her husband, the owner of a proud estate of his own. Coupled with her inherited lands, they would have been prosperous indeed.

The road widened further, and they saw fresh ruts where a cart had passed not too long before. Alejandro stared down at the tracks. "Always, when I see such marks in a road, I think of the death carts, laden with bodies of plague dead."

Kate reached up and made the sign of the cross on her chest. "God rest the souls of the departed and keep them."

"Amain," Alejandro said.

They pressed on, despite their sudden uneasiness. Up ahead, Alejandro made out what he thought was a flag tied around the trunk of a tree, perhaps at shoulder height. Travelers on horseback and foot alike would not fail to see it.

"Look there," he said, gesturing in that direction.

Kate looked over his shoulder. "Black again..."

Soon enough they were abreast of the flag, which hung weather-tattered on a dying tree. The bark had been stripped all around, probably by some gnawing animal. The poor tree had only a few leaves and was—in its own illness—a fitting support for the sign of plague.

Kate tightened her grip on his back yet again. "What shall we do?"

With the flag waving over his head, Alejandro considered the matter. It was a few moments before he answered her. "I think we shall proceed," he said.

"But—"

"Where better to hide than in the midst of something that will keep even the staunchest warrior at a distance?"

They rode on, leaving the flag behind them. They passed a few small cottages, set well back. A bit farther along, the road opened up into what appeared to be the center of a small village. They stayed back on the edge of the market area, watching in relative anonymity as the people of the town went about their daily business.

"I see no mourners, no death carts waiting, no black drapes on the lintels."

"Aye," Kate said quietly. "There is too much activity for there to be plague herein."

Soon people began to look in their direction, but no one approached, though passersby kept their eyes upon them until they were well past.

"Always," Alejandro observed quietly, "the women gather at the well."

"Where else are they to gather? They need water, for cooking, dyeing, washing, the grinding of flour—it is a necessary thing."

"Indeed."

He dismounted, then offered his hand in assistance to Kate, saying, "I think we shall stop here for a decent meal." He pointed to a tavern on one side of the square. "Perhaps we shall even stay a day or two, to restore ourselves."

Kate came to the ground and stood next to him. Alejandro tied the horse to a post, and the two travelers stood on the edge of the square and surveyed the bustling village as the inhabitants went about their business.

"I have not seen this much liveliness in a town for a very long time."

"Nor I," Kate said. "The place seems a prosperous little island unto itself."

It was only a short while before a young boy came up to them. He smiled in the awkward sort of way of boys and made a rough bow. "Welcome, travelers," he said, with all the innocence of youth. "I see that you have braved our flag."

Twelve, Alejandro judged from the look of the boy and from the squeak of his voice. At that age, Kate had been a wonder—so full of life and curiosity, despite their adversities.

"Yes, young man, we have, and we thank you for your kind welcome," Alejandro said. "What is the name of this village?"

"Eyam," the boy said.

"Eyam," Alejandro repeated. He glanced around the square, making sure the boy saw him do so. "A fair place, in my estimation. And what would be your name, boy?"

"Thomas Blackwell, sir." He bowed, with unseemly grace for his age and station. "The Younger."

For a moment, Alejandro said nothing. *Thomas Blackwell* danced in his mind, prodding some distant memory. Finally, it came to him:

AND HERE LIE MY TWELVE CHILDREN AND
MY WIFE OF MANY YEARS

He had seen the name on a headstone when he and Kate fled from Canterbury. Alejandro let the dark image slip away and smiled at the boy, thinking that it could not be the same man, so far away. "And how many years do you have, Master Blackwell?"

"Twelve," the boy answered, puffing out his chest. "And my father's name is also Thomas. He is called the Elder hereabouts."

"No wonder. One expects he is indeed older than his son."

This brought a chuckle from the boy. "Ah, kind sir, you are correct. My father is quite a bit older than I."

"And your mother?"

The boy laughed gaily. "Also older than I, though a bit younger than my father."

"Ah," Alejandro said. He appraised the boy with an up-and-down look. Kate stayed in his shadow, saying nothing.

"We are passing through your town, but we are in need of lodgings for a short while. Are there any to be found nearby?" Alejandro asked.

"There is a tavern, though they have no rooms to let," Thomas Blackwell told them. "Missus Tarnoble has tossed the mister out again, and he has put himself in there. Missus says that it will surely be convenient for him, as the tavern is where he spends his time anyway. So you are short of luck." Then his smile broadened. "But I venture that my father would welcome a paying boarder."

"So much the better," Alejandro said. "I favor lodging with a household. It is so much more—friendly."

The boy grinned. "It will cost you a penny, I daresay," he said.

"So be it," Alejandro answered. "I am tired, as is my daughter. A penny is a worthwhile expenditure for the comfort of a good home."

"Then follow me," said Thomas Blackwell the Younger.

"Allow us a moment first," he said. He drew Kate away. "I know you were but a child, but do you recall, when we fled from Canterbury—we came upon a grave..."

"It cannot be the same man."

"Daughter," he said, loving the sound of the word, "I have come through experience to believe that there is no such thing as coincidence."

She stared at him for a moment, then said, "You may well be correct in that belief."

Their curiosity thus stirred, they followed the boy through a square full of people, all going about their daily business. Nowhere did they see any signs of affliction. A stone cross with ornate carving, the edges dulled by time and the elements, stood in the center of the village square, not far from the tavern. A stone church dominated the village center and was surrounded by smaller cottages. People stared at them, seemingly without shame, as they progressed through it all; Alejandro felt their judging eyes upon him. But after a while their expressions softened, one and all, as if something about their appearance proved tolerable. He found it strange indeed.

All along the way, the boy Thomas Blackwell greeted the familiar people he passed with a marked jocularity that was not in keeping with the morose times in which he lived.

Nor was it in keeping with a plagued town. Alejandro leaned back and said to Kate, "This is a remarkably affable village."

"I think so as well."

Each one knew what the other was thinking—that this was a place where none of their pursuers would dare to venture, and that a respite from flight might be a good and welcome thing.

"Let us hope it can be arranged for us to remain here and rest a bit," he said. He pondered anew his remembrance of the name Thomas Blackwell. There were surely many Thomas Blackwells in England; it was a common enough name. But to come upon a black-flagged village where plague had *not* taken its toll, and to come upon the name of a man who had once before escaped its grip—it was unnerving, at the very least.

.   .   .

"Can you not regain their trail?" Benoit said, with audible frustration.

Sir John disliked the man for his grating voice as much as for any other reason. He wondered what de Coucy thought of Benoit's blatant impudence in bypassing his higher-ranking cousin and demanding an answer for himself. He cast a glance at de Coucy but saw no evidence of annoyance in the baron's expression.

Ah, well, they are only French, the knight thought. He called out to the master of the hounds.

"Count Benoit wishes to know why we cannot regain their trail," he said as soon as the man arrived.

"I do not know, m'lord. The hounds are confounded. This seldom happens, but with the ground wet from spring..."

Now de Coucy spoke; his voice was shrill and angry. "Well, lead the beasts on until they find their noses again!"

The houndsman bowed hastily and then rushed off with a worried look on his face, never having glanced into Sir John Chandos's eyes again. The knight cursed under his breath as the man shambled away, though his anger was more at de Coucy. But the houndsmen would not answer to the king should the quest be futile, as he knew it might well be; it was Chandos himself who would have to explain, with careful decoration, why his best trackers had not been successful in finding a Jew and a young woman.

He knew for certain that the king did not understand the skills his daughter possessed; he had never watched her stand before a target and place arrow after arrow in its center, after carefully adjusting the feathers to her own requirements.

Goose feathers, Sir John heard her say with her lovely smile, *serve best. Many favor hawk, but not I....*

Nor did King Edward truly fathom the depth of the Jew's intellect, having no such depth himself. Chandos's excuses would be well considered and believable, but they would not be entirely true.

His thoughts on a plausible explanation for what might be failure were interrupted by the sound of barking, distant and well forward. It was not the ordinary sound of pursuit but something more definitive: The hounds were excited. He rode ahead and saw wagging tails, for the animals all had their noses to the ground. The houndsmen wore brighter looks than those he had last seen on their faces.

Ducks and chickens pranced about the Blackwell yard as if they owned it—and by the odor, Alejandro guessed that they actually did. He stepped around their filth as best he could and followed the boy. As they passed by the simple cottage, they came to an outbuilding with a fenced corral of sorts. In it they saw a fine big hog. Perhaps in curiosity on hearing their arrival, a fat sow wallowed out from the small enclosure; she was obviously heavy with young, on the verge of delivering her litter. It was a prosperous household, to have separate lodging for the animals.

"Father!" young Thomas Blackwell cried.

After a few moments, a middle-aged man of some girth appeared in the doorway.

"We've guests!" the lad cried. He gestured in the direction of the travelers. "Paying lodgers!"

The father's face lit up. He stepped out into the sunlight, wiping his hands on a cloth. "Welcome!" he said affably. He nodded slightly to Alejandro and Kate.

"Thank you," Alejandro said. "My daughter and I are in need of arrangements."

Thomas Blackwell the Elder eyed them suspiciously. It was not the first time that someone had looked upon the pair and judged that there was no possibility of kinship between the two. The expression that developed on his face was one of skepticism that gradually changed to humor. A smirk threatened to blossom, but the man held it admirably in check.

"We've a comfortable loft above the house, if you don't mind the noise," he said. "I've four young ones," he added.

"I rather enjoy the sound of children," Alejandro said. He touched Kate lightly on the arm. "It has been far too long since my own daughter was young."

"Ah," Blackwell said. He looked Kate up and down, to Alejandro's chagrin. "Indeed," the man said, "I can see that."

He strode forward and extended his hand in greeting. "Thomas Blackwell, at your service, sir." Alejandro took it as Blackwell asked, "And what would be your name?"

"Alejandro," he said.

"A Spaniard," Blackwell noted.

To this assumption, Alejandro gave a nod. "And this is my daughter *Katarina*."

Kate glanced at him in surprise, though Blackwell did not see it, for he had been distracted by a squeal from the hog's pen. There was a bit of jostling going on for a position at the fence.

"You'll be waiting a bit more for your feed if you keep that up," he said to the swine. Then he turned back to Alejandro. "They're a right greedy pair."

"One can see that, judging by their size."

"There'll be a fine slaughter one of these days," Blackwell added. "Enough to keep the whole of Eyam in bacon for a good long time. We have a fondness for bacon fat around here. 'Tis a cure for plague."

For a moment, Alejandro said nothing. Finally, he said, "We have seen by your flag that plague has visited this place."

Blackwell spat into the hog pen, then wiped his face on his sleeve. "It has," he said, "though it was last year. A man came through the town, just as you do now, but he stayed at the tavern. None of us liked the look of him, truth be told—he was sallow and thin when he arrived. First this visitor took ill, then the landlady. She died right quickly, within a day. The landlord's daughter was stricken as well, but she recovered." With one meaty hand, he made a quick sign of the cross on his chest. "She'll not recover her beauty, I fear. The scourge has left a mark on her."

"And no more were afflicted?"

"No, thank Christ and all the saints. The girl took to her loft and drank her bacon grease until she was well cured, and by that action stopped the spread."

Kate stepped forward and said, "I heard a tale from a traveling beggar, who spoke of plague being presently in the north. That was a mere fortnight ago."

"You have come upon old Will, have you? He's been spreading that story for the better part of a year. We don't pay him any mind. We leave out food for him now and then, and he makes his way, God alone knows how, but he manages."

"But it was well south of here."

"The man has naught to do but ride," Blackwell told her.

"Then what he said was untrue."

"Not entirely." He reached into a sack and withdrew a handful of grain, which he threw at the hogs. They squealed in delight and began rooting in the mud with their noses immediately. "We are of a mind to *keep* it out, and the best way to do that is to tell anyone who will listen that it already lives here. Then it will not come, at least not by way of a traveler." He wiped his hands unceremoniously on the legs of his breeches. "I'll wager a night's lodging that you felt a few stares as you passed through."

Alejandro nodded.

"There are many who bemoan the lack of both commerce and congress, myself among them. There were some who thought it wise to flee, to avoid the pest altogether. But flee where, I say—anywhere you go it can come upon you. I know." He pointed his finger downward and said, in a bitter voice, "I put all of my children by my first wife and the lady herself into the ground. There is nowhere to flee."

So there it was. This was the very same Thomas Blackwell. And now he had a twelve-year-old son.

God is indeed good.

He put his supposition to the test. "Nowhere to flee—this is a strong statement you make, Mister Blackwell."

"Indeed it is, *Monsieur l'Espanol.*" He grinned momentarily, awaiting a response from Alejandro, whose nod of acknowledgment was reason enough to continue. "I buried them, one on top of the other, in one grave, not far south of Canterbury."

After a decent interval, Alejandro said, "Please allow me to express my sincere condolences to you. But I must confess—many years ago, when I traveled in that region, I saw the grave you made for them."

Blackwell stared at him, as if he were lying.

"It is the truth, Alejandro said. "You wrote an inscription: *And here lie my twelve children and my wife of many years.* I wept in grief for them and—perhaps more deeply—for you."

Blackwell looked toward the house in which he lived with his current wife and their children. There was an expression of desperate love on his face, but at the same time, there was a longing. Alejandro could guess what the man longed for—the return of the departed. It was a dream that would not be realized.

"Often in my own dreams," he said, "I have seen you laying all the children in the grave, and then their mother, with her arms outstretched to protect them. I pray for your family." He forgot de Chauliac's warning to him in the emotion of the moment. "I am a physician, and I have seen too many die of this scourge."

For a moment Blackwell stared at him. "I thank you for your dreams, kind sir. Your prayers are most welcome and appreciated. But I must tell you, that is not how it took place."

Alejandro did not really understand. "How, then, did it happen?"

"Well, it was a very curious turn of events, I must say. My wife died first—Janet was her name, rest in peace. She was a good woman."

"By how long, might I ask?"

"I cannot recall exactly how long. There is a part of my mind that will not allow it."

"It is God's way of protecting you, sir, from the pain of your memories."

"Ah," Blackwell said. "Of course, that makes perfect sense. I do remember that Janet died on a Sunday eve—we had all gone to chapel that morning, and those of us who could took the blood and body of

Christ. I have often thanked God that He provided grace for my family just before He called them to Himself. But my gratitude did not last long. You cannot imagine, unless you have lived a week like that one, watching all that you love die slowly before you."

Alejandro recalled the day that Adele died. The pain had almost been unbearable. She had died in his arms, but so had the children and wife of Thomas Blackwell—thirteen souls, whereas he had known the death of but one. The man's grief would have been immeasurable.

"You are correct, sir," he said. "I cannot imagine."

He said nothing to Thomas Blackwell for another moment or two; the poor man had rivulets of tears running down his cheeks, though Alejandro did not think that Blackwell was aware of it, since he made no attempt to wipe them away. He waited—more patiently than he would have thought possible—until Blackwell finally sensed the wetness and wiped his cheeks dry.

"I laid Janet's body out in the far end of the longhouse until I could dig a proper grave for her," Blackwell said. "I had the children to care for..."

In his mind's eye, Alejandro saw twelve children, each one a bit taller than the one who preceded him, each one running toward a pit in the ground. As Blackwell's sorrowful tale droned in the background, the physician saw each child morph from pink health to pale ashes and then leap into the pit, only to burst into a shower of gray dust.

"...but the grave was a good deep one, thank God, else their toes would be sticking up out of the soil."

The ignominy of that notion brought Alejandro back to the present; Alejandro tried to imagine Adele's toes sticking up out of the soil, or those of Hernandez, a giant of a man, who had helped him in so many ways.

"It was a week of pure hell," Blackwell said quietly.

A week, Alejandro thought. It seemed uncanny. "Kind sir," he said, "I shall pray anew for the souls of your loved ones."

"For that I thank you. A prayer is always appreciated." He crossed himself and closed his eyes, and when he opened them, his gaze was directed toward heaven. "Holy Father, please cast Thy blessings upon us, Your faithful servants who stand here without support, on the rough and unforgiving earth."

Alejandro let a brief moment pass in deference to the man's memories, then said, "Tell me, Blackwell. Just out of curiosity, have any of your children of *this* union succumbed?"

Blackwell crossed himself again, but this time he fell to his knees. He put his hands together and faced his God. "Heavenly Father, I give thanks to Thee that none has been taken." He rose again and said, "There are some families in the farms on the outskirts of town who have had their brush with the pest, but none in town here." Blackwell leaned closer and said, with a grin, "God has answered our prayers, plain and simple."

Alejandro kept his skepticism to himself and simply said, "There are many remarkable occurrences in this world. This is perhaps just one of them."

"Bloody right," Blackwell said emphatically. "We are a fortunate lot here, I would say—more fortunate than most, because the king's men will not venture in here while we purport to be afflicted. And for this we are most grateful."

Kate and Alejandro exchanged a silent understanding. They would stay in the haven of Eyam, perhaps for a few days, to plan the rest of their escape.

It was a sickly-looking fox at best, but de Coucy put an arrow into the poor thing anyway. He ordered one of the houndsmen to take the pelt, but even the most desperate furrier would not consider putting it into a cloak. The animal seemed almost to lay itself in the path of danger and put up little fight when the hounds cornered it. The houndsman displayed the bloody thing by holding it up in one hand. De Coucy's triumph was greeted with only lukewarm praise.

The houndsman hung the carcass over the back of his saddle. His horse did not seem to appreciate the smell, which was disturbingly more vile than one might expect from a fresh kill.

Chandos rode up to de Coucy and said discreetly, "No one will think less of you for getting rid of that thing. Certainly I will not."

"I will keep it," de Coucy said defiantly. "Better yet, my cousin shall have its pelt for his fiancée, and it shall become part of her trousseau." He looked to the same man who had brought it to him. "You," he said, "skin this thing and leave the carcass behind."

Chandos wanted to strike him. But the king would not approve of such a gesture, especially under the circumstances. He ordered the party to continue on.

They made camp that night about half a day shy of the Peaks. The hounds had picked up a fresh trail, and they had followed it, as there was nothing else to show them the way. In the morning when they awoke, the pelt was gone. *Stolen by a wolf,* the houndsman speculated. Everyone thought it a mercy. De Coucy said nothing, nor did Benoit. The unpleasantness was over, for the moment.

Kate awoke before dawn. The first thing her eyes settled upon was the thatched ceiling of the Blackwell cottage, and a surge of happiness rushed through her. She turned in the straw and saw three little girls lying there, all sound asleep, dreaming perhaps of sweets and treats and rag dolls to make their days happy.

"You live a fine life," she said in a whisper. They were not wealthy, nor were they privileged in any other way, but there was a bond of love and trust between the parents and children of this clan that seemed almost unnatural to her. One little girl mewed slightly in her sleep and turned a bit in the straw. Her blond curls were a tangle, and Kate wondered if the little child would cry out when one of her older sisters tried to comb the knots out of it.

I only hope your sister is more gentle to you than mine is to me.

She threw off the light wool coverlet and tiptoed across the wide planks of the loft. She moved quietly down the ladder and found Thomas Blackwell's wife already at work before the hearth.

"Good morning to you, madam," Kate said brightly.

Mrs. Blackwell nodded and smiled, then put a finger to her lips.

She leaned forward and whispered, "My husband is a bit under the weather this morning."

Kate leaned close as well and asked, with alarm in her voice, "Has he taken ill?"

"Oh, no, dearie, nothing like that. He just has a bit too much of the drink left in him this morning. He'll be fine in a few hours, I suspect. But right now he wants to toss back up everything he ate yesterday and more. I shouldn't be surprised to see a fair piece of his stomach somewhere on this floor."

Kate smiled with relief as she left the house and headed for the water trough. The ground was damp with dew, which wet the bottom of her feet. It was wonderfully quiet outside, not even a bird was chirping— the hour was still too early. When she had cleaned the sleep from her eyes and face, she went back into the house. "Is there some way I can help you?"

"No, miss, you just take your ease. I'll finish the porridge."

It seemed such a sweet and simple task, the making of food, one that Kate had been denied for all of her time in Windsor.

"It would be my pleasure to stir," she said.

After a long look, Mrs. Blackwell pointed the handle in Kate's direction. When Kate took it, Mrs. Blackwell wiped her hands on her skirt and sat down on a chair to watch.

"Well, isn't this a treat," she said. "A fine lady I am, if only for a moment."

"Indeed," Kate said as she turned the slurry over and over in the pot. The last time she had performed this task was in the longhouse outside Paris, for her husband and father. She did not look in Mrs. Blackwell's direction, lest the woman—a stranger—see her tears. One or two fell into the pot. She hoped they would not turn the porridge bitter.

After a few more moments of stirring, she turned back to Mrs. Blackwell and asked, "I was wondering, madam, if you might spare a few goose feathers."

·   ·   ·

Chandos rode at the head of the party as they followed the hounds. When he saw the black flag in the distance, he held up one hand to halt those who followed him. When the entire party was stopped, he turned to one of his men and said, "We shall proceed no further in this direction."

Amid the cacophony of baying and snorting, de Coucy moved forward, just close enough so that Chandos could hear him. "But the hounds..." he said.

"I can see that they are agitated," Chandos said. "Nevertheless, we shall ride no further." He nodded toward the flag. "I am not man enough to tempt such a fate as that, with the future son-in-law of my king in the party."

De Coucy glared at Chandos; the seasoned warrior stared back with even greater vitriol. It so unnerved the young French knight that he looked away for a moment. Finally he gathered his courage and said, "But she will escape!"

"Perhaps she will," Chandos said. "It would not be the first time she has slipped away. Nor, I am sure, will it be the last. She is as cunning as a vixen." He placed his gloved hand on de Coucy's arm to soothe him. "And more determined than a vixen not to be caught."

De Coucy brushed his hand away angrily. "Cunning she may be, but I will have her back again."

"Perhaps," Chandos said quietly. "And perhaps not." He rode off to confer with his lieutenant on their camping arrangements, after which he turned his huge black horse around and faced the company.

"We will make a detour around this village," he said. He pointed to the flag. "In view of this posting, I suspect our quarry will not have ventured therein. Perhaps," he said, staring at de Coucy, "the hounds are confused by the scent of yesterday's fox."

All eyes went to Isabella's unhappy baron.

"If, on the other side," Chandos continued, "we are unable to reacquire their trail, we shall return to Windsor and make our apologies to the king. He will not fault us for preserving ourselves and the new member of his family against the Death." He gave a quick nod to one of his lieutenants, who whistled loudly and gestured with his hand in the reverse direction.

The soldiers in the party turned about face as if they were one body. De Coucy and Benoit stayed beneath the flag, whispering feverishly between themselves for a good while before they fell in with the others. As he waited for them, Chandos stared up at the tattered warning flag.

I have no fear of plague, Kate had told him over one of their chess games. A tingling rose up in Chandos's spine, for he knew in his heart that they were in there.

Twenty-six

"We need to take a tissue sample to be sure if this is plague," Janie said as she stood over the mottled corpse. "It would be best to get one from the neck or the groin."

"This would have to be from a natural source," Lany said nervously. "Wouldn't it?"

"I don't think so. There's no natural reservoir around here."

"But there must be carriers in this area. He might have handled something that was infected, like a rabbit or a rat or something. People must be eating a lot of strange things these days."

"If we were out west in a dry climate," Janie said, "I might agree with you. But natural cases of plague are so rare here. In the past twenty years there have only been two cases."

Lany gave her a suspicious look. "And you know this because..."

Janie looked at her. "Because I once did some fieldwork on—" She was about to say specifically plague but changed her mind. "Infectious diseases. One of the, uh, projects I worked on concerned plague in the environment."

Lany stared back for a moment, sensing from Janie's clipped explanation that there was more to the story than she was telling, but she didn't press. "And you're relatively sure this is plague."

"No, but it has a lot of the characteristics. At least on the surface. And I've seen it firsthand."

"In a human being?"

She couldn't meet Lany's eyes. "In more than one."

"Someday you'll have to tell me about that."

Janie did not respond to the prompting, but instead explained the reasons for her suspicion. "Look at the groin," she said, pointing with the stick. "Massively swollen lymph glands and testes. And his neck," she said, moving the stick. "Visible buboes. If we'd taken a scalpel to those swellings just before this man died, they would have exploded all over us."

"*Ugh.*"

"You don't want to know. If we could get his mouth open, his teeth would be coated with a white film of bacteria. In his lungs you'd see pockets of dried blood that collected in the air sacs. His liver would be swollen, if he'd had *bubonic* plague, which from first glance this resembles."

She stood up and walked around the corpse, examining it with her eyes only from all angles. "Still, I don't know.... This is just so out of place. It looks like plague, but it really shouldn't be. Not here, not at this time of year."

She was quiet for a moment, as if mulling over something in her mind. "The bacteria we found on our SAM-pulls, and on the repeat samples Michael took...that looked like plague too. But it wasn't. And it looked a little like DR SAM too. But it wasn't."

"You're certain of that?"

"I am. Unequivocally."

"My God," Lany said. "What if this is a combination of the two?"

"There's no way to tell what it is unless we take a sample." She glanced up unhappily. "Unfortunately, I did what Steve suggested: I brought survival stuff, not field-research equipment." She looked the corpse up and down again, her frustration building. "My kingdom for latex gloves and a plastic bag," she said. "A nice sharp scalpel wouldn't hurt either."

Alejandro, she knew, would have found a way to make do with what was around him. She looked down on the ground nearby for something that might be folded or cupped. A large brown leaf, waterlogged and supple, presented itself.

Janie took out her knife and knelt low over the corpse. Using the leaf like Lany had, she grabbed a cluster of lymph nodes with her left hand and, with one swift move of the knife in her right hand, cut them free. She set the leaf faceup on the ground with the small slice of flesh in its center, staring up at her.

"I need something to tie it up," she said.

Lany brought forth a long green tendril of newly sprouted bittersweet. "I used to yank this stuff up from my flower beds. It's tough as nails."

"Great." Janie took it from her hand and wrapped it around the leaf until it was all secure. "Looks like a stuffed grape leaf," she said.

"I hope that holds," Lany said. "Otherwise, we're both in trouble."

"Hey," Janie said, almost bitterly, "not to worry. If it's plague, we're immune, right?"

With the sample stowed at the base of one of her saddlebags, Janie went to the water's edge and rubbed her hands clean until they were so cold from the icy water that she could barely feel them. She got back on the horse again with her teeth chattering. "We need to make up some time if we're going to do twenty miles today."

"Then we should probably go out onto the road," Lany said. "It'll be a lot faster. This river should bring us out to Route 32. I don't think it's even a mile from here to that point."

They continued along the riverbank. Since they'd discovered the corpse, sounds were louder, colors brighter, smells more overwhelming. Janie was supremely aware of every crack of a stick and every scream of a bird. When they finally reached the bridge for Route 32—

within a mile, just as Lany had speculated—they urged their horses up the embankment until they came to the edge of the cracked pavement. Lany looked up at the sky, then looked in each direction on the road. "East is that way," she said, pointing left.

The sounds their own horses' hooves made on the pavement seemed deafening. "This makes me nervous," Janie said. "I keep expecting a car to come whizzing around the corner at any moment. I feel like I want to get off the road."

"It is strange," Lany admitted. She glanced around, her eyes touching on abandoned buildings where roadside businesses once thrived.

Not far down the road, they came upon a cluster of dilapidated industrial-looking buildings, typical New England mills. The walls of a large brick building—an abandoned factory of some sort—came right up to the edge of the road. They passed in nervous silence, too close to the building for either one's liking. At the halfway point, despite her desire to get beyond the looming facade, Janie brought Jellybean to a sudden halt.

Lany turned back and gave her a questioning look.

"Shh," Janie whispered. Then, "Do you hear that?"

Lany concentrated on listening. "Water," she said.

"More than that. I hear something else—I think it's—*creaking*."

They tied up the horses and inched their way around the edge of the massive building. When they came to the back corner, they stopped and looked around carefully. The source of the creaking sound became clear instantly.

It came from a brand-new, fast-spinning waterwheel that rotated freely, pushed by the rushing current of a small river. There was a narrow bridge over the wheel, attached to the top of the building from which the wheel's axle protruded.

Two little girls played on the bridge. After a few moments, an adult woman came out onto the bridge and shooed them back inside, perhaps for a snack or a nap.

As if nothing had ever changed.

"My God," Janie whispered as the trio disappeared into the building. She let her gaze drift up the side of the building; it was five stories high, and along the side there were perhaps a dozen windows—twice as many, at least, in the other direction.

"A whole town could live in here," she said.

"Maybe a whole town does," Lany replied. "Maybe we should . . . go inside."

"No," Janie said urgently. "We have a mission. We need to stay focused. And we have a sample of what might be bubonic plague tissue in one of our saddlebags. We can't be exposing a whole group of people to that."

A whole group of people. It was the most delicious phrase.

But their excitement was quickly tempered.

"Look," Lany said, pointing up a hill.

Janie turned her eyes in that direction. She saw three graves with cross markers. The earth that covered them appeared to be fresh.

"I guess we know where our mystery man came from," she said.

"He'd have to canoe upstream to get to where we found him. He didn't look like he was in any kind of shape for that."

"Maybe he wasn't all that sick when he left."

"Then why would he leave?"

Janie looked at her and said, "Maybe it wasn't voluntary."

They went back to the horses and rode off at a quick but stealthy pace. From a safe vantage point, they stopped to look back. Janie half-expected to see eyes staring back at her. *Monastery* came to mind.

The horses, at their riders' urgings, stepped lively. The sun was past its zenith, leaving them perhaps five more hours of traveling light.

"When we get far enough out of town, I'd like to check in with the folks in Orange. Steve will be worried about us by now."

"Okay," Janie said. "They can send a message to Alex for me after that."

About a mile farther down the road, all evidence of civilization vanished, except for a small roadside picnic area with a table and benches, by some inexplicable grace still unrotted and sittable. They tied up the horses and stretched their own legs for a few moments, then sat down on opposite sides of the weathered table.

"Oh, God," Lany said as she began to press the buttons on the PDA, "I hope I can remember how to work this thing."

She held it in both hands carefully so as not to drop it and pushed buttons with both thumbs. "It's on," she said. "Now, I press *Select....*"

She fiddled for a few more seconds, then looked up at Janie with a grin. "There's a signal bar," she said. "My God. How long has it been since I've seen one of these?"

Janie came around to that side of the table. "Just one bar," she said. "But maybe that'll be enough."

"It'll have to be." Lany touched the keypad a number of times in rapid succession. Then she typed out a message letter by letter, a slow and laborious process for fingers out of practice.

> **OK so far, twelve miles out. Came upon potential friendlies. Send e-mail to TA from J.**

She wrote nothing about the graves; it would require too much explanation and would have to wait for their return. "Okay, now I send it. Here goes," she said. "Keep your fingers crossed."

She pressed the green arrow. A progress bar appeared, advancing slowly from left to right as the message was beamed through the air to the next cell tower:

Message sent successfully.

"Oh, my God, it worked!" Then, in a more tempered voice, she added, "At least it says it did."

Janie said, "Steve said they would send something right back if they got ours."

"Ten minutes, they said, so the battery doesn't run out."

They waited, counting the seconds of precious battery power.

The PDA emitted a small beep.

Janie almost jumped. Lany held the PDA so they could both read the screen.

Hello, Lewis and Clark, things fine here, message to TA tonight.
Invite friendlies to dinner. Smile. Keep up the good work, report in
before sleep if possible.

What sleep? Janie thought. There would be little sleep for her
tonight.

Fredo found Bruce in his laboratory in the biological sciences building.

"The teams are ready, boss," he said.

"Good. Has everyone gotten their positioning?"

"We handed it out about a half hour ago."

He drew in a long breath, then let it out again. "Well, I guess we're
all set, then. I'll be there in a minute."

"Okay, see you out there."

When he was alone again, Bruce sat down and rested his elbows on
the surface of the desk. He put his face in his hands and just sat there
for a moment, gathering himself.

I'm not a warrior, he told himself.

His deeper self answered, *You are what you need to be in any given moment, or you are dead.*

He rose up and left the lab, then traveled through the maze of
underground corridors that once teemed with students going from
dormitory to class to dining hall and back again, all sheltered from the
wicked winter weather that settled over the Blackstone Valley for more
than four months of each year. They'd had a bit of luck—the wells,
blessedly, had continued to produce good water; the enclosed quad-
rangles were sunny and fertile enough to grow their vegetables. And
there was a near-lifetime supply of canned and dry goods in the storage
areas adjacent to the dining hall.

Before joining his companions on the far side of the quadrangle, he
made one stop. He stepped inside one of the aviaries and was greeted
with the usual chorus of protests from the territorial birds of prey that
were housed within.

"Hello," he said aloud. A symphony of bird cries came back at him.

He put his hand into a small tank and brought out a salamander. He dropped the slimy thing through the bars; it landed on the floor of the cage, just below a wood branch, on which was perched a young eagle. The bird shook its leg a few times in an effort to dislodge the small metal box that was attached just above the foot.

"Better get used to that thing," Bruce said. "We won't let you go until you do." This was a chick from one of the eggs they'd taken from the veteran female 908; the young bird's behavior of late had been strange. "Let's hope you do better than your mama seems to be doing lately."

The bird screamed in its baby voice.

"That's right, squawk all you want. Did anyone ever tell you that you sound just like a dinosaur?" He clicked his lips to mimic the sound that the eagle's mother would have made in feeding him. "But I have to tell you, if we'd been around then, we would have survived all that climate change too, because we can *think*."

The baby jumped down off the perch and sucked in the salamander. Then he fluttered back up to the perch again. As he swallowed, he flapped his wings furiously.

Bruce moved along the cages until he came to one that housed a young turkey vulture. He opened a metal food container attached to the bottom of the cage and turned his head away in disgust as he pulled out a putrid hunk of rabbit flesh with a metal tong. He pushed it through the cage wire and held it in place until the bird had eaten the whole thing.

"That's right," he cooed, "eat up! We have plans for that stomach of yours."

He left the aviary and went out into the relative silence of the quadrangle. He looked up into the gray sky; a storm was in the air. It was bad news for the double deltas who would be arriving, starting today, if their interceptions were true. They would arrive with hearts full of good intentions. He and his cohorts would watch and, if their equipment would allow it, listen—hopefully without revealing themselves—to make sure that no harm came to them. He wondered if there would be anyone watching behind them and envisioned, with a small sense of irony, a daisy chain of watchers extending around the world, to Afghanistan, Iran, Eastern Europe, maybe all the way to China. Who knew where the Coalition's reach might have extended?

As he steeled himself for what might come, the hackles on his back were rising. He couldn't pinpoint exactly why, but it didn't matter. He'd know soon enough if the Coalition was primed to swoop down on their favorite prey. It was coming down to a war of the birds. He'd been through it in his mind so many times, and he always came to the same conclusion: that they were using some kind of bird to carry their new bug out into the world and inject it into the native rodent population. They'd discovered this by sending out their own birds, the beautiful eagles, with sensors on their legs. And in the end, it would be the turkey vultures—he hoped—that carried the seeds of a cure.

All he had to do was make it work.

"There's a house up ahead," Lany said. "Should we check it out?"

"Probably," Janie said. "There's not enough light left to go much farther."

With the horses tied up behind the house, they went together from room to room, Lany with her gun out, Janie with knife in hand.

"Seems empty," Lany said when they finished inspecting the second floor.

"I'd feel better if it was a little farther off the road."

"Me too, but I think it'll be okay." Lany snapped the safety in place and put the gun into the holster on her right leg. "There's a back stairway if we need to make a quick exit."

"Let's go get the horses, then."

They brought the animals inside the first floor of the house and closed the door.

They settled themselves into one of the upstairs rooms. Janie was about to light one of their small lanterns, but Lany stopped her hand before the match hit the wick. "Do you really need the light?"

After a few seconds, Janie said, "I don't suppose I do. But I'd like it. We need to eat."

"I just wonder if it might not be a better idea to keep it dark. We've got sandwiches; we don't need light to eat them. We know there are people out there now, and I worry about someone seeing us. We don't know if there are more groups, but it stands to reason that there would be—that dead man had to come from somewhere."

Janie knew she was right, but still she resented the darkness. She found some comfort in the meal, however; the sandwich of coarse bread and hard cheese might as well have been filet mignon for how delicious it tasted after a long stretch without food. When she was finished eating, she crept carefully down the back stairway, feeling each step in the blackness. Once outside, she moved a few steps away from the house and relieved herself, quickly and in the open. No mountain lion would get her now.

The darkness was stark, with no moon and a layer of clouds obscuring the stars. The chill night air assaulted her skin. She shivered as she made her way back up the unfamiliar stairs and dove into the sleeping bag with her teeth chattering.

With nothing to occupy her senses but the sound of insects outside, her mind went straight to pain.

Oh, Tom, I miss you so much tonight. Had he not lost his leg, he would have insisted on going along, double delta or not. She hugged her own arms around herself, but it brought no comfort. *And please, God, take care of my son.* Tears filled her eyes and nose; she sniffed and wiped them away with the cuff of her sweater.

"You all right?"

She sniffed once again. "No, not really. I miss my husband, I'm worried about my son, and I can hardly remember why I'm huddled here in the dark, far away from the things I love and need. I didn't really want to go on this trip, but once we got started, I was hoping it would take my mind off—everything. So far it hasn't made a bit of difference. And I just can't seem to get warm. I can't stop shivering."

Lany hitched herself, still in the sleeping bag, across the floor until she was very close to Janie. "Here," she said, "unzip your bag and hook it to mine. I'm plenty warm."

The conditioning of a lifetime made her hesitate.

But how many times had Alejandro slept in the same straw bed as another person, just for the warmth?

Somehow in the dark they managed to hook up their bags. Warmth returned, but the aches were not banished. She tried to hide the sound of her weeping, but Lany heard.

"Go ahead," Lany told her. "Cry if you want to. You don't have to keep a brave face for me. And no one will care tomorrow if your eyes are swollen shut."

Janie wept bitterly until, finally, sleep took her.

They rose up very early and got moving fast. The remaining distance to Worcester—geographically the most accessible place in Massachusetts—took four hours to cover. By noon, they were installed in a thicket of brush outside the armory, silently watching the comings and goings of more people than either of them had seen in years.

"Three dozen people waiting outside." Lany extended her hand and offered the binoculars. "Here, take a look."

Janie positioned the eyepieces and adjusted the focus, then watched intently for a few minutes. "Someone just came out the front door," she said. "He's talking to the people who are waiting."

She handed back the binocs.

"They're going in," Lany said as she looked. She set down the viewers. "What do you think we should do?"

"Run," Janie said. "As far and as fast as possible. This all scares me to death."

"It scares me too, but we're here, so we might as well finish what we started. We can leave the horses here and continue on foot, see if we can get close enough to hear what they're saying. Hell, we're supposed to be in there with them."

"Leave the horses? What do we do if someone steals them? Walk back to Orange?"

Lany considered that comment for a moment before responding. "You stay here, then, and I'll go closer. I'm smaller, anyway. They won't see me as easily."

She handed the binoculars to Janie. "Keep an eye out. Can you whistle?"

"Badly, but yes."

"Whistle if anything looks like it might be a problem."

"Okay."

Lany patted the gun on her thigh. Earlier, before they'd entered Worcester, Janie had watched her open the chamber and remove and then replace all the bullets.

"You've got your knife, right?"

Janie patted her own ankle.

"Good. I'll be back as soon as I can. No more than an hour." She took a few steps forward, then turned. "If I don't come back in an hour, you have to go back without me."

"I'm not going to leave you here alone—"

"Oh, yes you are. I would leave you alone if the situation were reversed."

Janie stared at her for a few seconds, then said, "Okay." As she watched Lany disappear into the brush, the cold terror of solitude settled over her. She raised up the binoculars again and watched as, one by one, the invitees—all presumably double deltas—stepped through the door.

It terrified her to see each person slip out of sight. Did these people all know and trust one another, or were they strangers, as Lany and she would be if they chose to join the party? And why would anyone step through a door not knowing what might await them on the other side?

She heard the voice of Myra Ross in her mind. Over a long-ago lunch, Myra had spoken of her passage from Berlin to Auschwitz. *We went into the boxcars because they told us to. They told us not to worry, that we would be safe.*

Chills and tingles, the icy fingers of warning, ran up and down her spine.

Janie wanted to stand up and scream to them. She managed to contain herself, though it took all of her will. She continued to watch, her mind exploding with silent *nos*, until a movement in one corner of the lens distracted her.

It was Lany, on the edge of the wooded area that surrounded the building. There was a chain-link fence; Lany was trying to squeeze her way through what appeared to be an opening. Janie watched as she put one leg through, then bent down, as if to slip inside.

And then, behind Lany, there was a man—a very large man with a ponytail.

Janie's heart leaped into her throat and she stood straight up. She tried to whistle, but it was as if she were trying in a dream—she had no spit, and her furious efforts resulted in no sound. She watched in horrified helplessness as Lany was pulled back through the opening in the fence and then disappeared from view.

Bruce walked slowly around the chair in which Lany was seated. No one was expecting the Coalition to send a woman; they'd been caught off-guard, just as the Israelis had been in the time before when the Palestinians began sending women as suicide bombers. He chided himself for his failure to see it coming. "I'll ask you again," he said, "where do you live?"

He got nothing but silence in return.

"Look," he said, "we know what's going on. I just want to know what your part is in the whole thing."

He placed her gun on a nearby table and the PDA next to it. He saw her eyes dart from one item to the other, and then she looked straight out, focusing on nothing.

"Good weapon," he said, "and pretty advanced communications. You must have a good-size cell. How many are there, two hundred, five hundred? More than that?"

She counted silently and came up with a figure of fifty-six between the two allied colonies. It seemed laughable that he should be estimating hundreds. She said nothing to his question.

"What do you have planned for the deltas?"

Still staring ahead, Lany said, "I should be asking *you* that question, don't you think?"

"And how am I supposed to know?"

Finally, Lany looked straight at him. It was hard to do; one eye was twisted by scar tissue, in keeping with that whole side of his face. The other side of his face hinted at handsomeness, once upon a time. She didn't really know which eye to engage—and despite the fact that she was his captive and ought to be spitting into one of his eyes or the other, it seemed impolite to ask.

But the questions he was asking *her* made no sense. "You were watching too," she said. She stood, bringing the chair to which she was handcuffed up with her. "You're one of them, aren't you?"

For a moment, he seemed stunned. Then the look of shock disappeared from the half of his face that could show such expressions. She had managed to unnerve him, however momentarily. He could not let that happen. "No," he said quietly. "But I think *you* are."

Lany threw back her head and laughed aloud. "Not me," she said. "I came here to see what they're up to."

Once again, he asked, "Where are you from?"

It was a number of seconds before Lany finished weighing the possible answers. "Let's just say we're not close neighbors. I live a pretty good distance away from here. Someone—I have no idea who—sent me an e-mail invitation to this meeting and I thought I'd better find out what was going on."

It wasn't precisely a lie; the e-mail had been sent specifically to *cop@orangecommunity.net*. But her captor didn't seem to buy it, at least not completely. He took her gun and the PDA and left her alone in the room.

Stay and wait; see if she gets out. Go after her. Go back to Orange. Go back to the mountain and forget any of this happened.

Janie was deeply rattled; all she knew was that she had to stay hidden, at least for the moment. A brutally honest assessment of her own capabilities and resources led her to the painful conclusion that it would be an act of sheer insanity to try to find Lany and rescue her. She could go to Orange and enlist their help in getting Lany back, but every bit of her wanted to go straight back to the mountain, to her son and husband.

I can contact Orange from there, she told herself. It was home, it was safe, it was where she belonged. She unfolded the map and looked over the routes.

Almost fifty miles, she calculated. Two long days. She left Lany's horse tied up; if she got free, she'd need her mount to get away.

"Come on, darlin'," she said to Jellybean. "Take me home."

There was a small window in the room, looking out into the quadrangle. It looked so different with its gardens and play areas and clotheslines than it had when she'd trained there years before. She followed a young man with curly dark hair with her eyes as he made his way across the grassy expanse. He carried a box of some sort and wore—if her eyes were seeing it correctly—some kind of leather shield on his arm.

Falconry came into her mind. But here, in the middle of what had once been a city? *They did it in castles,* she reminded herself. Castles were the cities of their time. Everyone she'd seen seemed healthy and well fed; maybe the falcons were trained to bring back small game, rabbits, pheasants, squirrels . . .

Rats, mice, ferrets, snakes . . .

Her mind pushed the distasteful images away. If they fed her, she would look carefully at what was on her plate.

The door opened; she moved away from the window quickly and stood in one corner of the room as her captor entered again.

He had two glasses in his hands. He offered one to her. "Lemonade," he said.

She stared at the glass as the shock set in.

"You have *lemons*?"

"And limes. We grow them in a special room that's environmentally controlled. We use solar power and ultraviolet lights." He raised the glass in offering again. She eyed it suspiciously. He took a sip from both glasses, one after the other. "There," he said. "Not poisoned or drugged. All natural, just like the good old days."

She came forward and took one of the glasses from him. "Thank you," she said. When the lemonade hit her tongue, it felt like heaven.

"Thank *you*," she said again, with more emphasis. "My God, that tastes good." She drank the rest of the lemonade in one long and thirsty pull.

Bruce smiled and sat down in one of the chairs. "Look," he said, "I'll get straight to the point. There isn't any time to fool around."

Oh, yeah, she thought suspiciously, *butter me up with lemonade, then pump me for information. . . .*

"We know there's a cell in New Jersey. We think that's the closest cell. Is that where you came from?"

Cell? New Jersey? She was completely confused.

"No, I . . . didn't come from New Jersey."

"There's another cell close enough for you to travel here?"

"What are you talking about, *cell . . .*"

"Don't play with me."

She stood, bringing up the chair again. "I'm not. And I truly have no idea what you're talking about."

"Then why are you here?"

"I told you already. We received an e-mail at—home. It took us to a Web site for double deltas. We read about the meeting."

Bruce let a few moments pass as he stared at her in an attempt to determine if she was as genuinely confused by what he was asking as she appeared to be. Finally, he tossed out the burning question: "Did the Coalition send you here to spy on this meeting?"

"*What?*"

"The Coalition. The group—"

"I know what the Coalition is. I used—"

She stopped.

"Used to what?"

She didn't reply.

"Look," he said, his frustration showing clearly, "I'm not accustomed to this interrogation stuff. I don't know the first thing about it. But there are things I need to know, and you've been out there. So how about this: I'll tell you what we know, and then maybe you can tell me a thing or two about you, by which I mean you and whatever group you belong to. Deal?"

The taste of lemon was still with her. They hadn't hurt her; this man, despite his hideous scarring, seemed to want to know what was happening in Worcester as much as she did. It was, after all, right in his backyard that the meeting was taking place.

The facility, at least what she'd seen of it, was as clean and well kept as it had been before, and full of pleasant surprises.

Trust your instincts.

"Deal."

"Okay," he said. He seemed quite relieved. "Okay, you go first."

"No."

He smiled slightly; the cracks on one side of his face intensified. "All right. If that's how you want it. . . . Here's what we know: This event was set up by an offshoot of the larger double delta organization. We don't know where they're located; their Web site doesn't say anything about that, for obvious reasons. For all we know, they are entirely a virtual organization, with no headquarters at all. Everything filters down from some core group, God only knows where. We suspect that the Coalition operates in the same way. From what we've received, we think there are other, similar events in a lot of places right now, maybe not at this precise time, but soon, or maybe recently. It's in keeping with their mission statement. I assume you've read it on their Web site."

She nodded.

"So here we have a meeting of double deltas. What a great target for the Coalition—what could be more infidel to their beliefs than a bunch of Lutherans and Irishmen? That's what the deltas are, primarily. It was a total fluke of nature that they weren't affected by DR SAM."

"Maybe it wasn't," Lany said quietly. "Maybe there's a larger plan. . . ."

Bruce remained silent for a moment. "Wouldn't it be nice if we could know whose side God is on. But I certainly can't say. In any case, the Coalition sees the delta survival in biblical terms—as if they'd all smeared themselves with lamb's blood and so the plague passed over them. We think they're sending another plague. And maybe this one will get the deltas too."

Twenty-seven

Thomas Blackwell the Younger listened with keen interest to the discussion that took place directly beneath him. He remained as still as a cat in the tall branches of the tree until the party of riders who'd gathered outside the town had all moved off, far enough so they would not notice him climbing down. When he judged that it was safe to do so, he scampered nimbly down the trunk, taking care not to break off any twigs, lest the snapping give away his presence. Despite his efforts at silence, leaves rustled as he descended. More than once he had to stop and hold his breath, for the last man in the group, the one on the handsome black horse, had turned to look back twice; both times his eyes came to rest upon the very tree in which the young boy had made his roost.

Every word that passed between the two noblemen had drifted up between the leaves, even their whispers. Young Blackwell understood clearly that they were distressed by the older knight's orders.

She is to be my bride! We must find her and the scoundrel who took her!

What does it matter if we find them or not—we will find you another bride. There is plague here!

Will you find me another princess, then, Cousin?

Bride—princess! An image of the golden-haired woman who had boarded in his father's home in the company of her supposed "father" flashed into his mind. Grand notions of some vast reward danced in his head as he scurried through the woods toward his home to tell his father what he had seen and heard.

He wove his way through the residents of Eyam, many of whom had gathered for their marketing. None of the town's residents appreciated the splatters of mud he raised as he ran past them in his haste. He maintained his fast pace, so when he finally reached the pigpen where his father was toiling, he had no breath for speaking.

"What bedevils you, boy?" his father said harshly. "You might have seen a ghost for all your agitation!"

"I have news!" he gasped. "Not a ghost, Father, but something near as marvelous—in the woods . . ."

"You've been up in that tree again, have you? I thought I told you to keep your feet on the earth, where they belong!"

The boy ignored the scolding. "But, Father, I saw soldiers! On horses, and they sat outside the village for a good long time, but they turned around and rode away when they saw the sign. I heard what they said, Father. . . ."

The elder Blackwell set down his bucket; his voice was quieter when he said, "Out with it, then."

"You'll not thrash me, Father, please. . . ."

"I'll thrash you at my pleasure, boy. Now, speak."

The lad blurted out what he had heard, then stood before his father, waiting nervously for a reaction. It was a few moments before the elder spoke again, but when he did, he kept his voice low. "Go do your chores," he said, "and say nothing of this. If you do a right good job of them, I'll not tan your sneaky hide."

"Yes, Father!"

The cart carried only a few bolts of cloth, for the drover had already delivered most of his load to other villages. The two big stallions who pulled the cart were now showing the wear of their long ride. As he rode past the warning flag on this last bit of his journey, the drover's heart began to beat faster. He had been told to wait for the tailor on the edge of the graveyard, though he did not understand why the goods could not be brought into the town, as he'd done with the rest of his load in other towns.

Up ahead he saw the man through the mist, and he was glad, for he could get a good start on the trip home before night fell again. He waved and received a wave in return. As the tailor hurried through the vapor, a chill went down the drover's spine, for the image was ghost-like and eerie.

As the bolts were passed out of the cart, the rough burlap in which they were wrapped gave off its usual disagreeable smell. Fibers of the coarse material rose up into the air, and the tailor sneezed violently several times. Birds alit from the treetops, frightened by the unfamiliar noise. In the cacophony of their furious departure, neither man heard the confused chirps of the small black rats that bounded out of the back of the cart and into the woods, toward Eyam.

The drover handed the bill of lading to the tailor, who gave it a quick inspection. "We hear that the Death still rages in London," the tailor said with a wan smile. "They're not poxed, one assumes...."

"God protect us, no," the drover replied. "Not that I'm privy to His intent." He gave the tailor a knowing smile. "I've seen your black flag. Perhaps you ought not be asking me if my load is poxed, when your own town is supposedly in its grips."

He offered the quill; the tailor glanced around once, then nervously scribbled his mark on the bill of lading. They exchanged a quick tip of their hats. The tailor gathered up the bolts and hurried off toward town. The drover watched the man for a brief moment—he had an odd bowlegged gait, made more noticeable by the burden of the bolts. Then he turned his team around, gratefully, to head back to London.

Still digesting his son's story, Blackwell picked up his bucket and began feeding the hogs once again. As he tossed handfuls of grain into the pen, he pondered what he ought to do with the unanticipated bounty his son had delivered. Should he tell the strangers that he knew the truth of who they were—at least who the woman was—and get from them what he could? Or should he keep still about what he knew and let them drift off when they would, without any kind of fanfare? They seemed like decent folks. The father was a bit too serious, but the young woman was likable enough. A beauty, and—if what the boy had overheard was true—a bride of some value.

He spent the better part of the morning pondering the dilemma his son's espionage had created for him but came to no conclusion on what ought to be done. The day passed as all his days did, with hard work and small reward.

Blackwell came upon Alejandro in the courtyard later in the afternoon. The physician was sharpening a very small blade, the likes of which Blackwell had not seen before. After a nod of greeting, the man from Eyam said, "That is an unusual device."

"Indeed." He held it up so Blackwell could see it better. "It is called a scalpel."

"Ah," Blackwell said. "What is it used for?"

"Cutting soft things, like, shall we say . . . flesh."

After a gulp, Blackwell said, "Well, then, it is worthy of maintenance. One does not wish to be cut with a dull blade."

With a cordial little smile, Alejandro returned to his sharpening.

Seeing that there was little more conversation to be had on the matter of the scalpel, Blackwell said, "My son climbed a tree this morning."

"Youth is a blessing, well spent in such activities. One can see so much from a lofty perch."

For a moment Blackwell watched in silence as Alejandro further perfected the edge of his tool. Finally, he came out with it. "He saw—and heard—a great deal from his perch."

Alejandro put the scalpel back into its leather sheath and looked up. "Oh?"

"A great deal, " Blackwell repeated.

As he tucked the sheath back into the pocket on this belt, Alejandro said, "I should be interested in hearing of this."

"He watched a party of the king's men at rest. He is sure they did not notice him."

"Your son must have been inordinately quiet."

"I taught him well," Blackwell replied. "He heard talk of a young woman who had escaped from Windsor," Blackwell said, his eyes narrowing. "A runaway bride, he heard said. A *princess*."

"Is that so?" Alejandro said, his own eyes returning the look of suspicion. "I pity the unhappy bridegroom who has been left behind."

"No doubt." Blackwell stared directly at his guest. "Perhaps you have heard something of this event in your travels."

"Not I," Alejandro said warily. "Not a word of it." He drew the knife out of the sheath again and ran his finger crosswise against the grain, as if testing its sharpness. "But I would be sure to report it to you if I had, in view of your apparent interest."

The eyes of the two men locked in a measure of mettle.

Chandos and his party of trackers made camp an hour's ride east of the plague village—Eyam, so a sign had said. There was a sick feeling in his gut as they made their way around it, and he was glad when the place was well behind them.

In the deep woods, away from the place of danger, he felt no more assured of his safety. They would arise the next morning and search for one more day, but Chandos was certain it would be a futile exercise. Perhaps, the knight mused in silence, if Edward had acknowledged the girl at an earlier age, her heart might not be so hard to him now. But now there was nothing to be done, nothing at all.

Alejandro was eager to be away from Blackwell after their strained encounter. When he went to the kitchen, where he had last seen Kate, Mistress Blackwell informed him that she had gone off in search of medicinal herbs.

"You'll find her on the edge of the graveyard just north of the church," she told him.

He walked through the town, staying within the shadows when he could, his senses heightened to any indication that others in town had seen or heard the soldiers. But there was little activity, certainly nothing to cause alarm, so he continued on.

Suddenly he heard heavy breathing behind him. He turned to see a bowlegged man shouldering a stack of wrapped packages. By the man's red-faced laboring, Alejandro judged that the packages were heavy. He stopped and let the man catch up to him, and as he passed, Alejandro said, "Good day."

The burdened man said nothing, though he did nod in reply. He seemed to be in a great hurry.

Strange, Alejandro thought as he watched the man stumble under the weight of the packages. *Why did he not have a cart, or someone to help him, or perhaps even carry the load in two trips?*

He was about to call out an offer of help when the man turned into a narrow alleyway. Two or three steps into the alley, the man shifted his burdens so they could be balanced with one hand and scratched at his back with the other, all the while moving along. He stopped at a door at about the halfway point and set his burdens down. After a few seconds, the door was opened, and the man brought his packages inside.

It was a perfectly ordinary occurrence, and yet something about it made Alejandro's spine tingle. He stayed at the end of the alley for another moment, struggling with his own desire to investigate further, until he remembered that he himself was the subject of curiosity. He left the village square and walked past the church to find his daughter.

The dogs had no success in picking up the scent of the fugitives outside the village. By noon, there arose a considerable amount of grumbling among the bored soldiers. When Chandos announced to his troops as the sun made its downward arc that they would return to Windsor, the chants of approval were loud and energetic.

Excepting, of course, from de Coucy and Benoit, who insisted that they press on, despite the fact that one of the trackers seemed suddenly to have taken ill. It was all they could seem to agree on; they had fought with each other constantly in low tones since the party had left the edge of Eyam.

Ignoring his noble charges, Chandos halted the party and took the master of the hounds aside.

"Your fellow seems rather . . . unwell."

The man cast a quick glance at the pale and sweaty tracker. "I would agree with that assessment," he said. "He is, naturally, most disturbed by our—"

Before he could complete the sentence, the tracker groaned and clutched at his belly. Chandos and the master of the hounds turned to him just in time to see him fall over on his side.

They rushed to him; the man lay on the ground with his knees drawn up tight against his chest. Together they laid him out flat. The man's eyes stared blankly upward, so Chandos slapped him lightly on the cheek to get his attention. The tracker closed his eyes, then reopened them quickly. He turned his head to the side and vomited.

The rest of the men in the party stepped back, almost as one. Chandos stood his ground for a moment, then, thinking better of it, backed away. He pointed to two of his soldiers. "Make a stretcher," he ordered. "We will bring this man back to Windsor immediately."

De Coucy brought his horse alongside Chandos. "The man may be plagued. We cannot take him back."

"And what would you have me do, sir? Leave him here to the wolves? I see no buboes on him. For all we know, he has eaten something disagreeable." He paused briefly, then said in a cold voice, "Perhaps he has partaken of the missing fox."

Benoit came up beside de Coucy. "Slay the man here, and then you may leave him with the assurance that he shall not be aware of it when the wolves have at him."

Chandos had his sword out and against the vile little man's throat before he could draw another breath. Not a motion was made among the others in the party, all of whom watched from their distance as Chandos inched the tip of the sword slightly forward. Benoit drew back in the saddle, but Chandos merely extended his arm farther, so the point remained in the fatal position.

One thrust, he thought. *One sweet thrust and the world would be rid of this vermin.*

Then de Coucy was speaking again. His calm, quiet voice sounded distant to Chandos, for it seemed that there was no one there but himself and Benoit.

"Surely," he heard de Coucy say, "we can come to some reasonable agreement on how to proceed."

Chandos was certain he would not agree on anything with this man, save that which was undeniable—say, the position of the sun. With his eyes still steadfast on Benoit, he heard de Coucy's proposal.

"I myself shall take this ill man and the rest of the party back to Windsor. I have need of the time to prepare for my wedding." Then his voice became quieter. "You are in command of this foray, sir, and will order us as you like. But perhaps you could continue your quest for another day or so, with the aid of my dear cousin. Our search, after all, inures entirely to his benefit. One has no idea of what may come to pass with a bit more effort. A lucky event, if God will allow it."

So, Chandos thought, chuckling to himself as he pulled the sword away from Benoit's throat, *perhaps the tie of blood is not so strong between them as the king thought.*

"For the love of God, husband," Mistress Covington said. "What have you done?"

"Woolens," he said defiantly. "From London. Nothing more than that. How can a man earn a living if he is denied the supplies of his trade?"

"It was agreed not to bring anything in for the moment! It is only a short while until—"

"Good heavens, woman," he said. "Do you think the plague itself rode in on these bolts? They are wrapped, and have been since they departed London. Now, don't breathe a word of it to anyone, or I'll box your ears but good."

For three days in the previous month, she had hardly been able to hear for the ringing in her ears. She curtsied stiffly and said, "Yes, husband."

"That's a good girl," he said. He pulled her roughly close and pressed a hard, unloving kiss on her forehead. The poor woman stiffened but did not resist otherwise.

One day, she thought as she left him to his bundles, *God will see to it that you are punished for your unkindness.*

The elders of Eyam congregated as usual in the public house across from the church in the center of town. Each one had a flagon of ale in front of him, in preparation for conducting the town's business. All politicking in Eyam was conditioned by a good dose of the drink, which made the efforts ever so much more pleasant and the outcomes of their deliberations far more sensible, at least in the eyes of the direct participants. There were seven, all of whom took the task of caring for Eyam far more seriously than one would expect from observing their methods of government. It was around the very table at which they now sat that the seven had decided to create a ruse of plague with a black flag, to keep out shipments of goods that might bring plague into it.

The physician who was sent there, they were told by a man who had once served as a guard at Windsor, *would not allow anyone or anything in or out, without first a quarantine. And we survived the winter, without a death save one, of a man who had ventured outside.*

They were on their third round of ale pots when Mistress Covington came rushing into the public house, with a look of terror upon her face.

Thomas Blackwell was finishing his pint in the tavern and listening to the deliberations among the council of elders when the tailor's wife rushed in.

"God's mercy," he whispered to himself after hearing the tale of her husband's sudden illness. He ordered another pint and drank it down fast.

One of the elders followed her. When he came back a few minutes later, his face was white with terror.

"He brought in bolts from London."

The remaining elders were on their feet within seconds. Blackwell watched the lot of them run out the door. Where they planned to go, he could not imagine. He only knew that he must go home, for he would drive his wife and children like cattle to the ends of the earth, if necessary, to keep them from the plague.

Alejandro and Kate were sitting at the long table in the main house, sorting the herbs they had gathered. Some they would leave for the mistress of the house; the rest they would take with them. They were otherwise prepared to depart at first light. When Blackwell arrived all lathered after his sprint from the village, Alejandro half-stood, anticipating another difficult encounter.

But no challenge materialized. Instead, Blackwell blurted, "Covington the tailor—he is ill. The elders say he is plagued."

Alejandro stood fully and asked, "Where does he live?"

"Behind the church, off the alleyway—he brought in woven goods from London! His wife told the elders that he has had three shipments over the last month, all delivered secretly. God curse the man!" He sat down hard on a bench and put his face into his hands. After a long and troubled sigh, he said, "He may have brought death into our midst."

Alejandro remembered the bowlegged man he had seen with his heavy burden, who scratched at his back as he hurried down the alleyway. He could only imagine what was in Blackwell's heart. He put a hand on the man's arm. "Please, you must take me there," he said.

He followed Blackwell back to the public house. All seven elders of Eyam were deep in conference, their heads close together. Blackwell removed his hat and cleared his throat to interrupt, and the elders turned toward him in unison.

An aged man with a full white beard spoke first. "Not now, Thomas, we are engaged in a serious—"

"I know what you're discussing, Uncle," Blackwell said. "I saw Mistress Covington when she came in, all a-truth."

"Then you'll know we haven't time for trivial matters."

"It's not a trivial matter I bring to you." He pointed back over his shoulder. "I've a houseguest, in case you hadn't noticed."

The white-haired uncle looked Alejandro over and said, "Aye, it was noticed. And not appreciated. There is discouragement against it, as you know."

"I'm on the outskirts," Blackwell said, as if that might justify his disobedience. "And I've come here to tell you, this guest may be of some help to us."

All eyes turned to Alejandro, who stepped forward. "I am a physician," he said.

There was an immediate change in the expressions of all the elders. A space was made between two of the men at the table. "Well, then. That is another matter entirely. Sit down, sir," Blackwell's uncle said. Blackwell himself was left standing as Alejandro assumed a seat.

"We would know if it is plague that ails Covington," the uncle said. "We cannot be certain ourselves."

"I must see the man in order to make that determination."

They conferred among themselves for a moment, until Blackwell's uncle said, "You're not afraid to do so?"

"I am as afraid as any man ought to be of plague, but I will take what precautions I can."

No one seemed interested in knowing what those precautions might be.

The elder looked up at Blackwell. "Nephew, will you lead him there?"

"Aye, Uncle, if that is your wish."

"You're a good lad." He turned to Alejandro. "You'll bring us your report?"

"Immediately."

Blackwell—visibly disturbed—put his hat back on his head and moved in the direction of the door. Alejandro followed and soon found himself following his host down the same alleyway that he'd seen Covington negotiate a few hours before. Blackwell stopped when there were still many paces left to reach the door.

"There it is," he said, pointing.

Alejandro knew that Blackwell would not go any farther. "I can do my work without your presence. It would be wise for you to wait here." He left his distraught companion where he stood and walked to the door of the Covington household. He rapped on the wood planks of the door and heard muffled voices within. The door was soon opened by a frightened-looking woman; behind her, clinging to her skirts, was a young girl. Both wore hollow, desperate expressions.

"Be gone with you, stranger," the woman whispered. "We've a sick man within."

"I am a physician, sent by the elders," he said. He pointed to Blackwell.

The woman looked out the door and saw Thomas Blackwell. "Oh, Blessed Virgin," she said. She opened the door wide, and Alejandro strode through. Stretched out on a pallet before the hearth lay the tailor Covington.

He stood over the man and looked down and saw immediately all that he needed to see. He said nothing to the man's wife.

"He scratched and scratched himself, like he had the scabies," the woman offered. "Once before, when a spider got him, he swelled all up like that. But this time, he's much worse. I try to keep the cobwebs down, Lord knows, but with all the other work—"

"Madam, this was not the work of a spider," Alejandro said. He turned and looked her square in the eye. "Your husband is gravely ill, which I am sure you know already. It is my considered opinion that he suffers from plague."

The woman gasped and pressed her hand to her mouth. She closed her eyes and began to blubber.

"You yourself, as well as your daughter, are in danger of acquiring the malady. Nevertheless, to avoid contaminating others, you must remain here in the house. Do not leave, or you will expose others to the same dangers."

"But I must get bacon grease! I've none in the kitchen."

"It will not work," Alejandro said.

"It cured Mistress Harrison; she drank a full beaker, thinking in her delirium that it was water. She was sick one more week, and then she was cured!"

"I assure you, madam, that bacon grease is no cure for plague. You must not drink it, or you will do grievous damage to your intestines."

"We'll have no need of intestines if we die!"

The little girl began to whimper.

His heart went out to the child, but there was no way to avoid the truth of the situation. Soon, both of them would fall ill, and both would most certainly die.

"We'll leave that in God's hands," Alejandro said. "But please, do not waste your time on such quackery. It will come to no good, and may do much harm."

"But my husband," the wife pleaded. "Is there nothing you can do for him?"

"Nothing," he said mournfully. "I know of nothing that will ease his distress. There are some means by which you can keep him comfortable until fate plays its hand. Wipe the sweat from his brow—the water will cool his fever—and avoid sharp noises, for they will pain his ears."

"How long..."

"One day, perhaps two. But no more than three. By then you will know if he will live or die. He may drink ravenously, or he may disdain water altogether; it will be one or the other. What I can say with surety is that this man must not leave this house. Nor should you."

As Sir John Chandos watched de Coucy depart with the ill man and the rest of the party, leaving him alone with Benoit, he wondered what would happen to the poor fellow. It was *fait accompli* that Edward Plantagenet would rather perish in battle than face the humiliation arising from such a gross failure of hospitality as inviting the nobility of Europa to the wedding of his daughter, only to have them succumb to plague within the walls of his castle. It was not the deaths the monarch dreaded but rather the ignominy, for, truth be told, there were many in attendance that he would rather see dead.

Sir John laid his head on the hard ground and covered himself with a thin blanket. On the other side of the fire, Benoit snored and snorted, then mumbled in his sleep. Chandos wondered as he drifted into sleep how the events that would soon unfold at Windsor would affect the fate of Britain. He came to the conclusion that he could not know and that his worry would change nothing. Despite the foulness of the man with whom he presently kept company, Chandos much preferred sleeping under the open sky to the lavish accoutrements of tents and pallets he was forced to endure when he traveled with the king. The discomfort of the hard ground on this night would be a penance for the things he was about to do, for the sins he would commit against his monarch, a man he still, albeit begrudgingly, loved like a brother.

When Alejandro returned to the public house, the elders of Eyam did not leave him to stand but moved aside and bade him sit among them.

"The tailor is indeed plague-struck."

By now there were dozens of people gathered around the meeting; moans of disbelief arose from them. Kate stood at the far side of the crowd, flanked by Mrs. Blackwell, who wore a look of absolute horror on her face.

"When you leave here tonight, go directly to your homes and remain there. Thus will you prevent the spread."

One of the elders said, "Many have gone to their homes before and perished. We are powerless."

Above the frightened din, Alejandro said, "No, you are not."

The tavern went quiet. "You have more power over this than you can imagine." He paused for a moment. "I'm told that you've heard the tale of a physician who kept plague out of Windsor by allowing no one to go in or out."

There were *ayes* all around, until another of the elders said, "Rumors have a way of gathering substance where there is none in reality. How are we to know if it is true?"

"Quite simply," Alejandro said.

He did not, in that moment, fear discovery; there was work to be done in Eyam.

"You can ask him. It was I."

Twenty-eight

"There's every reason to believe that meetings like this are going on all over the world, but we only know for certain what's going on here. And we don't really have a handle yet on how the Coalition might respond to the deltas organizing, as it seems they are. But if they're sending out a new plague, there's every reason to think that they're targeting the deltas as well this time."

For a few moments, Lany was quiet. An argument raged within her head—tell him, or not?

Tell.

"I think we may have seen it."

Bruce pulled a chair directly in front of her and sat down. "Speak," he said.

Lany spent a few moments arranging words in her head so she would tell him enough but not too much. "We discovered a body along the way, a man. His body was decomposed, but not too badly—the skin was spongy, like it had been frozen and then thawed. Had a kind of freezer-burn quality to it. We opened his clothing and looked at as much of him as we could. The person I was traveling with —"

"You weren't alone?"

"No."

"Where is the other person now?"

"I don't know. We separated just before you found me. If I were her, I'd be long gone. I hope she's all right. But in any case, she said she thought it looked like plague but that there was no natural vector for it around here, especially over the winter."

"She's right," Bruce said.

"So the guy we found had to have contracted this—whatever it is—in a manner that wasn't completely natural." She paused for a moment. "On the way here, we passed by a settlement in an old mill. There were fresh graves, three of them."

"Any idea how large the settlement is?"

"Not really. We only saw a woman and a couple of kids. But it was a pretty big building; if the whole thing was occupied, it could have been hundreds of people." She paused to consider what three new graves might mean. "If there are hundreds of people there, then I guess I would consider three simultaneous deaths to be high but normal. If there are less, though..."

"Then three is a lot."

For a few minutes neither of them said a word. Then Lany spoke. "We detected a new strain of bacteria out in our area—in lots of places, some of them quite remote. We figured that it was getting out there naturally in the rodent population."

"If it's the same one we're tracking, I can tell you that rodents carry it but it has to get into them somehow. Birds are my guess; they're low maintenance, high return. But I don't have a handle yet on which species they might be using. It's very slow to develop, whatever it is."

"Maybe the man we found was one of their field people," Lany said. "We were wondering if he was an outcast from the settlement we saw, but with the graves there, you'd have to make the assumption that they're taking care of their ill, or at least trying. Could there be a Coalition group around here? Maybe this is one of them." She recalled the eerie Internet site about the community that died to the last soul. "If this was a Coalition guy and he contracted this thing they cooked up—no matter how—he'd be a problem. I'm guessing they'd try to eliminate him. There was a canoe near the body; why would someone be canoeing down a river in winter, while he was sick, except to escape?"

"You could be right," Bruce said. "Some of the groups in the Coalition have long histories of sacrificing their own members as a means of achieving the greater goal. It's also possible that this guy was infected as an experiment, to see how it would unfold. Maybe he even knew about it, like the suicide bombers all did. And maybe he changed his mind."

"It could just have been a handling accident. Remember Reston?"

"Who doesn't?" he said. "They rewrote the book on procedures after those monkeys got sick."

After a pause, he said, "I knew a member of the Coalition, in London."

She eyed him with some suspicion. "I wondered how you had all this information about them. None of it was ever published."

"I didn't know he was involved, but he told me, not too long before he died. Of something else, by the way, that he ironically picked up through a handling accident." The small laugh he made after this revelation was weighted with bitterness.

"I don't know why I'm telling you this, I've never told anyone before, even someone who I was—very close to." He paused for a moment, then continued. "This guy was trying to recruit me. I told him no."

"Obviously."

"It was pretty confusing to me when it happened. He was someone I looked up to, at least once upon a time."

"I wish I could say *bummer* that he's dead," Lany said, "but it sounds like a case of poetic justice."

"Yes," Bruce said, "but no. It's murky."

He seemed lost in sorrow for a few moments, then regained himself. "Now you have to tell me how you know about the Coalition."

Oh, hell, she thought. A deal is a deal. "I was on the A-team of biocops."

He folded his arms across his chest. "My goodness."

His interest was obvious, but the story was too long to tell with other, more urgent matters at hand. "That's a story for later," she said. "Right now it's not germane. Let's concentrate on the immediate, like this thing you think they might be cooking up."

He nodded. "It's nasty. We have some concerns that the deltas may be at risk from this thing."

He saw her involuntary shudder.

"There's a double delta among you, then."

Fifty thoughts collided within her brain. Her cop's instincts took over and sorted them out, according to their relevance. In the end, she went once again with her gut feeling that there was much here to be learned and that this fellow was a good man and ought to be trusted.

"Two," she said. "One of them is me."

"Then you have a lot riding on this."

"My life," she said. "No more than anyone else."

"Okay, let me put it to you this way—the world has a lot riding on *you*, and all the other deltas. The Coalition is vulnerable right now. When things fell apart for everyone else, they fell apart for them too. It's not really the same group anymore. Oh, the core philosophy is the same—wipe out anyone who doesn't believe as we do—but the founders are all gone now. But don't be fooled—there's still some strength there, and despite what you found, it's a safe bet that they're much better at avoiding contamination themselves. They've picked up splinter groups along the way, other elements of the lunatic fringe that also have God on their side. They had to, to keep their numbers up. There are a lot of wackos with specific axes to grind, and they're all just waiting their turn at the wheel. There's going to be a big showdown one of these days. It looks like they've blended two killers—part plague, part DR SAM. But this new model doesn't depend on whether or not there are receptor sites it can attach itself to—it bypasses them completely. The resulting illness develops more slowly because of that, but when it does it looks and acts like plague. That's why the double deltas may not be immune or resistant—because this organism doesn't use the receptor sites to hitch a ride like DR SAM did. It develops much more slowly because it has to do all its own work."

He hesitated. "We picked up a sample a number of months ago, just like you did. Based on that, I'd have to conclude that they've been field-testing it for some time now—that's probably how it got into the area where your friends found it. We weren't looking for it; it was pure coincidence." He lowered his head. "We lost one of our people to it; otherwise we might not have even known it was out there. Like your friend said, it looked like plague."

"Was he following one of them?"

"She. And no. She came into contact with it outside of here. Since then we've all pretty much stayed inside, unless we absolutely have to go outside. The only reason we were out today was to observe the delta meeting—hopefully without them knowing we were doing so. We grabbed you because we thought you were doing the same thing and we didn't know why. We were there to protect them, and we didn't know what you might be up to."

"But if you haven't been outside much, how do you have so much in-formation? . . . One person's infection couldn't provide that much data."

"We take remote readings."

It all seemed completely absurd to her. She said, in a voice that bor-dered on snide, "What, do you send out little robots or something?"

Bruce gave a wistful little laugh. "I wish," he said. "They'd proba-bly be more cooperative. But we do send out emissaries, of a sort—we use eagles."

"*What?*"

"Eagles."

Bruce saw the stunned look on Lany's face but misunderstood.

"Come on," he said, "I'll show you if you'd like to see them."

He took out a key ring and unlocked the handcuff that held her to her chair. "I'm assuming you'll behave. And you should believe me when I tell you that you'd rather be in here with us than out there on your own right now."

"Look," she said, "I'm not your enemy. Can I at least use the PDA to call in to my folks and let them know I'm safe?"

He gave her a long look. "Maybe later."

She followed him out the door. Two young men fell in behind and stayed with them in an almost military fashion as they made their way through a labyrinth of tunnels and hallways. They passed labs and classrooms and offshoot hallways Lany thought might have once led to dormitories; it was all vaguely familiar. After nearly five minutes of meandering, they came to a stop outside a metal door. Lany looked in through the glass window and saw dozens of cages. She heard occasional shrieks, though they were dampened by the glass and the thick door.

"Welcome to the aerie," Bruce said as he pushed the door inward.

The shrieking intensified dramatically when they stepped inside. Lany put her hands protectively to her ears and wrinkled her nose against the smell. She followed Bruce to the first cage.

"This little lady's about six months old," he said, pointing to a magnificent young bird with shiny feathers and a proud, sharp beak.

"She's gorgeous," Lany said. "But I don't get it. Do you train them?"

"We try," he said, "but we haven't had much success. They operate pretty much on instinct. We have to work within their biological parameters."

He moved along to the next cage and pointed at the eagle's leg. "When they're fully grown, we put those things on."

There, attached just above the ankle, Lany saw the small metal box. She caught her gasp before it got out.

He brought her to a small cafeteria. There were several other people there, mostly youngish men, who all stared at her.

Bruce pointed to the serving area. "Go ahead, help yourself," he said. "There's plenty."

There were green vegetables and ripe red tomatoes. Lany was awestruck as she filled her plate. "Where does this all come from?" she said when she sat down.

"From our greenhouse in the winter; in summer we grow things in the quadrangle. We have water and power and sanitation, all within this little area."

"Are there more people than this?"

Bruce's broad smile highlighted the oozing cracks on the burned side of his face. "Eagles aren't the only thing we breed here."

It was a complete society all contained within the university—mind-boggling to a woman who'd had to settle for what seemed in comparison a pioneer life. "How have you kept this all hidden?"

"Very tight security. No one goes in or out unless we're completely sure of them."

"You weren't sure of me," she said.

His expression changed. "We still aren't." He looked directly at her with the eye on the good side of his face. "You won't leave until we are."

She became very quiet on hearing this and gave herself over to the food on the plate in front of her. She ate in silence for a while; Bruce remained at her side, saying nothing. When she had finished her food, he started in on her again.

"So," he said, "we went first. You know a lot about us already, and we know a little about you. Now that you've had a good meal, a tour, some lemonade, time to tell us more about *you*."

Lany sat back in her seat, quiet and thoughtful. "Soon," she told him, "but first I think there's something else I should tell you." She paused again, then said, "We took a tissue sample from the body we found."

On seeing his dismayed look she quickly added, "But the person who was with me is used to handling infectious materials, so she knows how to avoid contamination."

Bruce rose up and began to pace. After a period of what appeared to be intense thought, he turned again to Lany. "What will this other person do when you don't come back?"

"I don't know," she said, "but if it were me in her place, I'd get the hell out of here."

.   .   .

Get home hung in Janie's forebrain like a mantra. The distance she needed to cover was thirty miles at least; she'd gone perhaps twenty in the frantic ride out of Worcester. "Hill towns," they'd once called the communities between that city and their mountain; now she understood why.

She needed to travel quickly, but she was riding a horse whose ankle had given out not all that long ago; as she pushed Jellybean over hill after hill, she wondered why she hadn't left the mare behind and taken Lany's horse instead. It was habit, nothing more, that made her get up on Jellybean's back. Habits had a way of coming back as bad news. She hoped this one wouldn't do that.

In the last of the day's light, she stopped at a river that ran perpendicular to her route. She got off Jellybean and led her down the embankment so the horse could drink. The water was clear and cold and inviting, and she'd drunk what was left of the flat boiled-clean water that was in her canteen an hour before. With her thighs on fire from hours of riding, she crouched down at the water's edge. Her rippled reflection stared back at her, but even through the distortion she could see the lines of exhaustion in her own face.

Cryptosporidium, Giardia . . .

"Stop it!" she said aloud to the bad-habit thoughts. Jellybean turned her great head in Janie's direction and whinnied quietly.

"Not you. Me." She dipped her cupped hands into the water and brought up a delicious mouthful. She drank until she could drink no more.

Under cover of darkness, she led them to the place where they'd left the horses. And even though she was coming to believe that she was in the hands of the good guys, Lany Dunbar was secretly pleased when they found only her horse at the edge of the wooded area, and no sign of Janie or Jellybean.

"Looks like your friend did what you would have done," Bruce said.

By now, Lany thought, Janie would be well away, hopefully safe and on her way back to—

Orange, or the mountain?

She raised one leg as if to climb aboard the horse, but Bruce caught her by the arm. "Just lead him."

There were several young men along to ensure her cooperation. They all moved a step closer. "I'm not going to bolt," she told him.

He smiled. "I didn't think you would. But a horse without a rider makes less noise when he walks."

It was a reasonable argument. "Okay. Sorry."

They went back by a different route, one that took a bit less time. They reentered the university compound through a service garage in the rear of one of the buildings. One of the followers took the reins of Lany's horse and led him away.

"We should get you settled," Bruce said. "You're probably going to be with us for a while."

He brought her to a dormitory room, furnished just as she would have expected. "Your own bathroom," he said, pointing to a door. "You'll probably want a shower. The towels are clean. Someone will come get you in the morning. Then we'll talk some more." He stepped backward toward the door. "Well, good night. I hope you sleep well."

"Wait," Lany said as he neared the door. "One more thing."

He turned back; his ravaged face shocked her anew.

"Why eagles? If you can't train them . . ."

He stopped, his hand on the door handle. "They can't just go out in a bunch of airplanes and drop it. We don't all intermingle the way we did before, so the Coalition can't depend on a rapid deployment through normal social interaction. Eagles eat rodents," he said. "The boxes we put on their ankles pick up the presence of bacteria when the eagles eat their prey."

"The eagles eat infected rodents, but they don't get sick?"

"No. They have a different immune mechanism. Most birds don't get sick from the things they carry, except the bird flu, of course. They probably become carriers, but they keep to themselves, so it's not much of a worry. We use all sorts of protection when we handle them."

"But how do you get the readings? Do those boxes send out some kind of signal?"

"Only location signals. We know where they go, but we can't tell if there's contamination through the signals; we have to examine the boxes to find out. But we do that when they come back."

Again she didn't understand. "They return here, like homing pigeons?"

He shook his head. "They come back here because they know there's easy food, and they come back to mate. We only release females; we keep all the mature males here. Eagles are like any other species— they take the shortest route to genetic continuity. There aren't enough wild males out there to service all those ladies we've released. In a couple of years some of the young males that are hatching out there now will mature enough to start mating in the wild, but until they do, the females come back here. At least, most of them do."

In her mind's eye, Lany saw the headless bird on the ground near Tom's body.

"I need to send an e-mail," she said. "Right now."

Janie understood, as she prayed for safety, why people got religion. She would fall down on her knees and worship anything that got her through this terrifying night. She was somewhere along Route 9, in a dilapidated barn that was just far enough off the remnants of the road so it couldn't easily be seen but close enough for a fast departure, should it become necessary. Her hunger made her want to press on, but exhaustion would not permit it.

She laid her stiff and aching body on her blanket and wrapped what she could around herself. The dirt floor was hard; the few bales of straw she found were damp on their surface, so she didn't risk opening them up in the darkness. The god she was about to start worshipping was the only one who knew what might be lurking inside the old straw.

A mouse scampered by just inches from her head; she heard its tiny footsteps through the otherwise stark silence. "Go away," she said, and wondered how long it would be before she started talking to herself.

·   ·   ·

It was late into the night when Lany finally finished telling Bruce, along with Fredo and another of his "lieutenants," about their two little societies.

"I'm so sorry about the bird," she said. "But she was attacking Tom. He was still halfway up the pole. I didn't know what else to do."

Bruce said nothing about the bird. "This Tom is . . . *whose* husband?"

"Janie's. The pole came down on top of him. He lost a leg."

Bruce sat back in his chair.

"It was terrible. Their son watched the whole thing."

"Their son."

Lany wondered momentarily why he seemed so focused on this one detail but dropped the thought to continue pressing her case for sending the e-mail. "They have samples of new bacteria that they found in an area near their compound," she said. "It could very well be the same thing that the Coalition cooked up. I need to warn them about it."

Bruce snapped back to the present. "You can't. Someone from the Coalition may intercept it and then they'll know we're onto them. We can't risk that."

"Maybe I can get the idea through to them without actually saying it in so many words."

"How?"

She thought frantically, trying to come up with something. "They called the specimens they collected SAM-pulls. I can use that. They'll figure it out, but no one else will."

"No," he said. "That's too obvious."

"Please," she begged. "My son is there. I lost both of my daughters to DR SAM. I can't lose him too."

She saw hardness in his face. *Give them names*, she thought, *make them human so he'll soften. Just like with kidnappers.* "Please just listen to me. There are other people there too, Caroline and Michael, their little girl Sarah . . ."

She saw his expression change. For a moment, this scarred man she knew only as Bruce seemed lost in some deep sadness. Then he stood up, quite abruptly, and looked down at her. "All right," he said, his voice shaking. "Figure out what you want to say, and if I think it won't give us away, we'll send it." His comrades stared in shock as he turned and went out of the room, slamming the door behind him.

Janie heard the sound of wings flapping overhead and opened her eyes to see a yellow finch fluttering up to the rafters of the barn. She came up on one elbow, wondering why it was light when she'd only intended to sleep for a short while. By the stiffness in her joints, she knew she'd been asleep for several hours, at the very least. The barn floor was cold, and her back was one big ache as she rolled first to sitting, then slowly rose upright.

Jellybean stood placidly where Janie had tied her. The horse snorted on seeing her awake.

"Yeah, I agree," Janie said. "Let's get out of here."

The sun hadn't yet breached the horizon; there was a thin layer of frost on the ground as they worked their way across a meadow to the road. The horse's breath turned into little clouds of mist; Janie pulled up her collar and nestled her chin into it against the cold. The mare trotted along at a good clip, quickening her pace without command. They passed by abandoned farm stands and crumbling barns with their weather vanes tilted and rusty. A field where stalks of corn once grew tall enough to hide a basketball team lay drearily fallow. In less than an hour, they came off Route 9 and took the familiar back roads that led to the river.

An hour after that, Janie saw the bridge.

She guided Jellybean up a rise for a clearer view. She took out her field glasses and focused them on the near side of the bridge. The metal rails were red with rust from nearly a decade of neglect. She lowered the glasses and focused on the trusses, which were now inhabited to bursting with nests of all kinds. She lowered them again and saw the encampments.

Her heart sank. The horror of her passage over that bridge with Tom came back in full. The banks below the high structure were already thick with encampments then; they'd almost turned back for fear of what might happen if they crossed. By the grace of some unseen benign force, they'd gone over and then later back again with barely a scratch. But those were the early days; whoever remained under that bridge now would likely be hardened by years of deprivation and far more desperate. And she was alone, with only a knife and bow as weapons, with no man to protect her, astride a horse that could go lame anew at any moment.

Easy prey.

But the next bridge was ten miles north; she would have to cross there, then come all the way back down the river to the same position on the opposite shore in order to reach the road that led up the mountain. She scanned the shore, looking for some kind of barge or ferry, hoping against hope that some new-world entrepreneur would have put something of the sort in place. She would barter something—anything but Jellybean—for passage across the river. But there was nothing. Going north to the next bridge would mean another full day of travel; there simply wasn't time.

She went completely off the road to the riverbank and then down to the water's edge. The bank was gentle, and the riverbed was visible under the water for at least thirty feet before it faded out of view. The bridge was positioned in this location, as Tom had pointed out, because at one time this had been a ford. She stared at the cold water. The current was swift, driven by the spring rains and snowmelt. But the river was naturally shallow, as low as three feet in some places along the ford. There was a gap of perhaps thirty feet that Jellybean would have to swim before her feet would hit the shelf on the opposite side.

If I pole us along while she's swimming, we might make it. She took a quick look around the water's edge for a long branch and saw a young tree that had been felled by beavers. The teeth marks were fresh on the unweathered wood. The trademark circular gnaw pattern forced the end of the sapling to a point. It was as if the beaver had known they would be coming and had left them a perfect pole.

She dismounted and used her knife to cut away a few remaining small branches, then got back up on Jellybean. With gentle words, she urged Jellybean down the slope. The horse moved slowly but with amazing balance. They reached the water again, and Janie brought her to a halt.

She spoke gentle reassurances as if the horse could understand her; no one else was available to hear her dilemma.

Or so she thought.

"If we go into that water, we're going to have to get home today so I can get warm again."

She patted the horse on the neck. "So what do you think?"

The horse snorted.

"I'll take that for a yes." She loosened the straps on the saddlebag and made something akin to a backpack that rode high on her shoulders. Then, balancing the pole across her lap like a high-wire artist, she heeled the mare in the sides and they headed into the water.

To TCMEKASET from L. Don't pull Sam.

Evan stared at the e-mail. "It's got to be from my mother," he said. "But it doesn't make any sense. What do all those letters mean?"

Michael stood behind him, still in his pajamas. The chime had sounded in the early hours of the morning; it was still enough of an anomaly that everyone came awake. "Us," he said. "Our first intials. But *Don't pull Sam*..."

As Michael was pondering the meaning of the strange message, Evan went through all the letters silently. "You're right," he said. "It's got to be us. But there's no visible reply address. She couldn't have sent it from the PDA, or the address would show."

"*Don't pull Sam*..." Michael said again. "Wait a minute—she doesn't want us to take samples."

"But why?"

After a pause, Michael said, "I don't know."

They both went silent. Their concentration was broken by Alex's arrival.

"Does it say anything about my mom?" the boy asked.

After a look of concern at Michael, Evan said, "Not really. But sometimes no news is good news. I'm sure she's fine."

Jellybean heard the interlopers before Janie did. The horse began to prance nervously at the edge of the water; Janie thought she was just hesitant to enter the cold current.

Janie cooed, trying to soothe the horse. "It's okay, baby . . ."

And then the sound of snapping twigs made her turn her head around. She saw two ragged men barreling down the embankment directly toward her. One had a rope in his hand.

He wasn't interested in her, he wanted Jellybean! She herself would be expendable, just another mouth to feed.

"Heeyah!" she shouted. She slapped the reins down on the mare's back, and Jellybean bolted forward into the frigid water. She glanced back at their pursuers when Jellybean was knee deep; in the roughness of their entry into the water, both men had been splashed. The shock of the cold water had stopped them momentarily. But it wasn't long before they started after them again.

"Come on, Jellybean, go!"

The horse plowed into the river. The two men followed apace. She turned and shoved the pointed pole at them; when one grabbed on to it, she shoved backward with all her might, and the point went into his chest. Blood blossomed on his shirt, and he let go, sinking into the water. The other man took up his comrade's cause and tried to grab the pole, but Janie pulled it out of his reach just in time. He slowed and fell back, and finally turned away to help his fallen companion.

Janie turned and looked to the opposite shore. It was still a thousand miles away. When the water began to seep inside her boots, she began to understand just how cold she would be for the next several hours. By the time the water hit her knees, she had already lost all feeling below that point. It was an effort to heel the horse with the current pulling at her legs, but they had to keep moving.

She lowered her upper body to lay against Jellybean's neck, knowing she would need the warmth of the horse's flesh as the water rose. The horse was still stepping but seemed with each step to float up just a bit. Finally, one step touched nothing; Janie could feel the slight dip of the horse's body as the river bottom went out of reach. The water hit Janie's belly, and she almost cried out with the shock of it. A wave of nausea ran through her, and she retched, but nothing came up, because there was nothing within that could be expelled.

As soon as Jellybean's hooves left the river bottom, she began to swim like a champ, but they began to drift downstream with the force of the spring current. Janie plunged the pole into the water on the downstream side of the horse, pushing forward and in opposition to the current at the same time. Still, they drifted, at a rate that was a lot faster than Janie had anticipated; they moved south nearly as fast as they were moving west.

"Come on, baby," Janie shouted above the sound of the current. She worked her legs against the mare's side with as much force as she could manage and shoved the pole over and over again into the silt of the river bottom. They were aiming for a sandbar on the other side, but at their rate of drift, Janie saw that they might miss it. Beyond that, the river widened; the shore would be much farther away.

She prayed, through blue and chattering lips. *Thy will be done, but please, let me get home to see my husband and my son again.* She clenched her teeth and shoved the pole into the muck with all of her heart and soul.

Twenty-nine

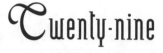

My beloved Alejandro,

I pray that this morning finds you and your daughter both safe and free. It finds me a bit sick to my stomach; this, I know will pass, but not soon enough.

De Chauliac has given Guillaume a wonderful knife! Yesterday he had some fine pieces of wood delivered, and he presented them to him for his whittling. The boy is just as pleased as he could possibly be to have these splendid things, and it is just in time to soothe his spirits, for we have had some unfortunate news. His playmate, the child of one of the cooks, took ill with the pox and has not been brought to the house since the first of his pustules appeared. I was terrified at first for Guillaume; each day I have examined him thoroughly, and by God's grace, or so I thought, he showed no signs. On the fourth day of my examinations, he showed me the place on his arm where, according to him, "*Grand-père* scratched my arm to ward off the pox." You will of course be required to explain this on your return, which I hope and pray will be soon.

Our progress on the Cyrurgia continues. This morning, may God be praised that the work went quickly, we discussed and recorded Father Guy's theories on the matter of foul breath. Were this not a serious tome, my dear, I should have laughed most heartily! Of course you will read this yourself on your return, but I cannot restrain myself from recording a line or two, to lighten my spirits; even Father Guy laughed when he read what he himself had written.

In the curation of stinkage of the breath there are two rules, the com-mon and the particular. The common is of the diet and of the purgation. Be it made after the kind of the humor from which the stink or filth cometh. It is showed that stinkage of the breath and the taking thereof in the likeness of smellings of fishes is an evil token in sharp fevers. And the substances of gruel and all broths and sops and garlic and onions make evil breath.

Bring your sweet breath back to Paris that it might once again mingle with my own.

By the middle of the next morning, the tailor's wife began to feel poorly. She took to her bed at the height of the sun, with only her young daughter to attend her. When the terrified child opened the door to Alejandro and Kate the next day, she blurted out, "I did what you told us to do, but my mother and father are no better at all!"

They followed her to the hearth, where there stood a bucket and a cloth. The path of water drips ran along the rough plank floor to where the parents themselves lay on their pallets of straw. Alejandro knelt down between the two and pulled their blankets down. There was no need to touch either one, for their buboes were well visible, and his eyes told him all he needed to know.

He glanced up at Kate and saw in her expression a clear concur-rence with this opinion—there was little reason to be encouraged. "You have been tending to them well," he said to the girl as he rose, keeping his doubts to himself. He made an effort to smile, though he was cer-tain the gesture fell short of his intent. "You are a brave and good child."

Kate took him lightly by the arm and pulled him away from the hearth. "I know only too well what trials await this child," she whispered.

You must not let me spit out the medicine, he heard himself saying to her, a thousand years before. *No matter how I protest, I must swallow it.*

He cursed whatever force of nature had changed Mother Sarah's waters from healing sulfur to the bland, innocuous liquid it had become. He glanced back at the little girl, who now knelt between her two parents with the cloth in her hand. She dutifully wiped away the sweat on their brows. She was a spindly waif with long blond hair and large, round eyes of a fine light blue, so much like Kate in her childhood. His heart ached with the understanding that the child might well not live to become a grown woman, as his daughter had.

As if she could read his thoughts, the girl looked up and asked, in a trembling voice, "Am I going to become sick too?"

The truth, both knew, would frighten the girl. Kate touched her gently on the shoulder and said, "Only God knows if that will happen. You must look to Him for that answer. Continue to do what you have already done. This will help your mother and father greatly."

"It will help them to live?"

After a short hesitation, Alejandro said, "I say again, that is for God to decide. Now we must go."

A look of utter panic came over the child's face. "Please, can you not stay, even just for a little while?"

"I am sorry, child, but others are sure to become ill and we must prepare. We will come again tomorrow."

Her brave little nod brought tears to his eyes.

Outside in the alleyway, Kate clutched his arm and leaned against him. "Oh, *Père*," she whispered, "I hated to leave her."

"As did I, daughter. But there is nothing to be done. And what I said was true. We must prepare."

None of the Blackwell children was outside the house when they returned.

"I'm keeping them inside," Blackwell said when the question was posed. "I'll not lose these children, I swear it."

"You had best let them out again, then," Alejandro said.

Blackwell narrowed his eyes. "I do not understand. In the tavern, you said we must all keep to our homes."

"I know, and this is wise for those who live close to one another, as do those who live around the market. But here, where you have a good distance between yourself and the next cottage, it is wiser to let them outside."

"But the humors of plague—"

"—are just as likely to live inside your house as out. Perhaps more so."

He was on the verge of telling the man about the sight of rats scampering out of a burning house in which seven souls lay dead; the vision from long ago would haunt him forever. But it had been difficult enough to convince the learned de Chauliac, who still would not entirely acquiesce, insisting that the humor traveled on the breath of one victim and then into another. *We are both a bit right* was the tenuous peace they had eventually reached on the matter. And though Blackwell was no fool, he was unlikely—in the midst of the blossoming horror— to listen to well-considered scientific explanations.

Quietly, Alejandro said, "We will minister to any of your family who fall ill, should that happen."

Blackwell's voice trembled. "I shall pray diligently that no such ministrations will be needed."

"As will I," the physician said.

By noon of the following day, six more people in Eyam were ill, and dozens more were showing signs. Alejandro and Kate worked long into the night caring for the sick and dosing out what comfort they could. When they were on the point of exhaustion, Alejandro went to the town elders in desperation.

"We cannot continue in this manner," he told them. "We run from one house to another to give aid to the ill. Can we not bring the afflicted all together in one place for care and comfort?"

The elders spoke among themselves briefly, until one said, "How many are now afflicted?"

"Perhaps thirty. And more will succumb, have no doubt." Alejandro let out a long breath. "In those homes that plague has not touched, the people should remain. But where it has already entered, the pest will show no more mercy here than it did in London—all the members of those households will almost certainly take sick. They must accompany their own to the place of quarantine. Until they become ill, they can help to care for their loved ones."

Another man said, "We have only the church with enough size for that."

"And when the church is full?" asked the first elder.

On seeing their horrified looks, Alejandro added, "It will become full, I assure you."

They argued among themselves quite heatedly as the physician waited, his impatience growing with each word uttered. They reached no accord on a location for those who would not fit into the church but instead turned to a more obvious one.

"Who will take these instructions to the people?"

Again they argued, as if Alejandro were not there. Finally, when his patience was completely gone, he shouted above the din.

"*You* will take it to them."

There was immediate silence. He glanced around the table until he had looked into each man's eyes, and then said again, quietly, "You will."

There was no arch of victory to receive the returning warriors, for they had come back with nothing to show for their efforts but a sick man. The poor castellan was left alone with the groaning tracker while everyone else departed. De Coucy's words still rang in the castellan's ears: *See that the sick man is taken care of.*

He moved slowly and carefully toward the stretcher and leaned over it, wondering what de Coucy had meant with that vague order. There was a sheen of sweat on the sick man's face and he was markedly pale.

He coughed every minute or so from deep within his chest. Not knowing what else he ought to do, the castellan hurried off in search of old Nurse, who was known to be wise in such matters.

When he found her in the princess's apartment, the old woman was—despite her age and frailty—dragging a laundry maid by the ear and shouting curses over the girl's laziness and ineptitude.

"You must come with me," the castellan said, "for I am in dire need of your counsel!" He pulled her to the window and pointed toward the stretcher. It was ringed by a circle of curious onlookers, all of whom stayed well back.

When the nurse saw the ill man lying there, she crossed herself rapidly. She dismissed the laundry girl, who ran off whimpering, and then turned back to the castellan.

"He must be quarantined," she said, stepping back into the salon.

"But what if it is plague?" the steward asked, his voice terrified.

"How shall one know that from this height?" she cried. "I am no physician, nor is there one on the premises. You had best send for the queen's astrologer. Let him decide what must be done. But right now this man must be separated, or else we shall all die."

The castellan watched as she ambled off again, not knowing what was in her heart. But he knew how easy it was, after decades of serving Plantagenets, to hide one's true feelings.

King Edward sat in his ornate chair with his wife by his side and listened carefully as her court astrologer expressed—in quiet tones so the others in the courtroom would not hear—his learned opinion on the medical status of the ailing tracker. The king considered the practitioner a charlatan, for on several occasions he had steered the queen on paths that the king regarded as regrettable. To make matters worse, the astrologer had a thin, high-pitched, grating voice. He was at least as accurate as the palace physician in matters of the corpus, sometimes more so, but neither practitioner, in the king's opinion, was worth the spit to polish his boots.

"There is currently an intemperate juxtaposition of Saturn with

Venus; these two opposing forces have taken hold of the man's internal organs by using his spleen as a gateway. It is a most unfortunate affliction, one from which I fear he may not recover. His humors are starkly out of balance."

"Speak plainly," the king whispered. "I would know if this is some sort of contagion."

"I cannot say, sire. I shall require some time to do additional readings."

"How much time?"

"Perhaps a day or two—the calculations are grueling. . . ."

The king stood slowly; his gout was flaring painfully after the rich excesses of the celebrations. The small, thin astrologer moved back involuntarily upon seeing the substantial monarch at his full stature.

"Get out," the king said.

"Edward!" Phillippa protested. "He has come at my request to help us—"

"He is no help at all," the king said, interrupting his wife. He lowered his voice again, lest anyone else hear what he was saying. "I am more confused than I was before we consulted him. We have a palace full of guests. . . . Imagine the consequences if plague should enter these walls when all the royalty of Europa is in attendance for the wedding of our daughter!"

For a few moments, Phillippa was speechless. Then she whispered, "You might at least have had the courtesy to allow him to finish his explan—"

"I am the king. There is no requirement that I be courteous. And I have heard quite enough of his gibberish about confluences and influences and malfeasances." He looked around the court for a moment, searching out of habit for his old friend, but remembered unhappily that Chandos was not present. He sat back in his chair and turned to a page. "Find Gaddesdon," he said harshly, "and send him to me, at once."

The page ran off to find the king's physician. The observers in the court all moved aside to let him pass, then closed ranks around the king again. The king smiled and gestured to the musicians to play, and the conversation resumed among the courtiers and dignitaries as if nothing at all had happened.

Some of Eyam's residents went willingly to their confinement; others protested vehemently and had to be dragged. By the third day of the outbreak, there were forty souls whose affliction by plague was certain, and twenty-five beyond that with the same terrifying symptoms. The church was filled to near capacity. By the end of the fourth day, more than half of the townspeople were confined, including four of the elders.

When word of the pestilence spread to the surrounding towns, there came offers of assistance—most shouted across the very same graveyard from which the pest made its entry on Covington's bolts. Soon people from the unafflicted towns to the immediate north of Eyam were bringing supplies: sheaves of wheat, loaves of bread, bags of lentils, hard cheese, all left in a pile at the edge of the graveyard. Once a day, one among the well would go forth to retrieve the supplies. The only person to leave Eyam was the drover of the death cart.

The scourge continued, spreading like fire through the town. The melancholy hopelessness plague had brought to a thousand small towns settled over Eyam like a shroud.

Until the seventh day.

"How are you today, pretty one?" Kate said.

Her question had been spoken rhetorically; she expected no response from the little girl who lay before her on a pallet on the church floor. When she had last examined the girl, her child seemed very near to death.

"Very much better, thank you," the little girl said. The voice was weak, but Kate still heard the conviction in it. She stepped back in surprise.

"Remarkable," she whispered.

She gave the child a drink of water, then left her. When she found Alejandro, she pulled him by the arm out of the hearing of the man to whom he had been tending.

Over his protests, she said, "You must come with me to see something."

He followed her to the place where the child lay, now awake and smiling. Kate fussed for a few moments with the child's hair and stroked her head, then stepped back again.

"She is recovering," he said in a stunned whisper.

Kate nodded. "Yesterday she was so ill that I thought we would surely be placing her in the cart this morning, perhaps even last night."

She glanced around the church at the dozens of people who lay sick and—presumably—dying. "I have noticed something odd, *Père*. Many in this village ought to have taken ill by virtue of their proximity to the afflicted, but they have not been stricken."

He had been so busy tending to the sick that he had simply not seen it. "You are right," he said with wonder in his voice. He looked around for himself to confirm what Kate had put forth. Husbands tended to wives without falling ill themselves, and children—the tailor's little daughter, for one—looked after afflicted parents without so much as a sniffle.

"Unless the nature of plague has changed," he said quietly to Kate, "and I see little evidence of that in those who have already been taken, there must be something about Eyam that protects its residents."

The man from Eyam stood over the pile of goods that the people from the north had left only a short while before. It would be a heavy load to carry into town, but he was glad to do it, for he was hungry and there was fresh bread in the supplies. He could smell it; he began to salivate.

What would it hurt, he thought, *if I took a loaf for myself?* He considered how good it would feel to have a full belly and indulged in self-assurances that one loaf of bread would not make a difference to a town full of people, many of whom were too sick to eat.

He followed the scent with his nose and found the bread in the third bundle. The loaf he pulled from the satchel was still warm, its crust not yet hardened—it must have been taken from the oven just as the offerings were being loaded.

He wrapped his hands around the warm bread and enjoyed the warmth; it was a chill afternoon, under gray and threatening skies. He put the loaf to his nose and took in the rich, grainy smell. Just as he was bringing it to his mouth for the first bite, the loaf exploded.

The man shrieked aloud and dropped what crumbs remained in his hand, then looked in the direction of the arrow's origin.

A short distance away in the woods, Sir John Chandos chuckled. He tucked his bow into a loop on his saddle, then held out his hand to Benoit, who scowled in disgust as he put a coin into it.

"You are not wise with your wagers," Chandos said. "One hopes you will fare better at what comes next." He motioned for Benoit to follow, then spurred his horse and left the cover of the woods. They rode to where the stunned man stood, his hands still raised and trembling mightily.

" 'Thou shalt not steal,' " Chandos said as he approached. He stopped a few paces short of the thief and stared down at him.

The man fell to his knees and said, "Keep your distance, sir, there is plague within!"

"I am well aware of that," Chandos said. "I have seen your flag. And I am touched by the kindness of your neighbors in sending supplies to the afflicted. I shall convey a report of their generosity to the king, who will, I am certain, reward them. As for yourself, I shall convey a report of your actions to the people of your town, who may not look kindly upon them. It is disgraceful that you should steal what is intended to be shared around."

"I'm entitled to my portion, sir," the trembling man said. "I was just taking it a bit early, that's all."

"Indeed," Chandos said. "Quite early, it would seem."

His horse snorted and pranced in place; the man scooted out of the path of his hooves. Chandos looked down at him and asked, "How are your townspeople faring in this scourge?"

"Well enough so far, sir, though we are all still afraid for our souls.... We have brought out many dead."

Chandos glanced at the row of fresh graves. "I offer you your king's condolences, as well as my own. But tell me," he said, "is there a midwife or a barber in town to bleed those who have fallen ill?"

The man became excited. "Why, no, sir, neither, but by a fine stroke of luck we have instead a physician—a traveler who came to town not a week before the outbreak began. And there is a lady with him—his daughter, he says."

"An extraordinary stroke of luck.... How is it that a physician just happened to be in the near surrounds when plague made itself known?"

Though he was clearly frightened by the strange and impressive knight, the man found reason to ponder the curiosity Chandos had put forth. "I cannot say, sir."

"No, I suppose you cannot. It makes one wonder, though, if he perhaps brought it with him, with the purpose of gaining glory by caring for the ill."

On this matter, the man had a ready opinion. "Oh, no, sir. The elders say it came in on Covington's bolts of woolens. He brought them in from London, against the edicts."

"Well, I am sure that is the case, then, if the elders say so. I'm certain this physician himself had nothing to do with it, no matter how coincidental." He leaned forward and said, his voice lowered, "I will share an intelligence with you, for the good of your town. I have heard of a traveling physician, for he passed through the area around Windsor in the company of a handsome blond woman. The man is a Jew, and the woman a witch. We have heard that they possess the same poison that brought the Death to wells throughout France."

The man gasped. Chandos allowed a moment for him to absorb what he had just been told, then gave a nod to him and said, "Well, good day to you, sir. Do not steal anything more, for if I learn of it, I shall come back with a ready blade to steal your hand. I shall pray that your town fares well against the pest. And that the interlopers will not work too much magic upon you."

He turned his horse around and slowly cantered off with Benoit following. After a few steps, Chandos turned to his despised companion, who had said not one word throughout the encounter.

He gave Benoit a smirk and said, "You did well."

The man was not in Eyam for five minutes before he began speaking of his encounter with the fearsome knight. The rumor spread like wildfire throughout the population; it flew through the church and the tavern as if it had wings. The whisperings were always the same:

A witch and a Jew—they have brought it in with them.

Alejandro and Kate were taking a brief rest on a bench in the market square when the elders confronted them.

"Is it true, what they say," one asked, pointing a finger of accusation, "that you brought plague to the innocents herein, just so you could make a name for yourself in treating it?"

Alejandro stared blankly at the man. "You have me baffled, sir. I know nothing of the matter on which you speak."

"The plague didn't come until you were here. Perhaps it did not come on the woolens at all, but through some poison! And now you're treating us, and some are living."

"There is nothing we have done that—"

Another elder stepped forward. "This is all your doing."

Alejandro and Kate stared at each other for a few horrified seconds. "We know nothing of what you are telling us," he said. "But we have come to the conclusion after our observations that there is something about Eyam that impedes the spread of the pest. This is a remarkable thing, we realize, but—"

"It would be the more natural course of things that they should die," the third elder said. "You interfere in God's plan, like Satan himself."

"The course need not be entirely natural. We have seen in the past some means of dampening the curse—"

"There, you see! *Witchcraft.*" He pointed his finger at Kate. "She is a witch." Then he turned to Alejandro. "And you are a Jew."

Father and daughter stood.

The elder's eyes narrowed. "You are the Devil and she is a witch, and you are using your evil poisons against us," he hissed.

After a quick glance at each other, Alejandro and Kate turned and ran off. They were followed by a chorus of curses and a shower of stones.

Blackwell was astonished by the news. "I will admit to my suspicions, but this I can scarcely believe of you."

"You must believe me that we did not bring plague with us."

"But the dark knight said you are a Jew. . . ."

Alejandro looked directly in his eyes. "I am."

"Though you do not act like a Jew."

Alejandro did not say what was in his angry heart: *And how is a Jew supposed to act?* He said instead, "All of my actions have been to help the people of this town. At my own peril, and that of my daughter."

Blackwell said, "Aye, I've seen that myself." He watched as Alejandro stuffed his belongings into his satchel. "You'll be needing supplies," he said. "I'll give you what I can, though it will be little— without commerce, my stores are low."

"Do not deprive your family," Alejandro said. "We will fend for ourselves. We have done so many times before."

He reached into his purse and extracted two gold coins, which he pressed into Blackwell's hand. "For our keep," he said. "We thank you for your family's generosity."

Blackwell eyed the gold. "And you for yours as well, Physician and Princess," he said. And then he surprised them by saying, "I shall not betray you. Now go with God, before I change my mind!"

"We shall," Alejandro answered. He climbed up on his horse and pulled Kate up behind him. They rode out through the cemetery, leaving Eyam's secret undiscovered.

Sir John Chandos waited just off the road that led out of Eyam, knowing that his quarries would be driven out of town eventually as the seed of mistrust he'd planted earlier grew. He'd stayed there all day with Benoit at his side, trying his best to ignore the man, who would not give him any peace but complained of his discomfort constantly. He was hungry, he was thirsty, his backside was tired of the saddle....

The long wait was nothing new to Chandos, who'd seen many a war in which the adversary took its time in presenting itself. He had no regrets that he would not see the jousts and the jugglers at Isabella's wedding, though he would miss the wondrous voices of the singers who had been brought in to sweeten the air. He wondered if the musicians would have adequate talent to override the shrillness of the bride herself. One hoped she would remain quiet and not spoil her father's efforts. But that was unlikely.

His loyalty demanded that he stay here—miles from Windsor—in the company of a man he despised, to wait for a man he admired and a woman he did not, in his heart of hearts, want to catch. He let his mind wander back to Kate's childhood, when he had taught her to play chess and had created a fine adversary for himself.

He was drawn out of those pleasant memories by the sniveling sound of another complaint.

"I must have water, or I shall die!"

That happy event could not occur soon enough, Chandos thought as Benoit dismounted. He watched the man pull his water bag off the saddle and head toward the small stream that flowed along the road's path.

Alejandro guided the horse through the woods at the fastest pace he thought safe, knowing that they must remain within that cover for as long as possible. But soon enough they found themselves on the edge of a cluster of trees, the last bit of cover before the road opened into a meadow. It disappeared after that into another stand of trees on the edge of a deep wood. But to reach that safety, they would have to cross over an open area.

They dismounted and went as far to the edge as they could. For a long moment, they both scanned the opposite woods with their eyes, looking for any sign that Sir John was within and waiting for him to emerge.

"I see nothing," Alejandro said.

"Nor do I," Kate whispered in reply. "But I can feel in my bones that he is out there."

When a bevy of birds rose up from the woods across the meadow, Alejandro knew that she was right.

"There," Kate said, pointing to the small stream where Benoit was getting his water. "I see no one else."

"But Chandos will be close by." Alejandro shaded his eyes and looked again, touching on every detail of what lay before him.

A glint of light caught his eye. "Look to the right, perhaps ten paces from Benoit. I see a shadow that cannot be a tree. Only one."

Kate looked for herself. "I see him."

"Can you make the shot?"

"Benoit, certainly," she said quietly. "But then we will reveal ourselves to Chandos, and he will take himself out of range."

She looked back again. "He will try to come to Benoit's aid. Otherwise, he would be shamed before his king. And in doing so, he will be vulnerable."

"Then shoot Benoit first, for we must kill them both."

Kate looked at him; the expression she wore was one of complete desolation. "*Père*, I am not certain that I can do this...."

"Then he will find us. He will kill me and take you back to Windsor. God alone knows what fate would await you there."

She looked out from behind her tree for a moment, then looked back at Alejandro. He saw the tears threatening in her eyes. He nodded gravely, as if to reassure her that what she was about to do was necessary. She swallowed hard, then turned back to her quarry again.

She saw Benoit, who had filled his water bag and was walking along the edge of the road to where his horse was hidden—or so he thought—in the trees. She nocked the arrow into the string of her bow and took careful aim. She pulled back slowly until the bowstring was taut and quivering, and then, with her breath held, let the arrow fly. Before she could even lower the bow, Benoit fell, with an arrow in his chest.

"He is down," she said. And as she had predicted, Sir John made himself visible. She positioned the arrow against the bowstring and peered along its length to sight her quarry. She had a clear shot as he dragged Benoit's body into the woods. She pulled back the string.

But her hand shook, and after a few seconds, she lowered the bow.

"I cannot," she said quietly. "I have it not in my soul to kill him."

Alejandro said nothing, knowing that his own heart would have overruled his hand, just as Kate's had.

Thirty

Alex hadn't seen or heard Caroline, so great was his concentration on his prize. So when she asked him what he had in his hand, he quickly closed his fingers around the metal treasure and put his arms behind his back.

"Nothing."

"Let me see it, please." Caroline stuck out her hand.

With aching reluctance, the boy put the metal box into her hand. Caroline stared at it for a moment, then looked at him. "What is this?"

"I'm not sure."

He wasn't exactly lying, but he wasn't telling her the entire truth either. He'd wanted to open the metal box since the night he took it, but the opportunity had not presented itself. Today, with Kristina occupied with Evan and his mother still away, his dad resting, and most everyone else out working on the spring planting . . .

He'd labored over it for the better part of an hour with a tiny screwdriver, and had finally achieved success. After examining the contents—about which he understood nothing—he was just replacing the cover when Caroline appeared.

He stared up at her unhappily, keeping silent but thinking, *Why did you have to come along just now?*

"Where did you get it?"

He looked down guiltily.

"Tell me."

"I took it off the eagle's foot. When Dad fell."

On hearing this, Caroline softened. She bent low, bringing herself to Alex's level. "This is important to you, then, I guess. I didn't know that when I asked you to give it to me." She turned the box over in her hands. "I just want to show it to Michael, and then I'll give it back to you. I'll take good care of it, I promise."

Suddenly he sneezed, hard. Then he coughed with a dry and raspy sound.

"Are you okay?" Caroline asked.

He shrugged. "I guess so."

"All right, good. Don't go getting sick on me, now."

"I won't."

He followed her with his eyes as she left the room with his prize.

The floating came to an abrupt end; Janie felt the sweet solidity of the riverbed shelf when Jellybean's foot made contact, just a few feet upstream of the point of no return. With each step they came higher out of the water, and soon they were completely on the shore. She turned Jellybean around and looked back at the opposite shore; one man was dragging his wounded cohort along the riverbank, toward the bridge encampments.

Water poured off the horse and out of Janie's soaked garments in a cold, hard flood. With her rider still on her back, Jellybean shook herself from head to toe. Janie clenched her teeth together through the long vibration so she wouldn't bite her tongue. Then Jellybean took off again, as if she sensed the urgency of their journey. Janie brought her to a halt with a tug on the reins, then climbed down.

She removed her wet clothing, every soaking piece of which fought her by clinging desperately to her skin. She could barely feel her hands as she wrung the water out of her pants and coat. Each squeeze was torture as hot blood tried to rush back into her frozen fingers. She turned her boots upside down and poured out what water remained, then banged them against a tree trunk to shake off what more she could, each whack sending a jolt through her spine. Only those items she'd placed at the very top of her backpack remained dry; her extra pants were soaked, as was the wool sweater she'd brought. She had dry socks, underwear, a shirt, and a blanket, one end of which was slightly damp. She wrapped everything else in the jacket and tied it into a dripping bundle. Then Prairie Woman Janie Crowe got back onto Jellybean in her underwear, socks, and shirt, and wrapped the blanket around her.

Twelve shivering miles, she thought, *all uphill*. She looked for the sun and found it directly overhead, to her south. It was just past noon.

Michael shook the metal box and listened for loose parts. He heard no rattling.

"I don't know what it is," he said to his wife. "But I'm inclined to open it up to see what's inside. It might be some kind of tracking device. If it is, there'll be a chip of some sort."

He held it out at arm's length so his aging eyes could make out the inscription that was etched on one side of the metal frame. "908," he said. "I wonder what that means."

"Maybe it's part of a series. A tracking number for a repopulation program or something. Whatever it is, they're probably not tracking it anymore. Just make sure you can get it back together again, or you'll have to be the one who explains to Alex."

"Yes, dear," he said. It would be the least of his worries. He set the object down on the table and went to get his tool chest. Alex watched from the doorway as Michael went after the cover on the metal box with screwdrivers and pliers as he himself had done before.

"Bloody thing is built like a Sherman tank," Michael said as he struggled to get it open. Finally, the top sprang off and landed about a foot away. From his place in the doorway, Alex gasped. He ran forward and picked it up, then brought it back to Michael.

"No harm done, I don't think," Michael said after a quick examination. He set down his tools and peered into the workings of the mystery box.

"Get me my spyglass, will you, love?"

Caroline went off dutifully and came back with the magnifier. "Here you are, Sherlock."

"Thanks." He put the glass over the open box and looked closer. "There's a chip, all right. And some kind of tiny transmitter." He set the glass down on the table and looked at his wife. "Right about now, if there's anyone paying attention—which is doubtful—someone out there thinks we're an eagle."

"Boss, there's something funny happening."

Bruce left Lany alone and stepped out into the hallway.

"908's back online again."

The bird had been off-line for a while after their determination that she was walking.

"She's going on and off," Fredo said. He pushed a pin into the map at the location indicated by the coordinates.

Bruce looked at the topography. "She's on the mountain," he said. "Has she ever done this before?"

"Not that I know of."

Just then the transmission stopped completely. For several minutes there was no signal at all. Then, just as abruptly, it began again.

"I don't get this. They only stop when you open them. Even if the bird is dead, the thing will keep going until the battery wears down. And that hasn't happened yet."

Bruce hurried back to Lany's holding room.

"You said you killed an eagle, that it had a box on its leg."

"Right."

"Did you take the box with you?"

"No. We left her there."

"With the box on her leg still."

She nodded her head in confirmation.

A few seconds later she said, "Wait a minute. I sent Alex back to get the hatchet. I left it on the ground near the pole."

"Alex? The little boy?"

"Yes."

"Could he have taken the box?"

"Not without—" She stopped, remembering that he had blood on his hands and wondering at the time if he'd touched Tom without her seeing it happen.

Bruce finished the sentence for her. "Not without cutting off the leg."

"Here you go, sport, good as new." Michael put the box in Alex's hand and patted him on the head. "Put it someplace safe, why don't you."

He took the little cube of metal and walked into his parents' bedroom. His father was sleeping—*again*, he thought. He put his metal treasure into the wood box on their bureau.

Janie couldn't tell where the sun was in the sky any longer; the trees on either side of the mountain road obstructed her view. She clung precariously to Jellybean's back, only looking up now and then to see that the mare was still on the correct course. She hadn't been this way in several years; even in her near delirium, the deterioration of the road surface astonished her. Chunks of blacktop were all she saw as they moved up the mountainside, because it was too much of an effort to lift her head.

She wrapped her frozen fingers in Jellybean's silky mane; that was the only way she could hold on. The reins were trailing down the horse's neck, swaying rhythmically as they climbed upward. Janie could feel each plodding step; she began to wonder if the horse would have the steam to make it all the way. She had no idea what she would do if Jellybean gave up.

But the mare pulled through. Thirteen hours after their sunrise start, they reached the compound. The gate was locked, as Janie expected it would be. Still astride the horse, she reached out and took hold of the bell chain and pulled, over and over again. The gate opened and she saw

Michael, who reached out and took the reins. He pulled Jellybean inside and closed the gate just as Janie slid off and fell to the ground.

"He had to have touched the blood, then," Bruce said with alarm. "He had to have cut the leg off to get the box, and there had to be blood."

"The bird was already dead," Lany said. "I cut her head off. Her heart wouldn't still be pumping."

"How long before?"

"I don't know, exactly. Maybe fifteen minutes."

"At that point, blood would probably still be settling in her extremities. If he had to pull to get the box off, whatever was in the leg would ooze out." He breathed in deeply. "If that bird was infected, he could be too."

"Do you happen to know what the infection rate is in your birds?"

"No. We haven't tested them. None of them has gotten sick, so there didn't seem to be any point. But they can be carriers, we know this for sure."

Lany stood up and started to pace. "We have to get to them somehow and let them know. Another e-mail—a carrier pigeon! *Something*. We just have to tell them!"

Bruce put his hand on her shoulder. "Please," he said. "Don't panic. This takes a very long time to develop—weeks, maybe, from what we've seen. It's slow-moving and slow-growing; the difficulty is that by the time there are symptoms, the disease has a good hold."

"It was almost a month ago when this happened."

"You didn't tell me that."

"You didn't ask. Oh, God," she moaned again, "does it respond to anything, any antibiotics?"

He hesitated, though he wasn't sure exactly why. "We just started working on something we hope will work, but it hasn't really been put to a test yet. We have a few leftover antibiotics available to us, some streptomycin, aureomycin, a few more of the common pre-SAM drugs, but none of them has been terribly effective. It seems to mutate as fast as we attack it."

Lany flopped down in a chair and closed her eyes. She let her head hang over the back of the chair. "This is a very—special little boy. We can't let him get sick."

Bruce wondered what was so much more special about him than any other child but did not ask.

"What the hell are we going to do?" Lany moaned.

In the silence that ensued, the chirping of her PDA in Bruce's pocket sounded like the Liberty Bell.

J home solo. ????????????????????????

"She got back," Lany cried gleefully. "*Home*, they said. She must have gone to the mountain. Oh, thank *God*. She'll be there to take care of Alex if he gets sick. God knows what she'll be able to do for him, but she'll do it better than anyone else can."

Bruce didn't say anything immediately. After a few moments, he said, "You can send back if you want to. Just write, *Safe*—nothing more. It'll have to do."

"Okay," Lany said. "Thank you." She immediately touched in the allowed letters and pressed *Reply*. When she saw that the message had been sent, she closed the cover on the PDA and started to put it in her own pocket.

"No, sorry," Bruce said. He held out his hand, palm open. "I think I'd better keep it for a little longer."

She handed it to him, reluctantly, and felt its void when it was out of her control. He replaced it in his pocket, then picked up a chair and positioned it directly opposite her. He sat down and faced her full-on, as if he meant business.

"This woman Janie," he said. "What was her last name?"

Lany was struck by the immediate thought that his interest was too strong to be entirely casual. "You know," she lied, "I don't know. We never use our last names—there doesn't seem to be any point."

"Ever heard her mention her maiden name?"

"No."

"And her son, what was his name again?"

She hesitated, and then said, "Alex."

"How old is he?"

"Seven."

"So he was born after the second round."

"Yes."

"You said she could take care of him," he said. "What was her profession?"

Lany clammed up. "I don't know these people all that well, so I'm not really sure...."

"That's all right," he said quietly. "It's not important."

Caroline put two large, smooth rocks on the stove to warm them and then carried them in a pan to Janie and Tom's bedroom. She lifted the covers and saw that Janie was still shivering mightily, though she was swaddled in the bedclothes. She slipped the pan next to Janie's legs and replaced the covers.

"Hot rocks, just like in the good old days," she whispered to her friend. "You'll be warm soon."

Tom sat in the chair next to the bed, but Janie did not come out of her delirium for several long hours, during which Alex remained there as well. As his father watched, the boy checked his mother's pulse, took her temperature, listened to her breathing, and recorded everything diligently on his chalkboard. When he fell asleep snuggled against his father, Caroline and Kristina took turns watching over her vital signs. When she wet herself in the middle of the night, it was Caroline who cleaned her, changed her nightdress, and refreshed the bedclothes. When Janie opened her eyes in the middle of it all and whispered her thanks, Caroline smiled and whispered, "Payback, bud. Payback. Remember London, what you and Bruce did for me?"

An hour before dawn, her trembling finally stopped. She opened her eyes to see her husband and son entwined in sleep on the cot. She raised herself up on one elbow to get a better look at them.

Tom looked older than when she'd last seen him, less than two weeks ago. She wondered how that could be. But there was more peace in his expression than when she'd left for Orange. She saw only one crutch resting against the wall near the cot; it was progress, and she hoped it meant that he was coming out of his depression.

Thank God.

She wanted desperately to hold him. But rest was what they both needed. "Alex," she said quietly. She reached out and touched his arm, and he came awake.

"Don't wake your father."

He got out of the cot with small careful movements and slipped under the covers with his mother. He wrapped his small arms around her, his flannel sticking like Velcro to hers.

Bruce left Lany in the watchful care of Fredo and one other man and went to his own quarters. When he looked in the mirror after splashing water on his face, he thought to himself, *She wouldn't recognize me.* He removed his pants, and they fell to the floor with a *clunk*. He picked up the forgotten PDA and flipped open the cover.

Why not? he thought.

Following the prompts, he typed in a brief message:

Pass to J from B: Leeds

He pressed *Send* and let the message fly, for better or worse.

Steve Roy stared at the computer screen. "*B. Leeds?* Who the hell is that? And pass what? There's no message."

"I don't know," Linda said. "Whoever B. Leeds is, he's got fat fingers. He hit the colon instead of the period. Just pass it along as it is— it must mean something, or Lany wouldn't have sent it."

"Maybe she didn't send it."

They looked at each other for a moment. Finally, Steve said, "I'm going to pass it along. Maybe it means something to the two of them that we don't know about. She sent back that she's safe, and that's a relief, but we still don't know what happened out there, and if they have some kind of a new code going between the two of them, I don't want to mess anything up." He typed in a few commands and passed the message on to the compound. "But I'll tell you what, I think it's time we paid a call to the other side of the mountain." He patted Linda's shoulder. "Let 'em know, will you?"

Kristina was the first to respond to the chime.

"It's a message for Janie," she said.

She got up from the computer and went to the bedroom, where everyone was asleep.

She came to the bedside and sat down in the empty chair. Janie opened her eyes.

"How are you?" Kristina said softly.

"I feel like I climbed Mount Everest," Janie answered in a weak voice. "I am so tired I can't even think." Then she struggled to one elbow. "But Lany's still out there.... I've got to let them know that she's been taken...."

"We already sent them a message that you came back alone. They sent one back that she's 'safe,' but we don't know anything more than that."

Janie lay back again. "Safe..." she said. "Thank God."

"But there's a new one that came in, which they want us to pass to you. It's odd; no one can figure it out. We think maybe part of it didn't come through."

"What did it say?"

"*Pass to J from B: Leeds.* No one can figure out who B. Leeds is. It came in on the PDA, so Lany has to be there with whoever sent it."

Leeds. Something clicked in Janie's still-woozy brain, but she couldn't make it out. She sat up slowly and got out of bed, taking care not to wake Alex. "I better take a look at it."

She padded through the lodge in her pajamas, still a bit unsteady, and went to the computer. Kristina stayed close to her. She sat down at the desk and looked at the message, which was still on the screen.

"He doesn't type very well," Kristina said. "He hit the colon instead of the period."

"Wait a minute, there's no colon on the PDA keyboard."

"Maybe it was sent from a computer."

Suddenly, Janie's brain came back. "Even on a computer it doesn't make sense," she said. She looked hard at the keyboard. "You have to hit the shift key to get the colon, otherwise it's the semicolon. You don't hit the shift for the period."

Kristina leaned closer and looked at the message again. "It's definitely a colon."

"Then it had to be intentional."

Pass to J from B: Leeds. Janie stared at it.

Leeds. B. Leeds. B and Leeds.

"Oh, my God," she whispered.

Bruce, and Leeds. They'd had their first date in Leeds while she was in England, in a restaurant that was housed in a building that had once been a toy factory.

But it couldn't be.

"It can't be."

"What can't be?" Kristina said.

"I—I'm not sure yet, give me a minute."

She hit the *Reply* button and typed in the word *toy*. She hit the *Send* button, then folded her arms across her chest as if she had to protect herself from something. She sat at the computer for a little while, rocking back and forth, staring at the screen, waiting for a reply. When it seemed that none would come, she stood. "I've got to go back to bed. I'm still exhausted. If anything comes in, let me know."

Alex was still in the bed; he hadn't moved from the position he'd been in when she left him. She lifted the bedclothes and felt an immediate rush of warmth. She looked for the warming pan; sometime in the night, Caroline had removed it.

Janie put her hand on Alex's forehead. It was hot and dry, and his cheeks were bright red.

The message light flashed.

"Hello, Janie," Bruce said to the PDA in his hand. "Long time no see."

A few moments later, he found himself standing outside Lany's door between the two watchers, not remembering how he'd gotten there. When she answered his knock, he sent Fredo and the other man away.

"Would you come with me?" he said.

As she followed him, he talked. He didn't bother with questions about how she'd slept or if she was less upset than she'd been when he left her the night before. He went straight to the heart of the matter.

"The woman you were traveling with is Janie Crowe." He put the PDA down in front of her. The message light was flashing. She picked it up and was about to open it, but Bruce stopped her. "Wait just a minute. Don't look yet. This morning I sent a message to her, using a word that I thought might prompt a reaction, if it was indeed her." He glanced down at the flashing light. "It'll be a short message. If I'm right, it will probably say *toy*." He looked into Lany's eyes and said, "Go ahead and open it. If that's what it says, then I think there's a trip west in our future."

With her eyes still on him, Lany reached down and picked up the PDA. She opened the cover and pressed the *Receive* button, looking down just long enough to read the single three-letter word on the screen.

"Son of a gun," she said. She glanced up at him. "What should I do?"

"Send back *factory*."

Thirty-one

Sir John wished it had been the Jew, and not Kate, who had taken the detestable little French count out of this world, but it had been her hand that fashioned the distinctive arrow that he'd pulled from Benoit's chest, and her hand that would understand how such an arrow ran through the air. The head was merely wood, not the forged iron that King Edward's archers sent flying into the air, but it was hard and well shaped, strong enough to do the job for which it was intended. It had smashed right through Benoit's ribs and lodged in his upper chest, and for a few moments, great gushes of blood spurted out. When Sir John yanked it out by the shaft, the cracking noise had sickened him.

Benoit's still-dripping body was draped over his horse, his eyes hideously open. The only sound was the buzzing of the flies that swarmed around the wound. Sir John sat astride his own mount and waited, with seasoned patience, in the woods at the side of the road, knowing that sooner or later Alejandro and Kate would have to move from their hiding place.

The lush spring foliage was good cover; he hid to one side of a stand of brush with his sword unsheathed. It had been hours since the birds had betrayed their position, affording Kate the fatal shot. Sir John marveled at their patience, but at some point they would have to move. He would be there when they did.

The shadows were long when they finally passed him. The horse on which they rode was quiet and looked to have been well trained, for the animal moved carefully over the tree-sheltered road at his master's urging with very little sound. Chandos nodded in respect as his quarry passed, giving them the silent *well done* that they were due. But now he had them.

Alejandro did not realize Chandos was directly behind them until he heard Kate's gasp of surprise to feel the point of his sword pressing into the middle of her back.

"Turn the horse around," he heard Chandos say. "Slowly."

Alejandro brought the horse to a stop and then guided the animal through a half turn so he was facing their captor.

Behind Sir John, draped over his horse, was the grotesquely contorted body of Benoit. By now, Alejandro knew, the rigor of death would have begun. He let out a long sigh on seeing the dead man but said nothing about him. Instead, he looked directly into Chandos's eyes. "We meet again, sir, after all these years. Under different circumstances, I would say it is a pleasure."

With the sword still extended, Chandos said, "I would return the same sentiment to you, Physician." He glanced to Kate. "My apologies, lady, if I caused you any injury just now; it was not my intent to do you harm."

"All pleasantries aside," Alejandro said, "you must tell me, what precisely *was* your intent in raising your sword, if not to cause harm?"

A moment passed. "To effect a delay. I would have you reconsider."

"You would have me reconsider what?"

"Taking the lady away."

"Ah, yes, well . . . I am sorry to say that I cannot. She is my daughter, and I will not be separated from her, sir."

"She is, *sir*, the rightful daughter of the King of England by papal decree, which—though you may not realize it by virtue of your heathen status—is as good as the word of God Himself. You are kidnapping her, a crime against my king, and now also against God, both punishable by death."

Death. The word settled over him like a shroud. For what had he come all this way and through all these years? Certainly not to find death; no, it was for a continuation of a life that he already knew would seem too short, no matter how long it ran. And to attain it, they would have to escape this man.

But with two on the horse, they could not outride him; Alejandro knew that Chandos would happily leave the remains of Benoit behind and make chase if they attempted to run. Still, he stiffened in his saddle; on sensing the defiance in his posture, Kate clutched him more tightly.

"She is as much my daughter as if she had sprung from my loins. Certainly more so than she is the child of the man from whose loins she happened to spring, by some cruel twist of nature. Tell me why I should not remove her from this island, with all its threats against her safety."

"Because if you attempt to do so, I will engage you in combat, and you will be vanquished. And because if you release her, I will protect her, I swear a holy oath, without harm to you. I will allow you to escape— the king will not fault me if I return without you. He only wants his daughter back again."

Alejandro deliberately ignored the offer; he pointed at Benoit, then turned his attention back to Sir John. "What sad fate befell your comrade? He looks rather unwell."

With his free hand, Chandos pulled the arrow he had taken from Benoit out of his own quiver and tossed it forward. Reacting instinctively, Alejandro plucked it from the air. He examined it briefly before tossing it back.

"Goose feathers," Chandos said. "I have seen such a design before in an arrow."

Now it was Kate who stiffened.

"Of course, I cannot be absolutely certain who it was that used this missile; in the haste of your departure, you might have dropped it, and it may have been picked up by a highwayman, who used it on the unfortunate count." He smiled cynically. "Or something like that."

"Most assuredly, that is what happened," Alejandro said. "But tell me, just for the sake of satisfying my curiosity, by what means will you manage to protect my daughter?"

After a long pause, Chandos said, "I will take her to wife myself."

It was an answer for which Alejandro was totally unprepared. He had expected to hear a vow of championship, or perhaps a bargain with the king.

"But—you are an old man!"

Chandos laughed aloud. "You might look in the glass, sir."

"I am her father, not her husband."

Chandos dismissed Alejandro's protests and pressed his offer. " 'Tis not unusual for a man of my age to take a young bride. Experience is a desirable quality in a husband, or so I am told. If the lady will have me, her safety and standing within the royal family will be assured." He looked at Kate, though he was still speaking to Alejandro. "I promise that I will treat her kindly and with respect. She will never lack for anything that she should desire."

"But you are near thrice her age, and a man of war! She is—"

"She is what—a woman of pious tranquillity? Let us speak truthfully. *I* know her to be a woman of great virtue and honor, but there are those who would claim—with some basis—that she is a witch. She is a traitor to her family, and—if my suspicions are correct—a murderess, though only those present here need ever know that. She can reasonably be accused of many vile and punishable deeds. Such a woman would require whatever protection she could find."

Alejandro remained still and silent, stunned by the viciousness of Sir John's diatribe. Still, it was guaranteed that one of them would live through this encounter.

He turned back and faced his daughter.

"*Père*, please..." Kate said quietly. "This is a matter for me to settle."

·   ·   ·

She climbed down from the back of the saddle and went to Sir John's side, where she stood on the ground and looked up at him. "Your words are harsh, sir, but I cannot deny that you speak the truth of what I have become. I would beg your indulgence; under different conditions, I might have chosen a more ordinary path. I might not have been forced to live as an outlaw against the king, but you of all people should know that it was the king himself who forced that upon me. And yet, knowing all these terrible things, you do me the great honor of requesting my hand. And were our circumstances different, your offer would be a matter of great pride to me, worthy of serious consideration, and the difference in our ages would be of little import." She glanced at Alejandro briefly. "I would press my father to accept your proposal on my behalf."

Alejandro tried to speak; she shushed him by holding up her hand. "But I cannot imagine any situation in which my sister will choose not to torment me. Her hatred of me is merciless and, it would seem, insurmountable."

"I have some influence with the king," Sir John said in a soft voice. "I would intercede on your behalf. And Isabella will soon depart for France with her husband. Her vitriol arises from covetousness; she is envious of your kind nature, your beauty, your intelligence.... These are but a few of the many attributes that I have come to admire in you, now that you are a woman grown."

A blush rose up momentarily on Kate's cheeks, but her expression quickly hardened. "You are kind beyond what I deserve, and for that I thank you, again and again. But I am no longer the sweet little girl you knew from times before. I have seen much in my travels and I know the ways of this cruel world too well. You will not find me to be a cultured lady of the Windsor court, if that is your desire. I will always seek to be away from that place; it holds no attraction for me. And I will not leave the father of my heart ever again, no matter how hard our path."

Chandos looked at Alejandro for a moment before directing his gaze to Kate again. "I beg you to reconsider. You would live in the comfort afforded by a husband of means."

"I will tell you what I told my sister: I have already wed, and I will not wed again until I find the same love that I had in Guillaume Karle."

The sword wavered slightly. "And you did not find this sort of love with Chaucer?" When she did not reply, Chandos added, "There was an attraction between you and him, easily seen, even by one such as myself, who takes little note of the romance that surrounds him."

Quietly, she said, "No. He is a worthy fellow, but—no."

Alejandro said, "She has made her sentiments known. She will not wed you."

Kate watched in silence as the tension built between the man she called Father and the man who would be her champion, given the chance.

Finally, after a long sigh, Sir John said, "Well, I suppose the matter is settled, then." He raised his sword again with such swiftness that neither Kate nor Alejandro saw it until it was resting on Alejandro's chest.

"Since your decision is not to my liking, you shall both come back with me and face the consequences of your crimes."

My sweet companion,

I tremble now as I write these next lines and pray that I shall not have to add another, yet more tragic, within the next few days. Guillaume is stricken by measles. So many have gone ill, one can only think of the plague years. I myself am unaffected; as a very small child I took ill with a long fever and a red rash, and I must now assume that I have already had my visitation. One day you and I must try to determine by just what magic it is that some ailments visit a person only once, even though all around him are afflicted.

The poor child was so hot yesterday that I could hardly touch his forehead. He coughs incessantly, and though I give him tea of sassafras, he cannot seem to help himself. Yesterday, he sat up in his bed and began to scream for you; your manservant came to summon me, and I ran to Guillaume as fast as I could. When I entered his room, he had left his bed and was cowering in the corner, pointing to the floor and ranting about some dark swarm of insects that he thought he saw. I told him that I saw nothing myself, but he would not lie down again until I took a broom and swept at them. I swept right through the air—there was nothing to be banished, but in his mind's eye, there was an encampment. He is calmer now, but his fever still rages, and his poor little body is a sea of red welts. One day perhaps we shall have some magic to scratch into his skin to ward off the measles as you did the pox!

And now I am truly alone, for de Chauliac has returned to Avignon. Damn the pigeons with their little messages! He left some days ago, with promises to stay only as long as necessary and not one moment more, for he would be here to celebrate when you return. Hurry back; my heart aches with missing you.

Chandos took their knives from them before they set out again. They stayed one length ahead, and with each step toward Windsor, their misery grew.

When it was too dark to ride any farther, Chandos told them to stop. He made Alejandro put his arms around a small tree, then tied his wrists together.

"Gather some faggots," he told Kate. "But hurry back, for if you take too long, the physician will pay dearly."

Sparks rose up from the small fire he built between them. The ghoulish glow of the flames cast a cruel light on Sir John's lined face, which was now devoid of all his previous sympathy and bore a dark and determined expression. Alejandro remained completely silent, lest he anger or provoke the man into doing something regrettable.

He was relieved when Sir John pulled out a strip of dried meat and began to eat it. The knight tore small strips off the length of beef and offered some to Kate, who accepted it with a nod of gratitude. Before Sir John could protest, she rose up and put a piece of the food into Alejandro's mouth. Thereafter, Chandos gave her no more.

An hour passed in near silence as Alejandro and Kate watched Chandos finish his rough meal. A short time later, the knight rose up and went to his horse, where he found a flagon among the items in his traveling bag.

"Wine," he said. He held out the flagon in offering. "Will you have some, Princess?"

She refused it with a wave of her hand.

"As you wish." He drank alone, all the while watching his captives. Soon a melancholy overtook him, and he began to speak in a bitter tone. "I do not blame you for taking Count Benoit out of this world. Were he to be my spouse, I expect I would have done the same. He was a snake of a man, at his best."

"Why," Kate asked, "were you and he alone in hunting us?"

"Because the good Baron de Coucy was eager to return to his fiancée, and because there was an ill man among our party who had to be brought home."

This caught Alejandro's attention. "Ill how?"

Chandos took a long pull on his flagon, then wiped drops of wine from his lips. "One cannot say. He was quite feverish when last I saw him, three days ago. By now I imagine he has gone to his reward, whatever that might be. It is quite within the realm of possibilities that de Coucy has found a reason to leave him by the side of the road somewhere, but I instructed my men to bring him back to Windsor." He drank again, then said, "If they managed to do so, there will be a bit of a tumult, but that cannot be helped. I will not leave a man by the side of the road to be picked at by vultures before his flesh has even gone cold."

Neither Kate nor Alejandro responded.

"Well, I can see that I will get no conversation from either of you. A pity. Discourses around a fire can be quite entertaining."

Sir John leaned the open flagon against a nearby rock and rose up, still remarkably steady on his feet, in view of how much he had drunk. "I'll need to make water," he said after a while. "A consequence of the drink. I shan't be a moment."

He saw Alejandro's eyes upon him.

He stopped before turning away, to say, "Do not make the mistake, Physician, of assuming that I am inebriated."

He turned to a nearby tree, setting his sword against one side of the trunk so he could see it clearly.

Alejandro frantically searched the nearby ground with his eyes as Sarah's words came back to tease him. *There are many beneficial things that can be obtained by simply looking at the ground. . . .*

But not this . . .

The vial of laudanum was still in the pouch attached to his belt. Chandos had not found it noteworthy when he searched him. It might well be, he knew, their only opportunity. Alejandro caught Kate's attention and gestured with his eyes toward the right side of his belt. For a moment she did not seem to understand. And then finally his meaning became clear to her.

She glanced at Chandos, who still stood with his back to her. She rose up quietly and went to Alejandro. When she found the small bag, she pulled it free with a quick yank.

She poured half of the vial of laudanum into the flask, then hid the half-empty vial in the pocket of her own breeches, just before Sir John turned around.

"There," he said. "I am myself again. Now, were we discussing something? Plague showing itself as an unanticipated guest at Isabella's wedding?" He laughed bitterly. "Now, there is something one can drink to!"

He took another long pull on the flask, downing its entire contents. He tossed the flask aside and leaned down on his elbow.

"You might try to sleep, lady," he said to Kate. "There is a long road ahead to Windsor. I myself shall remain awake, but do not worry, I will not take advantage of you in the night." He laughed briefly, and then his expression hardened again. "I am not the sort of man who would do so in front of a woman's *father*."

She lay down dutifully on her blanket, keeping her eyes on the knight.

In a few minutes, his eyes began to flutter; his head dropped down and then abruptly jerked up again as he fought off sleep.

"I am suddenly so tired," he said. "Perhaps I should tie you as well, so I can sleep myself." He came up to sitting and then made to stand, but his legs would have none of it. He sat back down again. A look of confusion came over him, and he slumped to one side but steadied himself on one elbow. He reached toward his sword, as if it might somehow stave off the sleep that threatened to overtake him.

But even the sword of a great warrior was no match for the dram of potion that coursed through his veins; he rose no more and soon drifted into a deep sleep.

To the sound of his snores, Kate untied the rope that held Alejandro to the tree. Once freed, he went to Chandos and listened to his breathing.

"He sleeps as the dead," he said.

And when he awakened, both knew, his head would pound so badly that death would seem welcome.

The body of the sick man still lay where it had been brought, to a seldom-used stable at one of the far corners of Windsor. The castellan had ordered two of his men to take the tracker there while he was still alive and to leave him water and food, should he awaken again. But he never did; for several days his corpse lay where he'd died, in the May heat, until finally the smell was too powerful to ignore. His blanket was wrapped around him, and the stretcher from which he had never risen was used to pull him out of the stable. He was rolled into his grave with only a hurried blessing by a priest, who stood as far back from the hole in the earth as decency would allow.

The wedding of Isabella Plantagenet and Enguerrand de Coucy had taken place without so much as a sniffle from any of the guests.

De Chauliac stared into a bowl of holy urine but saw nothing amiss. He sighed to himself; the weight of this pope's worries would produce a bevy of complaints, the same as in his predecessors.

"Just as I thought," the Frenchman said to Guillaume de Grimoard, who had, at his investiture the previous year, taken the name Urban, as four other popes before him had done. "It is a flaring of your rheumatism. You must rest, Holiness, or this malady will cause you even greater distress."

"Surely it can cause no greater distress than those matters that are before me for decision, *Guigio*—this mess with England will not go away! I have missives from Edward—almost daily, it seems. Each time I hear of a bird landing on the roof, I tremble to think what we might find strapped to the ankle! He raves over matters that are too old for consideration, and will not leave me in peace."

Matters too old for consideration. De Chauliac set down the bowl of urine and straightened up. "I have given orders for you to be treated daily with a small amount of laudanum. This will dull your pain and calm your temperament. However, you will notice over time that its effects will diminish, so the apothecary will increase it slightly according to my recommendations. And he will administer poultices favorable to the production of bile. Tell me, Holiness, what matters does Edward press?"

"It seems his arrangements for the marriage of Benoit to the daughter I restored have not come to fruition. He wishes for me to support him against the claims of the *famille de Rais* in Bretagne. Of course, I cannot do this without offending them mightily. I am not fool enough for that." He sighed and held out his arm. "Shall I be bled?"

De Chauliac took the arm and gently placed it on the armrest of the throne. "I think not at this time. My findings on examination of your urine indicate that such treatment is not warranted."

The pope seemed disappointed somehow, but said, "Very well. I am relieved, I suppose, to know it is nothing more serious that plagues me. One does worry with one's physician at such a distance as Paris. Tell me, *Guigio*, how goes the Cyrurgia?"

"As well as I could hope," de Chauliac told him. "But I am eager to get back to work; I must beg your permission for another absence."

"Which, of course, you shall have." The pope raised his staff and passed it back and forth a few times, then made the sign of the cross over de Chauliac's bowed head. "Go," the pope said, "and do your work."

As de Chauliac backed out of the audience chamber, he was passed by a cardinal carrying a large stack of papers. The pope's expression soured as the cardinal approached; de Chauliac knew the next summons would not be long in coming.

He hurried through the palace to his own apartment there, and when he arrived, he quickly changed into his traveling clothes again, leaving his physician's robes behind. Outside the door, his escorts awaited.

"Come with me," he said. They followed him through the streets of Avignon on foot, until they arrived in the Jewish Quarter. When they came to the street where Alejandro had lived, he told them to wait.

He went down the narrow street himself, bringing stares of wonder, for he was a giant compared to the people he passed. When he came to the door that had been Alejandro's, he stopped.

He backed up a few doors; a small boy was at play not far from there.

"I seek a woman named Rachel," he said to the boy.

The boy pointed to her door, then ran away.

De Chauliac tapped on the door and waited. It seemed a long time until the door opened, and then just a crack; he saw only a portion of the face that looked out at him, and that was in shadow.

"Do you know who I am?" he said.

The door was opened fully. The woman nodded and beckoned him in.

"Is he dead?" she asked quietly.

De Chauliac did not answer her question. "I have come to see the father, if I may."

"He is resting."

"Then he must be awakened, for I have not much time."

Rachel eyed him with suspicion for a moment, then said, "Wait here."

After a few moments she returned. "He is awake." She pointed toward a small room at the back of her house.

De Chauliac bent over as he passed under the doorway. There in the bed lay a very old man, raised up on a pillow.

"My son speaks of you as if you were God Himself," Avram Canches said. "Have you come here to deliver sad news?"

"I have no news, else I should already have seen to it that you were advised," he said. "But I have made a promise to your son that I would care for those he loves. I have come for you, sir, if you will allow me to take you to Paris. If Alejandro returns, you will be reunited. If he does not, I will see to it that you are afforded all the necessary comforts."

Avram was silent for a few moments as he considered de Chauliac's offer. "Tell me," he said finally. "Is there someone such as Rachel in Paris? It is only by her devotion that I am alive to hear your generous offer. Perhaps you should extend it to her as well and save yourself the bother of finding three people to do what she as one can do with ease."

"I cannot speak to your question, sir, I regret to say." De Chauliac glanced back to see if Rachel was within hearing. "There are good reasons why it may not be so."

Avram eyed the Frenchman for a long moment; he was deeply saddened by the realization that the hoped-for marriage between his son and Rachel would not take place. But this would certainly be his last chance to see Alejandro.

"You had best tell her that yourself."

He did so. Tearful Rachel would not accept the gold that de Chauliac tried to press upon her, nor would she take any from Avram. De Chauliac thought he had never seen a more desolate look on a woman's face than the expression she wore as his young soldiers placed Avram Canches into the straw-laden cart they had brought for him. She stood in the doorway and watched in silence with her shawl wrapped around her as Avram Canches began the last long journey of his life, to Paris.

Alejandro spread the beautiful map out on the ground before them.

"How marvelous," Kate said. "It is as if we were angels hovering over the earth."

"To have this, I believe there must be angels hovering over us! One is surely named de Chauliac." He pointed to the area of the Peaks. "We are near here, I think."

A look of terrible unhappiness came onto Kate's face. "Oh, *Père*," she said, "we have come so much farther north than I thought!"

"Yes, too far north. But now we are free to ride south, and we must do so quickly. If Sir John comes out after us again, he will not be alone, nor will his temperament be benign." He ran his finger straight down through the center of England, settling finally just above the Isle of Wight. "This port of Southampton will have shipping—to Normandie and Bretagne. From there we can ride to Paris."

"But it will be so long before we reach there!" She paced out the distance on the map with her fingers, and for a few moments she was silent as she figured the time in her head. She let out a long and sorrowful sigh; Alejandro knew that she was thinking of her son, of how long it would be until she finally saw him with her own eyes.

He folded the map and stowed it away in his satchel. "If we go southeast to Dover, your son will likely never see his mother or grandfather again. He has waited seven years for you; a bit longer will not be his undoing."

The horse went lame just outside Coventry. The animal had brought him all the way from Avignon and knew all his master's quirks and idiosyncracies, but he'd suffered under the burden of two riders, and it was time to give him a rest. In a small town on the northern edge of the Salisbury Plain, where they could ride at a good pace with the proper animals, they found a miller whose simpleminded son needed a gentle mount. The man had a stable full of horses, for he was fond of breeding them, to see what sort of progeny would come of each match.

"Give us two that can ride all day and pull at their tethers through the night, for the love of the next day's ride," Alejandro told him. "We have a long journey yet to go."

The new horses performed admirably as Alejandro and Kate headed south, keeping Oxford with its royalist fervor well to their east. After many days of steady travel, they found themselves in the heart of the great plain. The hills that had impeded their progress through the midlands gradually gave way to an expanse of rolling rises carpeted in the lush, waving grasses of spring.

The next evening, as they were about to end their day's ride, they saw in the distance an odd formation.

Kate peered south, shading her eyes. "I cannot make it out. Some sort of building, I think. There are people within it." She turned and looked at Alejandro. "What if it is an encampment of soldiers?"

He considered the possibility for a few moments, then said, "We should dismount and walk closer for a better look. We are far too visible on horseback."

They pulled the horses along and came, after a time, to a place where the earth rose just enough to conceal them. They left the horses and made their way to the top of the rise, and crouched in the grass to observe the oddity that lay ahead on the plain.

"It seems to be nothing more than a stand of large stones," Alejandro said. "Not a building at all. But their circular arrangement—"

"*Père*," Kate said as she herself stared at the stones, "this is the Hedge of Stones! I have seen it in a drawing; a minstrel came to court, many years back, and he carried with him a parchment rendering of this very arrangement."

"An apt name," Alejandro said. "They have built a fire in the center. I see a priest among them, and there are women." He looked for another moment. "But I see no soldiers."

They decided, after watching the gathered folk for a while longer, that there was nothing to fear from them.

They remounted their horses and rode toward the stand of stones, and as they neared it the people who were gathered there came together and watched their approach.

Sir John Chandos entered the king's study and found the monarch poring over a pile of papers. The page Geoffrey Chaucer sat at the secretary, quill in hand, awaiting the king's words. Chandos went down on one knee; the king made a wave of his hand, and the knight stood, with some difficulty.

"My fellow of the Garter returns at last," Edward said. He did not bother to look up but concentrated his attention on the stack before him. "The tumult of celebration has barely faded, and now come the bills." He picked up the top parchment and waved it around. "Fifty-three pounds for a veil," he lamented. "What can I have been thinking to allow such profligate spending? Ah, well, new taxes will have to be imposed. Thank God my own dear wife is not Godiva—she is too old to ride naked through the streets in protest." He placed the bill for the veil back into its proper pile. "You were wise, Chandos, to stay away."

"Begging your pardon, sire, but it was not by choice that—"

"Do not underestimate my knowledge of my retainers and what they do outside my observation," the king said, finally looking up. He glanced pointedly at his scribe. "You are excused, Chaucer."

The lad stood and bowed, then turned and headed for the door. As he passed by Chandos, their eyes met for a very long moment. He saw the knight's eyes narrow just slightly and forced himself, with great difficulty, to make no reaction to the unspoken accusation he saw in them.

"He's a good lad," the king said as Chaucer disappeared through the door. "Despite his quirks. Diligent and, I hope, loyal."

Chandos paused a few seconds before saying, "You have always inspired true loyalty, sire. In myself especially."

The king gave him a look of frank disbelief. "You are an old friend, and I will forgive you that insult to my intelligence. Now, sit," he ordered. "Tell me, through your *loyal* eyes, what transpired in the north."

Chandos had thought long and hard, as he rode back through the midlands with Benoit's corpse in tow, of what he would tell the king. He had decided along the way that he would tell him de Coucy's cousin had met his death at the hands of robbers, who thought them fair game since there were only two.

He would not tell him of the pounding headache he had upon awakening to find Alejandro and Kate gone, or of how that misery had persisted for a full day beyond his awakening.

He would not speak of his surprise to find that they had left him all of his weapons and half of his dried beef. Nor would he speak of how he had found himself covered with his own cloak against the rain that fell during the night. The king would not appreciate knowing how his stalwart comrade-at-arms, the hero of many battles, had fallen prey to simple trickery. Nor would he begin to understand Chandos's gratitude for the kindnesses they showed him, though he had shown them little grace himself.

He would not tell him of the desperate offer he had made to Kate, or of her refusal.

"They are gone, sire" was all he could say.

"Gone? Just gone, and that is all?"

"I heard of them in Eyam, Derbyshire, north of your hunting grounds. I have found out that the people there banished them from the town. That is the last news there was."

"And it was then that you sent the rest of your company back?"

Chandos nodded silently.

"Your fellows, no doubt, appreciated being present for the festivities. It was—*brave* of you to continue the search on your own, sacrificing your own enjoyment, having company only with Benoit, may the idiot rest in peace."

"I am not much a lover of celebrations, Your Majesty."

"Of this I am only too aware." He rose and came directly in front of Sir John. He stood over him and looked down with his eyes full of mistrust. "Tell me, Chandos, in your experienced opinion, what is the advisability of sending out another party? Surely these two cannot simply vanish into the ether. Sooner or later we will find them and bring them to justice."

Chandos remained silent for a moment, considering what he ought to say. When he had formulated a response, he stared hard into the king's eyes. "You are my liege, and I your most loyal subject. But beyond that, sire, you and I are old friends, as you have just said."

The king made no immediate reaction beyond a narrowing of his eyes. Eventually, he said, "As much as any king can have a friend, I will aver that I have one in you."

"I have stood by you and your son in many a conflict, and in honor of that I would ask your permission to speak plainly."

With uncharacteristic quiet, the king said, "Permission is granted."

Chandos shifted nervously. "It is my considered opinion that one ought to leave the matter be."

"Explain," the king said coldly.

"The lady will never bend to your will. She much prefers the company of the Jew to that of her own family here. And with all due respect to yourself, for you are a fine and capable ruler, I must say that in view of the turns her life might have taken here, her preference is more than understandable."

The king took a moment to digest what his knight had said. "Your tale of robbery lacks credibility. I must ask you now, did the Jew kill Benoit?"

Very quietly, Chandos said, "No, sire, he did not. Of that I am certain."

"If he did, then she is as much a part of it as he, even if it was he who pulled the bowstring. De Coucy, quite understandably, wants revenge for his cousin. He is making new demands."

Chandos recognized the slight nervousness in his king's voice. "The marriage was consummated, was it not? Therefore, you have no need to consider his demands. If he wants revenge, then let *him* go out and search."

In a hundred years of hunting, Chandos thought in his heart, *de Coucy will never find them.*

The king was quiet for a few moments, until he said simply, "Thank you, Chandos. You may return to your saddle, which seems to suit you so well, and do whatever pleases you. Tell Master Chaucer that we will resume."

Chandos stood, made a curt bow, and left.

Beloved companion,

It is my joy to write that Guillaume has recovered. How I wish this glad news could break free of the page and fly on to you and Kate! He does not care for strong light just yet and keeps to himself in his room. His playmate has recovered from the pox, but he is badly scarred on his face, and when Guillaume first saw him, he was frightened. I reassured him that his friend was indeed the same person and that inside his heart he has not changed. But I wonder if that is true—how can one live through the depths of horror and the disfigurement of the pox, especially as a child, and emerge intact? The world would forever be an altered place for one whose face elicits a gasp on first sight.

Now it is later, and I am filled with joy! How I wish de Chauliac was here, for he would rejoice with me! There has just come a message from Chaucer; you have escaped and must now be on your way here!

Thirty-two

Lany didn't understand what Bruce was telling her. "You followed Janie from London?"

"Well, not exactly. I tried, but I got bounced back to London by U.S. Customs in Boston. I should say *we* tried, because we were together at that time, as a couple, you know. . . ."

He paused and took a long breath. "We'd known each other years ago; I hate to tell you how many years. We were students. In the midst of all the chaos we went through in London, we got back together again. Things seemed to go faster with everything coming apart around us."

Quietly, Lany said, "They sure did."

"I'd been living in England for several years when the first outbreak happened, working for a medical institute there. I should have gone back to renew my passport and make sure all my citizenship issues were in order. But it was so . . . interesting in London, the way they handled the first outbreak—so different from the States. They put in place all these immigration restrictions and made a real effort to keep out anyone who didn't have a clear right to be there. Not like the U.S.; anyone could get in, even after we had a grip on what DR SAM was all about. I'll admit, I wanted to be in the thick of it all. But it cost me to do that."

"Too bad they sent you back."

"Yeah. Janie had her lawyer—Tom, ironically enough—work on getting me in, but the regulations were so strict after the first round that he couldn't do it. I guess I should wonder now whether his heart was really in it. I'm guessing it wasn't."

"Tom's a very good man," Lany said. "Fair and honest. I didn't know him as a lawyer, but I can't imagine him working against the interest of a client."

Bruce didn't comment immediately. "I guess not," he said finally. "But I wasn't really his client; Janie was. He married her. You can't work any more in someone's interest than that. In any case, I had to go back; he kept working on getting me a visa. It was more than a year before it finally came through, but by then the second round was well under way. I managed to get on the last flight out of London to Boston. I didn't know what was happening here; we weren't getting any information in London. And she didn't tell me about Tom, she just told me that she didn't think it was going to work for us. If I'd known what was happening between the two of them, I probably wouldn't have come at all."

He gestured toward his scarred face. "But we were already in the air when the controllers in Boston shut things down and deserted their posts." He pointed at his scarred face. "The plane crashed, as you might already have guessed."

"This is so astonishing," Lany said.

He told her about the harrowing month they'd spent chasing down plague after Janie had inadvertently dug it up, how it had gotten loose, and how close it had come to working its way into the people of London. She listened in silence as he spoke of Caroline's terrible illness and their race against time to save her with the ancient remedies they'd found in the cottage in Charing Cross, of her lost toes and numb fingers, and the terrible depression she'd suffered.

"We burned the place as we fled," he said. "We had no choice; someone would have taken over the cottage, without knowing anything at all about what was there. When she was well enough, we took

Caroline down to Brighton on the English coast to recuperate; she had a rough time of it."

He spoke of the journal of a medieval physician, which Janie brought back to the United States.

"She said she'd seen plague firsthand," Lany said. "But she never told me the details—no wonder! What a story."

"I didn't really do it justice, and there isn't time now either. If her boy has been exposed to that bacterium a month ago because of one of our birds, we need to get out there." He looked down in shame. "If that child dies because of something I did, I will not be able to live with it."

"You won't have to worry about it," Lany said. "She'll kill you herself. She has a lot riding on that boy."

Now it was Bruce who didn't understand.

"Alex," she said. "Short for . . ."

It was a few seconds before Bruce made the connection to Alejandro. "My God. You can't be serious."

"I am."

Bruce was very quiet while Lany related what had been told to her about how Alex had come about. When she'd finished, she told him about Tom's accident, the amputation Janie had done, and the effect it had had on her.

But he made no comment on Tom; instead, he focused on the boy. "So he's not their child together. . . . He's not anyone's child, really." Then, with uncertainty, "Not that it matters."

"I don't think any mother ever loved or adored a child as much as she does that boy, myself included. And trust me when I tell you, I love my son. He's all I have left, of three."

At that point, Bruce drifted off into a private place, where he stayed until he sorted out this thoughts. When he found his voice again, he said, "I wondered if it might be . . . something like that; I assumed it would have to be an implant of some sort, because she had a tubal ligation, and it would have been impossible for her to conceive in the old-fashioned way. But this my God, now that I've heard it, I'm having a hard time believing it."

"No harder a time than I'm having with the story you told me."

It was a moment before he said, "We look back almost seven hundred years, through the eyes of someone who lived through a very difficult time, and now we're living something like it. I can't even imagine what history will say about us and what we did."

"We're not done doing it yet."

He stood. "Well, then I think we should get to it." He picked up the PDA. "The batteries are pretty low, but now I need you to send that message for me, and add a line. On the first line, send one word: *factory*. On the second line, send: *B+L A2D*."

Lany peered at him. "*Factory* I don't get, but the rest—it's easy: Bruce and Lany arrive in two days. If anyone intercepts it, they'll figure it out, you know, as easily as I just did."

"So be it," Bruce said. "If someone in the Coalition intercepts it, they'll have to find us out there in that wilderness. They're a little busy with the deltas right now, so go ahead, send it."

Lany did as he asked, then put the PDA down on the table and said, "We've been sending from this location—anyone with the right equipment might be able to track us."

He picked up the PDA, opened the back cover, and tapped it against his hand. The batteries dropped out. "Not anymore."

"He's hot as a pistol," Janie said to Tom. "His temperature is over a hundred and three." She shook him gently; he didn't respond.

"Alex," she said, shaking him harder.

He opened his eyes and looked at her. "What's my temperature, Mom?"

She almost didn't want to tell him; he knew too much of what it meant, for which she had only herself to blame. "It's one hundred and three," she said finally.

Alex thought about that for a moment, then said, "Uh-oh."

Kristina tapped quietly on the door frame before saying, "There's another message. For you again."

Janie rose up and looked to her husband. To her unspoken question, he said, "Don't worry. I'll be here."

"I'll be right back."

Her hand trembled as she clicked on the *Open message* button.

B+LA2D

She managed to close the program before she fainted.

It took less than an hour to prepare for the journey west, for they'd made a habit of keeping the basic supplies in one place for easy assembly. "You never know when you're going to have to leave on short notice," Bruce told Lany. He gave her back her gun and brought out one of his own.

And then he packed up a supply of the serum he'd harvested from the turkey vultures. He held the last vial up to show Lany; the liquid was a light emerald color.

"Turkey vulture bile," he said.

"What?"

"Turkey vulture bile," he repeated. "They put out enzymes that can kill just about any bacterium they might come into contact with, and the enzymes can adapt to mutated viruses."

"Cut it out."

"It works, believe me. How do you think they've survived this long on what they eat? Carrion! Loaded with bacteria. This is the best hope we have if he picked up the bacterium from the eagle."

He gripped the vial tightly, as if it contained God's blood. He held it closer for Lany to see. She regarded the green liquid with a look of amazement.

"Let's hope it will work."

"Let's hope more that it won't be needed."

Before they left, he surveyed what they'd packed. After a long sigh, he said, "There's something else we should bring along. I wasn't sure we'd have room, but I think we do."

She followed him through a maze of corridors and pathways until they came to a door with a small block-lettered sign:

PROSTHETICS LABORATORY

Inside, they walked through a forest of limbs, all hanging from straps on the ceiling and walls. Arms, legs, feet, hands . . . in every imaginable size and color.

"At what point on the leg is Tom's amputation?"

"Just below the knee."

Bruce rummaged through a series of boxes, finally pulling out three different metal contraptions. "Cups," he said. "They'll have to construct the lower part from wood to be the right height, but these will make it more comfortable."

An hour later, four travelers left the Worcester Technical Institute on horseback, exiting through the same entrance they'd used to bring Lany's horse in when they captured her. They took a circuitous route out of Worcester and went a bit south before heading west. They rode on the shoulder of a ruined highway that went straight west without straying off-route to the north or south.

Early the next day, they crossed the bridge in a group of four. There was safety in numbers, because no one bothered them.

There was a scrape on Janie's forehead where she'd hit it on the arm of the chair as she slumped over in a faint. Kristina went to the icehouse and came back with a large chunk, which was pressed alternately on Janie's own forehead and then her son's. His fever had remained high all morning.

All Janie could think as she pressed the ice pack on her head was *This cannot be happening.*

She sat at Alex's bedside, her mind racing back and forth between the uncanny message and her son's distress.

You're not sick, you're really not sick. . . . She willed this thought toward him, as if he could pick it up through some form of sickbed telepathy.

It's not really Bruce, it couldn't be Bruce. . . .

Tom hovered in the doorway, balanced on his crutch.

"He seems to be sleeping it off," Janie said hopefully.

"That's good," Tom said. "He needs to sleep; he's got to be exhausted." He paused a moment. "Do you want to tell me what happened this morning? Why you fainted? I know you've come through a real trial, but..."

His voice trailed off, as if he didn't know how to finish.

She struggled for a moment over what she ought to tell him. It didn't take long to decide that the simple truth would serve everyone best.

"There was a message..." she began.

"From Lany?"

"No. From Bruce."

For the next several hours, as her son sank into a deep sleep, Janie did not move from the bedroom. Food was brought to her, but she barely touched it. Both Caroline and Kristina offered to take her place in the vigil, but she turned them away.

It's my fault, she told them. *God is punishing me. My will be done,* she said. *I brought him here, and now God is going to take him away from me. It's all my fault.*

No one could convince her otherwise. They all watched with terrible sadness as Janie bathed and cleaned her son. She checked every few minutes to see if the dark discolorations that were developing under his chin had grown any larger. She spooned broth into his mouth, only to see it dribble out again. He was pitifully small in the large bed and seemed to grow smaller with every minute. She tried now and then to wake him, but he would not come around to consciousness.

There was nothing she could do; a sense of total helplessness overwhelmed her. Finally, in desperation, she rose up and rushed out of the room, brushing past everyone else without a word.

She came back with Alejandro's journal in her hands. With trembling hands she opened the fragile binding and set the book on her lap. As Alex moaned and writhed in pain, she read steadily, page after page, revealing to him the life he had once led, hoping it wasn't too late. She didn't know if he could hear her and, if he could, whether he would understand.

Shortly before dawn, Alex came back to consciousness for a short while. As Janie clutched the shivering boy in her arms, he whispered into her ear, "Who is Kate?"

She pulled back and smiled at him, hoping he would not see her tears. "Someone you will love very much someday."

May it please the—

She stopped herself in mid-thought.

No. *God willing.*

Thirty-three

While struggling over a line of poetry, Geoffrey Chaucer was interrupted by an unexpected knock on his door. He opened it to see one of his fellow pages, a young boy still in training, who held an envelope in his hand.

"From your banker in London," the boy said.

Though he was confused because he had no such acquaintance, Chaucer took the letter with thanks. After the boy had gone, he examined the seal; it bore the crest of a well-known London banker.

"Well," he said as he tore it open, "perhaps I have an anonymous patron somewhere...."

The letter contained no advice of good fortune but something Chaucer craved even more.

My Dearest Geoffrey,
No doubt you have wondered what has become of us; I will tell you what I can without revealing too much. We are assured that the man who will forward this letter to you is very discreet, as befits the stature of his customers, one of whom happens to reside in Paris.

By now you must know that Sir John Chandos returned to Windsor without us, unless by some stroke of good fortune you have managed to get away from that vile place and are thus blessedly ignorant of its intrigues. The good knight caught up with us in a town called Eyam, well to the north, where we went in the hopes of confounding our pursuers. Benoit was with him; I cannot say what happened to him in this letter for fear that it might one day come back to haunt me, but I will say that the man suffered an appropriate fate.

Chaucer skimmed through the details of the events that transpired in Eyam.

We escaped from Chandos and traveled south for many days. On the Salisbury Plain we came upon a group of travelers, pilgrims *en route* to Canterbury. We had intended to continue all the way to Southampton, but one of the travelers advised us that we would not find easy passage there, as the ships were mostly given to cargo, and those seeking only personal passage might be looked upon with interest. Though we feared Dover, we did not think it wise to risk the southern ports and decided it would be best to travel with these people, realizing that we would not seem so notable in such a group. We did not tell them anything of our own history, except that we are father and daughter, returning to our home in France after staying a time with relatives in England. It is for the most part the truth, and no one seemed to feel a need to question us further.

They were an affable and interesting group, among them a priest, a nun, and practitioners of many professions: miller, reeve, carpenter, and more. There were women as well, one of particular note, for she was large both in girth and in personality. She had a singular wit about her, and she could always pull a laugh out of me. Her opinions were many and strong, and she required little prompting to reveal them. Also in the company was an elderly knight, a gentle, quiet man, whose last desire in life was to say prayers in the holy cathedral for the soul of his daughter, who had just passed to God. Though he was kind and thoughtful, he seemed sometimes to be entirely devoid of spirit, and when asked of his daughter's demise, he would withdraw into some terrible place of sadness, and none of us could bring him around again.

Despite this one darkness, our journey was uneventful, perhaps even of a quality that one might call good! These people, with their joys and woes and opinions, made the long ride far more tolerable than it might otherwise have been. I shall always remember them and all the tales they told to entertain one another.

I have never seen my father so spirited and happy as he was on that part of our journey. He has a lady love who awaits him in France, and he brightened a bit each day that we came closer to our passage. When we reached Canterbury, we parted ways with this jovial group, quite tearfully, and headed by ourselves to Dover.

But before we left Canterbury, we sought out the grave of the lady Adele de Throxwood, who was my sister's woman when she was of a younger age than I myself am now.

Chaucer thought back to the day of the masque, when the shade of a woman had appeared to him in the woods of Charing Cross. Perhaps it was she.

" 'Twas a long journey you took to reveal yourself," he whispered to her spirit.

This good lady was *Père*'s lover when he was here before, and more than a friend to me; it was she who stood by him as he nursed me back to health when I lay sick with plague in the time of the Great Mortality, and she who shielded me from the wrath of my cruel sister. He wept bitterly as he stood before her grave; there was little I could do to comfort him. But when we slipped out of Canterbury, he seemed more at peace, as if a burden had been lifted from him.

When we came to Dover, we inquired as discreetly as possible about conditions in Calais; we came to understand that there were many English troops there still, just as there had been when *Père* crossed over in April, and we decided that it would be wiser to pass over to Bretagne in Normandie instead of Calais. My heart was heavy when we took this decision, for the voyage over sea was a great deal longer and would land us at more of a distance from Paris. But *Père* convinced me that we would stand a far better chance of success if we did not have to pass through an English stronghold; in view of our circuitous route, there had been plenty of time for news of our escape to cross *la Manche* before we could do so ourselves.

And so we went by ship, south through the channel to Bretagne, and I suffered mightily from seasickness. When at last we stepped ashore, I fell to the earth and kissed it! After buying decent horses, we made our way to Nantes, which we found to be quite a charming place. The Bretons do not consider themselves French, nor do they give their allegiance to England, which lays claim to that region just now. They are Bretons, first and last, with a language and a spirit all their own, and for that I admire them. Therein lies the rub for the king, I suppose; he had hoped through Benoit to gain something of a foothold there against the *famille de Rais*. He has lost it, may God be blessed.

I daresay I found that place so appealing that I would consider going to live there, if *Père* will agree, once our business in Paris is settled. We could make a good life, with little fear of betrayal, for no one has any love for those who would claim us.

We rode overland for what seemed an eternity. We stayed on the last night before reaching Paris in the little village of Versailles. . . .

"Tomorrow," Kate said with longing. She laid her head on her rolled-up cloak. "Tomorrow I shall see my son. My heart is so full that I can barely contain myself! *Père*, you must tell me—how shall I act when I see him? He does not know me, nor I him."

Alejandro reassured her as much as he could. "Every night since he was a baby, I have told him about his wonderful mother. I have told him how you look and spoken of the sound of your voice; I have described your character, all in great detail."

"But he has never *seen* me," she repeated.

"And his love for you will be no less for it. I have kept you in his mind every day; there must be an image in there that he goes to for comfort and reassurance. The very first thing he asked me when I told him I would go to England was whether I would bring you back."

He saw no evidence in her expression that his words had brought her any comfort.

"You have never seen him either," he said. "Will that change how you feel about him when that happy event finally comes to pass?"

She shook her head. "But what shall I do if he does not *like* me?"

Alejandro laughed softly and stroked her hair. "Of that there is no possibility. He will love you as I do, I promise."

He did not speak of his own fears, of what might happen when Philomène saw *him* again after so many weeks of separation. Would she welcome him into her arms and her bed again, or would time have allowed doubts to enter her heart?

Soon enough, he would know.

They entered by nightfall, passing quietly through an open gate on the western side of Paris. There was no post of soldiers to question them, as there was little for the king of France to fear from the English with their princess so newly wedded to the Baron de Coucy. The monarch's biggest worry, Alejandro knew, would be his own people's discontent. The respite in the English war meant that his soldiers could spend their time in quashing the small rebellions that rose up from time to time in the countryside, those dim, heartbreaking echoes of the failed rise of the *Jacquerie*.

They followed the road that ran alongside the bank of the Seine, knowing that there was little chance of interception by any authority—they looked all too common, a traveling man and woman, riding peacefully. There was no need to cross the river, for they were already to its

south. They came upon *l'hôtel de Chauliac* through the same road where
Kate and Guillaume Karle had stood on the night, long ago, when they
first began to plot Alejandro's escape.

As they neared the spot where the handsome young couple had
stood, Alejandro turned to Kate and said, "If it will not upset you,
daughter, I would have you wait here."

The request took her by surprise. "But why, *Père*—"

"For your son," he said. "Please."

"All right..."

He left her quickly and entered the courtyard. After the groom
took his horse, he ran into the house. He stood in the foyer for a moment and looked around; no one was about. He could feel Philomène's
presence in his bones, tugging at him, but he ignored the urge to find
her and instead went quickly up the stairs.

His manservant rose up immediately with effusive greetings.
Alejandro gave the man a quick embrace.

"The boy?"

"Asleep, and dreaming happily, one hopes."

"Happier soon," the physician said with a wide smile. "I have
brought his mother."

He left his manservant in fervent prayers of thanksgiving and entered the room where Guillaume lay peacefully asleep.

His heart soared in anticipation of the happy reunion.

"Guillaume," he said, gently shaking him. "Wake up!"

The boy turned in the bed and looked up. Then he sat up on his elbows, his eyes wide in disbelief. "*Grand-père!* You are back!"

Alejandro embraced the boy fiercely, then led him to the window.
"Look," he said, "down below."

The boy gave him a questioning look, but after Alejandro's encour-
aging nod, he glanced out onto the street.

There below he saw Kate, still on horseback. She raised her arms
up and waved at him, almost frantically, and blew kisses through the air
to him.

The boy could scarcely speak. "Is that...is she—"

"Yes!" she cried from below. "Yes! Wait there, Guillaume I will come to you!" She kneed her horse in the side and disappeared in the direction of the courtyard.

Guillaume ignored her order and ran down the stairs, skipping steps, with Alejandro close behind. The boy tugged the heavy door open and fairly flew out into the courtyard. When he saw Kate dismounting from her horse, he stopped abruptly and stood still.

She faced him, and said, "Hello, Guillaume, my son."

He turned around and looked to Alejandro.

"Go, child, and give your mother a kiss."

He ran, his feet barely touching the cobblestones, and leaped into her waiting arms.

Alejandro took Kate and Guillaume upstairs to their turret room, where they talked for many hours. The kissing and weeping and hugging continued well into the night; miraculously, the rest of the household did not come awake. In time, Guillaume began to doze in his mother's arms. With the reluctance that comes from too long an absence, she laid him down in his own straw and pulled the covers up over his shoulders.

"Sleep here, beside him," Alejandro told her. He pointed to his own bed. "I shall find a place to lay my old bones." He looked out the window. " 'Tis nearly dawn, in any case."

He left them in the room and closed the door behind him, then headed immediately to Philomène's room.

For a moment, he stood there with his heart racing. Finally, he summoned the courage to tap lightly on the door.

He waited. No one came. He tapped again, a bit louder, but still no one came. He pushed the door open slowly and saw, to his horror, that the room was empty.

In a panic, he went down the stairs and searched for her in the library. Each failure drove the fear that she was gone deeper into his soul. Eventually he made his way to the kitchen, where the scullery maids were already at work on the day's bread. He spoke urgently to one of the older maids, a woman named Mathilde, who he knew had been in the household for some time.

"Please," he said, "the *mademoiselle*? Is she gone?"

Mathilde gave him a knowing smile. *"En bas,"* she said, pointing toward the stairs. "In the surgery."

He had been thrown down the same staircase, eight years before, by de Chauliac's guards, and now he nearly threw himself down in his eagerness, but this time there would be no bent ankle for him at the base of the steps. A candle burned in a sconce against one of the sweating walls; he took it from its resting place and, by its light, he found Philomène's cot.

He saw that de Chauliac had made a comfortable place for her, with a table and chair and a small commode. Alejandro stood over the table and saw several pages of de Chauliac's manuscript, far more neatly stacked than he himself would have done.

And then he stood over the woman herself. Alejandro was stunned once again by her loveliness; she seemed even more beautiful than he remembered. With one light breath, he blew out the flame of the candle, then pulled aside her coverlet, and as she opened her eyes, he slipped into the linens beside her.

She wrapped her arms around him and pulled him close, and clung to him with all her might.

"Oh . . ." she breathed. "Oh, my love, you are here. I can hardly believe it. . . ."

They were speechless with joy; their hands were upon each other, frantically touching, to be sure it was not a dream.

"But why are you down here, and not above in your own room? I took a fright when I found it empty."

"By choice," she said. "I often awake in the night, with dreams of you, and the work helps me to keep my mind occupied."

And then Philomène took his hand in hers and drew it to her waist. She placed it upon the slight rise that had formed in the place where once the hollow of her belly had been. "But let us speak of other things now."

Alejandro rose up on one arm and hovered over her; his expression was one of utter disbelief.

"Are you—that is, I mean to ask—"

She laughed lightly and kissed him. "I am."

They were surrounded by their little family—Kate, Guillaume, and Avram Canches—but Alejandro saw only Philomène. He barely heard the words of the sacrament that Guy de Chauliac read from a book of Christian rituals held open before him. Kate and Guillaume stood next to them and witnessed the marriage with wide smiles upon their faces.

The servants and maids stood by, dabbing their eyes, for it was an occasion of much happiness, and there was great affection among them for the man and woman being united by the master of the house. There was great cheer when the ceremony was completed; footman and scullery maid alike were there to offer congratulations to the happy couple.

And though it was just a formality, the pair was sent to their bedchamber in a shower of good wishes, for their first night as husband and wife.

Philomène's labor began one afternoon as the December sun was just slipping away. Ignoring her husband's admonishments, she had refused to confine herself well in advance of her labor as other women did. But on that morning she had felt quite agitated, and though she knew her time was near, she could not explain the uneasiness that took hold of her. When in mid-afternoon her waters broke, she sent Kate to summon Alejandro away from his work with de Chauliac.

The pains began in earnest two hours after the sun had fully set, when the household was nearly all abed. All through the long, cold night, Philomène struggled and pushed, with Kate at her side and Alejandro pacing nervously outside the door.

But the child would not be born.

·   ·   ·

For a short while, Philomène managed to rest. In the brief quiet inter-
lude, Alejandro said to de Chauliac, who had joined his vigil, "Does it
not seem strange, colleague, how you and I—both physicians—have
found ourselves once again waiting outside the door while a woman
moans within?"

De Chauliac barely had time to agree before her moaning began
again.

"How long has it been now since her waters broke? It seems an
eternity."

"It is, quite nearly," de Chauliac said. "More than twelve hours
now."

Alejandro lowered his head. There was shame in his voice when he
said, "We have put you to so much trouble. I am sincerely sorry if you
have lost any of your influence with Avignon...."

"Do not give it a thought," de Chauliac said. "If I have, which I
doubt, I will not miss it much. This pope is not the man that Clement
was. Clement, may he rest in peace, was far more—beneficent. Oh, he
had his moments of jocularity, and God knows he was fond of his secu-
lar pleasures, but for the most part he was a devout fellow with the
good of his flock at heart. This one sits in his chambers and counts
God's money, with which, I truly believe, God does not concern
Himself."

"That is, I think, why He made man in His image, to count His
money."

De Chauliac smiled. "That is a unique point of view, colleague."

At that moment a long and woeful moan arose from beyond the
door. When the stressful contraction was finally over, Alejandro let out
the breath he had held—quite unknowingly—for its duration. "I cannot stand to see her in pain," he said. "Is there nothing we can give her?"

"Not in my pharmacopoeia," de Chauliac said.

Two hours later, as Philomène lay exhausted in her own sweat, Kate
came out, looking defeated and pale.

"No matter what I do, I cannot manage to bring the child forth. I have not the experience—we must have a midwife who has seen enough births to know what is required. Send Mathilde—she is known to be wise in such matters."

De Chauliac hurried off to find the most senior of the maids, so she might be sent on the required errand.

Less than an hour later, the midwife arrived, bustling with urgency. She was followed by a strapping lad who struggled up the narrow staircase with the stout and heavy birthing chair. Alejandro stood just beyond the door to the birth room with de Chauliac behind him and watched the woman as she moved her large girth down the hallway. She stopped just outside the door and removed her shawl, revealing her face fully.

He nearly gasped but held it back. She looked into his eyes for a moment, and he saw the same look of recognition on her face.

But in a marvel of containment, the midwife did not show her surprise either; instead, she said simply, "We meet again, Physician. Do I attend to your daughter this time as well?"

"No," he said, his voice even and controlled. "My wife."

"Ah," she said. "Mathilde tells me that she has been at her pains for the best part of this day and part of the last. Is that true?"

"It is. But she has been well attended, for my daughter has—"

The midwife interrupted him. "You ought to have summoned me sooner. Let us hope we do as well this time."

Shaken, the Frenchman and the Jew slipped downstairs to the library. De Chauliac ordered wine to be brought, and they drank it down quickly, to numb the shock of what had just transpired upstairs.

"We ought to have considered this possibility that we would come upon someone from Lionel's household," de Chauliac said. "What fools we are!"

"She was only known to us as a servant there," Alejandro said, "a maid with skills in birthing. Not specifically as a midwife! One assumes that she has taken up the trade, now that the household is empty and she has lost her employment there, and she did well enough with Kate in birthing Guillaume, but still . . ." He downed the wine in one long gulp, then placed his hands flat on the table. "She must not be allowed to leave this house until we have made arrangements to leave ourselves."

"But it would be madness to travel with an infant, and with your wife weak from childbirth. . . ."

With steel in his voice, Alejandro said, "I will do what must be done to protect my family."

"We cannot keep her here; she is a free woman, and someone will surely miss her!"

"Was I not a free man when you kept me here? And was Kate not a free woman when Lionel and Elizabeth stole her from me?"

For a moment the bitterness of that time hung in the air.

"If we cannot detain her," de Chauliac said quietly, "then we shall bribe the woman, buy her silence."

"For how long? Such a one as she cannot keep silent about her triumphs—you must recall her from Guillaume's birth: She is boastful and loud—"

"—and she is common. A sack of gold will close her mouth. Just long enough."

Alejandro did not seem convinced. "One hopes."

Alejandro heard desperation in Philomène's voice.

"I am spent," she told him. "I can do no more on my own."

"What would you have me do?"

"You must take the child from me, by cutting me open, as I took the child from that poor woman."

Instantly, Alejandro said, "No, this will not be done. Not by my hand."

She drew in a long breath and clenched her teeth together in a grimace. When the pain finally subsided, she said, "Would you have me lay here in my own filth and die in pain, knowing that I leave you with no child to show for it? God's mercy, Alejandro, do to me what was done to Caesar's mother, so that the child might survive."

His voice trembled. "No, my love, if I do this, you will die—"

"Beloved fool," she whispered, "I know what may happen. You must cut the child out of me, or both of us shall die."

He turned away, his heart beating so rapidly that he could hardly breathe.

"Please, husband, I beg you; had I been a bit more diligent, a better physician, the woman and her child might have lived. . . . And had I had the knowledge I now have—that you can have before you by virtue of de Chauliac's drawings—it would have worked. But I cut too deep, I know that now, but you can do it better. . . ."

The midwife stepped forward. "A woman, a physician . . . This is forbidden, by God and the law!"

She turned toward the door but managed to take only one step before Kate had her firmly by the arm.

"Let go!" she said, struggling to free herself.

But Kate held her fast and spoke a gilded warning, very close to her ear. "Your help will be needed, so you must stay. Someone must pull the child out when the cuts are made. You are a midwife, so that task should fall to you, with your considerable skills."

Now de Chauliac and Alejandro flanked the woman, one on each side. She swooned, then fainted; the two men guided her limp body down to the floor so that she would not be hurt.

Kate slipped out of the room, to gather what was required.

The birthing chair was set aside; the lad who carried it for the midwife was sent away with a coin in his hand, stunned by his sudden good fortune. The footman at the front door was ordered not to let anyone in or out of the *maison*. De Chauliac's drawings were found in the library and brought to the birth room. The instruments of surgery were laid out, clean and gleaming, on a cloth at the foot of the bed. The midwife had been brought out of her faint. All was ready, save the surgeon himself.

Alejandro stood over Philomène's exposed abdomen with the knife in his hand, his face ashen and his hands trembling.

"I cannot," he said. He looked to de Chauliac. "Colleague, will you . . ."

Reluctantly, de Chauliac took the knife from Alejandro's hand and assumed the necessary position over Philomène's abdomen.

"Forgive me, *Madame*," he said to Philomène. "Are you ready?"

"I am," she whispered. "God help me, I am."

Too much blood, there is too much blood, Alejandro thought as he watched the red liquid spill out of the incision.

Too deep! The cut is too deep, she will die and my child will be lost. . . .

But the cut was perfect; de Chauliac worked quickly but carefully, slicing only through the skin, making certain that he did not cut the muscle below it. Though her terror was calmed by laudanum, it was plain to all that Philomène felt every bit of what was being done to her. She bravely clenched down hard on a wooden spoon, biting to keep the exquisite pain at bay so she might remain still. She wept aloud as layer after layer of her skin was rent by the fine sharp knife in de Chauliac's hand.

Alejandro held her arms down, so tightly sometimes that he feared he would break the bones. Kate wiped her forehead and smoothed back the tendrils of hair that stuck to her sweaty skin.

With his hands still at work on Philomène's belly, de Chauliac glanced at Kate. "Hold up the drawing of the uterus," he ordered. "To my right side, so I can see it clearly."

She found it among the other drawings and gave it to the midwife, who held it up in de Chauliac's line of sight. For a moment he seemed unsure of what to do; then, with a deep sigh, he pulled aside the muscles to expose her uterus. The tight, shiny surface of the organ undulated as the child, eager to be born, moved within it.

"May God guide my hand," he said. He pressed the knife into the taut and distended outer surface of her womb.

The servants heard Philomène's screams all the way to the basement kitchen. She let out one long, keening wail, and then she went silent.

·   ·   ·

Though he was still in a state of shock, Alejandro took the infant in his arms after the midwife wiped away the remains of the birth and declared the child healthy and sound. He carried the precious bundle out of the room, as he had done at Guillaume's birth, while de Chauliac removed what was left of Philomène's ruined womb.

He found his grandson waiting outside the door, with a terrified look on his face. The boy, like everyone else, had heard the screams.

He kneeled down and presented the baby to Guillaume. "I would like you to meet your—"

He stopped, not knowing what to say. This child, his daughter, was sister to Guillaume's mother. "Your aunt, I suppose," he said.

He pulled aside the cloth that covered the baby's face, so Guillaume could see her. The newborn opened her lips slightly as if to speak but made only a small mewing sound, then closed her mouth again. Guillaume smiled and tentatively touched the baby's cheek.

"So soft," the little boy said.

"Yes," Alejandro said. He remembered the feel of Guillaume himself in his arms when the boy was but a few moments old. "Just like you."

And just like her mother.

He rose up and left his grandson alone, then took the baby to Kate. He went to his own room and wept bitterly, alone.

Thirty-four

They made their way up the mountainside in just more than half the time it took Janie to cover the distance on Jellybean. As the sun set, Lany and Bruce, followed by their two companions, came through the gate into the courtyard of the compound.

Caroline was the first to see them. She stood very still for a moment and looked at Bruce, not saying what was in her mind, that he was not by any measure the same man he'd been. But she let the disquiet caused by his appearance go and walked straight up to him.

After a long embrace of welcome, she pulled back and smiled.

"Have I thanked you recently for everything you did for me?"

Sarah came running up behind her but shrank back behind her mother's leg in fear when she saw Bruce.

"It's okay, baby," Caroline said to her daughter. "This is an old friend of mine and Janie's." She rubbed Sarah's shoulder. "He's come here to help Alex."

Her look to Bruce completed the sentence: *Hasn't he?*

Bruce nodded.

"Well, follow me, then."

Bruce looked around in wonder at the place where Janie had spent her life for nearly all of the time since he'd last seen her. When they reached the lodge's main room, Caroline said, "Wait here for a moment."

She went to the bedroom. Janie was sleeping, draped over the bed-side. Tom was in the chair, with his good leg stretched out in front of him. He, too, was asleep, but his stirrings told Caroline that his sleep was fitful. She closed the door behind her as she entered.

With Caroline's gentle touch on her shoulder, Janie came awake. She sat up and rubbed her hands over her face. Her first act was to take hold of Alex's wrist; wild relief rushed through her when she felt his warmth.

She turned around. "They're here?"

Caroline nodded.

Janie glanced back at her son, then looked to Caroline again. "I couldn't wait for them to get here; now I don't know if I'm ready."

"Take a moment to get yourself . . . awake, before you come out. I'll go back out and keep them company until you're ready."

Ready or not, the moment had come. Janie stood and walked over to her husband, who was awakening in the chair. She stood and faced him.

"I love you," she said quietly. "Nothing will ever change that."

He pointed to the place where his leg had been. "Not this?"

"Tom . . ." she groaned. "Please . . . don't—"

He made a small wave of his hand, then nodded toward the main room. "Or that?"

She was quiet for a moment, but when she spoke, her voice was firm. "There's been a lot of water under the bridge since then."

Tom's gaze drifted to the floor. "Yes. There has. And despite every-thing we've been through, we've done pretty well." He looked up again, seeking confirmation from his wife.

"Miraculously well."

"But this changes everything, you have to admit."

She was about to say, *No, I don't have to admit that,* but she knew it would come out sounding angry. Instead, she said simply, "We have a son, a home, a family—even if it is unusual—a life that we've worked hard to create. And there isn't anything that would make me put it all in jeopardy. This is a *good* life; if you want the truth, this is as content as I've ever been. Oh, I miss the work I did before and the way I was able to do it, but I'm getting a practice back together again." She smiled. "It's not so bad being a country doctor. It's hard sometimes, but truly— this is enough for me. We get by with what we have and we have more every day. I need you and Alex, and Kristina, and everyone else. I don't know what I would do without you."

Tom hobbled forward on his crutch. When he reached her, he leaned it against Alex's bed and balanced on one foot. He wrapped his arms around his wife and held her close.

"Wait," Caroline said when Janie finally came out. "There's something I should tell you before—about Bruce . . ."

Janie stopped short. "What?"

"He's—not the same."

Janie took her hand off the doorknob. "What do you mean?"

"His face . . . Janie, it's mostly scars. Something terrible must have happened to him. I had to bite my tongue to keep from reacting."

Janie stood there for a moment. She said a quiet "Thanks," took a deep breath, and went into the main room.

He was there by himself; Lany had seen to it that everyone else found something to do elsewhere. When Janie entered, he had his back to her. When he heard her steps, he turned and faced her fully.

The line of his scarring went straight down the middle of his face. One eye was off-kilter; a large tear dripped from the outside corner. She stared at him for a few moments, saying nothing.

Finally, he spoke. "You look . . . wonderful."

"So do you."

"Janie, please . . ."

She closed her eyes for a few seconds, then opened them again. She stepped forward and took one of his scarred hands in hers. She kissed the rough tissue lightly. "In my eyes, you will always look like you did the last time I saw you."

"I wish I could remember myself that way."

She laughed lightly, then pressed his hand against her cheek. A tear slipped from the corner of her eye; Bruce used his fingertip to wipe it away.

"I hope that didn't hurt you," he said. "My skin, it's so rough...."

"If it did, I wouldn't be able to feel it anyway. I'm completely numb."

"Understandable." He reached into one pocket and brought something out in his closed hand. "Give me your hand," he said with a smile. "I brought you a little gift."

He put the lemon in her hand. With a look of astonishment, she turned it over and examined it. Then she brought it to her face and took a long sniff of the fragrance.

"Oh, my God, where did this come from?"

Just as she was about to sink her teeth into the peel, Caroline hurried into the main room. "I'm sorry," she said, "but he's been saying things, words that don't make any sense."

As Janie turned to go back to the sickroom, Bruce caught her by the wrist. "I brought something else," he said. "It might help."

The two men stood face-to-face for the first time. They stared at each other for a few moments, each one wondering if his own imperfection was the greater. After a time, Bruce extended his scarred right hand.

"I want to thank you for everything you did to try to get that visa," he said.

Tom balanced on one crutch and put out his own hand for the shake. It was firm and genuine. "I'm sorry it took so long," he said.

Bruce laughed quietly. He shook his head and said, "No you're not." He glanced at Janie briefly, then smiled back at Tom. "And if you really did drag your feet, I can't say that I blame you. I probably would have done the same."

For a few seconds no one said anything. Then Alex stirred in the bed, reminding them all of why they were in that room.

"We have work to do," Bruce said. He slipped his backpack off his shoulders and began to fish around in it. He pulled out the vial of green gold that he'd brought from Worcester.

"We have to get this into his stomach somehow. It's an enzyme base, but I haven't been able to figure out how the effective part of it leaches out. I can't think of any other way to give it to him."

They fashioned a feeding tube of sorts and slipped it into Alex's throat. Janie prayed her silent thanks that her son was not conscious to experience the extreme discomfort he would feel on having the tube slide down his esophagus. When the liquid was gone from the vial, they pulled it out again.

Tom and Janie sat side by side and held each other's hand, with Bruce standing behind them; all three watched over the second coming of Alejandro as he mumbled out the details of what his mother had read to him, sweating out Alejandro's memories. The familiar names poured out of Alex's mouth all night long as the medicine that Bruce had brought with him from Worcester spread slowly through his body.

They kept their vigil as Alex called out in anguish to Adele and whispered the name Philomène with loving reverence. Janie mopped sweat from his forehead as he arched his back and cried out to Eduardo Hernandez, Sir John Chandos, Guillaume Karle, and all the others whose paths he had crossed in his first iteration. She wiped the tears from his cheeks as he called to Kate and heard his pain as he spoke to Avram Canches. He said "De Chauliac," over and over and over.

It was not until the next night that he opened his eyes again. His first word then was *Mom*.

"You've got a good toothbrush, so don't forget to use it, and ask Bruce to boil it for you once in a while."

"I'll make sure he does it," Lany said.

Janie glanced up at her with a silent *Thanks*, then looked back at Alex again. "I know you'll remember to wash your hands."

"Of course I will," Alex said. "You only tell me a hundred times a day."

"That's my job," she said. "I won't be there to do it, so you'll have to remember on your own."

"No I won't," the little boy said. "Bruce will remind me."

Yes, I suppose he will.

"Okay. Go make sure you have everything I told you to pack."

He ran off.

"Where's Bruce?" Janie said to Lany.

"In the lab, I think."

Janie left the main room of the lodge and went to the lab. As Lany had said, he was there, looking over some results of tests that Kristina had done on Alex's blood.

She stood in the door for a moment, until Bruce noticed she was there.

"Hey," he said.

"It's getting on time to leave," she told him. A fretful look came onto her face. "I reminded Alex about brushing his teeth, and—"

"We'll take good care of him, I promise."

"Are you sure you need him? I mean, isn't there some other way. . . ."

"You tell me," Bruce said. "Is there some other way?"

After a quiet pause, Janie said, "No. I guess there isn't."

"His blood mounted a terrific immune response to that bacteria. If we can figure out how it all came together, we might be able to create a pharmaceutical shortcut that—"

"Just take his blood."

"You know the response will develop over time." He came closer to her. "He wants to go. He's excited. Lany will be there, and I will too, and there are lots of other children."

"He's going to pester you about continuing his medical education—"

"I look forward to teaching him. He's a brilliant little boy and he can make a huge difference in the world. Please, Janie, don't stand in his way."

"This is payback, isn't it? . . . I stole your heart, now you're stealing mine. . . ."

"Stop it. It's not like you're never going to see him again. If this works like we think it will, things will open up—the Coalition will be powerless, because they won't have that weapon of mass destruction. Your son will have neutralized it."

She was quiet for a few moments. "Please, the second you get there, let me know."

"I will, I promise. We're going to Orange first to pick up a few more people, then we'll stop in that mill complex you and Lany saw on the way to Worcester. I think we should make contact, find out if they're friendlies, ask them about the graves. And if they are, we'll have a whole new bunch of allies."

And so on, and so on, and so on. She knew he was right, but to watch her son go out the door at the tender age of seven was so excruciating that Janie could barely face it.

Bruce steered her away from the pain. "Tom's doing well with that new leg."

"Yeah, he is. He says it fits really well. I can't thank you enough."

"Well, you'll have to pay me when things are a little smoother. I'm expecting to have some of this scar tissue replaced. You're the only surgeon I know."

"Just say when."

"After we get settled and get this whole process in place with Alex. There's plenty of time."

Janie smiled. "There is, isn't there?"

Bruce smiled back. "Yeah. And by the way, did you notice..."

He pointed toward the terrariums. There were blossoms on the lemon tree.

Thirty-five

~ 𝓈 ~

Kate and Alejandro stood in de Chauliac's courtyard and watched the midwife hurry off with a small fortune in gold clutched tightly to her breast. No one, least of all the woman herself, would deny that it was a bribe and nothing more. Her payment for the work of birthing would have been no more than the hundredth part of what she carried away with her.

"How long do you think she will keep our secret?" Kate asked.

"Until the gold is gone. Then she will be back for more, have no doubt."

"And suppose we do not give it to her? . . . It cannot last forever."

"Then she will sell our tale to someone who will give her what she wants. She will first reveal me as the Jew who humiliated her former mistress in a feigned romance, and then if that does not bring enough, she will reveal that Philomène practiced as a physician. De Chauliac will not be able to help us, nor should he. We must not allow our misfortunes to taint him. His integrity must not be compromised. There is much work to be done still on his Cyrurgia, and he must have the luxury of all the time he needs."

Kate shook her head slowly back and forth. She sighed deeply and drew her shawl tightly around her, as if she felt chilled. "Then we do not have much time. We must be gone soon, so he can reasonably deny us should anyone challenge him." She put a hand on Alejandro's arm. "I long for the day when we can stay in one place without fear of discovery or betrayal."

"As do I, daughter."

Alejandro entered the nursery and found his baby daughter in the arms of the wet nurse.

"She has just finished," the young woman said as she handed the baby to him. She rose up. "I will leave you now."

Alejandro thanked her. When he was sure she was gone, he kissed the child on the forehead and cooed, "Come, little one, let us go and visit with your mother for a while."

Philomène still lay on the bed where she had suffered through the agony of surgical childbirth; she had been too weak to move. Kate and the maids of the house had kept her as clean as they could, but despite their efforts, the dank odor of confinement still hung in the air, and it assaulted Alejandro when he entered. He set the baby down and opened the window, shaking his head as he did so, for each time one of the maids came in to attend to Philomène, the window would promptly be closed to ward off bad humors. And though the physician was certain that such bad humors existed, he knew that air would do her more good than the Paris miasma would do her harm.

He lifted her coverlet, then carefully took up her shift, so he could see the dressing on her wound. Philomène opened her eyes to thin slits when he did this. He smiled reassuringly. "The seepage is still clear. This is a very good sign."

She said nothing, but nodded her head very slightly.

Then Alejandro leaned over and put his nose close to her abdomen. He took in the odor that emanated directly from the dressing. After considering its nature for a moment he said, "I detect no odor of infection. It seems a miracle, but you are healing."

She turned her head to one side; he could not see her face, but he knew that her expression would be pained. He took hold of her face gently in one hand and turned her back so she faced him.

"You worry me with this melancholy of yours," he said. "You must maintain good spirits to promote health."

Her voice was barely more than a whisper. "What can you know of the shame I feel? I am no longer a woman. The parts that make me feminine are gone."

"And you are alive. Need I remind you that had de Chauliac not done what he did, you might have lost all your bodily fluids? Such an imbalance would surely have led to your death. I will thank him forever for what he did."

He stroked her hair. "You are all the woman I will ever want or need," he said. He left the bedside and picked up the baby again. He brought the baby to the bedside and held her close to her mother.

Philomène's expression brightened immediately.

"Look what you have given me. Ariella Meryle."

Philomène reached out and pulled the swaddling aside. The baby's hair was a deep, rich black, and her skin was rosy. "Little blackbird," she said. "I pray that she shall not have to fly away too often."

Alejandro let her enjoy the baby for a moment, then said, "That may be her legacy. Soon she will have her first flight, I am afraid."

He recounted to her the events of the day when Ariella was born, of their bribe to the midwife, and of his distrust that the woman would keep her promise not to betray them. "We have bought some time, nothing more," he said. "Soon enough, she will sell us away. So we must prepare."

A good cart was bought, and four excellent horses. De Chauliac himself oversaw the modification of the cart's interior; several thick quilts of soft goose feathers were laid in place, and then pillows were added, so Philomène and Avram might ride in comfort on the rutted roads that led away from Paris. Tools and equipment were hidden among the quilts and the pillows, as well as several empty water bags. Alejandro assembled a cache of herbs and medicinals, which he hid in a box beneath the cart's seat, along with several knives and the strops on which they could be sharpened. Kate readied a strong bow and a quiver of arrows so all were just to her liking, and then added an extra bowstring.

When all was prepared, the cart and the horses were tucked into the stable, to await the day of their betrayal.

Not too many days later there came a visitor, a priest of the Benedictine order. Alejandro watched, out of sight, as de Chauliac took the man into his library and closed the door.

He was not present an hour later when the priest emerged from the library and was escorted by de Chauliac himself out into the courtyard, but he was summoned by the Frenchman shortly thereafter.

"I fear to ask what transpired," he said to his colleague.

"And that is well, for there is nothing to tell, other than that a certain woman, a midwife by trade, came to him and made a most unusual confession. He did not say what she told him, for it is a sin of the gravest magnitude for a priest to reveal what was said to him in the confessional."

He paused, then said, "But we know what she said to him. And if she is speaking to him, she may have spoken to others, who are not similarly bound by the rules of their faith."

Sadly, Alejandro said, "It is time, then."

"I am afraid so."

The sorrow of their imminent separation hung in the air between the two friends, until finally Alejandro said, with great humility, "We must part again, colleague, perhaps for the last time."

"Perhaps," de Chauliac said. "It pains me to realize this."

"Myself as well. I cannot begin to thank you for the many blessings you have given me. I will not recount each one, for it will take all of the day, and there is much to be done now."

A wistful smile came onto de Chauliac's face. "What am I to do without the comfort and inspiration of your company?"

"You shall do as you have always done," Alejandro replied. "You will study and learn, as will I, knowing that I must keep up with you or perish in trying."

Alejandro stood in the foyer of the *maison* and faced his colleague of many years, a man who had once been and was now again his teacher. For a time, when he discovered that Alejandro was a Jew after sending him to England in the Great Mortality, they had been enemies. But when their paths crossed again, it seemed to both that God had put them together for a reason, and as their mistrust of each other waned, their friendship grew. De Chauliac was now and would always be the greatest friend he had ever had. He glanced out through the open door to the courtyard and was quiet for a moment as he regarded his waiting family. Kate, the daughter of his heart, Guillaume—her son and his grandchild—Philomène, his wife, now carrying their child in her arms, and Avram, his ancient father.

He turned back to his friend, the enigmatic Frenchman who would forever inspire him. "We have come through many trials and triumphs together, de Chauliac. I wish there were more to come, but alas, I think it shall not be. Again, I must thank you, for your kindness, your stern-ness, your patience, and your succor when I thought I could not go on." And then a mischievous smile came over his face. "But more than any-thing else, my dear friend, I must thank you for doing what even my father could not manage."

De Chauliac looked at him in confusion. "And that is what?"

He glanced out into the courtyard. "You arranged a suitable mar-riage for me." And with that said, Alejandro embraced the man who had accompanied him through two decades. He let him go, then went out into the courtyard to join the others. Alejandro could feel the weight of de Chauliac's eyes on his back as he headed out of the court-yard with his beautiful and precious family, toward their new life.

Thirty-six

———

"This is unique," Alex Thomas Macalester said to his mother. "They'll never believe me back at MedGlobe when I tell them I got to stand over my own grave."

"Please," she said. "Don't rush things. It's not yours, it's his."

"A technicality."

"It might not be a good idea to tell them anything about this."

Alex said, "You're probably right."

They walked through the cemetery until they came to the place where his original lay buried.

Janie got down on one knee and brushed debris from the headstone. The inscription was weather-worn by centuries of intense Bretagne weather. She looked up at her son.

"You're sure this is the right one?"

"*Alejandro Canches,*" he read. His voice was very quiet and subdued. Janie noted a slight tremor.

After a moment, she said, "Does it say anything more than his name?"

"Yes, it does," Alex told her. "After his name it says *Physician.*"

Janie moved, still squatting, to the next stone. "Is this his wife?"

Alex squatted down next to her and sounded out the Hebrew letters. "*Pi-lo-men.* It's got to be her."

They were both quiet. Janie's head was bowed, as if she were praying. Alex put a hand on her shoulder. In a few moments he felt, but did not hear, her sobbing.

After a moment Janie began to rise, with some difficulty; Alex rose up quickly and helped her.

"Thanks," she said. "The knees aren't what they used to be."

"You know you can have them both replaced anytime you want to."

"I know. But that would mean I'm old. And I keep telling myself I'm not."

"Might work. But it probably won't."

She looked down at the graves for a moment, then looked at her son. "I wonder what she looked like."

"Why?"

"Well, I know what he looked like, and I know what *your* wife looks like, so . . ."

"She probably didn't look anything like Sarah. And I'm certain that my Kate doesn't look anything like the original."

"You don't know that."

"And I don't really care much either."

"I'm just curious, that's all."

"So was he," Alex said with a smile. "It got him into a lot of trouble."

The train from Nantes to Avignon floated on its air cushion; the ride was smooth and relaxing.

"I'm so glad we had the chance to do this," Janie said. "I know it means you had to take time away, and I appreciate it."

"MedGlobe can get along without me for a couple of weeks," Alex said. "I think I finally figured out how to delegate. I don't feel like I have to oversee everything personally anymore. There are lots of good people keeping an eye on things while I'm gone."

"Good. You can't do everything there. I used to worry about you when you first started up. I don't think I ever saw anyone work so hard."

"There were still Coalition cells all over the place. I had to save the world, Mom." He laughed and squeezed her arm affectionately. "It's in my blood, remember? In more than one way."

"How could I forget?"

Janie looked out the window as the scenery whizzed past, and considered how precisely Alex had walked in the path of his original, step by careful step. His own world was a safer place now because the people who worked for his brainchild, MedGlobe, kept a close eye on emerging microbes and hunted down the ruthless people who conjured up the bad ones.

She turned back to him. "Do you miss Guy and Kate?"

"Oh, yeah. But Sarah's got everything under control. They probably don't miss *me*."

An electronic voice came over the loudspeaker and made an announcement, in a succession of languages: *Next stop, Montpellier.*

The starkly angular building that housed the university library seemed incongruous, situated as it was in the middle of an ancient city. Mother and son in turn placed a palm against the reader and stepped through after the gate slid open.

"Le Cyrurgia Magna de Guy de Chauliac," Alex said to one of the librarians.

"*En haut,*" the woman replied, pointing upstairs.

They rode the escalator to the second floor and followed the signs for *Collections Historiques*. They found the manuscript in a glass case under soft light. A placard below it said it was a copy found in Nantes in the fifteenth century. For a few moments they stood in front of the display, just looking at it.

IN GOD'S NAME, HERE BEGINNETH THE INVENTORY OR GATHERING TOGETHER OF MEDICINE IN THE PART OF SURGERY, COMPILED AND FULFILLED IN THE YEAR OF OUR LORD 1363 BY GUY DE CHAULIAC, SURGEON AND DOCTOR OF PHYSIK IN THE FULL CLEAR STUDY OF MONTPELLIER . . .

Alex said, "I wish I could touch it."

"You did."

And then Janie and her son said in unison, with a wide smile, "No, that was him."

"Just like he described it. I'm kind of glad we didn't look at any photos of the place before we came here."

"It sure is white."

"That's what he said." He looked up and used his finger to air-count the towers. "It kind of has that New England farmhouse add-on look."

After the papal palace, they visited the narrow alleys and tiny houses that once were the Jewish *ghetto*.

"My God, these people must have been small," Alex said as he stood before the medieval temple. He ducked under the lintel, pressing his hand on the symbol of holiness on the door frame, and went inside. There were a few rows of seats facing the front dais, on which there stood a small podium. It was silent and calm in the small room; a filtered light came in through a narrow window at the front above the door. Alex looked down at his feet in the sand of the floor and wondered what the boots of the man who'd stepped over that threshold seven hundred years before were made of.

Janie looked up from her street map of Paris and pointed at the sign. "*Place Paul Painlevé*. This is it."

They found de Chauliac's home just a few doors from the Cluny Museum.

A small plaque was embedded into the stone of the courtyard's outer wall, just to the right of the gate. "*Musée de Chauliac*," Alex read. "How appropriate." The courtyard was barred with an iron gate, which proved to be locked when he tried to open it. Janie rang a bell; they waited for a few minutes, but no one came.

They walked around the courtyard to the adjacent street. It was, like most streets in the ancient sections of Paris, painfully narrow. When they looked down its length, they saw the metal pillars that barred entry by vehicles. Janie took her son by the arm and led him into the street, then turned him around so he faced the small dormer.

"This must have been the spot where Kate and Guillaume Karle stood. He wrote about looking out of the dormer room." She looked upward and pointed. "That's the only one I see that faces a street."

Chunnel or boat?

Boat, definitely. That's how he did it, so that's how I want to do it.

But their crossing from Calais was smooth and fast on the hovercraft, not the tortured odysseys that Alejandro had known. In Dover they boarded another, which floated them down the Thames past Canterbury. They stepped off at a transit pier and were shepherded into the Customs area, through which all entering travelers were required to pass.

As they stood in line waiting their turn, Janie looked around. "There are a lot more people here than when I came into Heathrow."

The people moved forward, one by one, through a door marked *Palm Reader*. Janie chuckled when she saw it. "That used to mean something entirely different," she said to her son. Eventually they passed through that door themselves, into the room where the official business of entry took place.

They were third and fourth in the line; the examiner at the podium seemed to be taking his time questioning the man who stood before him on the indicated spot. Words were exchanged, and though Janie couldn't hear all that was being said, she understood by the demeanor of both parties that the conversation was not pleasant or agreeable.

Immunizations . . . history of communicable disease . . . pregnant. Reasons for rejection.

"He's not giving him his hand," she whispered to Alex. "I wonder why." Suddenly a bell rang, and metal plates slid up from the floor almost in the same instant. Small air bags burst out of the tops of the plates and pressed against the man's lower legs, imprisoning him without injury. Within seconds, two guards with chemical weapons burst out of a side door and rushed forward. They had the uncooperative traveler secured with aircuffs in a heartbeat. One of the guards reached down and touched something on the floor, and the lower assembly deflated, then disappeared into the floor again. They took their prisoner off as Alex and Janie watched in stunned silence.

When it was their turn, Alex stepped forward.

"Alex Thomas Macalester," the examiner said. "Welcome to England, sir."

Alex stepped aside with a nod. Then Janie stepped forward. She answered the examiner's questions politely, presented her palm for recognition, and then quietly asked, "If you don't mind telling me, what was the problem with that young man?"

The elderly examiner leaned forward and gave her a flirtatious wink. "We suspect this chap may be pregnant." He grinned widely, enjoying the ruse. "Pregnant."

Something had flipped a switch in this examiner's brain, and they would never know what. They would never know if the world had been saved once again by that small caution.

The examiner pressed the button that electronically recorded her entry into England on her palm chip, then smiled at the man behind her and said, "Next."

The oaks, remarkably, were still there, though they were showing their age—there were very few leaves on the twisted branches, even in the middle of the summer. They walked through the arched gate; a slight breeze fluttered the ankles of their pants.

"The cottage was about there," Janie told him, pointing to a spot about thirty yards farther.

"From what he wrote, I would have thought the distance was farther."

"Yeah, you would, wouldn't you? It was a lovely little building.

Thatched roof, stucco walls, a rough wood floor. It was such a shame it had to burn. But we had no choice—it was the only way to stop the spread."

They left the oaks and walked to the far end of the field.

"This was the spot," she said. She pointed to the ground a few feet away from a protruding rock. "Right here. We positioned the plugger right here and sank it into the soil. We brought up only a little piece of the shirt. The rest of it's probably still down there."

Alex was pensive for a moment, then he looked at his mother with excitement. "I want to dig it up," he said. "Let's go buy a shovel and get the whole thing."

He took hold of her hand and started to turn, as if to walk off the field. Janie pulled him back. "Alex," she said, "no."

"There's a piece of *me* down there."

"I know that. But leave it be, please. There are pieces of you all over this world. Not physical pieces," she said, "but pieces of your influence. You took up right where Alejandro Canches left off, braving problems that no one else would touch, creating new technology, new methods... MedGlobe is a wonderful organization, and it's your baby. His, through you. Let that be enough."

She lowered her voice and said one last thing.

"It'll be a better ending."

Alex Thomas Macalester stood quietly on the spot where, more than thirty years before, his "mother" Jane Elizabeth Crowe had dug up the small piece of contaminated cloth that set plague free in London. The shirt from which it came had been buried there, in the time of the Black Death, by the man whose genetic material was used to bring him to life.

The tale was complete.

"Let's go home," he said.

Thirty-seven

Sir Geoffrey Chaucer brought his horse to a stop with a quiet, "*Arrêtez,*" for this was a horse trained in French commands, unlike his own favorite mount in England. The animal stood still on a shaded path that ran along the north bank of the Loire, a few miles east of the city of Nantes. He held in his hand a worn parchment on which was written the poem that had brought him there, in a hand that he could not mistake even after so many years:

> *There lives a dame of age with hair of gray,*
> *Who thinks of times gone by most every day;*
> *And wonders if her dearest friend of old*
> *Has given up, or still retains, his soul.*
> *So much to say of all the years gone by;*
> *She shakes her head and breathes a troubled sigh.*
> *Shall she await the one who set her free,*
> *Beneath the two entwined and ancient trees?*
> *But no, she cannot travel in that land*
> *For fear of capture by a hunting band*

Of soldiers loyal to the late-crowned king
Who chased her once before, meandering
Through wood and square, with hounds and men at bow;
And where she ended up, they'll never know.
But to this friend she offers rendezvous;
If he is of a mind to see it through.
East three leagues beyond Château de Rais,
Where she is oft engaged on any day.

The river flowed peacefully below, and birds chirped in the silence of the forest. He barely heard the sound of an approaching horse until it was nearly upon him. He turned toward the sound and saw a hooded figure sitting straight and steady on the back of a dappled gray mare.

He heeled his horse in the direction of the rider and came alongside. The rider pulled down the hood and smiled.

He could barely breathe at the sight of her. "Madam . . . Karle."

She nodded gracefully. "That is still my name, *Sir Geoffrey*."

This brought a laugh from him. "I had not thought my knighthood would resonate at such a distance."

"All news resonates, given time," Kate said.

He regarded her for a moment. Though her hair was tinged with gray, it held some of the same shining gold color he remembered from their youth. There were lines on her face, but fewer than he would have thought. Her cheeks were still high and her lips full, and the blue eyes twinkled, even in the low light of the forest.

"Ah, madam, you take my breath away, for you are still a beauty. I suppose I ought not to be surprised by that."

"Pure luck," she said, though she smiled with a youthful blush. "I have been treated well by time. My father taught me well the ways of preserving health, and I have practiced diligently. Even now, in his absence."

"Oh, dear," Chaucer said. "I dared not ask. . . ."

"Last year, he took a shock."

"I am sorry. He was a remarkable man."

She smiled again and nodded her acceptance of his condolence. "It was a good death, if such can be said of any passing. I hope someday my own will be as swift."

"Your son, how fares he?"

"He fares well, I can say with complete confidence. He lives with me, not far from here."

Chaucer hardly knew what to ask in view of their unusual life. "Has he ... a trade?"

"He is a maker of furniture and other such things of wood. His artistry is impeccable."

"You are a proud mother, then. But you never . . . I mean, you did not—"

"Marry again?" She laughed. "No. A woman must leave her family to marry properly, and I was unwilling to do so. Knowing what you do of my family, I am sure you will understand my reluctance." She glanced downward for a moment, as if reliving memories. When she looked up again she said, "And the lady your wife? We have heard that she is a fine woman."

"Passed on herself, seven years ago." Now it was Chaucer who lowered his head. "Ours was not a perfect marriage, but what is said of her is correct—she was a good and decent woman. Our unhappiness was entirely my doing. God forgive me, thoughts of another occupied my heart from time to time. Too often, I confess." He looked up again, directly into Kate's eyes. "I could never completely put them out."

"I will confess as well," she said softly, "that you were in *my* heart. And my prayers, as I promised."

"Those prayers have had great power, apparently, for I have lived a favored life."

"One hears of your good fortune often, your appointments, the king's favors ... your fine writings! And I must tell you, I have read your works when I could put my hands upon them." She leaned in and said, with a twinkle in her eyes, "Really, m'Lord Chaucer, your *Canterbury Tales* have thrilled me! I need not tell you why! And your *Wife of Bath*, you have captured her to perfection. Of course, in your presentation, she wants a censor, I'm sure you will agree! But she is a marvelous creature, wise and worldly, and deserving of emulation."

He let her praise sink in, then said, "And *The Physician's Tale*? What think you of that?"

There was a pause. "I would have had a better ending," she said, "though it differed little from our knight of that journey. He would never tell us how his daughter died, and we never pressed him on it. It seemed a cruel thing at the time. But *your* knight—to kill his own daughter, so he can keep her from those who would harm her; he is in need of great blessing. It seems so—*extreme.*"

Chaucer spoke, as if to explain. "One must exaggerate, for drama's sake, sometimes. I wrote what I thought to be the worst possible scenario, praying all the while that God would have a better notion."

"Well," she said quietly, "your prayers certainly had power for my life, if not that of our poor knight." And with that, she pulled a book from under the folds of her cloak. She passed it over to Chaucer, who examined it with his eyes for a moment before giving her a curious look.

"My father kept a journal for many years. He left it—quite unintentionally—in Mother Sarah's cottage when we made our hasty departure after the first Great Mortality. He swore that it must still be there, that the daughter Sarah kept it from him when he asked about it on his return during the *pestis secunda*. I do not know if that is true, but as you may recall, he was not a man to put forth an idle notion." She nodded toward the book. "That which you hold in your hand is the journal his wife kept, beginning with his mission to bring me out, and ending only a few months ago with her own death."

"He married—I am so happy to know that!"

"Yes, she was the love that he left behind when he came out of Paris to retrieve me. He had a fine life with Philomène. She was also a physician, so they shared their love and their work."

Chaucer said, with surprise in his voice, "A woman!"

"Indeed, a woman; she was also a student of de Chauliac, though he kept it hid."

"It was a match meant to be, then."

"Truly." She pointed to the journal that Chaucer held in his hands. "There was sadness, at times, but he loved her with all his heart, and theirs was overall a most fortunate union. It is all recorded in there, including the events of our journey out of England for the last time. I would like to ask you to take it back there when you next return and give it to the daughter Sarah, and if she is no longer there, to her daughter. If you do not find them, then keep it for yourself as a token of my eternal friendship. I have read it a thousand times and memorized each word, so I will not feel its absence. Beg whichever Sarah might be there to copy the entries into my father's journal, if it still exists."

He started to open Philomène's journal, then thought better of it. "May I?" he said.

"Please," Kate said, "read it if you like. I need only return before nightfall, or Guillaume will fret."

Chaucer turned the pages carefully, reading small bits here and there, as Kate sat on her horse and watched his expression change with each snippet of the Jew Alejandro Canches's life, as described by his loving and devoted Christian wife, Philomène de Felice.

Our beautiful daughter thrives. She has just begun to speak, and my husband insists that she learn every language we know, starting immediately, though she can barely walk! Now is the time, he says, for her to take them all in. And so we speak to her in French, in Breton, in Latin with bits of Greek tossed in, in English, and, of course, in Hebrew. It is a wonder that she can speak at all, with all the curious words he throws at her each day. . . .

"A daughter! How wonderful! What is her name?"

"Ariella Meryle. Their little blackbird."

"Lovely," Chaucer said. He read on.

Guillaume is such a fine young man! We marvel daily at how he grows and prospers. Yet, there is something about him, a longing for privacy, perhaps, that makes him keep himself away from others. Alejandro thinks that he is worried, in some dark part of his soul, of being taken from his family again, or that someone he loves will be taken from him. I pray daily that he will overcome these feelings, if that is true.

Chaucer sighed and turned pages so he was further into the journal.

Avram Canches left this earth today. My husband was at his side when the great old man breathed his last and went to his reward. Tomorrow we shall put his body to the fire. This is against the Jewish way, but there is no Jewish cemetery in Nantes, and we dare not reveal ourselves by inquiring after one within the surrounds. . . . God will know that we mourned him properly; that is all that matters. . . .

Once again, Chaucer looked up from the journal. "He was reunited with his father, then."

"Yes. De Chauliac brought him back on one of his journeys to Avignon. That was a joyous day!"

"One can only imagine," Chaucer said. He read a few more lines. "And here is more joy!"

"Well, some . . ." Kate said. "Some bitterness as well."

The Cyrurgia is complete! We journeyed to Paris to join with Father Guy in a celebration. So much work has gone into its creation, but it will stand the test of time, I am sure of it! Centuries from now, physicians will still seek out the wisdom and beauty to be found in its pages.

But while we were there, Guy de Chauliac was called to God. My husband could not be consoled at the loss of his greatest friend. We could not attend his funeral, and this was a torture to us, but we heard that it was a remarkable event—Pope Urban himself presided.

Before we left Paris, we labored diligently for nearly a fortnight, and by the grace of God we were able to make a complete copy of the Cyrurgia. We took it with us when we returned to Nantes. Immediately upon our return, my good husband went to a small church, and though it was against his faith, he lit a candle in de Chauliac's honor. He wept without shame for the soul of our beloved mentor and friend. And since we had a copy of the Cyrurgia in French, my husband took it upon himself to translate the work into English. He spent the better part of the next year in doing so, but we are proud beyond description that our hands are upon it in such a significant way. . . .

Chaucer looked up from the journal. "Did the man never stop working?"

Kate laughed lightly. "Not that I can recall. He cast his influence on my son, I fear, though they are not of the same blood."

Guillaume carves in wood incessantly; he has made a secretary for us in the wood of the black walnut tree, and I swear I have never seen a thing of such beauty. We keep our papers in it, though they are few. Each day after I write in this journal, I put it away in one of the drawers, secure in the knowledge that it will be safe and dry. . . .

Dear Kate has become a peerless midwife; there is no woman in France who can bring a child into this world with more skill and care. She is called often to the house of *la famille de Rais* to deliver their children; they are a haughty bunch, with no idea that a daughter of the king of England is pulling the screaming infants from their noble French wombs, with little mishap. Yesterday she brought triplets into this world, and by the grace of God, all survived. It is a sign, Alejandro says, that God favors us. . . .

Today is the anniversary of the day we wed. My dear husband brought me a volume by the Englishman Geoffrey Chaucer, who conspired with him to bring our dear Kate out of England. God bless and keep this brave, courageous, and remarkable man! It is a delightful work, full of wonderful characters, each with his own history, each with a tale to tell.

But I do not care for *The Physician's Tale*. I want a better ending.

And the last entry, dated September 8, 1393:

My soul is hollow and void of all happiness. Yesterday my husband Alejandro Canches took a shock. He was in his surgery, which he modeled much after that of his departed friend de Chauliac. He was working over a glass plate of blood. He had put all manner of tinctures in it and was endeavoring to gauge the results of his experiments; it was the blood of a woman who had taken ill with plague and yet lived. *I have seen this before*, he said to me, *many years ago in England, and I must unravel the mystery*.

To his very last moment, my dear, sweet Alejandro sought knowledge and put his best effort into improving the lot of his fellow man, whether Christian or Jew. *We are all children of the same God*, he said, and he lived his life in keeping with that belief.

And so, Dear God, I ask you please, in your infinite wisdom, find a way to bring such a man into the world again, so it may benefit from his wondrous influence.

Sir Geoffrey Chaucer stopped his horse before the oaken gate, but only after he had drawn in a deep breath did he urge his horse between the two massive trees. A wind came up, but not the harsh one he'd known from his first passage through. The path to the cottage seemed different as well, much shorter and without the clutching roots. He wondered to himself if the place had the power to change over time; it certainly seemed so.

An old woman in a red shawl busied herself with a flock of chickens as he came into the clearing. She looked up at him and smiled in welcome.

"You've been here before," she said.

"How do you know that, Old Mother?"

"I can see it in your face. I am Sarah, as you might well know."

"Geoffrey Chaucer, at your service, madam." He nodded his head respectfully.

"Ah, the poet!" she said. "Well, come in and entertain me with your fine tales! I'll give you a drink. It's a hot day, and you'll no doubt be thirsty."

But Chaucer remained on the horse. "I thank you, but I've many errands to tend to before the sun sets. But I've brought you something. Can you read, Mother?"

"Now, how else would I know that you're a poet?"

"And can you write as well?"

"I can, indeed."

"Very well, then," Chaucer said. He took Philomène's journal out of his satchel and gave it to Sarah.

She opened it and glanced at a few of the pages, then looked up at him. " 'Tis not poetry."

"No," Chaucer said, "but it is an intriguing tale nonetheless." His eyes went to the book. "It is written by the wife of the physician who left his journal here...."

"Ah, I have heard about this.... My mother, in her senile ramblings, spoke of it often and with enthusiasm. But I myself have not ascertained that it is here."

"Indeed," Chaucer said. "Well, that being the case, you'll have no use for the book, then. A pity; his daughter thought perhaps that it might be of interest to you." He held out his hand expectantly.

Sarah peered at Chaucer suspiciously, scratching her chin as she did so. "I'll take another look among my mother's things," she said finally. "I've a notion it may be among them somewhere, though I can't say for sure."

Chaucer smiled. "Well," he said, "if you should happen to find it, perhaps you'll be so kind as to add a few entries." He leaned closer, as if confiding in her. "It will be far more entertaining if you do."

"Aye," the old woman said. "Another *Physician's Tale*? One hopes this one has a better ending."

Her eyes twinkled.

Chaucer tipped his hat to her and said, "That settled, I bid good day to you, Mother."

"What, without a story?"

"You hold one in your hands," he said with a smile. And with that, he turned his horse around and rode out along the path to the meadow. The oaks let him pass without so much as a puff of air. In the middle of the field, he got down off his horse and picked up a small handful of earth. He put it to his nose and took in its pungent odor, then placed it on the ground again and patted it reverently back in place.

About the Author

ANN BENSON lives in Connecticut with her husband and is the mother of two grown daughters. She is also the author of the acclaimed novels *The Plague Tales*, *The Burning Road*, and *Thief of Souls*. She is an avid and expert beader, and has written eight books on beadwork.